BOOK 3 *of the* WRAITH CYCLE

A FLAME OF SONG

T·R· THOMPSON

ODYSSEY
BOOKS

www.odysseybooks.com.au

First published in 2021 by Odyssey Books

A Cataloguing-in-Publication entry is available from the National Library of Australia
ISBN: 978-1-922311-45-0 (pbk)
ISBN: 978-1-922311-46-7 (ebook)

Cover design by Elijah Toten

A FLAME OF SONG

The spark that floats across the sea

To light a flame of song

A ship upon eternity

The cycle of fate turns on

Prologue

Thin fingers of mist reached up from thawing leaves into the pale sky above the Tangle, giving the light of the morning a dream-like, ethereal quality. No wind disturbed their path as they angled ever upward, warming and fading in the sunlight. It was a still, silent morning, the world holding its breath in anticipation.

The Elder One towered above the canopy of the forest, its high, narrow branches disappearing from sight into the low early morning cloud flowing down from the high stone cliffs that lined this far eastern edge of the forest. The air was cold and wet, a heavy stillness laying over the area, silencing the birdsong and animal snufflings that were the usual refrain here at the wild outskirts. Beyond the enormous trunk of the Elder One, the rocky peaks of the great mountain range known as the Spine stretched up into the heavens, their bare stony foothills delineating the eastern edge of the Tangle, a hard, physical border that halted its green spread.

The Guardian reached out to touch the trunk of the Elder One, listening for its quiet song. The multitude it carried within it spoke.

It is nearing time. Where are the others?

Be patient. They will come.

It is so quiet here. So still.

This place has ever been wild. No man ventures this far east. Not since the raising of the mountains themselves.

Raising?

Long ago, when perhaps even this Elder One was a mere sapling, the Tangle's borders stretched far to the east. An endless green blanket of souls. But the men of the east, the Daleishmen, they did not understand such things, and what they did not understand turned to fear. This fear led them to commit a great crime. They used fire to beat back the roots of the past. Only the raising of the Spine itself stopped the flames from taking all of the Tangle.

But raising a mountain range? How? Who did such a thing?

We did. The Guardian we once were. With a little help from the trees, of course.

There, just under his fingertips, the Guardian felt the tremor of the voice of the Tangle whisper to him.

Fluttering wings, high in the sky. They come to meet us; they come to die.

An eagle's cry cut across the silence of the forest and moments later, an enormous bird swooped down out of the grey mist to land somewhat clumsily on the wet grass. It hobbled slightly as it settled, then fixed the Guardian with a single piercing eye, as if daring it to say something about the less than graceful landing.

Nurtle. Jared. Welcome.

The eagle paused a moment, then bowed its head in greeting.

You wish to remain in this form for your final moments on this surface world?

Once again, the eagle waited as if considering how to reply, then bowed its great head again.

I do not think they can separate fully anymore.

They are true wildlers now. They have left the human world behind.

And their next journey awaits. Come. Let us help them.

The Guardian reached one hand to the eagle's thickly feathered neck and held the other hand palm outward against the trunk of the Elder One. The muscles of the eagle's neck knotted and tensed at the touch, some part of its mind rejecting the presence of this strange being, but another, stronger will descended on it, soothing its fear and lulling the wild mind of the beast into obedience and stillness.

Now, open yourself to the song.

The whisper of music changed then, seeming to widen and deepen and morph beyond mere sound into something physical, wrapping itself in the grey mist and twisting it around them, so that the air darkened as the light from the sun struggled to pierce the thick cloud that had formed around them. The hand gripping the eagle's neck flexed and stiffened as it felt the heat of life from the animal respond, pulling away from the physical form that held it and joining with the twirl and chaos that wrapped around them.

I see fire. Flames.

You see the past.

I see darkness. Death.

You see the future.

No. Not that. It is not an end I see.

Death is not an end. It is a looping path.

I see … suffering. Pain.

You see what once was and may yet be again.

I see … Wilt. And Higgs. But they no longer reside in the same mind.

You see our young spark, and the flame he has lit. Come. Return. It is done.

The Guardian opened its eyes to find itself alone in the forest, one hand still held palm outward against the ancient trunk of the Elder One towering above. The whisper of song had faded back into the depths.

It is done. They are gone.

No, not gone. Just … changed.

The morning cloud was beginning to lift now, the surrounding forest seeming to close in around them as its white veil was pulled clear. Slowly, the sounds of the forest returned as the mist faded and a gentle breeze rippled the leaves.

They are now a true part of the Tangle. May their roots sink deep.

Is this how all wildlers end? Merged into the forest itself?

Only those whose task is at an end. And only those deserving of true honour are passed into the Elder Ones.

So, this is their reward? Nurtle and Jared?

They are true servants of the forest. True wildlers. It is right that they be honoured so.

A gift of love. A place above.

And what of the others? What of Wilt? And Higgs? And—

They too will soon pass out of our sight. But come. This is not the place.

The Guardian turned and walked back into the forest, its body fading into shadow. A moment later, the Elder One stood alone, surrounded by its strange children, stretching itself silently in the warm sunlight of the morning.

Chapter 1

The sounds of battle—clashing steel, grunts and gasps from urgent, lunging strikes leaked into Daemi's dreams, illuminating the grey mist she floated within, lightning flashes of memory blasting the fog clear. She duelled with the other guards in Redmondis, the scars on her back tearing open as she held off one, then two, then three opponents. She fell backward, one hand holding herself up off the ground, the other thrusting her long knife up and into the belly of the wolf that passed over her, drenching her in hot blood. She stood alone within a sea of black claws reaching for her, her body a blur of movement as she struck at the nightmare forms.

Gloomclaws.

The voice in her mind snapped her eyes open, and she lay still, letting her breath slow and the world around her form into some sort of logical shape. She was staring at a bare timber ceiling, the low beams casting barred shadows across the walls in the morning sunlight. Five long thin fingers, reaching for her.

Waiting to snatch you into their fist.

She was lying on her back. How was that possible? She hadn't been able to rest that way since …

Daemi sat up, one hand sliding under her pillow for her blade, the other darting quickly over her back, searching out the scars that had marked her since Redmondis. There was nothing there. Her skin was smooth and cool, just the hint of numbness remaining where the scars had once been.

Her blade wasn't under her pillow. She looked around the

small chamber, the bed she lay in taking up half the room, the only other furniture a small desk with a basin resting on it and a single chair angled toward her as though it had been vacated just minutes before. Hanging from the back of the chair were her belt and sword. Her weld blade.

The desk was pushed against the wall and above it a single window allowed in both the sunlight that lit the room and the noise that had woken her. As she sat and listened, it was clear the sounds were of soldiers training, sparring rather than fighting; the shouts and grunts of encouragement and correction, not panic or fear.

A dark shape darted into view at the window, the large cat leaping easily from the sill into the ceiling beams, coming to rest just above the foot of her bed, its eyes twin black pools that threw her reflection back at her, its tail waving slowly back and forth.

Daemi locked eyes with it and knew.

She was in Sontair, the capital. She had travelled here with Heather and Frankle—the sudden memory of the journey and the dipping, soaring flight sent a wave of nausea rolling up her stomach—and had met up with Lodan. Had sought out Wilt only to be confronted by the—

Gloomclaw.

The creature that had attacked them underneath the castle. She had tried to hold it off, but it was too fast. Then something came between her and it, saving her. She had felt the wounds on her back tear open. Wilt. Wilt had been there.

She stared back at the cat and waited for some other confirmation, but none came.

The door of her chamber flew open and Heather burst into the room, her face breaking into a wide smile as she saw her patient awake and sitting up.

'Well, it's about time!' Heather swooped in before Daemi knew what was happening and wrapped her in a tight hug. Daemi sat very still as Heather patted her back, not sure what she was supposed to do. After a moment, she realised that Heather wasn't just embracing her, she was examining her, checking her back for scars.

'They're gone,' Daemi whispered, her voice hoarse and strange in her throat.

'I know.' Heather leaned back and released her, scooting backward to perch on the foot of the bed. 'Frankle and I …'

'You healed me. Better than even Petron could do.'

'Oh, I don't know about that.' Heather ducked her head, but it was clear she enjoyed the compliment. 'We just had a bit more to work with. Besides,' she nodded at the cat staring down at them both, 'we had some help.'

Daemi followed her eyes. 'Wilt.'

'It is Wilt, isn't it?' Heather whispered, her voice awed. 'I don't know how. Or why. We were hoping you would be able to help clear some of that up.'

The cat stretched slowly on the beam, its silver claws sliding out from its paws and gleaming in the sunlight.

'I don't … I'm not sure how I can explain it.'

'Of course, not straight away!' Heather smiled. 'I'm sorry, you only just woke up. There's a lot to catch you up on.'

A particularly loud clang of blades rang out and Daemi got to her feet and moved to the window, aware of Heather watching her. Studying how she moved, how weak she still was.

'How do you feel?' Heather asked.

'I'm okay … I think. Just a little fuzzy.'

Through the window, Daemi could see a large training ground where a mass of soldiers was being put through their paces. There were hundreds of them.

'It's impressive, isn't it?'

Daemi nodded, but held her tongue. There was something about the way the soldiers on the training ground moved in lockstep that troubled her. Something about the sight of them dancing back and forth through their drills spoke to the silent emptiness she could feel turning slowly within her, hidden in shadow. Waiting.

In time. All in good time.

She glanced back at the cat staring down at her, its tail still swaying slowly under the ceiling beam.

Heather caught the look and frowned. 'Frankle will be pleased to hear you're awake. And Lodan, of course.'

Daemi stepped back from the window and sat down on the bed again, her cheeks flushing slightly. 'Oh yes?'

'Of course! They've both been bothering me endlessly about you. It's part of the reason we moved you out of the castle. At least here we could get some peace.'

'How is he?'

'Lodan?'

Daemi's blush deepened as she shook her head. 'Frankle. How is Frankle?'

'Oh, he's as happy as a clam. Found his way into the queen's— the former queen's, I should say—study. Tells me there's all sorts of things in there. I've been hoping to get a look in there myself, but he's pretty much commandeered the whole room. Says it's wielder business. I've let him think he's in charge for the time being. Now that you're up and about though …'

'You plan on sticking your nose back in.'

Heather grinned. 'Of course.'

Daemi lay back on the bed, a sudden wave of dizziness crashing over her.

'You rest.' Heather stood up. 'Take as much time as you need. There's plenty of work around here to keep us all busy.'

Daemi nodded and reached out to grab Heather's sleeve. 'Heather, thank you. For everything.'

Heather smiled and patted her hand, then slipped out of the room as Daemi's eyes fell closed and sleep overwhelmed her.

Inside the tall silver castle that was the jewel adorning Sontair's crown, past the seemingly endless courtyards and halls and dining rooms that formed its outer circle, beyond the enormous throne room with its ostentatiously carved columns and ancient tapestries lining the walls, past even the hidden viewing chambers and greeting halls that made up the former queen's private wing, a small, almost unnoticeable wooden door interrupted a bare white wall. It looked for all the world like a broom closet, or perhaps a servant's powder room, a place to be ignored by all who passed it. In fact, if one wasn't specifically looking for it, one might find their eyes sliding across the door completely, as though the timber of the door itself somehow repelled awareness, convinced the unaware mind that there was nothing particularly interesting here.

You should move on, look elsewhere. Leave it be.

Frankle had first found the door days ago, only a few hours after beginning to explore the castle proper. Daemi's recovery was well in hand by then, and Lodan and the court officials he had somehow come to an agreement with were too busy to worry about what a young wielder like Frankle might get up to. As long as he was out of the way.

It was the weld music that had led him to it. A whisper of song, almost past hearing, a sound that would twist away from you if you tried to pin it down, like smoke in the breeze. Frankle had come to recognise it from his time in Redmondis. He'd first heard it when Delco and Higgs had formed the silver barrier wall in the wielder's tower, and again later when helping to track down Wilt's weld blade. The more he heard it, the easier it was to identify, and since they'd arrived in Sontair and settled into the castle, his ability to recognise it seemed to have increased tenfold.

If he thought about it, the song was there when he and Heather found they could form moonsteel—weld blades to arm the soldiers of Redmondis—and again later when they were on Wilt's trail here below the castle. When the nightmare creature had attacked them and Wilt had somehow managed to step in and save them all.

Gloomclaw—that was the creature's name, he knew now. It was just one of the pieces of knowledge he had discovered once he had followed the music to the unmarked timber door and discovered the riches hidden behind it. The queen's private study. And so much more.

He now sat silent on the floor, his head bowed over a large stone bowl filled with water, its surface still and quiet, tracing his fingers slowly over the carvings that marked the bowl's edge. His lips moved slightly as his fingers read the words, though he held back from actually voicing the words aloud. Not now. Not yet. Later, perhaps. When he knew more.

Frankle was careful. He knew the dangers knowledge could hold for those without the proper training. The consequences. He'd seen more than enough of such things in his time.

In an instant, he was transported back to the past, huddled in the corner of his room in the wielder's tower in Redmondis, covered in blankets and old clothes, trying to still his breathing as the sound of marching feet and the cries of his fellow students grew louder and louder. They were searching for him, searching out all the wielders in the tower, rounding them up and leading them down to Cantor Cortis.

He felt the fear again, the thrill of it, the electric shiver up his spine as he closed his eyes and sweated in the hot, confined space he had chosen. They would find him, of course. They had to.

Frankle saw his fear begin to take on a shape then, a black vortex spinning up to speed and reaching for him.

He sat back and exhaled, pulling his eyes from the viewing bowl and stopping his fingers from tracing the last remaining words carved across the bowl's lip. He sat very still for a full minute, letting his breathing return to normal.

There was something there, some connection between the memory of that time and the darkness in the depths. No, more than that, between fear and what lay beneath.

He rolled to his feet and hurried over to the large desk that lined one wall of the room, covered in papers and scrolls and large, dusty tomes. There had been something here, something he'd hurriedly read in his first skimmings of the papers the queen had left. Something about—

There. He pulled a single leaf of paper free from the pile and focused on it, reading slowly now, trying to understand what it was the queen had scrawled so hastily.

Fear is the key. The key to the depths and what lies beneath the ice, where the serpents once dwelled. It calls to them, leads them to the surface. But more than that—when used properly, it could … The boy knows more than he realises. We can use him to unlock the past. We must try.

The boy—she had to mean Wilt, hadn't she? But what does unlock the past mean?

Frankle sighed and pushed the paper back into the pile. Like so much he had found here, it was at once exciting and infuriating. He knew enough to realise the knowledge captured here was valuable, but not enough to fully understand it himself.

Petron. He would be able to understand it. If only he were here.

Frankle grabbed the apple he had filched from one of the kitchens on his way through this morning and chomped into it distractedly. As soon as the sweet juice from its flesh entered his mouth, he realised he was ravenous. For the next few moments, all he thought about was eating, devouring the apple in quick, messy bites until all that remained was the skinny core.

When had he last eaten? Was it lunchtime already? It was so easy to lose time here.

There were no windows in the study, no distractions allowed from the outside world. The room was lit by hidden lightwells set high in the ceiling, sending a blank, even whiteness across the room that Frankle had already found tiring. Just staring around the room made his eyes heavy.

His eyes fell on the biggest curiosity he had found so far: a large stone gateway set against the back wall. It glowed faintly green in the light, as though the stone itself was luminous, and more strange carvings lined its edges. He tossed the apple core onto the table.

A gateway—a door, perhaps? If one read the words lining its barrier, would it open? Where would it lead?

Frankle stood before it, hands on hips, chewing his lip in indecision. He didn't know enough even about this. Not enough to try. One had to be careful when dealing with the depths.

'It's wonderful, isn't it?'

Frankle almost jumped at Heather's words. 'What? Oh yes. Wonderful. When did you get here?'

'Just now.' Heather smiled and began picking slowly through the papers on the desk. 'It looks like you've been busy.'

'There's a lot here. How did you find me?'

'Oh, simple really.' As if that was answer enough.

She often did that, Frankle had begun to notice. Gave half answers, hints at things she knew and he didn't. It was infuriating. It was meant to be, he supposed.

'I thought—' Frankle cut himself off and frowned, not sure he should actually speak the words. 'I thought I was the only one who could hear it.'

'Hear what?' Heather turned her full attention on him, that strange half smile still playing on her lips.

'The weld song, the … you know. The sound that led me here.'

'I'm sure I don't know what you mean.'

Frankle just stood in front of her, hands on hips, unsure what to say next.

After an excruciating few moments, Heather relented and pulled a small bowl out from one of her pockets. 'This led me here.'

Immediately, Frankle forgot his frustration as curiousity took hold, and he stepped forward to get a better look. 'Is that a sounding bowl?'

'It is.'

'I've heard about these. But don't you need something to make it—'

With her other hand, Heather pulled her necklace free from her collar and rested it inside the stone bowl. As soon as the gemstone touched the bowl's surface, a haunting melody began to emanate from it, filling the room with its song.

'A heartstone,' Frankle found himself whispering.

'That's right.' Heather pulled the necklace free of the bowl and tucked it back inside her shirt. 'You know more about crafting than you let on.'

'Not nearly enough.' He turned and gestured at the stone gate. 'Just look at this. Crafter work, surely.'

Heather stepped past him and ran her fingers over the markings along the edge of the door.

'It's a conduit, I think. I've read about these.'

'Read? Where?'

'In Redmondis. Some of the crafter lessons mentioned them.'

Frankle groaned. 'Of course they did. Wouldn't do to let us wielders know anything about them, would it?'

Heather flashed him a quick smile and turned back to the gate. 'I'll have a look over my notes. I'm sure I'll dig something up. Do you recognise this stone?'

'Only that it's more than just stone.'

'It's the same as those cells we found in the dungeons. Made to hold wielders. I think it comes from Redmondis.'

Frankle stepped up beside her, their shoulders lightly brushing against each other.

She was right; there was something more to this stone as well. A whisper of—

Heather leaned into him and knocked him sideways. 'Anyway, it's almost suppertime. I've come to fetch you.'

'What? Already?'

'Come on, we have a special guest tonight.' She leaned close to him and sniffed. 'And you need to wash up. You smell like old parchment.'

Heather turned on her heel and stepped out of the room, leaving Frankle to pack the scattered papers together into some sort of organised chaos.

It wasn't until he was leaving the room that the thought occurred to him.

Why had Heather's heartstone led her to him?

Chapter 2

By the time Frankle had washed and changed and tried to do something with his mop of hair, the sun had set and the sky outside his bedroom window was darkening into night.

He even changed his robe; Lodan had dropped off a pile of fresh clothing days before that looked close to his size, another prize discovered in the extended search of the castle apparently still going on. He picked a plain blue robe that didn't have too many ostentatious trimmings and stood in front of the mirror, studying himself.

He looked like a servant. A well-dressed one, perhaps, but still a servant. Young and thin and lost inside the world of men. He sighed, pushed such thoughts from his mind, and stepped out of the room.

The recent upheaval in the castle hadn't done anything to reduce the various activities going on within its walls. Servants scurried to and fro through the corridors Frankle passed down, none of them meeting his eyes, all focused on their duty and trying their best not to be noticed. He knew the feeling. In times of trouble and change, it was best to stay quiet and still, like a mouse peeking out of its hole, whiskers twitching, nose tasting the air.

The previous night, he had managed to chase down one of the young cleaners assigned to this wing of the castle and tried to wheedle out some information. The boy didn't know much, and wanted to tell Frankle even less, but eventually he seemed to recognise something of a kindred spirit in the young wielder and let slip that the latest rumours were about the king himself, still bed-bound, spending his waking hours raving quietly to himself, his bed surrounded by officials all waiting for him to pass. Apparently, the entire court was in an uproar. Whispers about Redmondis and assassins and attempted military coups were gaining strength.

Still, best to leave such worries for Lodan and the others, like that guard captain Frankle had seen Lodan with a lot recently.

Captain Mont, that was his name. Better not to get involved at all. Once Daemi recovers, we can get out of here, back to Redmondis. Back to the safety of its high stone walls.

That thought brought his mind around to dinner and the special guest Heather had mentioned. Did she mean Daemi?

His question was answered as soon as he pushed open the heavy door to the dining room they had claimed as their own, a relatively sparse affair close to the kitchens and plain enough to afford some privacy. The table was set for six, and already sitting at one place was Daemi, her head bowed, her hands clasped in her lap.

'Daemi!' Frankle blurted, hurrying over to her. Without waiting for a reply, he wrapped her in a hug.

She returned the squeeze quickly, then pushed him back, looking him over. 'Frankle. You look different.'

Frankle smiled, then realised he felt exactly the same way about her. She looked strange. Older. Damaged, somehow.

Daemi seemed to recognise the change in his expression, and a scowl twisted across her lips. 'I'm fine. The scars have closed completely, thanks to you and Heather.'

'Oh. I'm glad to hear that.'

Daemi's eyes darted to the fireplace set in the back wall and the large black cat that was splayed out in front of it, watching them.

Frankle felt it immediately, the spark that flashed between Daemi and the cat. 'Heather told me we had a special guest. I'm glad it's you.'

Daemi smiled again and waved him into a seat. 'Yes, well, that's enough soppiness, don't you think? Tell me what you've been up to these past few days.'

Frankle was just about to launch into an excited listing of all the treasures he'd discovered in the queen's study when the door swung open again and Heather stepped in, grinning, followed quickly by both Lodan and Captain Mont, their heads bowed together in a whisper. They broke it off as soon as they entered, and Lodan strode over to Daemi, clapping her on the shoulder.

'I'm pleased to see our patient has recovered! We could do with some good news around here.'

Frankle looked back and forth between Heather's expectant grin and Daemi's cold, slightly flushed demeanour. But there was something different now.

Her smile faded and her eyes slipped past Lodan to look to the cat again, as though in support. It lazily reared into a stretch in reply.

If Lodan noticed, he didn't mention it, simply waved the guard captain to the head of the table and sat down next to Daemi. 'You all know Captain Mont by now, I think. I wanted to invite him along tonight especially. To see Daemi upright for one, and … well, the rest can wait until after we've eaten. Rest assured, Captain, the food here is hearty and hot, and most important of all in these halls, safe.'

Captain Mont nodded to each of the others before taking his seat, then turned his full attention to Daemi, looking her over coolly, his practised eye noting the way she held herself even when sitting for dinner.

'Daemi, I'm told you are a guard captain in Redmondis. Should I address you as such?'

'Please don't.'

Captain Mont bowed in recognition and grinned. 'And that, Lodan, is what I was saying about the benefits of being a stranger in these parts. No formalities to tie you down.'

'No connections either, Captain, and rest assured my people are doing their best to cut any needless red tape that may be holding you back.'

'Oh, they are, it's just there's such an awful lot of it in this place.'

Captain Mont grimaced and shook his head. 'Almost makes me miss those days in the Tangle. Almost.'

'Were you stationed there for long, Captain?' Heather flapped her napkin open and lay it across her lap. Frankle copied her instantly.

'Long enough, young lady. Long enough. Still, it proved interesting in its own way.'

His attention was caught then by the cat, which had scurried over and climbed into Daemi's lap. It stared at the captain, its black eyes locked onto his.

Captain Mont shook his head suddenly, as if waking up. 'I'm sorry, what was I saying?'

'The Tangle …' Heather prompted.

'Oh yes. Dark days, even darker nights. Strange creatures haunting the shadows—'

'Gloomclaws.' Daemi cut him off.

'I'm sorry?'

'The creatures, the … things that attacked you. Attacked us here. They're called gloomclaws.'

Frankle nodded quickly in confirmation. 'The queen left notes in her study calling them the same thing.'

Lodan leaned forward, his eyes suddenly keen. 'And what other titbits of knowledge have you two been keeping from the rest of us?'

Frankle flushed. 'The queen left a lot of information in her study, not all of it very organised. There's a lot to get through.'

'But I take it you're enjoying the task?' Lodan grinned.

'Oh yes! Just this morning, Heather and I—'

'Lodan doesn't want to hear about every little thing we discover, Frankle,' Heather cut him off abruptly and turned back to Captain Mont, wrenching the conversation back to him. 'I'm told you met our friend in the Tangle, Captain. Wilt.'

'Yes. Yes, I brought Wilt here into Sontair. Unfortunately, I lost track of him almost as soon as we got here.'

The captain stared at the cat then, his lips moving slowly, as though he had forgotten what he had been trying to say. A moment later, the spell seemed to pass, and he snapped back to full awareness.

'I've been pecking at Lodan here like an old maid, trying to get him to tell me where Wilt has gotten to now. I'm worried for him.'

'Rest assured, Captain, he is not in any danger here,' Daemi answered calmly, absently stroking the cat in her lap.

'So, he is here, then? Still?'

Daemi's mouth twisted into a frown and Heather stepped in. 'It's not that simple, I'm afraid, Captain. You see, Wilt has some … special powers. He saved us when we stumbled into the creature—'

'Gloomclaw,' Daemi corrected.

'—the gloomclaw we found in the dungeons here. Apparently, the queen had been keeping it as some sort of pet, or experiment, or something. It would have killed us if it wasn't for Wilt's intervention.'

'These powers you mention, Heather. They wouldn't have anything to do with what became of one of the queen's advisers in front of the entirety of the king's court, would they?'

The room became very quiet then. The captain looked at his hands, gently rearranging the place setting in front of him.

'Um—' Frankle began, and Heather instantly kicked him under the table.

'It's not something any of us fully understand yet, Captain. We're working on it.'

The silence stretched out, filling the room. Then the door to the chamber swung open, and the first of a retinue of servants stepped in, each carrying a large steaming tray of food. In moments, the room was filled with the rich scents of roasted meats and vegetables.

'Well,' Lodan finally spoke after the servants had breezed back out of the room, 'I say we put off any further questions until after our meal. I for one am starving.'

For the next half an hour or so, conversation was minimal as they each dived into their food. Even Daemi seemed to step back into herself as she ate, her shoulders settling and her spine straightening. Every now and then, she slipped a morsel of meat to the cat waiting in her lap. By the time they had each eaten their fill, the table looked like a battle zone.

As soon as Lodan slid his chair back from the table, the door swung open again and the team of servants cleared the table in moments, the final one placing a large pot of steaming coffee in the centre of the table and bowing his way out of the door.

Captain Mont clapped his belly appreciatively and sighed. 'You weren't wrong about the service here, Lodan. Your people could teach even the court servants a thing or two.'

'When jobs are at a premium, Captain, those who hold them grip them tightly.'

'Too true.'

'Now,' Lodan turned to each of them, 'I mentioned we were expecting a special guest tonight. Not to detract from your good selves,' he nodded in turn to Captain Mont and Daemi, 'but there was someone else I thought we should meet.'

On cue, the doors opened again, and two armed men entered leading a third, bent over and covered with a blanket, shackles clinking as he was led to a seat at the table and pushed down into it. At a nod from Lodan, the two soldiers backed out of the room, their hands never straying too far from their blades.

'And what sort of special guest comes so garbed, Lodan?' Captain Mont sat forward, all his attention on the prisoner.

'One I think we will all be keen to question,' Lodan replied, and reached out to rip the blanket free.

Huddled in the chair was a thin, red-robed man, hands and feet locked into what looked like slightly greenish stone chains, face bent down and away from them, as though even the dim firelight that lit the room was too much for him.

'Raise your face.' Lodan's voice was one of command, very different from his timbre only moments earlier.

The man obeyed, his thin, sunken cheeks and pale, almost silvery skin shining in the light.

'Open your eyes, wielder.'

Frankle let out a gasp of recognition as the man's lids opened to reveal his glowing, golden eyes. 'Cortis.'

'What's that?' Lodan turned to Frankle.

'Cantor Cortis. In Redmondis. The prefect we told you about, who tried to overthrow the Sisters. His eyes were just like that.'

'You see, Captain? Already we are making progress.'

'But what is the significance, Frankle? Why would this man's eyes be so—'

'It's something Cortis did to his followers—the ones closest to him, anyway. They became wolves, part of his pack. Their eyes were the first thing to turn. Others, the ones who resisted him …'

Frankle shuddered at the memory of the pile of writhing half human forms at the base of the wielder's tower, the result of failed transformations that Cortis had abandoned.

Frankle's words seemed to encourage the prisoner, and a grin of triumph twisted across his face.

'They were weak. Too weak to face the truth they were offered. Just as you are.' The man's voice was barely above a whisper, but it twined about the room, slithering into their ears.

The cat on Daemi's lap leapt up onto the table and crept slowly toward the prisoner, its black eyes never leaving his face.

'Leave us,' Daemi spoke, her eyes also locked onto the prisoner. 'Frankle, you stay. You can assist.'

Heather was the first to react, pushing her chair back and gesturing Lodan and Captain Mont to do the same. 'It's okay. I think I know what they're going to do. Let them have the room.'

Captain Mont looked like he was about to argue the point, but at a glance from Lodan, he nodded and followed them both out of the chamber, shutting the door behind them.

The prisoner's brash confidence seemed to drain away as he stared into the cat's eyes.

Frankle sat very still, watching Daemi's face. 'Are you sure?'

'Yes, Frankle.' Daemi reached out and took his hand in hers. 'Come. Like this.'

Frankle closed his eyes and dived into the chaos of the depths.

That's right, like this.

The voice was Delco's, just as it had been before, but Frankle knew that Wilt was the one calling him on, through the swirling currents that sang to him, down into the strange peace of the space beneath the depths, onto the ice barrier that stretched out below them, marked only by a single black spot. He sunk helplessly toward it, trying to swallow the panic that surged into his throat.

It's okay, Frankle. We won't let you fall.

Frankle trusted him, trusted Daemi, trusted his memory of Delco and the strange connection he could still feel between the cat before his eyes and the man he once knew.

Come. Walk with me.

Frankle felt his feet touch onto the ice. He looked down at them, and thought he caught a flash of movement somewhere beneath, through the blurred lens of the frozen surface.

Don't look down.

Instantly, his eyes flicked forward, obeying the command.

You have grown in strength, Frankle. Even so, those sights are not for your eyes. Not yet.

He felt his feet begin to move over the ice, slowly at first, testing each footfall to ensure it held his weight. The cat trotted slowly beside him, much surer on his four feet.

We will break into his mind together, but you must leave me there once the task is complete. Fear not, I will return easily enough. You must take Daemi with you. I do not want either of you to feel responsible for what must be done.

Frankle saw a flash of vision, a drained face, cadaverous, black skin sunk against bone, dead eyes staring. He shook his head, and the image faded.

Come. Take me with you.

Frankle bent down and the cat jumped easily into his arms.

Now. Let us begin.

A surging vortex, a black snake twisting out from its centre, striking down onto the helpless mind of their victim, then a chaos of memory crashing over them.

He stood in the circle, one of the chosen, each strong enough on their own to be named wielder. He felt the triumph of it, the glow of power inside his mind. Burning and bright and too much to hold, so that it leaked out through his golden flecked eyes.

Interlinked, their minds joined together in the way the queen had instructed them. A chain far stronger than the sum of its parts.

He reached his arms up as one with the others in the circle, and the net began to form. Surrounding the shadow in the centre of the circle, trapping it, holding it on the surface plane. Not allowing it to sink back into the depths.

Cold sweat broke out on his forehead as the net surged and warped, the blackness in its centre pulsing back at it, a tickle of darkness scratching over the surface of his mind. He could feel it staining him, leaking into him through the barriers he had put in place. It was too much for them to hold.

Back, Frankle. Away from that. Go forward.

The silver blade cut through the air in front of his face, so close he could feel the whisper of its passing.

'Moonsteel.'

Vargul frowned. 'A weld blade. Use its proper name.'

He nodded and kept his eyes on the treasure as Vargul swept the blade through the air again. 'How?'

'The assassin from Redmondis was carrying it.'

'But how did it find its way into his hands? Surely they haven't mastered—'

'No, this came from the east, beyond the Spine, across the Eternal Sea. Look here.' Vargul pointed at the top of the hilt, where a small flame motif was etched into the base of the silver blade. 'The queen has others like it. The flame marks this as a blade forged in the fires of Pankesh, where all true wielders hope one day to serve.'

He nodded, hoping his ignorance of the topic wasn't showing on his face. He had heard about the strange folk of the Eastern Dales, but talk of an Eternal Sea and Pankesh were mysteries to his sheltered mind.

'I think this blade was owned by none other than Cantor Cortis himself,' Vargul continued, his eyes shining.

'So, the assassin?'

'Do not fear. I have him under control. Come, let us show our brothers what we have found.'

There, Frankle. That is what we need. Come now, I do not think we can hold this mind open any longer.

A crack and a shift and another vision opened.

He sat in the dark, huddled in the corner of the room, waiting for the sound of his door swinging open. It came every night; it would come again tonight.

A silence, a coldness, a blackness too deep to breathe in, so thick it choked him and clawed its way into his eyes, wiping the world away. Then the pain.

Frankle. Enough, you must go.

Oh, the pain. Like he was impaled on a spear of flames, licking his insides, burning up and out through his eyes.

Now Frankle, leave this nightmare where it belongs.

The door swung slowly open, and he looked up.

A sudden wrench and Frankle was out, back above the swirling chaos of the welds, surging out and breaking back into the surface world, the deep coldness that had found him dripping away.

'Breathe, Frankle.'

He opened his eyes to see Daemi leaning over him, her eyes edged with concern.

'Are you okay?'

He thought about that for a second before nodding and sitting up. 'I'm fine. That was—'

'Dangerous,' Daemi finished for him. 'I hope you found out what we wanted to know.'

Frankle gasped as he saw the shrunken figure of the prisoner slumped in the chair across from them. His skin was blackened and drawn, like something had sucked the years out of him.

'We're not going to get anything else out of that one.' Daemi clapped him on the back and pulled him to his feet. 'Are you sure you're okay?'

Frankle nodded, his eyes not leaving the husk in front of them. 'Did I—'

'No.' Daemi looked over at the cat crouched on the edge of the table, its black eyes staring through them. 'That wasn't you.'

'Were you there with me? Did you see?'

'I saw. Come now, you need to rest.'

Frankle was about to protest again when he almost collapsed as a wave of exhaustion seemed to pull his legs out from under him. 'Um, perhaps you're right.'

'Leave this for the others. We'll worry about what to do later.'

He slumped gratefully against Daemi's shoulder as she led him from the room.

'And the others?' Captain Mont sat forward, his eyes never leaving Daemi's face.

'I don't know. There was only one other there. Vargul.'

'He's—' Lodan began.

'Already accounted for,' Captain Mont finished for him. 'But there were others here, other advisers.'

'None that have popped their heads up,' Lodan continued. 'As soon as one does, we will know about it.'

'We should have waited.' Captain Mont sat back and slapped his thigh in irritation. 'Let the dungeons do their work on him. Now there's nothing left.'

Daemi shook her head. 'You wouldn't have got anywhere. He had been trained by a Sister.'

'The queen?'

'That's where we need to focus. Frankle has been working through her study. Apparently, she left a lot of information there, for those with the wits to understand it. I say we contact Petron in Redmondis and get him to send a team here to study it, find out what we can.'

Lodan frowned. 'That's all very well, but how long will it take them to get here? We need to act now, not in a month's time.'

'There are ways.' Daemi replied, and glanced across at the ever-present cat watching their exchange.

Old ways. Silent ways.

Chapter 3

At first there was only cold. A deep, groaning cold inside his very bones, locking him in place and driving all thought from his mind. A chill so deep he was numb to the burning pain of it, unable to respond as he felt the ice around him shift and crack and begin to slide free. Then a pulse of heat, waking him, opening his eyes to the glowing golden thread in front of him. Singing to him, calling him on, upward, toward the light of the surface. A single shining doorway out of the dark.

Higgs opened his eyes.

A heavy hand clapped onto his shoulder, forcing him to his knees, then holding him upright as a wave of nausea rode up his insides and cold, salty water vomited out of him. Just salt water, nothing more inside him, the red stone at his feet washed clean by it.

'Get it out of you. You don't want to leave any of that inside.'

His stomach spasmed again in response, a thin, warm stream of bile falling from him.

'Breathe. Remember to breathe.'

He sucked in a long, shuddering breath, amazed at the feel of it, the deep ache in his lungs slowly subsiding as they flexed back into life.

'Good. Now rest. Recover. The Novus will judge you soon enough.'

The hand on his shoulder lifted and he heard boots move away, out of his line of vision. A metal door clanged shut, then the steps slowed again and he could just make out the same gruff voice repeating the commands to some other poor sap, getting them to empty themselves and live again.

Live again. He was alive.

Higgs raised his head and looked around, trying to blink his eyes into focus. The light was dim, a dull red glow covering everything—his eyes didn't seem to want to follow orders—his vision was blurred and smudged as though he was staring out from deep underwater.

He felt himself sinking, impossibly heavy in the darkening waters. The shape on the ice above battered at the surface, its four paws clawing uselessly at it.

—Wilt, fight it. Stay with me!—

Higgs coughed and collapsed forward again, squeezing his eyes shut against the vision that had overwhelmed him. He put his head between his knees and gasped for air, slowly getting his breathing back under control.

After almost a minute, he tried again, raising his eyes slowly this time, taking one sight in at a time.

Red stone floor. Red stone walls. A barred door—a different, darker shade. Green perhaps. His eyes refused to focus on it. He shuffled forward awkwardly and reached out to touch it, fingers shaking as he tried to hold them still.

A spark of recognition as his fingers brushed the stone bars. A hint of green light pulsing in response.

Another clang as the door in the adjoining cell slammed shut, and he shrank back into his huddle, but the sound of boots on stone moved in the opposite direction, away from him. The voice was just a whisper now, too low to pass through the thick stone walls of his prison. He rocked back on his heels, concentrating on his breathing, on the wonder of air moving in and out of his lungs once more.

How was it possible? How was he here? How was he anywhere at all?

Where was Wilt?

Sontair. They had been in Sontair. He had taken control of Wilt, hiding him deep, allowing Vargul to break in and seemingly dominate his victim's mind. Then they had escaped, Wilt's wraith form taking over, its black hand sliding into Vargul's chest, feeding on the man's final thoughts as it drained him, trying to track the power that controlled him, infected him, bloomed within his mind and finally abandoned its servant to death. The dark power that recognised Wilt clung onto him, pulling him down below the barrier at the heart of the depths, into the cold ice. Into death.

But something had found him again. A vision, a memory, from before Redmondis. From Greystone, when the assassin had been sent to kill Wilt. They had slipped into his mind and found the shining golden weld that controlled him. Grasped it, pulling themselves up and out of the ice and ending up …

Here. Wherever here was.

He was breathing easier now, his lungs no longer protesting each shuddering breath, though a dull ache remained inside his chest, as though he had strained the muscles around his lungs. He coughed and a hot clench of pain shot through him.

'You. Boy.'

A voice, different from the one before. Very different. A female voice.

'Boy? Can you hear me?'

It was coming from behind the stone wall, from the cell next to his.

'Come. Before they return.'

Higgs scrambled forward to the corner of his cell, where the dull green bars disappeared into the strange red stone of the wall. He tried to respond, but his voice didn't seem to want to work. All that he could squeeze out was a thick rasp of a groan, like the final dying breath of an old man.

'Ah! I thought I heard them bringing someone else back. Can't talk yet?'

Higgs caught himself shaking his head in response as he tried to clear the strange lump in his throat.

'Must have gone too deep. It will take a while for your body to recover.'

He managed another grunt in response.

'I only went shallow this time. Easy task.'

Another clang rang out from farther down the corridor outside his cell door, and Higgs heard the owner of the voice scramble away from their shared corner.

'Get back. They return already. Hope you can answer the Novus's questions or it'll be back to the Pit for you.'

The voice stopped then, and he could hear marching feet approaching. He slid back away from the door and bowed his head, eyes locked on the floor.

His vision blurred as he stared at the dull red stone, and he felt himself swaying in place, unable to hold himself still even in his crouched position. He squeezed his eyes closed and concentrated on breathing, trying to will himself to stay conscious.

The bolt on the door of the cell next to his shot back, and he heard a short, whispered muttering, then a single clear voice addressed the girl.

'Weldfarer, you return. What is your name?'

Higgs heard her reply but couldn't make out the words.

'Good. And your task?'

Another murmur, and Higgs almost toppled over as he leaned toward the wall to try to hear.

'You were successful?'

No reply then, at least none that he could hear. Perhaps she simply nodded.

'Good. You may rest for now. The Novus will no doubt call on you again soon.'

A swish of movement then, as of a long cloak brushing against the stone floor, and another loud clang as the door of her cell slammed shut again. The booted feet moved closer and Higgs bowed his head between his knees as the door to his cell creaked open.

Suddenly a gloved hand was under his chin, forcing his eyes up. He blinked furiously, his eyes filling with tears as something bright blinded him. A familiar, golden light. Then a mutter of anger, and his chin was thrown back down.

'This one has ventured far too deep. He has forgotten how to see.'

The voice was strong and severe, a rasp of age at its edge. Instantly, the image of Cantor Cortis popped into Higgs's mind, but this voice was different. Similar, but not the same.

'Your name, weldfarer?'

He coughed again as the words refused to form in his throat.

'No voice either? How was he allowed to lose himself this way?'

The question seemed to be directed at the other, and he heard the first voice again, the one that had awoken him.

'The mules brought him to me as is. I know not of his time elsewhere.'

The gloved hand grasped Higgs's chin again, and this time he could almost make out the shape of a face through the golden blur.

'A waste, letting them drown themselves this way. He should have been better prepared. Back to the Pit with him. We will reform what has been lost.'

'As you command.'

He must have lost time then, for the next moment both bodies had left his cell and he was blinking his eyes at the stone ground, trying to will his thoughts into focus.

Pit? What was going on?

'You. Boy.'

It was the girl again, back at the front corner of his cell.

'Couldn't answer? Nothing for it now. Try to regain what strength you can. You'll be back in the Pit soon enough.'

Higgs thought about crawling to the corner to try to talk to her, but a wave of exhaustion swept over him. He inched further away instead, back to the cold stone wall at the rear of his cell, huddling into himself.

'You got out of there once. You can do it again.'

Her voice seemed to drift into his mind like a dream. He wrapped his arms around his head and curled into a ball, shivering as he tried to will some heat into his body.

Body. His body. Somehow.

She whispered something again, but Higgs had already turned away from her voice, away from the world itself, as a blank wall of unconsciousness slammed over him and he knew no more.

Chapter 4

Daemi ducked low under the swinging blade and stepped into a thrust, her weld blade cutting easily through the plate armour of the training dummy and sinking deep into the central wooden pillar that was its trunk. Her blade had struck home in the exact same spot six times now, each thrust driving a little deeper, and the weight of the heavy blades in the dummy's 'hands' were beginning to make the entire structure sway as it waved them back and forth in a futile attempt to slow her down.

Beads of sweat dripped down her forehead, and thin clouds of dust had kicked up into the stale air of the empty gymnasium, blurring the air into a dream-like landscape of shifting shadows. The only sounds were the pads of her feet, the short staccato drums of her blade striking home, and the mechanical whirring of the automatic dummy she trained with. That sound was beginning to roughen around the edges, a new twang entering its choir as the session dragged on.

A sneak strike shot out from the base of the pillar at her feet, and she leapt it easily, spinning into a slicing cut that struck one of the dummy's four arms completely free, its blade throwing more dust into the air as it cut into the dirt and rolled away into the shadows.

The dummy was clearly lurching now, its weight distribution all wrong as it continued to spin. Daemi stepped closer still, determined to end it. Three quick cuts later and the whir of its motor cut out completely, some vital hidden gear severed, the dummy's spin slowing to a sad, lazy collapse to one side as if drunk.

Daemi stepped back and caught her breath, rolling her shoulders to relax her back.

She felt off, wrong somehow. It was her back, she realised, the lack of scar tissue limiting her. She kept waiting for the bright flare of pain from her scars opening, but her back was unmarked and whole again. She had to keep working to get used to the lack of limitation in her reach.

A slow clap echoed from the dimness of the doorway, and she backed away from the broken training dummy, sliding her blade back into the sheath on her hip.

'Looks like Captain Mont will need to get his training machines serviced.'

Lodan stepped out of the shadows, a wide smile on his face. 'He told me they were the latest invention of the crafters here. Not cheap either. You could make this an expensive hobby.'

Daemi nodded in greeting and reached for her towel, wiping the sweat from her face and neck. 'Your Captain Mont asked me to move my training in here. Apparently, I was making the other soldiers nervous.'

'I'm not surprised.'

'These machines of his are too slow, too predictable.'

'Perhaps we could get Heather to look at them. Sharpen them up a bit.'

Daemi snorted. 'At least it would give her something to keep her busy.' She threw the sopping towel onto the back of a chair, just missing the black cat perched there, eyeing her.

'You shouldn't let her teasing bother you. She only does it to get a rise from you. She's doing her best to hide a damaged heart.'

'I know.'

Daemi stretched again, Lodan watching the muscles on her shoulders pop and ripple.

'You move more and more like him, you know. Even though I never saw Wilt wield a blade like that. It's … imposing.'

'You bested a gloomclaw yourself. Perhaps we two should take a turn in the circle.'

'Oh no.' Lodan chuckled and held his hands up in surrender. 'What is the saying? Something about discretion being the better part. Besides, I don't think I was anything other than a passenger when Wilt took control.'

'He did, didn't he? Take control of you. Even though he wasn't there.'

'I believe it.'

Lodan nodded toward the cat staring back and forth between them. 'Just one more mystery to add to the pile, I suppose.'

'Wilt was never much of a fighter.'

'But you are.'

'It's the only thing I've ever been good at.'

'And now, somehow, part of him and part of you have merged. Isn't that right?'

A frown twisted across Daemi's face. 'I guess so. It's … complicated.'

'And Higgs?' Lodan stepped closer, eyes intent. 'Is he there too?'

The cat took that as its cue and padded silently up to Daemi, leaping up to her shoulder and burrowing itself into her dark curls.

'No.' Daemi patted the cat idly, her eyes elsewhere, staring at a spot somewhere other in time and place. 'He's … elsewhere. At least for now.'

'But you can sense him? Feel him?'

Daemi turned away and started to gather her things. 'Like I said, it's complicated.'

'Ah.' Lodan sighed and tilted his head. 'This must be that famous Redmondis doubletalk I've heard about.'

'I'm sorry, I really don't mean to be so vague. It's just—you know how some things are beyond words? The more you try to describe them, the further from the truth you get? It's like … there are thoughts that I can hear. Understand. But it's almost like they're my thoughts too.'

'From the cat, you mean?'

'Yes. But whether that's Wilt talking directly to me, or just me imagining what I think he'd say, I can't tell. There's a part of him here.' She rubbed the cat's back again and it arched against her palm. 'But it's not all of him.'

'So where is the rest of him, then?'

'I don't know, not for sure. But I'm going to find him.'

Lodan nodded, as though he was expecting her to say just that. 'I doubt we could stop you, even if we wanted to. Come then. I've got something to show you before you leave.'

They walked around the edge of the training yard, careful to stay out of reach of the various wooden weapons cracking into each other as the company of soldiers stepped through their routine. The cat was still curled around Daemi's neck, dark eyes hidden beneath her hair. Daemi studied the soldiers as she passed, instantly picking out any flaws she saw, determining weak points and strategies for attack.

Lodan turned to watch her, waving her up beside him as they walked. 'You really can't help yourself, can you?'

'What?' Daemi finally pulled her eyes away from a particularly intense bout just beside them. 'Oh, sorry. Force of habit, I guess.'

'It's more than that, as I think you know.'

'These soldiers are young. Green. They need to spend a lot more time here before they head outside Sontair's gates.'

'Ah, but time is one thing we do not have. Young men and women willing to fight—that we have in abundance. Come.'

Lodan ducked into a doorway and led Daemi up a tight spiralling staircase to the upper floor. 'Captain Mont kindly gave me a room here. Space is at a premium, as you know.'

He opened a door into a small, bare chamber, only a bed and desk crowded into it.

Daemi looked from one to the other and back to Lodan. 'And what is it you wanted to show me?'

Lodan grinned knowingly and held up his hands. 'Come now, you've been spending too much time listening to Heather.'

He walked over to the desk and opened one of its drawers,

pulling out a round necklace and placing it on the desk in front of Daemi. 'What do you make of that?'

Daemi leaned over and studied it. It looked like a medal of some kind, beaten silver shaped into a circle. It gave off a slightly bluish tinge. 'Uh, it's pretty, I guess. I'm not one for jewellery myself.'

'It was a prize for winning the flagball tournament in Greystone. With Wilt. Pick it up.'

Daemi did as she was told and as soon as her fingers brushed the metal, the blue tinge brightened into a vivid glow. 'Huh. It reacts to the holder.'

'It reacts to Wilt,' Lodan corrected.

Daemi held the medal in front of her, looking back between it and Lodan. 'To Wilt?'

'The Prefects—Cantors—of Redmondis used them to identify Wilt. When the prize was placed over my neck, it didn't react at all, but as soon as Wilt stepped forward it turned blue.'

Daemi watched the strange medallion spin slowly in the air in front of her before placing it back on the desk. Immediately, the blue light dimmed back into a dull gleam.

'But it's already blue.'

'Exactly.' Lodan smiled. 'I noticed it for the first time weeks after Wilt had left. In Greystone. When—'

'When Wilt was with you. Inside your memory.'

'Yes.'

Lodan brushed his fingers across the medallion and its blue light seemed to flicker in response. 'It's been this way ever since. Like Wilt left something in me.'

As if in response, the cat suddenly leapt down from Daemi's shoulders onto the desk and sniffed tentatively at the medallion

It looked up at Lodan and Daemi, its black eyes reflecting their faces back at them. Then it reached out a single paw and placed it in the centre of the medal.

A bright blue flash lit the room, blinding them both. The cat leaped back onto Daemi's shoulders, burrowing into her neck away from the burning light. Daemi blinked frantically to clear the stars in her eyes, and Lodan was bent over the desk, covering his face with one hand.

In moments, the blindness passed, and they both looked around the room, which seemed much darker now that the light had left it.

'I guess that seals it,' Lodan muttered, scooping the medallion off the desk and sliding it back into the drawer. 'Remind me never to do that again.'

Daemi was still blinking, a liquid silver pulse edging her vision. 'What does it mean?'

'It means that wherever Wilt is now, he's with us also. In part, at least.' Lodan looked at the cat bent around Daemi's shoulders. 'Some of us more than others. Perhaps that explains the pull you feel to find him. I feel it too.'

'Will you come with us?'

'I cannot.' Lodan walked over to the small window that opened on to the training ground below. 'You said so yourself: these soldiers are too young. The people here, they need my help. They need the Grey Guild. This is where I need to be.'

'We each have our own fate.'

'Do we?' Lodan turned back to her, a sad smile lighting his eyes. 'And are you so sure it is your fate you follow?'

Heather was sitting on the floor of the study, a large, heavy tome on her lap, head bowed and lips moving silently as her finger traced along the narrow scrawl that filled the page. It was heavy going, this particular subject not well known, and she had had considerable difficulty tracking down any reference to conduits at all. Their very existence was questioned, most modern crafters assuming they were figments of some wielder's over-active imaginations rather than anything concrete.

The concept was simple enough. If a weld can be used to invade other's thoughts, in effect, some part of the wielder's consciousness is transferred across the weld. If this transference could be widened, the welds could be used to transfer more than just thought.

A strong enough wielder with a working conduit could travel instantly across a theoretically infinite space instantly.

Unfortunately, as any crafter worth their salt knew, what wielders thought theoretically possible and what crafters could actually form from those ideas were often two very different things. It was all very well thinking something into existence. Some poor sap had to actually build the thing. And even then, if there was some problem with the conduit, some mistake made in its creation, then the unlucky wielder who stepped through it could find themselves stranded in the depths forever, or perhaps even worse, step out the other side missing some vital part of their anatomy.

And of course, even if everything went perfectly, there was no way of knowing where the conduit would send the wielder. Each entry point had an exit when the conduit was first formed, but who could tell if that exit point still existed? Perhaps what was once a doorway into a harmless bedroom on the other side of the world now sat on the bottom of an ocean.

No. No, there were far too many possibilities for disaster here.

Heather shook her head and looked at the stone doorway in front of her and the strange carvings etched in dull green stone around its edge. 'What mysteries do you hide?' she whispered.

'Talking to yourself, are we?' Frankle closed the door behind him as he shuffled inside. 'First sign of madness, that.'

Heather sighed and closed the book. 'It's the only way to have an intelligent conversation around here.'

Frankle grunted in reply and started rummaging through the mess of parchments scattered across the desk. 'Been making yourself at home, I see.'

'Of course. You know you really should try to be more organised.'

'Found anything useful?'

'Not there. But here, here's something.'

Heather stood up and dropped the book in the centre of the table, sending dust and papers flying. She opened it to the page she had been studying and pointed to the sketch in the bottom right-hand corner. 'Look familiar?'

It was a drawing of a doorway, much like the one they had found, though not as detailed. It had markings around its edge, but they seemed very different from those carved into the green stone in front of them. At the bottom of the sketch was a single line: conduit (speculative).

''Speculative?' That doesn't inspire much confidence.'

'Oh, just you wait until you read some of the results of their experiments. They get quite descriptive.'

'So, it's true then? They do exist?'

'They did. In some form, anyway. This volume is centuries old. Even I struggle to read some of it, and I'm the smartest person I know.'

'Really.'

'They were never perfected. Too dangerous by far. I mean, the idea is great but ...'

'But the queen had one. Someone made it for her.'

'If it even works.'

Frankle looked up from the page and walked over to the stone gateway, tracing his fingers lightly over its edge. 'Oh, it works. Can't you hear it?'

Heather looked at him and frowned. 'Hear what?'

'The weld song,' he whispered, as though not wanting to interrupt it.

'Are you sure you're all right, Frankle?

'Perhaps that's the part we're missing ...' Frankle continued to muse, then snapped out of it and smiled at Heather. 'You should know all about it.'

'What do you mean?'

'Your heartstone. You forged it, made the two stones as one, linked together. Partners.'

'Well, it wasn't quite as simple as that—'

'But the principle is the same, isn't it? You need two of them. I think this conduit is the same.'

'You mean there are two of them?'

'I mean that if there's one on this end, there must be another one.'

'Makes sense.'

'And if they were formed together, then the other one is probably back where they were both made. Doesn't this stone look familiar to you?'

Heather eyed the doorway again, the greenish tinge to the stone seeming stronger now, as though the presence of Frankle had somehow woken it up.

'Redmondis.'

'Exactly. Just like the shackles and cells in the dungeons here. The stone is from Redmondis. Perhaps this door—'

'Conduit.'

'—conduit, is how it all got here in the first place. We know the queen was from Redmondis.'

'Huh. Makes sense I suppose.'

Heather closed the book and held it to her chest as she stared at the conduit. It was definitely reacting now, the edges of the door positively glowing. Frankle was tracing his fingers across the carvings, his head cocked as though listening.

'Frankle?'

'Hmm?'

'How do we know there's only one other door?'

He stopped and looked at her, head still slanted to the side like a curious puppy. 'We don't, I suppose.' He smiled, his eyes lighting up with an eager glow she found instantly, troublingly familiar. 'Only one way to find out.'

Chapter 5

He dreamed of standing on a rocky shore in the shadow of a high stone wall, the eyes of the guards patrolling far above not dropping down to their level, locked instead on the swaying trees of the Tangle on the far side of the river.

—You. What is your name?—

Wilt.

No. Not Wilt. Wilt is here, beside him, searching at his feet for ammunition. Finding a good-sized rock now, slipping it into the smooth leather cradle of his sling, spinning it a few times in the air to judge its weight, the wind whipping past his ear and tugging at his hair with each revolution. Staring back out at the trees again with that look in his eye, aware of them staring back.

—You. What is your name?—

Higgs.

No. Not Higgs. Higgs is gone. Higgs died in Wilt's arms inside the fortress in Redmondis, the black tip of the weld blade pushing through and out of his chest, hot red blood spraying out across his friend's face. A deep red bloom spreading across his chest, soaking him in an instant, painless chill.

—Is this your name?—

He feels his hand plunge into the shallow water at the river's edge, ice cold, shocking his fingers into numb stiffness as they fumble among the pebbles at his feet, searching out something they know is there but cannot grasp.

—No. Not water. Is this your name?—

His fingers spread wide in front of him now, soaking in the heat from the campfire happily dancing in front of him, the shadows of his bones showing dark against the orange glow of the light. The cold melts away instantly, replaced by a warmth that moves quickly past comfort into danger, almost into pain as he reaches toward the flames. Soon he can reach no further, shying away from the heat, his body knowing not to proceed any further, despite the wishes of the voice inside his mind.

—No. Not flame. Is this your name?—

He is on the shore again, back from the flowing river's edge, the wind rushing over it and crashing up against the city walls like a wave, pulling his hair back from his face and driving tears out of his eyes as he faces it. The same wind that only moments before blew through the trees of the Tangle, sending them waving and calling him onward, inviting him into their shadows and secrets. Lifting him, pulling him into the sky to dip and dive with the thrill of flight, until nausea rolls up inside his belly and his mind rejects it, wrenching him back down to the stable ground.

—No. Not air. Is this your name?—

He digs his hand into the wet dirt at his feet, pushing past scratching, bruising rock and the sharp-edged bones of long dead creatures washed ashore, carried who knows how many miles from the mountains in the north to end up here, under the walls of Greystone. He feels the warm mud squeeze between his fingers as he grasps at it, feeling a faint tingle of acknowledgement inside his fist but no acceptance. No spark of recognition.

—No. Not earth. Could it be?—

His fingers know the truth of it without thought, wrapping themselves around the stone and pulling it free, shaking the water and sand free to hold it up to the sunlight, the late afternoon glow glinting off its smooth, cold surface. It was the perfect size, the perfect weight, as always. It was his gift.

Stone.

He feels it pulse inside him, the pull of possibility, the call to shape and reshape, to craft and form.

Stone. That was his name.

—*Stone. That is … unusual. There has not been one so named in time upon time. In an age. But there is no denying it. Stone. You are Stone.*—

Stone.

—*You. I know you.*—

Higgs felt himself be pulled up and out of sleep, hands first, the heavy shackles around his wrists cutting into his skin to send a scream of consciousness tearing through his mind, blowing all shreds of the dream clear.

He looked down at the source of the pain, blinking his eyes free of tears to stare at the single large clasp locked around both wrists, forcing his hands together in supplication. The bindings were formed from green stone that sent a thrill of memory through him. He had seen these before, through other eyes. Some other place. Some other time.

The shackles jerked forward, and he trotted after them, trying to lessen the pain of their pull. A dull red glow filled the air around him, bright orange light flaring out from cracks in the stone walls he passed, plumes of smoke and heat billowing out of them every few moments, like the breath of some massive, panting beast as he was led down its gullet into its bowels to be consumed.

He tried to look around and make some sense of where he was, but the shackles jerked again, pulling him into a jog now, forcing him to concentrate on keeping his feet as he stumbled along. His legs were numb, the muscles in his thighs tingling with heat as the blood pumped through them, warming them back into life.

A sudden gash yawned wide in the stone wall he was pulled past, and he caught sight of a large, open chamber, sunk down into the depths. A steep-walled pit, its edges pointed with sharp rock. Orange light flared out of it, and he could just make out a long, snaking river of fire at the base of the pit, strange shadowed forms shuffling along beside it, and—impossibly—other shadows dancing within the flames. Another jerk and the vision was ripped away as he was pulled past, the tunnel sloping down now, his feet struggling to keep up with the sudden momentum of his body.

The tingle in his legs shifted into a low burn, the pain in his wrists forgotten as this new fire licked at his mind. He stumbled, only just catching himself and bouncing back off the wall beside him, bruising his shoulder painfully.

The shadows in front of him were complete, the chain that pulled his shackles disappearing into a total blackness that his eyes could not penetrate. Still, they pulled him onward, ever deeper down the path.

He could feel his mind slowly chugging up to speed, trying to form cogent thoughts but slipping away again, as though something thick was wrapped around it, resisting all attempts at coherence, forcing the thoughts back and away to keep his mind open and empty and pure.

Higgs looked down at his wrists again, reaching for the memory there. Familiar. Where had he seen them? Why did he know them?

Stone.

The pull on his wrists stopped and his hands fell down to his waist as the chain dropped to the ground. He stared into the blank shadow, his breath coming in gasps, the air hot and wet in his lungs.

You. I know you. You are Stone.

The shadow waited then, as if expecting some sort of answer. Higgs nodded, unsure what else to do.

You are the first in some time. You will be alone. You will be watched. You will be judged.

The rock wall beside him cracked suddenly, a thin darting opening fleeing up the centre of it and pulling open to reveal another high-walled pit falling into the depths. He stood at the edge of it, peering down into the dim shadows to try to make some sense of what he was seeing. There was no path, no way down past the razor-sharp rocks that lined the pit's walls.

You will remain. You will be watched. You will be judged.

The shackles on his wrists clicked open suddenly and dropped to the floor. As soon as they left his skin, he felt his full mind return.

The shadow moved behind him then, a sudden force propelling him through the gap and out into the open air, his arms flailing uselessly as he fell toward the shadows and the waiting rocks below.

His first clear thought was fear. The second was pain. The third was lost as his mind fled into the waiting darkness, away from this world. Away from this time.

Chapter 6

Petron could feel the changing seasons on the tips of his fingers, an icy kiss of winter just starting to slide down the northern mountains. He stood right at the edge of the opening to his chamber, high in what was formerly the Black Robes' tower in Redmondis, leaning out into the wind that rushed up the cliff face like ocean surf crashing against rock. A distant smile played over his lips as he wiggled his fingers, eyes closed, mind elsewhere in the wash and rush of flight.

A high cry in the distance snapped his eyes open, and a single black shape formed in the sky, growing larger with every wingbeat, until he had to step back from the edge to allow the great eagle space to land.

'Good morning, Stax.'

The eagle tilted its head, watching him with one bright staring eye as it fussily arranged its wings.

'What news?' Petron smiled.

Stax scratched its claws into the rock as though stamping its feet, and Petron relented, reaching down into the corner of the chamber to retrieve the bucket of meat scraps he kept there. He tossed one into the air and the eagle snatched it hungrily.

'Winter is on its way,' Petron continued. 'The Tangle's aspect is darkening. Soon the great green sea will be cloaked in white.'

The eagle didn't respond, simply cocked its head again, waiting for another morsel.

Petron sighed and threw another hunk of meat. 'You'll have to forgive an old man his musings, Stax. An all too human trait.' He placed the bucket back in the corner and shuffled over to the fire to fuss with his teapot.

'It's loneliness, I suppose. Not something you feel anymore, I'd bet. Just another of your advantages.' He poured a steaming cup of tea, and a warm, spiced scent filled the air. He sipped the brew carefully, smiling as it warmed his stomach. 'Still, being human does have its positives as well.'

Petron looked at the giant eagle, properly studying it as it lifted one foot to scratch quickly behind its head. 'You've gained weight.'

Stax dropped its foot and stared at him with both eyes, fluffing out its wings in response.

'Oh, I don't mean it as an insult. It suits you. Makes you seem more … regal.'

The eagle seemed to consider his words before accepting them, then resumed its preening.

'My fault, of course. Too many snacks.' He placed his tea back on his desk and flipped idly through the stack of parchments laying on it. 'But I do enjoy your interruptions. Takes me away from all of this.' Petron stared dully at a page before tossing it back on the pile. 'Nothing new in these reports, anyway.'

The eagle let out an ear-splitting cry, the very air shaking, and Petron stumbled against his desk, almost sending his tea splashing across the pages. He caught the tilting cup just in time, burning himself as boiling water splashed over the back of his hand.

'What the—'

The door to his chamber opened, and a young boy and girl walked in, smiling as they watched him dance and curse.

'Now, now, Petron.' Heather smiled. 'That's no way to greet old friends.'

Heather stood at the opening to Petron's chamber, one hand clutching the bucket of meat scraps, the other stroking the head of the great eagle Stax, who seemed happy enough with the attention but always kept one eye firmly locked on the treats.

'And how are you, Stax?' she whispered, fingers sinking into the thick feathers at the eagle's neck. 'What news from the Tangle?'

She pulled out another chunk of meat and watched as Stax carefully plucked it from her fingers. 'Your eyes are glowing even brighter than I remembered. Or are you just pleased to see me?'

Stax shook his head quickly, tossing the meat into the air and gulping it down.

'You know, you remind me of another friend of ours, in Sontair.'

Petron was sitting by the fire, Frankle slumped into a chair beside him, a steaming mug of tea cupped in his hands. The young boy looked exhausted, his eyes drawn and dark, sharp cheekbones jutting out from his face.

'I suppose you have a story to tell me?' Petron prompted.

'What?' Frankle started, as though he had been about to doze off. 'Yes. The conduit.'

'Conduit?' Petron leaned forward, eyes sparkling. 'Now where have I heard that before?'

'See, Frankle?' Heather called out. 'I told you Petron would know something about them. Takes us crafters to actually read the studies you wielders hypothesise.'

'In Sontair. The queen, the former queen. She was one of the Nine Sisters.' Frankle smiled apologetically. 'Sorry, Petron, it's a little hard to put into words.'

Petron reached out and took the tilting cup from Frankle's hands before he spilled hot tea all over himself. 'Start at the beginning then, Frankle. I find that's always the best place.'

A full hour later, Heather and Frankle had filled Petron in on the major news from the day they had left Redmondis weeks before. They told him all about their journey, the unexpected greeting they found waiting for them in Sontair, the news of Wilt and the queen, and the troubled state Sontair was in. By the time they had caught up to where they were now, and the treasures they had found in the queen's study, Frankle was almost out on his feet, his eyelids seeming determined to close no matter how much he tried to hold them open.

Petron finally took pity on him and led him to his bed on the far side of the chamber, Frankle falling into a deep sleep before Petron could even cover him with a blanket. Once he was sure Frankle was settled, Petron crept back over to the fire and gestured questioningly to the heavy kettle happily boiling away over its flames.

'I'm all right, Petron. Frankle did most of the work.'

'Yes, this conduit you mentioned. Tell me about it.'

'Well, you heard Frankle's description. The only thing to add is that I could feel the stone, the life in it, especially when Frankle touched it. It was like it woke up in the presence of a wielder.'

'And when you stepped through?'

'It was … strange. It was almost like when we work together to form moonsteel, wielder and crafter combined. I see what Frankle sees, but only flashes of it. Chaos, mostly. Sometimes a rushing river, far below our feet. And fear—I can always feel fear touching the edges of our minds.'

'All wielders have to learn to control their fear, especially inside the depths. It can lead them too deep, so that they lose themselves in the rush.'

'But this was different. It wasn't Frankle's fear I felt. This was … darker.'

Petron sat back in his chair, staring at the flames dancing in the fireplace. 'Did you see anything else?' he whispered.

'Cold. I felt cold. And something solid beneath our feet, like we'd dropped out of the hurricane into the eye of the storm. Then there was … it's silly.'

'No, what was it?'

'A warmth against my leg.'

'Like a spark from a flame?'

'No. It was like an animal brushed past me.'

Stax picked that moment to lean his head down against the back of Petron's chair, staring at Heather, his eyes glowing golden in the dim evening light.

'An animal?'

'A cat, I think.'

Petron leaned one hand up and patted the great eagle's head, eyes still locked on the fireplace. 'Was it Wilt?'

'Yes. At least, part of him.'

'And then?'

'And then chaos again, another push through the rush and tumble, then we stumbled out the other side.'

'Here? In Redmondis?'

'Yes. Underground. It was a bare room, just the conduit on one wall. It looked exactly the same as the one we had walked through. On the other wall was a door, which led into a series of rooms, then up a sloping path, quite dark. But the walls glowed a slight green. I recognised it.'

'The same stone the conduits were formed from.'

'That's right. And when we got to the end of the passage, we walked out into the cold afternoon air of Redmondis. Not far from here.'

'You were in the Sisters' compound.'

'Do you … do you think the Sisters created the conduit?'

Petron frowned and shook his head. 'No. No, this magic was beyond even their reach. This is far older.'

'So how did the conduit get there?'

'Perhaps they found it. Perhaps it was there before they took control.'

'But you never knew about it?'

'Redmondis holds many secrets. Still does. And not all of them should be uncovered. Look at Frankle there.'

Petron waved a hand over to the bed where Frankle lay. 'Just that single trip has exhausted him completely. And he's becoming one of the stronger wielders we have. You are helping him, you know.'

Heather shook her head. 'I was just along for the ride.'

'That's not true. You are becoming closer, you two. Even an old man such as I can see it.'

'I … care for him.'

'But …'

'But Higgs is still out there. Somehow.' Heather grinned up at him. 'You see much for an old man.'

'Well.' Petron clapped his hands on the arms of his chair and pushed himself to his feet. 'Frankle looks like he will sleep through the night, at least. That gives me some time before we go.'

'We?'

'Of course, child. Why else did you come all this way? I'm going back with you. Besides, I've always wanted to see Sontair.'

It took a full three days for Petron to get everything in order. He seemed determined to wrap up as many loose ends as possible before the trip, in case returning turned out more difficult than expected. It was a good thing too. Frankle ended up sleeping soundly for two nights and a day. Petron took to forcing a thin soup through his lips as he slept, and even that only seemed to disturb him slightly. He drank and muttered and rolled over, back into sleep.

Heather took the opportunity to catch up with her crafter friends and restock some of her supplies. In truth, it was strange to be back in Redmondis. She felt … out of place. What she had once called home now seemed so much smaller than she remembered. Limiting. After the first uncomfortable day within Redmondis' walls, she took to spending most of her time in Petron's chamber. Watching over Frankle and feeding Stax a seemingly endless supply of meat scraps.

Stax too seemed keen to spend as much time as he could with them, and not just because of the treats. He went so far as to lay his enormous head on the bed beside Frankle, watching him with those deep, golden eyes, until Petron lost patience and shooed him back to the edge of the chamber.

By the time Frankle finally woke, Petron was growing impatient. Even so, he insisted they give Frankle another day and night after waking to fully recover.

When he had finally opened his eyes and sat up, Frankle was

very confused about where he was, the events of the previous few days seemingly having left no mark on his memory whatsoever. It was only after some determined prompting from Heather that he recalled parts of the trip at all, and even then they were only glimpses.

He remembered touching the edge of the conduit, feeling it wake beneath his fingers, the solid wall framed by the border of the doorway fading into a strange grey glow, as though a cloud had been captured and held inside its borders, wisps of air boiling and turning in place before them. Then clasping Heather's hand in his own, taking a long deep breath and stepping through. Then …

Darkness. Cold. A yawning, terrifying emptiness, beyond even the pull of the depths, a feeling of trespassing somehow, and therefore danger, as though they were sneaking into a place they did not belong and where someone—something—knew they were there.

Then somehow being led out again, travelling without moving, another hand in his own pulling him toward a waiting door and pushing him through.

'And do you think you will be able to do it again? Find your way back?' Petron busied himself cleaning up the dishes from their breakfast, but studied him as he answered.

'I … think so. I don't really think I did much to get us here the first time. It's the conduit that did all the work.'

'Not all of it,' Petron corrected. 'It took a wielder of some power to wake it. And another to lead you out again.'

'Wilt?'

'Perhaps. But come. Our answers will not be found here. Heather for one is very keen to return to Sontair, and I will be more than happy to leave these stone walls behind for a while. Besides, I want to take a look at this study you mentioned. I can't trust you children not to make a mess of things.'

Finally, the morning came when they were ready to go. Petron had handed over all that he could to the other masters and heads of the school, Frankle had almost completely recovered his strength, and Heather was champing at the bit to return to Sontair and the relative action and chaos it represented in contrast to the chill calm of the new Redmondis.

Petron grudgingly accepted an escort of guards to lead them to the Sisters' chambers—he knew there was no point protesting—but as they reached the great doors that marked the entrance to its underground passages, he put his foot down and insisted the guards remain behind. Only they three would continue on.

To be certain, he made a great show of sealing the doors behind them as they stepped through, warning the guard captain of dire consequences should any overly curious soldier choose to try to follow them in.

As they walked down the slight incline of the passage, Heather turned to him and smiled. 'Do you think they believed you?'

'About the door, you mean?' Petron cocked one eyebrow and let an answering grin twist across his lips. 'I learned early on that people fear what they do not understand. And that fear can be very useful indeed.'

Frankle was walking ahead of them, seemingly lost in his own thoughts. His head was bowed, and he led them through a snaking path of doorways without raising it, as though he was guiding them along by feel.

Heather noticed Petron's concerned glance and patted his shoulder. 'It's not far now. Even I can almost—'

'Oh yes.' Petron's eyes brightened, and he lifted his head, sensing the first scratchings of power in the air.

'It's already awake.' Frankle sounded concerned, and he broke into a trot for the last few turnings, finally pushing open a plain, innocent-looking wooden door into a bare room, lit by a dull green glow emanating from the conduit framed on the far wall.

'Well, this is different,' Heather remarked as they walked in, studying the glowing green markings around the border of the conduit.

'Frankle, step back please.' Petron's harsh voice cut across them, startling Heather and stopping Frankle's hand as it was about to reach out to touch the frame. He hesitated for a moment, shaking his head as though waking from a dream, then shrugged and stepped away, letting Petron go forward.

Petron patted him gently on the shoulder as he stepped past. 'It was calling you, Frankle. You have to be careful.'

'I know.' Frankle nodded, looking slightly guilty. 'I don't know what I was thinking.'

'That's why I'm here.' Petron smiled and turned to study the strange markings.

Heather watched impatiently as he bent toward the frame. It seemed an age before Petron grunted and stepped back, shaking his head.

'I don't recognise the writing, though it is ancient. There's one word here—' He pointed to the top right corner of the conduit. 'Which looks a lot like the Daleish word for pathway, but it's misspelled, or perhaps an older version of the term. It looks like the plural form, though.'

'Pathways?' Heather prompted.

'Yes, but …' Petron shook his head and sighed. 'There's so much knowledge we have lost.'

'Well, I know one place that might be able to shed some light on things for us,' Frankle offered.

'Very well.' Petron stepped back to give Frankle room. 'Lead the way, young wielder.'

Without a second thought, Frankle stepped past, and the conduit seemed to instantly respond, the stone wall it framed morphing into a white, roiling mist.

Frankle reached backward and waited for Petron and Heather to grasp one hand each, then took a final deep breath before stepping through. 'Here goes nothing.'

He led them into the conduit and into chaos.

Chapter 7

Daemi laid the weld blade on her bed beside her pack and draped her heavy Redmondis cloak across them both, then stepped back and surveyed the collection with a silent frown. She placed her hands on her hips and stretched her shoulders, enjoying the pull and stretch of the muscles across her back. She could afford to carry more; she was stronger now, but packing light was a habit she had a hard time breaking.

Too much. Start again.

She sighed and pulled the cloak free, letting it fall to the floor as she upturned the pack and shook out its contents again. There had to be more she could cull from this.

The black cat lay silently in the ceiling rafters, staring down at her and swaying its tail back and forth patiently. It knew as well as she did that she was stalling.

'I know, I know,' she muttered, refusing to turn to meet its gaze. 'Last time, I promise.'

Minutes later, the pack was restocked, a third of its previous items scattered in the corner of the room where Daemi had tossed them. She bucked the weld blade onto her hip and weighed the cloak in her hand, imagining herself marching for days on end with it draped across her shoulders. It wasn't necessary, not in this climate, but she couldn't deny the reluctance she felt at leaving it behind. 'The last sign of Redmondis.'

Captain Mont had gifted her new hardened leather armour, almost as strong as the heavy plate she was used to wearing but five times lighter, much more suited to the southern climes and, she realised not five minutes into her first training session wearing it, much more suited to her fighting style as well. She was quicker now, blindingly so, her instincts and training seeming to urge her body on to new heights of skill. It was something to do with Wilt as well, she knew, something in their connection that shaded her style, morphing it into a feline form that only enhanced her abilities. She was faster and stronger than she ever had been.

Eventually, she dropped the cloak onto the floor and kicked it into the corner to join the rest of the discarded items. 'Time to move on.'

Daemi hefted her pack once, then slung it onto her shoulder and turned to leave the room.

'Leaving us already?' Lodan was standing in the doorway, one shoulder leaning against the frame, his arms crossed neatly in front of his chest and a mischievous grin plastered across his face. 'Didn't think I'd let you leave without a proper goodbye, did you?'

Daemi stood watching him, not sure what to expect, until Lodan stepped forward and wrapped her in a tight hug. 'Be safe, Daemi.' He gave her a quick squeeze and stepped back, nodding up at the cat still perched in the rafters. 'And keep an eye on each other.'

She finally found her tongue and whispered a reply. 'You too. And look after Heather and Frankle for me. For us.'

Lodan turned to her side and walked out of the room with her, one hand still resting on her shoulder. Daemi imagined she could feel the heat of his hand through her leather armour, though she knew that was impossible.

'You aren't going to say goodbye to them?'

She pushed the thought out of her mind and shook her head. 'They'll only want to come with me.'

'And would that be such a bad thing?'

'They're too young. Besides, you've seen Frankle. You've noticed the change in him. He needs to stay here and rest. Recover.'

Lodan sighed and dropped the hand from her shoulder. 'You're probably right. Though I don't look forward to breaking the news to them. Whenever they extricate themselves from that study Frankle found.'

Daemi smirked. 'Leave them to it. They may find something interesting together.'

Lodan glanced up and returned her grin. 'Ah, you see, Heather's been rubbing off on you after all.'

Trouble.

As soon as the thought popped into Daemi's head, a black streak blurred past their feet and disappeared around the curve of the corridor.

Daemi broke into a run immediately, not questioning the sudden rush of panic that flooded her. Lodan was right on her heels, instantly understanding that something important was afoot.

They charged through the wing of the castle, taking sharp turns seemingly at random, the cat always a few steps ahead of them, holding itself back to allow them to keep pace.

Hurry.

Daemi put her head down and ran, pulling clear of Lodan as her speed took over. Moments later, the cat pushed through an open door and Daemi almost crashed into it as she slid to a stop.

The study. The queen's study Frankle had found. This was it.

She glanced around, surveying the room quickly to try to identify the source of the panic she could still feel coming from the cat. It stood on the far side of the chamber, right in front of what looked like a stone doorframe. Its ears were bent forward as if listening, and as Daemi watched, the hackles on its neck slowly raised.

'What ... what is it?' Lodan gasped as he reached the door and stumbled through, one hand on his sword.

'I don't—'

Suddenly, the border around the doorway lit up, the stone glowing green and seeming to pulse.

Come.

The cat didn't wait to see if she understood. It sprang toward the doorway and vanished into it.

'Stay here,' Daemi yelled, then charged after it.

Lodan stood dumbfounded as she seemed to disappear into the wall in front of them. As soon as she did, the greenish glow around the frame faded.

He stepped up to the strange door and tentatively pushed his hand into the centre of the wall it framed.

It was solid stone.

Petron knew that his eyes were open, but all he could see was darkness. He could feel Frankle's hand in his, the heat of life fading into a piercing cold that sent an ache of pain shooting up his forearm and almost forcing him to pull his hand free. Then a rushing, the sensation of movement, as though they were hurtling through space, flying through a black sea of nothingness.

The world around them lightened into a grey mist of rolling clouds rushing past them as they fell. They opened out into a pure white expanse, a floor of ice rushing toward them, and Petron couldn't help but close his eyes as they hit.

'Petron?'

He opened his eyes. They were standing on a thick sheet of ice in a blank, vast expanse. Heather was beside him, but Frankle was gone. He flexed his hand where he had held Frankle's. It still ached with cold.

'Where are we, Petron? Where's Frankle?' Heather was rubbing her own hands together, a pained expression on her face, her voice holding just this side of panic.

'This didn't happen last time?' Petron's breath misted as he spoke.

'No. I told you, I didn't see anything last time. I think something's wrong.'

Petron could feel it too, a dawning fear that scratched at his mind, growing stronger with every moment. He concentrated on stilling his thoughts before they took him away.

'There!' Heather pointed into the distance. 'Is that Frankle?'

Petron turned and squinted. Just at the edge of his vision, a dark shape was forming in the white expanse, growing slowly larger. It wasn't Frankle.

'Heather, stay behind me.' Petron pulled a thick chunk of chalk from inside his robe and started to scratch a design onto the ice in front of them. When he looked up again, there was no mistaking it.

'Gloomclaws.' Heather's voice was a thin whisper, her eyes locked on the terrifying apparition.

The dark shape had split, at least five separate forms bearing down now, the sharp angles and claws of the creatures becoming clear as they charged toward them.

Petron stood and clapped his hands in front of him, chanting under his breath as he did so. Heather felt a sudden heat warm the air, though nothing appeared to have changed.

He turned and grabbed Heather's hand. 'Run! I don't know how long the barrier will hold them!'

They ran, or at least tried to. Their feet slid on the ice as they tried to gain purchase, and it was only because Petron was holding her up that Heather managed to stay on her feet at all. She looked around, panic giving her legs new strength as she saw the gloomclaws clearly now, only a hundred yards or so away from them and gaining every second.

'Don't look back!' Petron pulled her along, trying to get his old legs to move faster.

There was a flash of light and a crumpling sound, and Heather couldn't help but glance back over her shoulder again. The gloomclaws had reached the barrier Petron had formed, one body seemingly crushed up against an invisible wall, the other four gloomclaws scratching and pulling at it, trying to break free. Then one of them was over it, and Heather faced forward again, pure panic filling her brain with fire.

'Petron! They're still coming!'

'There! Ahead of us! Can you see?'

Heather tried to peer ahead as she ran, but her eyes were streaming with tears. All she could see was a blue glow, getting stronger.

She was sure she could hear the clatter of the gloomclaw

behind her, gaining with every moment, almost close enough to tear into her.

'Daemi!'

Petron fell, pulling Heather down with him, and they both slid face first across the ice. Heather glimpsed a body flying over them. They came to a stop lying face down, both panting for breath, and Heather rolled over to look back.

It was Daemi, weld blade in hand, the sword shining a bright blue as it whipped and swooped and cut into the gloomclaws in a blur of precision movement.

Something pushed on the back of her head, and another shape pounced over her. A cat, charging to join Daemi in the fight. Wilt?

The air was still glowing blue around them as she pulled herself to her feet and reached down to help Petron regain his footing. As his cloak shifted, she could see the source of the glow, the weld blade slung against his hip shining through the mist.

'You have a weld blade too?'

'Of course. Everyone in Redmondis carries one now. You and Frankle have done more than you realise. But now is not the time.' Petron grunted as he pulled himself up, his eyes locked on the chaos of battle waging only metres from them. 'Come on, I don't think we can help her.'

Heather nodded and grasped Petron's arm as he took a first step and groaned in pain. 'Are you all right?'

'I'm old, girl, that's all. Let's move.'

They stumbled on, away from the battle behind them, trying to make some sense of where they were headed through the thick mist that closed in, growing denser with every step. Petron pulled his blade free, the blue glow lighting the space around them, but that too faded with each step.

Eventually, Heather gave up trying to pierce the white mist that surrounded them and kept her eyes on her feet as she struggled to maintain balance. Every few steps, a black shape shifted under her, something moving in the waters beneath the ice. Each time she saw it, a thrill of fear pulsed up her spine.

'Petron! Where are you?'

It was Daemi, her voice strong and clear. Just the sound of it gave Heather new heart.

'Here, Daemi!' Petron's gruff shout replied, and moments later a fading blue glow revealed two shadows trotting toward them.

Daemi looked them both over quickly, then stepped up to Petron and slung one of his arms over her shoulder. 'Fancy meeting you here.'

'Don't fuss now, Daemi, I'm perfectly—'

'Hush, old man, we don't have time for pride.'

Heather caught her breath at the blunt reply, but Daemi was clearly in no mood for argument. Immediately, their pace picked up, Heather having to concentrate on shuffling into a trot to keep up.

'Where's Frankle?' Daemi asked, wrapping her arm around Petron's waist now and almost pulling him off his feet as she hurried.

'We don't … I don't know.' Heather replied, her voice coming in short gasps now.

'There's nothing for it now. More gloomclaws will be coming. Hurry.'

The blue glow from Daemi's weld blade had also faded now, but Heather could feel the thrill of fear tingling through the air, like the charge in a storm before a lightning strike. The mist only seemed to thicken until it felt like they were pushing against it as they moved, the mist clinging to them and trying to hold them back.

Then, as suddenly as it had closed in, it faded, and they stepped into a clearing, an open space on the ice and a single doorway standing in front of them. Another conduit.

'You first, Heather. Go!'

Heather's feet obeyed Daemi's command immediately, and she stumbled through the doorway, Daemi and Petron on her heels.

A shift, and a sickening lurch as the world twisted sideways, and she tumbled out the other side, into the real world.

Heather almost fell flat on her face as she tripped out of the conduit in the queen's study, just acting fast enough to sidestep the body that lay right at her feet.

'Heather!'

Lodan's surprised shout brought her gaze around to him, crouched at the head of the figure that had almost tripped her.

'Help me with him!'

It was Frankle, his face pale, his skin cold and almost painful to touch. She reached down to help drag him clear as Daemi and Petron stepped through the conduit, the cat right on their heels.

'Frankle!'

As she blurted out his name, his eyes opened, and twin black pools stared back at her.

Chapter 8

Higgs sat at his desk, scattered papers and trinkets spread out in front of him, peering down at a thinly scrawled parchment, squinting as he read and randomly picking up items from the collection to hold in his palm. His lips moved silently, and his thumb brushed back and forth over each object in turn, until a decision was reached and he placed the item back in the pile and reached for another.

Outside the window, a cold wind cut over the Tangle far below, crashing into the cliff face and rushing up the steep walls to pour into his chamber, the flames in the fireplace dancing and growing into a roar. The sun was low on the horizon, a dying yellow light leaking in through the open window, fading with each passing minute so that he had to hunch closer and closer to the page in front of him to make out the words.

His hand found a heavy glass ball, and as he stroked it, it warmed slightly in his palm, but then resisted any further call. He frowned and returned it to the pile, careful not to let it roll off the desk. Not this one. Not yet.

Higgs's fingers tripped lightly over the other objects before coming to rest on a rough-hewn hunk of rock. Immediately, he sensed it, the letters on the page in front of him seeming to blaze brighter as he read, the stone in his hand burning in time with it, melting into the requested form.

Stone. Living rock. He could feel it, the life inside it, the shape waiting to get out.

He closed his eyes and dove into the memory.

Wilt knelt on one knee and cupped his hands for Higgs to stand in. Once Higgs was balanced, he stood and threw his leg upward, propelling the small boy high into the roof beams. Higgs grabbed on and scrambled into a steady position. He looked down at Wilt and almost smiled.

'What about you?'

'Don't worry about me. Head to the hatch.'

Wilt pointed to the small hatch in the roof and Higgs started to edge toward it, arms outstretched for balance.

Wilt quickly looked around and sprinted toward the corner of the room. He ducked past two groups of men before they knew he was there and ran full pelt directly at the wall. Just before he hit it, he jumped, his right leg landing four feet up the right wall, then he pushed off again toward the other wall, and his left leg hit another four feet higher. Then, as if it were nothing at all, he pushed off again, springing away from the walls now, and turned in mid-air to face the closest roof beam. His hand hit it dead on, and he allowed his body's momentum to swing him up to land feet first on the next beam across, coming to rest just under the roof hatch as Higgs arrived, wide eyed.

'Where did you learn that? You looked like a—'

'Cat,' Higgs whispered the word as he pulled back from the memory, still so sharp and clear in his mind. As if it were only yesterday.

A cat. That was the form. That was what called to him, from inside the stone.

He kept his eyes locked on the page in front of him, murmuring now as he read, the stone in his hand morphing into the shape he commanded. A set of claws grew out of it, curling against the skin of his palm as they sharpened.

Higgs finished the page and looked up at the perfect cat's paw that now sat within his hand, the stone cooling slowly as it accepted this new form.

Good. Use the memory. Shape the stone.

He could feel the world around him dripping away, the scene passing on with the tide, back into the depths of memory.

Higgs stood in almost total darkness, a dull red glow leaking down from somewhere high above the only illumination. He was surrounded by stone, encased in it, his feet clamped into place. His hands, too, were sunk within the column of rock in front of him, the red glow pulsing brighter now as he pulled them back, free of the rock, holding something between them.

It was a cat's paw, just as in his vision.

An unusual form, but none can question its accuracy.

Where has this weldfarer been to be twisted so?

What does it matter? We must recognise the skill of it. He has earned his ascension.

No. Not yet. Not with this wild form. He will only be lost again. Another.

As you command.

Higgs twisted in place, the rock around his ankles not allowing him to move any further, and dropped the cat's paw to the side, forgetting it the moment it rolled away into the shadows.

Not failure, but not success. He must try again. Try to remember.

'Foul!'

Higgs's voice cried out over the excited rumbling of the crowd, heads turning toward him as he jumped and waved furiously. He dove forward, shoving bodies out of the way as they shifted between him and his view of the pitch. That guard had flattened Wilt, miles from where the ball was, and he seemed to be the only one watching who saw the injustice of it.

Wilt lay on his back, stars flashing and bursting in his eyes as he shook his head clear. Higgs's high voice called him, and he rolled to his feet, ignoring the pain in his legs where the guard had caught him, moving from a shuffle to a trot to a full sprint as he saw Griggs on the far side of the pitch, ball in hand.

—What is this? This split in perspective, this shattering of memory.—

Another large body moved in front of him, blocking his view entirely now, and refusing to budge as Higgs dug his shoulder into the small of the man's back. He looked down and saw the purse hanging from the man's belt, practically begging to be taken. He reached down and tugged at it, hard, not trying to be the least bit subtle. The man spun around to catch the would-be thief, and Higgs slipped around him, leaving the purse where it was—it had felt a lot lighter than it had looked anyway—and stepped forward, away from the confused patron, grinning as he congratulated himself on his now uninterrupted view of the game.

He had the ball in his hands now, Griggs's pass having curled its way imperiously over the heads of the rest of the players straight into his path. The guard goalie, a behemoth of a man, ran straight for him, and he knew without thinking about what he was going to do.

He let the ball go, rolling it toward the charging man, the goalie's eyes widening in surprise and locking onto it. Then Wilt spun, stepping one foot and then the other onto the top of the ball, twisting around and away from the goalie, the guard's momentum unable to shift in time to match.

—A far deeper connection than we have seen. A sharing of minds.—

—This time has not yet been. This weldfarer has journeyed far.—
—Blasphemy.—
—That is for the Novus to decide.—
—How is this possible? What form can result?—

Higgs watched Wilt spin past the goalie and turn toward the centre of the pitch, knock the ball past the last two defenders straight to Lodan, leap over another flying tackle, and flip in the air to land already running.

He felt the grasping hand on his shoulder trying to pull him back, but shrugged it away. He wasn't going to miss one second of this. The pull became a shove, and he was thrown forward, almost falling face first in the dirt as a heavy body crashed past him, out of the crowd and onto the pitch. Higgs looked up, determined to make the culprit pay, when he saw what the man held in his hand.

'Blade!'

The voice brought Wilt back from the silent moment of victory, the flag still clutched in his hand. He turned toward the cry and saw death charging at him, a silver blade clutched in its hand, crazed, dead eyes staring at him. Through him.

—Hold. Beyond this muddle of perspective. That one. He does not belong.—

—He carries a weld blade.—

—His eyes. Could it be?—

—Another weldfarer. An assassin. But why?—

—Call him back. The Novus must see this.—

He felt the pull, the call of the light far above, and tried to resist it. Tried to hold himself still and calm and cold, a stone on the floor of a rushing river, clinging to its fellows as the water tore at it, urging it onward. Then a hand reached down and clutched it, only it, as though it knew exactly where to find the right one, the perfect size, pulling it up and out of the waters, toward the light of the surface world.

Chapter 9

Petron folded the warm damp cloth in half and placed it carefully on Frankle's forehead, gently wiping a stray hair back into place as he did so. His patient's eyes were closed now, the black ink that filled them having faded slowly over the hours that he had lain in bed being tended by Petron and Heather. When Petron had last pulled them open to check, they were clouded and grey, but improving, and he was confident it would only be a matter of time before Frankle returned to them from wherever he had ventured on the other side of the conduit.

'How's our patient doing?'

Petron turned toward the voice and nodded as he saw Lodan step into the room. 'Improving. I think more due to simple rest than anything I've done.'

'I doubt that.' Lodan crept quietly up to the bed, careful not to wake the slumbering young wielder. He reached out his hand to Petron. 'I'm—'

'Lodan.' Petron smiled and grasped Lodan's hand in his. 'I know. I get the feeling you know who I am as well.'

'Petron. It's strange, isn't it? I didn't have to be told. I saw you and knew you immediately, though we've never met.'

'One more mystery of the welds and all who come within a certain young wielder's orbit.'

'I knew him primarily as a thief, but what little I've been able to understand from Daemi and Heather seems to point that way. You know part of the reason Redmondis is still held in such distrust is the fact that nothing to do with it ever makes much sense to simple folk like me.'

'Oh, I expect you're not such a simple man. Besides, for many years, Redmondis encouraged such confusion. All the better to keep control. I've been doing my best recently to help change that.'

Petron stood up from his seat and guided Lodan away from the bed to the simple table and chairs that sat beneath the small window on the far wall.

'So, I've been hearing. What little news we get from the north has certainly improved over the last few months. We could use all the help we can get right now.' Lodan leaned his head out the window, where twenty feet below a crowded courtyard teemed with people in the early dawn light. 'The sun's less than an hour old and already the crowds pour in.'

'The attacks are still happening?'

'Every day brings new reports. I thought when Wilt killed the gloomclaw the queen had been holding that the troubles would die down, but they only seem to have worsened.'

'The barriers holding back such creatures have weakened past the point of repair. We saw that ourselves travelling here.'

'So we should expect more and more refugees to come, when we cannot house or feed those already here. And eventually ...'

'Eventually they will come to the walls of Sontair as well.'

'I often wonder what has kept them at bay so far.'

'That I may be able to help you with.' Petron sighed as he sat in a chair, turning his back on the window to keep one eye on his patient across the room. 'Fear. Fear is the lure, the siren song for such creatures. Here, within these walls, where there is at least a semblance of security and safety, such fears are controlled. But should they grow ...' Petron held his hands out and shook his head. 'Again, it is only a matter of time.'

'So, it is hopeless? I refuse to accept that.'

Petron peered at Lodan, standing at the window, his fingers gripping the edge of the windowsill as if he were ready to rip it apart, his strong jaw clenched in defiance. 'These people are lucky to have you.'

Lodan pulled his eyes away from the scene outside and relaxed his hands, rubbing them together with a rueful smile. 'I'm not used to being thought of as one of the good guys.'

'Ha!' Petron laughed and clapped his hands together. 'Nor was I … but I learned some time ago that I don't have much of a say in the matter. Come.' Petron stood and started toward the door. 'We should let Frankle sleep in peace. I'm sure Heather will be back to check on him soon enough. I only managed to shoo her off to bed a couple of hours ago. In the meantime, we two victims of circumstance should talk, and see how Redmondis and Sontair might begin to help each other for a change.'

Lodan's grim face broke into a smile as he followed Petron out of the room. 'I was hoping to talk to you about just such a thing.'

The coals in the low-burning fire bloomed into orange light as the door to Frankle's chamber opened and a chill night breeze was sucked into the room through the open window.

Heather hurried over to the window and pulled it fully closed, then bent down to tend to the fire, poking it back into life. When it was burning satisfactorily, she slid back the hood of her cloak and turned to the sleeping figure on the bed.

The cloth on Frankle's head had slipped free and fallen to the side of his pillow, but other than that he seemed to be sleeping soundly, his breath coming in long, regular pulses, the rhythm untroubled and steady.

Heather arranged herself on the small stool beside the bed and reached into her cloak, pulling out a small bowl that she placed beside his head. Next, she pulled out her necklace from under her tunic and over her head, dropping the whole thing into the centre of the sounding bowl. Immediately the music began, a slowly lilting tune that seemed at once triumphant and yet sad, a strange, melancholy music that filled the room.

Frankle turned in his sleep to face the small bowl, yet his breathing didn't alter and his sleep remained untroubled. Heather watched him silently, waiting to see if her guess was correct. If she was right, it should only take a few moments until—

There.

Under Frankle's closed lids she could see his eyes begin to shift and stutter into movement, haltingly at first, then speeding up as the dreams took hold. In seconds, they were positively dancing underneath his lids, jerking back and forth in a rapid frenzy of movement, so much so that Heather reached out with one hand, only halting its movement toward the bowl when she realised his breathing remained unchanged and steady. Whatever visions he was experiencing as a result of the heartstone's song, they didn't seem to be causing him any real distress.

She let the music play, closing her eyes as she listened to it, wondering briefly if she was to try to sleep as well, what dreams would come—if that was the way to call Frankle back from wherever he was.

'Early start this morning, I see.'

She hadn't heard the door open and started in her seat as Petron stepped into the room.

'Here. Drink. You're not going to sleep anyway.' He handed her a steaming cup and she smiled as the spicy scent of it tickled her nose.

'Hmm.' Heather sighed as she sipped, the cinnamon heat of it warming her as it slid down her throat. 'Where do you find these concoctions of yours?'

'This particular brew comes courtesy of some of my forest friends. Nurtle showed it to me—you remember her?'

'The eagle. The wildlers.'

'That's right.' Petron nodded and leaned over Frankle to check on him.

'He seems much improved.' He stood back up again and pointed at the sounding bowl, still playing its music, though lessened in volume now. 'Is that a heartstone?'

'Oh!' Heather reached out and snatched the necklace out of the bowl, ending the music abruptly.

'No, leave it, Heather. It seems to be doing him some good. That is, if you don't mind an old man listening in?'

'No, no, that's … fine.' She let the necklace drop back into the bowl and the music began again.

Petron walked over to the window and retrieved a second chair, placing it beside Heather. He cocked one ear as he listened to the music, as though listening for something within it, something only he could hear. 'That's the heartstone you made with Higgs, isn't it?'

Heather nodded quickly, a sudden hot flame of guilt lighting up her cheeks.

'And yet it works here now, with Frankle. Curious.' Petron nodded to himself, waiting for Heather to reply in her own time.

'I … I noticed it right away once we got here. To Sontair, I mean. The heartstone was reacting as though—'

'As though Higgs was here. As though he was alive. You know that's not true though.'

'But something must—' Heather stopped herself as she heard her voice rising. She sipped her drink again, gathering her thoughts. 'Something was causing the reaction. Some part of Higgs. Something within Wilt.'

'And now within Frankle? I wonder …' Petron tapped his fingers idly on the side of his mug as he stared at Frankle, weighing possibilities. 'I must admit very little to do with Wilt surprises me lately.'

Heather turned to him, her eyes glowing in the firelight. 'I think Higgs is still there, within the welds, a part of Wilt that he refused to let go. And I think Frankle is part of it as well.'

'And you hope that through Frankle you will somehow be able to reclaim Higgs?'

The bluntness of Petron's question shocked Heather into an embarrassed silence.

'You know, Heather, I lost someone I loved as well.'

Heather ducked her head, a single bright tear gleaming on her cheek.

'I understand the need to … fight back. But let me give you one piece of advice. Be careful not to lose what is right in front of you in pursuit of a dream.'

The music from the sounding bowl had begun to fade, and it was only once Petron had finished talking that Heather realised it had now fallen silent. She looked down at it, wondering what had gone wrong.

Frankle's eyes were open and staring at her, both of them clear and bright and seemingly untroubled. As she stared back into them, she felt the world tilt suddenly, and Higgs stared back out at her from behind his eyes.

'Uh, good morning?'

Then it was gone, and it was just Frankle looking at her, glancing between her face and Petron's and trying to understand why they were both sitting apparently watching him sleep. 'Have I missed something?'

Frankle sighed in satisfaction and pushed the empty bowl away from him, patting his belly absently. He leaned back and stretched, and only then noticed the six sets of eyes staring at him in amusement.

'Another?' Heather asked as she reached out to gather up the dishes.

'What? Oh, no, thanks. I'm all full.'

'You sure you don't want to try for a new record?'

'Record?'

'That's the fifth bowl of stew you've eaten, lad.' Captain Mont was grinning at him. 'You must have hollow legs.'

'Oh.' Frankle rubbed his belly again. 'I didn't realise.'

'Your little adventure through the conduit took more out of you than you realise. You need to be careful, Frankle.' Petron smiled and sipped his tea, only his eyes showing a note of real concern.

'Yes, that,' Captain Mont continued. 'If you'd be so kind to get on with the story, I have a lot of duties to attend to this morning.'

'Story?' Frankle looked lost, trying to spin his brain back up to speed.

'What happened when we stepped through the conduit, Frankle? We thought we'd lost you.' Petron set his teacup aside and leaned forward. 'Tell us what you can remember.'

Frankle looked around the room; Petron and Heather sat to one side of the table, Captain Mont and Lodan at the other, Daemi at its head, all seemingly there for him. He suddenly felt embarrassed. 'Oh, sorry. I didn't realise—'

'Just begin where you can, Frankle,' Lodan prompted. 'Petron said you opened the conduit in Redmondis. Took hold of their hands and stepped through …'

'And then we lost you,' Heather whispered. 'I felt a flash of pain in my hand where I had held yours, an intense cold, then you were gone.'

'I was? I don't remember.' Frankle's voice faded as he tried to concentrate. There was something there, a memory floating just out of reach.

'Do you remember falling?' Petron asked.

'Falling. Yes. Through a white fog.' His words grew in volume as his thoughts cleared. 'Down toward the ice.'

'And then we landed …'

'What? No.' Frankle shook his head, his eyes still elsewhere, staring back into memory. 'I didn't land. I went through the barrier. Under the ice.' He shivered involuntarily at the thought, a thrill of cold tingling up his spine. 'I was under the ice, looking up at you, then something pulled me away. A golden light.'

He shook his head again, angry at himself for not making any sense. His thoughts were a blur, a rush of images and panic. He remembered reaching out, hearing Wilt's voice, then he was out again, on the other side.

'I was … I found myself somewhere else. It was dark, very dark, but warm. Like a cave. Sort of like Redmondis, where the Sisters had been, I mean. Underground. I was soaking wet.'

Captain Mont started to interrupt, but Petron waved him into silence. 'Go on, Frankle. What else do you remember?'

'There were bars. Prison bars. It was a dungeon of some sort.

I remember walking toward music, a familiar song, and looking through a cell door. There was someone else there, on the other side of the bars. It—' Frankle caught himself and stared at Heather. 'It was Higgs.'

'Higgs?' Lodan shot to his feet. 'But Higgs is dead. You told me he was dead.'

Petron waved him back again, never taking his eyes off Frankle. 'Go on, Frankle. Don't try to explain it. Just tell us what else you saw.'

'That was it. He spoke to me. Recognised me. Seemed just as shocked as I was. Then … it was like I was dreaming, and someone woke me up. I was ripped away. There was cold again, deep cold, then I woke up here.'

He was staring at Heather still, watching the effect of his words.

'Did you see the gloomclaws?' Heather asked.

'What? No, where were the—'

'Gloomclaws,' Daemi finally spoke, and the cat that had been perched in the shadows of the ceiling pounced onto her lap. 'On the ice. We fought them off.'

'We?' Frankle echoed, his face a mask of confusion.

'Is that all you can remember, Frankle?' Petron asked, his voice gentle.

'I, uh … yes. I think so.' Frankle sat forward and held his head in his hands. 'It's very confusing.'

'Well.' Captain Mont slapped his knees and stood up. 'Confusing is certainly one word for it.' He turned to Lodan. 'Lunch in my chambers? We have a lot of work still to do organising the latest arrivals. In the meantime, I have a long list of more practical matters to attend to.'

He nodded once to Petron and Daemi, then smiled at Frankle and took his leave.

Frankle watched the door close behind the captain and sighed. 'I'm sorry. I think I disappointed him.'

'No, Frankle.' Lodan shook his head. 'He's just very busy right now. He knows you're doing your best.'

'Yes, quite so. And with more rest, more memories may come.'

Petron stood, and the others took that as their cue. 'Come now, let me walk you back to your chambers. I still have a few days before I need to think about returning to Redmondis, and I want to spend as much time as possible in the queen's study. I suspect there is still a wealth of secrets waiting to be uncovered there.'

Frankle was about to argue but as he stood, a wave of dizziness swamped him and he had to catch hold of the arm of his chair to keep his footing.

'Here.' Petron took Frankle's hand and placed it on his forearm. 'It's about time I led someone else around like an invalid for a change. Come.'

They shuffled out of the room, leaving Daemi, Lodan, and Heather standing around the table.

'Well?' Heather asked.

'Well what?' Lodan answered.

'When do we leave?'

'Leave? Why would—'

'To find Higgs,' Daemi interrupted, putting the cat down on the surface of the table. 'As soon as Frankle is strong enough to travel.'

'Wait a minute, you can't just—'

'We have to, Lodan.' Daemi turned to him, as if what she was saying should have been obvious. 'Don't you see? He saw Higgs. Besides, I think we need to get Frankle as far away from Sontair as possible before the gloomclaws find him.'

Lodan stared back and forth between them, trying to wrap his head around what they had obviously already decided. 'You think they're looking for Frankle?'

Yes.

Daemi started as the thought bloomed in her mind. She reached down and stroked the cat slowly, staring into its eyes. 'Wilt thought that the gloomclaws, the power that controlled them, sent them, was searching for him. Could sense his presence. But it may be that they were seeking out any wielders.'

'Either way, we have to leave,' Heather agreed. 'Can you imagine what would happen if they came here, to these crowded streets?'

Lodan dropped his eyes and nodded. 'No, you're right. I've seen what those things can do.'

'In the meantime, we ready ourselves as much as we can.' Daemi's voice was once again one of command. 'Heather, you must do what you can to assist Petron and Frankle. Lodan, I'm sure you know better than I how best to help Captain Mont.'

'And you two?' Lodan asked, looking at the cat Daemi was still patting.

'You remember the adviser Captain Mont captured, the one we … questioned? There are others here, hiding where they can. If the gloomclaws are called to wielders, then they have to be rounded up and accounted for. So …' Daemi met his gaze, her eyes flashing with a dangerous hunger that Lodan had never seen before, 'we are going hunting.'

Chapter 10

'Psst!'

Higgs's eyes flickered open at the sound. He was lying crumpled in the back corner of his cell, the dim red light unchanged from the last time he had woken in this place, the very air seeming to seethe and bleed.

'Psst! Boy!'

The voice was coming from the front of the cell, beyond the dull green stone bars. He shifted and sat up, his bones groaning in protest and the muscles in his back twisting with cramp.

'I can hear you moving in there. Back so soon?'

Higgs pulled himself forward and leaned close to the corner to better hear the whisper. He coughed, his throat burning with thirst.

'Still can't talk?'

It was the same voice as before. The same girl. Noble sounding, superior, though her accent was strange to him, the esses hissed slightly, as though she was speaking in a language not her own.

He closed his eyes and concentrated, forcing the words to form and come spilling out over his lips. 'I … I can talk.'

His voice was little more than a sickly croak, but it was there.

'Ah, progress!' The ess sound hissed again, stretching the word out, twisting in the silence like a snake. 'They brought you back up already. You must have done something to impress them.'

'Where—' Higgs coughed again and tried to swallow to soothe the tearing inside his throat, but his mouth was completely dry. 'Where am I?'

'Where?' The girl chuckled, though there was no joy in it. 'You *have* lost yourself, haven't you?'

A door clanged open further down the corridor, and a tramp of heavy boots began to march toward their cells.

'No time now. They come. Be silent. Be still.'

Higgs heard the girl back away from the corner of their cells and he did likewise, huddling against the cold damp rock, dropping his head to keep his eyes fixed on the ground. A moment later, the steps stopped right outside his cell.

'Here he is. What little there is of him.' The rough voice was strong, echoing off the stone walls, impossibly loud to his ears. 'What's he done now?'

'He has been summoned, that is all you need to know.' The second voice was much softer, but carried with it a quiet authority that was unmistakable. It, too, was one he had heard before, inside his mind.

The lock snapped, and the gate to his cell swung open with a high whine. Higgs looked up automatically and caught sight of two men, one a large guard and the other a shorter, robed figure, his face completely covered by a hood. As soon as he raised his eyes, the guard stepped forward, arm raised to strike.

'Lower your eyes!'

Higgs ducked his head and squeezed his eyes closed, his body clenched in anticipation of a blow that never came.

'Be still, Grell. It is permissible.'

The robed figure stepped past the guard and bent down to raise Higgs's face with his gloved fist. Higgs stared into the shadow of the man's cowl, but could see nothing. It was like staring into night itself.

'Come, weldfarer. You have journeyed deep. The Novus awaits your tale.' The robed man stood up and backed out of the cell as the guard stepped forward, heavy stone shackles in his hand.

Higgs stared down at his hands, his wrists enclosed once again in the green stone shackles, his fingers almost blue with cold and shaking slightly as he tried to flex them each in turn. He was alone again, standing in a circle of light in what felt like a very large room, the surrounding air much lighter, less close and stifling than it had been everywhere else since he had awoken in this place. Whatever this place was.

He could feel the effect of the shackles on his mind, holding it up at the surface, bobbing crazily like a cork in the ocean, unable to settle or sink into any one thought. A constant scratching panic turned inside him, swirling ever faster, but he refused to allow it to overwhelm him. He looked down at his fingers again, trying to focus only on them, holding himself calm and separate.

They were his fingers, he was sure of that much. Small, thin, clever. At least, when they weren't frozen with cold and cramp. His entire body felt clumsy and sluggish, always a step behind his mind's orders.

Perhaps his body was simply out of practice. Perhaps it had to learn to live again.

You see much, little one.

The voice inside his head blasted all other thoughts clear, a cold gust of power that shocked his mind into stillness.

Do not be afraid. Now is not the time for fear.

Higgs stared around the room, trying to pinpoint the source of the voice, but his eyes were unable to penetrate the thick darkness outside the small cone of light he stood within. Suddenly the heavy shackles dropped free of his hands, and immediately his mind rushed back to fill the waiting space inside his head.

That is better, is it not? You must understand our servant's precautions. One never knows what one might face when a weldfarer returns. Especially one who has voyaged so deep. You have caused quite the stir.

Higgs raised his hands to his face, scanning the cold skin with his numb fingers. It was his face. He really was back in his own body.

We sense your confusion. It, too, will pass. Time heals all wounds, does it not?

A deeply uncomfortable chuckle echoed inside his mind; a humourless, nasty snigger that sent a thrill of fear tickling up his spine.

You have questions. Let us begin there. Speak now.

Higgs almost blurted out his question before it was formed, the words seemingly pulled up and out of his throat without his say so.

'Who—' He coughed, his throat still burning in protest as the words tumbled free. 'Who are you?'

We? We are the Novus, is that not the name they now use? You waste your words, little one.

'Where then? Where am I? What is this place?'

You are in Pankesh. The centre of this world. The beginning and the end of it. Your kind call these lands the Eastern Dales. But that is not the right question either.

'How?' Higgs swallowed, forcing the saliva down his throat. 'How am I here?'

Ah. Such a large question from such a little one. But we will try to answer. You are a weldfarer; you know something of their possibilities. Let us start there. Come. Close your eyes. Remember.

He staggered forward and almost fell into Wilt's arms, his friend's face spattered with red blood—his blood. He looked down at the black weld blade protruding from the centre of his chest, a deep cold spreading out from it to cover him completely and drag him down into darkness.

All face death alone. We have witnessed such moments a thousand times over and yet it never fails to fascinate. But you. You were not alone. You were held back.

He turned away from the cold air that surged out of the far end of the long tunnel, back to his friend, padding forward on four feet to curl around the larger cat's legs.

You did not go gently. You returned and became something more than human.

He stood in the centre of the room, the chaos of battle swirling around him and the pool of grey, silent stillness he dwelled within. He reached toward the nearest soldier, his hand a nest of black welds, reaching into and through the man's chest and grasping his heart, wrapping it in ice as he drained it, watching the final moments of life flicker and die.

You became a wraith. Both of you. Minds entwined. Such power could not go unnoticed.

He stood outside now, under an open sky, in another time, another scene of panic and death. Again, his black hand reached for a victim, this one cloaked in red. Vargul, that was his name. This was the moment of his death.

You resisted our servants once more, but this time we were ready to greet you.

The ice locked around him and split him in two, suddenly alone, helpless on the surface, silver claws scratching uselessly at it as he watched his friend sink away from him, into the waiting depths.

But again, you surprised us. Somehow, he was found, inside that endless chaos. Somehow, he was found and returned.

A glowing, golden weld, dancing inside a song, beckoning him toward it, waiting for his hand to grasp it and to be pulled back to the surface, back into life itself.

So, you returned. But what of your friend? Your other half? Where is he hiding? Let us see …

The vision changed. No longer was he viewing the world through his own eyes; now he was floating near the ceiling of a strange room, a large open chamber, one wall entirely missing and a chill wind blowing in to flicker the flames in the fireplace into life. An old man pottered over the coals, muttering to himself as he fussed with the kettle. To his side, a small boy sat slumped in a chair facing the fire, the orange light of the flames dancing across his boyish face.

No. That is not the one. How is this poss—

A single black paw swiped across the vision, swatting it away, and the world snapped back into place.

Higgs was standing inside the circle of light again, head bowed, shoulders hunched against the seething fury that seemed to fill the darkness and reach toward him, itching to tear him limb from limb. It lasted only a moment, a silent howl of rage that cut through his mind, as though death itself had opened its mouth to scream.

And then it was gone, and he was safe inside the light.

You carry many mysteries within you, little one. Somehow, your friend has managed to disguise himself from us once more. This is … vexing.

With a snap, the stone shackles were back on his wrists, his arms jerked up and out to receive them as they wrapped around his hands, the chill stone heavy and cold against his skin.

You will remain here. A guest. A prisoner, if you prefer. Your friend knows you are here, that much is clear. He will come for you. To save you. Of that there is little doubt. And when he does, little one, we will be waiting.

Chapter 11

A constant rain fell on the crowded rooftops of Sontair, streams of water running together to rush down gutters and ageing pipework, sudden openings high in the walls sending thick waterfalls of oily rainwater splashing down onto the cobbled streets below.

Daemi stepped around one such overflow, shaking drips from her hair—the result of an earlier outpouring that had caught her unawares. 'A little heads-up would be appreciated,' she muttered under her breath, peering through the rain to the rooftops high above. A flash of movement told her the cat was still scouting ahead, making use of its sure footing on the slippery tiles.

Another. Just ahead. On your right.

The voice bloomed in her mind and Daemi stepped out and around another potential soaking, swinging her cloak back from her shoulder to reveal the hilt of the moonsteel blade on her hip.

'That's more helpful. Thank you.'

She still whispered the words aloud, unable, or perhaps unwilling, to allow herself to join in fully with the mindspeak connection the cat had established with her.

Something ahead. Keep to this path.

The voice was Wilt's, yet not Wilt's. It was as though he spoke from within a dream, an echo of his voice shaped and altered by the unfamiliar mind of the animal form some part of him now resided in. It was becoming clearer each day, the words and phrasing more human, more pronounced, though whether that was due to Daemi accepting the strange connection they shared or a change in the cat itself, Daemi couldn't say. All she knew was that it was changing, and something within her was changing with it. 'What do you see? I can't make anything out in this light.'

It was late at night. The alleyways they stalked through were deserted, the refuse and rubbish swirling in pooled rainwater the only sign of the masses of people that passed down these streets during the daylight hours. Captain Mont and his army had done a very good job of finding shelter and housing for most of the hundreds of refugees who still arrived daily, though at the cost of a general population that grew ever more frustrated and angry at their seemingly shrinking city. That was one benefit of the martial law that had been imposed since the death of the queen. Not many citizens argued with the point of a sword.

Daemi swung out and around another thick stream of water and suddenly the world shifted in place.

She padded along the rooftop, the shadowed world around her glowing grey and white, each shape defined, a thousand details that her human eyes missed immediately clear.

'Whoa.' Daemi stopped and grasped her forehead, squeezing her eyes shut against the vision that had overwhelmed her. 'That's … give me a little warning next time.'

She had seen what the cat could see. Looked out through its eyes on a world suddenly familiar and yet changed.

Here. Try again.

Daemi opened her eyes and felt the scratchings of the vision on the backs of her eyeballs. She took a deep breath and let herself fall into it.

The world was still now, the greys and whites of the night holding in place as the cat sat and waited for the other to accept what it saw. The night was bright and pulsing. A thousand shadows waiting to be explored.

Daemi pulled herself out and stumbled against the stone wall on her right, as she found herself back in her own mind. The world twisted and swirled for a moment, dimming back into darkness and shadow. 'Sorry. That's going to take a little getting used to.'

She rested one hand on the hilt of the weld blade and her vision settled, long slow breaths helping to ease the sudden knot of nausea in her stomach. 'What exactly are we looking for here anyway? How are we going to track these other wielders down?'

Not wielders. Not true ones.

'Okay.' Daemi straightened up and resumed her march down the alleyway. 'If you insist. What should I call them then?'

Dogs. Cortis's dogs.

Her lips twisted in a rueful grin at the words. Did the cat have a sense of humour, or was that Wilt? 'So, we're hunting down dogs. Very well. Do you intend to simply sniff them out?'

Almost. Come. Try again. And do more than just see. Listen.

Daemi's grip on the hilt of the weld blade tightened and it seemed to help steady her as the vision swamped her again.

The cat was moving now, its silver claws glowing faintly blue as they dug into the slick surface of the rooftop. Its ears twitched forward, and the constant patter of the rain dimmed as another sound took priority in its mind. Music. Very faint. It sounded like a song.

Daemi pulled her weld blade free of its sheath as she fell back into her own mind. Its blade glowed blue in the night. 'Like your claws. The blade, the weld blade, it helps ground me somehow. Helps make the connection less overwhelming.'

The blade. It senses them too.

'And that music. What was that?'

Weld song. Come.

The cat was off, following the sound, leaping over gaps in the rooftops as it hunted its prey. Daemi moved into a trot, her boots sending up splashes of filthy water from the puddles that were now pooling in the uneven cobbles of the street.

She could feel the presence of the cat ahead of her, a warmth in the cold night air, a connection that she could almost see hovering in the air between them like a trail of scent. Unfortunately, she couldn't move quite as directly toward the target as the cat could, and she felt herself falling further behind as she tried to hurry through the twisting alleys.

'Ugh.' She turned another corner and was doused once again with freezing rainwater. 'Slow down a bit, will you?'

Hurry. They are here. More than one of them.

Another snatch of vision flashed as she moved through the narrow alley. A small courtyard, a window glowing orange, a shadowed doorway.

The blue light of her blade was getting brighter with every step, so much so that she could see metres in front of her now, able to break into a full run finally as the strange glow illuminated the various barriers that loomed across her path.

Daemi felt the cat near her, around the next corner, perched silently on the rooftop above.

Hold.

She skidded to a stop and pushed her body up against the wall, instantly obeying the command. She could feel the mixture of excitement and danger suddenly filling the air and sheathed her blade to avoid any chance of the light it gave off revealing her position.

'Do they know we're here?' she whispered, her lips forming the words but only the slightest breath of air pushing through them.

No. I—

A sickening twist clutched her as the cat's mind rejected the utterly foreign concept that it had tried to form.

No. This is not the way.

'What do you mean? Are they in there?'

Daemi slipped over to the corner of the wall and peered around it. Sure enough, there was the window, lit up from a fire, and the doorway waiting for her to pass through.

Do you not feel it?

Her hand still clutched the hilt of the weld blade, and she tightened her grip further as the cat's meaning became clear. There was something there. Behind the door. Something waiting for them. 'A trap?'

Perhaps.

The cat sat back on its haunches, ignoring the rain that still streamed down, not moving its eyes from the doorway and the threat its instinct told it lay in wait.

There is another way.

Daemi could sense the thrill that ran through the cat's mind at the thought, and she almost gasped as a deep urge lit a fire of longing in the pit of her stomach. A hunger, almost sexual. Yet darker. Much more dangerous. 'What do you mean?'

The only reply was a glimpse of vision, a twisting hurricane of darkness swirling in place, sucking everything down with it into the void. As soon as it appeared, the vision vanished, wiped clear of Daemi's mind.

She gasped and realised she had been holding her breath.

Go.

Somehow, she knew what it was she had to do. There was no consciousness of it, but she followed the command that now guided her, moving as though walking in a dream. The rain still fell, but the world had fallen silent, all sound seemingly lost in the twisting void she had glimpsed. She stood up straight and set her shoulders back, pulling her cloak back over the blade on her hip, and walked out into the open courtyard.

A flash of shadow moved behind the orange glow of the window set in the wall in front of her, but other than that, there was no sign of the trap she knew she was walking into. Some part of her deep inside was screaming to stop, to take back control, but she could not. All she could feel was a deep, growing cold at the back of her shoulders, getting closer with each step she took toward the door.

She placed a gloved fist on the surface of the door, and in one movement pushed it open and stepped through.

A flash of bright light blinded her momentarily, and she blinked her eyes against the silver sparks that danced on the back of her eyelids. A glowing mesh, a silver net seemed to sparkle in the air in front of her, and she tried to raise her hand to her eyes to rub them clear, but something held her arms in place.

'So, my brothers, our precautions were not so in vain after all. Our web has captured a fly.'

The voice came from the far side of the room, near the glow that Daemi could only assume was a fire blazing in the hearth, and with the voice all sound came back into the world.

There were shuffling feet, a grunt of effort and a sudden piercing pain in her side as the point of a sword dug into her.

Daemi blinked furiously against the stars that still blinded her, and as her vision slowly cleared, she found herself staring at her feet, her soaked boots leaving a growing puddle on the wooden boards of the floor.

'And what do we have here? A soldier?' The voice was old, rasping with age or sickness.

'One of the new lot. Enemies of our queen.' The second voice sounded just as ill, yet different.

'Oh, more than that, I think.'

Something grabbed at her shoulder and ripped her cloak back, revealing the colours of Redmondis she still wore high on her arm.

'Redmondis.' A third voice, not as far gone as the others. The tone was one of command.

'Redmondis? Here?'

'Did you not hear the reports, the recent arrival the queen welcomed? The wielder.' The voice spat the word, as though the very shape of it on his tongue left a sour note. 'We warned Vargul not to try and meddle with him.'

'Wielders! But all of our plans, the coming storm—'

'Do not speak of it!' The command silenced the other immediately, and the third voice let out the soft whimper of a beaten dog.

'But this is no wielder.' The second voice spoke up again, eager to please.

The point of the blade dug harder into the leather armour at her side, threatening to split through the toughened material.

'No. Yet here she is.' A gloved hand grasped Daemi's chin and raised it up to the light. She blinked back the tears that still flooded her vision, and a pair of glowing golden eyes glared back at her. 'How did you come to find us here, little fly?'

For a moment, Daemi felt a glowing fire of something scratching at her mind, then it was pushed back and away by a pulse of deep cold. She shuddered helplessly as the feeling grew, creeping up from behind to take her over.

'What is this?' The golden eyes flashed in anger as the weld was so easily repulsed. 'Who—'

The last conscious thought Daemi had was a vision from outside the doorway, the world a swirling current of grey, the human figures inside the room glowing bright against the dark background. Calling to it to take them.

The wraith slid past the imprisoned figure of the girl locked in place, passing through the stone wall of the building with nothing more than a chill sigh. The other life that stood in front of the girl was taken without a thought, a clawed hand of a thousand twisting snakes reaching out and into him, grasping his heart and drinking from his life force.

Two more forms moved in sudden panic as their leader fell and the nightmare form loomed in front of them. They stumbled over each other and fell as the wraith reached out for them, its touch a burning flash of icy death.

In moments, they too were gone, the light of their lives snuffed out and their cold forms sinking down, invisible against the grey world of the inanimate. The wraith turned then, toward the one life still standing, waiting for it. It reached out for her.

A cry of pain, of fear, of hurt and anger and betrayal as the clawed fingers dug deep gouges in the back of her flesh.

The trap that had held Daemi in place fell away and she collapsed to her knees, her eyes clasped shut against the vision of the wraith. The memory of pain. Her breath shuddered, fogging out against the suddenly freezing air of the room, and she suddenly realised that she was alone. Alone and still alive.

She opened her eyes slowly, and the drained, skull-like face of the man who had only moments before tried to break into her mind leered back at her, the eyes set back in his skull twin pools of black.

Daemi?

The voice was clearer now. Wilt's alone.

Are … are you okay?

It was fading again, back down into the depths, back into an echo.

Daemi pulled herself to her feet and surveyed the wreck of the room. Three bodies lay on the floor, each a shrivelled mask of death. 'Yes.'

She saw again the flash of a black hand reaching for her, ready to drain her just as surely as it did the three bodies that now lay in front of her, and a cold shudder of dread tingled down her spine. 'I'm okay. Let's head back.'

With that, she turned away from the grisly scene, out into the streaming rain and the cool night air, the cat flashing between her legs and away, up to the rooftops above.

Petron stood back with a long sigh and clasped the small of his back as he stretched up and away from the base of the conduit he had been studying. He arched backward, twisting slightly as he tried to release the tensed muscles around his spine, eyes closed as he took deep slow breaths and struggled to will his aged body to comply.

'Careful now. You're likely to tip over.'

Petron grunted and stepped away, turning out of Heather's path as she pushed past him carrying a tray laden with bread and cheese.

'You missed breakfast again. Lucky for you, I have friends in low places.' She pushed the tray onto the corner of the large desk along one wall, scattering papers as she did so.

'Oh yes, breakfast.' Petron looked lost for a moment, and Heather felt a sick knot of pain twist in her chest at the sight of him. He looked so old all of a sudden.

It only lasted a moment though, then Petron was back again, his face gruff as he reached across to tear a corner off the loaf on the tray. 'You're making a mess of my studies.' He waved at the papers now lying across the floor.

'Oh, I think you're doing a good enough job making a mess all by yourself.' Heather slid onto a stool and began picking at the cheese. 'Progress?'

'Hmph?' Crumbs of bread fell from his lips as he turned back to the conduit he had been studying. 'Of a sort, I suppose. Not enough. Never enough. The queen left a trail of clues here, but I doubt even she knew what she was doing most of the time. This symbol here,' he said, pointing at a strange curving line at the top of the arch of the conduit, 'it represents time. Or water. Or travel. Or all three.'

He grunted again and took another bite of bread, ruminating on all he still didn't know as he chewed.

'Did you get that from all of these books?'

'What? Oh, yes.' Once again, Petron seemed to have been losing his train of thought. 'Sorry, it's just so frustrating to have found such a wealth of knowledge as this study, and yet to still have so much of it out of reach. Here, look at this.'

He stepped up to the desk and pulled a large tome out from under a pile of stacked books, dust billowing out from its pages as he flipped through it. Heather quickly stood and moved the tray of food out of harm's way, waving the air clear as she did so.

'Here.' Petron's finger traced down the page. 'Daleish again, like the symbols on the conduit. But this is a diary of sorts, a record of travel from the East. From the Daleish lands itself, I expect. It starts off incomprehensible, but then further on—' He flipped past a number of pages until he found what he was looking for. 'Around this point, it starts to make more sense. At least, a sort of sense. Listen to this.'

Petron moved his finger along the page, his lips forming the words silently until he located the right place. 'The great forest no longer bars the way. The flame of progress burns bright. Soon the very spine of the world will lie before us.'

'The spine of the world?' Heather prompted.

'No idea.' Petron shook his head. 'But look here: The gateways are connected. The stone is formed. The barriers weakened … Or broken, or not yet formed perhaps. The tense of the writing seems to move all over the place.'

'Barriers. That's what Frankle called the ice on the other side.'

'Yes.' Petron turned toward her, his eyes bright and alive now. 'Exactly what I thought.'

'And he said he fell through it. Is that because the barrier was weakened?'

'Or did him falling through it weaken it all the more?' Petron answered, his lips pulling into a grim smile. 'Did our very presence there weaken it even further?'

'The gloomclaws.' Heather stared at the conduit, her feet stepping slowly away from it on instinct. 'Do you think they can use these to—'

'No, Heather.' Petron's voice was kind now, and he patted her shoulder gently. 'I don't think that is what we need to fear.'

The hand on her shoulder slowed as Petron stared at the conduit, eyes moving slowly over the symbols that lined its border. Heather watched him silently, realising his mind was elsewhere again, lost in the contemplation of this strange new problem.

'You're just like him, you know.'

'What? Like who?'

'Frankle. He used to look like that when he'd spent too much time in here, amongst all this dust and knowledge. Just as distracted.'

'Well.' Petron stretched again, turning his back on the conduit in a physical effort to focus his mind. 'You may be right about that. But we have so little time.'

'How do you mean?'

'Well, I can't very well stay here much longer, can I? Redmondis may be able to manage itself for a few days, weeks perhaps, but any more than that and I'd begin to get nervous. Besides,' he shut the large tome he had been reading from with a thud, 'if we're going to move what we need to through these gateways, we have to learn how to control them. Sontair needs our help, our strength, and I'm determined to give it to them.'

'You want to use the conduits?'

'Yes. Redmondis has trained fighters armed with weld blades. Just what Sontair needs, especially if we encounter any more gloomclaws. We just have to get them here.'

'And you're going to lead them through?'

'Unless you have a better idea?' Petron smiled and tore another hunk of bread from the loaf on the tray. 'I don't think using Frankle as a guide again would be a very good idea, do you?'

Heather watched him eat, keeping the thrill of fear she felt at his words to herself.

Chapter 12

'You heard Daemi's report? What they found?' Lodan was pacing again, back and forth in a three-step loop in front of Captain Mont's desk, one hand clasped beneath his chin, scratching at the rough stubble of his unshaven face.

'I read what you sent me.' Captain Mont watched him from his chair, rubbing his own face now, surprised at the whiskers he found there. That would never do. He had to take better care of himself.

In one hand he bounced a lump of greenish stone, shaped like a cat's paw. He had found it holding down a pile of papers on his desk days before, and something about its weight in his palm gave him comfort as he worked. His fingers seemed drawn to tracing along its outline, slipping in between the sharpened claws that poked out of each toe.

'And the plan the ones they found mentioned? This "storm"? What do you make of it?' Mont continued.

Lodan stopped pacing and stared at the captain, his hand clenching into a fist that he punched into his other palm. 'My spies have heard nothing. They couldn't even find these hideaways, and Daemi managed to track them down in a single night. It's embarrassing.'

'Yes. Well, she did have some help.'

Lodan grimaced and resumed his march. 'A storm. An invasion, perhaps? An attack on the castle?'

'From where? By whom? My men have the guards under control. Even the bad seeds among them couldn't organise themselves into any sort of rebellion without us hearing about it before now.

No.' Captain Mont shook his head. 'That's not what this is.'

'Gloomclaws. The reports about them have started to dry up. Perhaps—'

'And this is what Petron is helping to prepare for, is it not? These weld blades he seems so keen to share with us. Our men train hard every day, your spies infest every corner of the city. I don't see what else we can do. Gods know I've enough other things to worry about without trying to dredge up new problems.'

Captain Mont waved his hand over the stack of papers on his desk, and Lodan scowled again.

'You're right, I suppose. I just wish we could do more.'

'Daemi is heading out again tonight, is she not? Let's see what other secrets she can uncover and go from there. In the meantime …' Captain Mont scratched at his face again. 'I think we could both do with a bath.'

Lodan nodded in reply but didn't make any move to leave the room. Captain Mont watched him continue to pace for a few moments, then turned back to the pile of papers on his desk, determined to try to make some sort of dent in them.

It never seemed to get any easier, this endless administration, passing out orders that others should have been able to decide on for themselves, make pronouncements based on half truths and limited information, all just so that someone else wouldn't take the blame when they inevitably went sour. He found the whole thing infuriating and exhausting. Sometimes he almost missed those days in the Tangle, leading patrols through its haunting shadows. Always on the trail of some otherworldly evil he still didn't fully understand.

He shuddered at the sudden stark memory of those ruined villages, the same visions that kept waking him up at night in a sweat, his fists clenching at the sheets. The blackened shapes scattered across the ground, waiting to be discovered. Staring back at him.

'Are you okay? You look even more tired than usual lately.'

Lodan's concerned voice cut through the daydream and brought him back into the present with a snap.

'What? Oh, yes, of course. Busy, you know.' Captain Mont sat forward and shuffled some papers, embarrassed at the attention.

'You should try to get more rest. You'll make yourself sick. This city can't afford for you to go down with a fever.'

'Oh, away with you, man. Go and get yourself a shave and a bath and leave me in peace. I'll survive.'

He didn't look up again until he heard Lodan leave and the door to the chamber click closed. Then he sat back with another long sigh and held one hand to his forehead, the other still juggling the paperweight in his palm.

The visions, the dreams that had started to haunt him, they were making the headaches worse. Perhaps he should speak to Petron about them; maybe he could conjure up some sort of medicine to help ease his troubled nights. He massaged his temples and took deep breaths until the images from the past faded again.

No. He would be okay. There was too much to do to bother Petron with such trivialities. It was time to get back to work.

He opened his eyes again and grabbed the nearest paper, scowling as he began to read.

The night was murky and cold, a dim glow lighting the castle grounds as low clouds slid across the face of the waning moon. The courtyard between the kitchen entrance and the side gate of the castle wall was deserted, but the servant still waited for another thick cloud to idle by before darting across it.

She gestured quickly to the lone guard stationed at the gate, her features covered by the hood of her cloak, and he barely registered her presence as she passed by. Another servant, finishing her shift and heading back to the lower city and the modest chamber she no doubt called home.

Fool. She scowled to herself from the shadows of her hood. Soon enough, he and all of his kind would find themselves on the wrong end of a blade. Perhaps even her blade, if the master would allow it. If she accomplished her task successfully.

She shivered in the sudden breeze as she passed through the gate and out of the protection of the castle walls, clutching her cloak around her chest, one hand checking again that she still carried the small pouch containing her prizes. Simple items, nothing contraband she could be stopped and questioned about. But prizes nonetheless. Hair clippings, a discarded glove, a half-eaten apple, the teeth marks still clear in its skin. All she had been asked for and more. The master would be pleased.

She reached the lower streets without incident and slipped into the nearest alley entrance, determined to take the longest, most indirect route to her destination possible, her path curling around and in on itself like a serpent, confusing and losing any potential pursuers. She doubted it was necessary, but the master had been insistent, and she knew to follow orders. They had to be even more careful now that they were so close to success.

Only last night, another group of them had been discovered. More than that. Ended with a finality that shocked even them. No prisoners taken for questioning. No mercy given. It seemed their enemy no longer played by such rules.

Finally, after more turns and misdirections than even she could count, she reached her destination. A simple wooden door in the shadows of a disused alley. She stood perfectly still a few steps from the door and waited. A low snort and a breath of steam clouding out from the darkness to her right told her the sentry dogs were aware of her presence. She felt a thrill of fear at having the beasts so close to her, grateful that the shadows hid their sadly twisted features from her eyes.

The door swung slowly open, and a shape moved into its light, waving her forward. She bowed her head and hurried inside.

'Did you bring it?' The rough voice was familiar, but she kept her head lowered and her eyes locked on the floor as she nodded.

'Give it to me.'

She pulled the small pouch out from under her cloak and it was snatched from her grasp.

Footsteps hurried across the room away from her, but she

remained in place as they examined what she had found. There were mutterings, at least three other voices, but as soon as the thought entered her head, she banished it. The less she knew, the better. Those who knew too much became targets.

'You have done well, child. Tell me. What is your name?'

She was shocked at the question, and hesitated before answering, but suddenly a cold, wet snout pushed against the back of her hand and she knew she had no choice.

'A—Asha, Master.' She whimpered as she spoke, and tried to bow her head even further, her chin burrowing into her chest.

'Do not be afraid, Asha. Droogo simply wants to get to know you.'

The snout moved from her hand to her legs, snorting as it inhaled her scent. A patch of stretched, balding skin moved across her vision as the dog brushed past her and finally moved away.

'Lift your eyes, Asha. You no longer need to be afraid of us.'

The words carried with them a command and she couldn't help but follow it, her head moving up, but her eyes snapping closed as her body refused to allow her to see what was in front of her.

'Ah, you still fear. That is unfortunate.'

She felt a scratching on her mind then, as of fingertips lightly drumming across her scalp, their cadence almost playful.

'Will you open your eyes, Asha? Or will you have me do it for you?'

A sudden needle of pain burned into the backs of her eyes and she gasped as she blinked them open. Then it was gone, just as quickly as it had arrived.

Three robed figures stood before her, a small table behind them. On it lay the pouch she had brought, its contents spread across the table's surface. A large, sickly looking dog shuffled behind the figures, disappearing into the shadows underneath the table.

'Do not worry about Droogo. He is simply curious.'

Her eyes flickered to the deeper shadows behind the table, where the voice came from. A shifting movement told her the master stood there, still out of sight. She sighed with relief. Perhaps she would not die tonight after all.

'And you, Asha? Are you curious? Curious as to what we have asked of you? Of what we might need such items for?'

'No, Master.' She bowed her head again as she spoke, unable to stop herself.

'Raise your eyes, child. I will not tell you again.'

With the voice came a cold spike of threat, sliding into her mind and down the back of her spine. Instantly she raised her head and locked her eyes forward.

'That's better.' The spike melted away, leaving only a dull numbness that throbbed slightly with each beat of her heart. 'Come now, you know something of what we hope to achieve. Our shared goal?'

Asha nodded silently.

'And what is that goal?'

'To overthrow this illegitimate regime. To reinstate the true faith. To expel every last hint of the Redmondis filth.' She chanted the familiar phrases automatically.

A low chuckle emanated from the shadows. 'You answer too quickly, girl.'

The three robed figures moved as one and slid their hoods back from their faces. Suddenly, she was staring at three aged men, their sallow skin gleaming sickly, their golden eyes reflecting back the dancing flames of the fire.

'You have done well. These items you have brought us will help guide the passenger. Now it is time for your reward.'

The three men stepped forward, and for an instant she considered trying to flee. A flash of panic tried to shock her body into movement, but it was no use. She was frozen in place, held in some invisible vice beyond her understanding.

A single tear rolled down her face as her vision was drowned in golden light, and a clawed paw placed on her forehead. Then a howl of triumph entered her soul, carrying with it a command that she couldn't help but follow, her bones snapping as her body collapsed into its new shape, and her human mind mercifully knew no more.

Daemi watched the large dog pace slowly across the entrance to the alley, then turn and march back again, its eyes never leaving the ground as it shifted back and forth through the sliver of pale moonlight that angled down one wall and across half of the cobbled street. At first glance, it looked like just another stray, larger than most perhaps, but Daemi had been watching it for more than a few minutes now, and she had seen such beasts before. Seen them and fought them and driven them out of Redmondis. She had hoped never to meet one again.

It wasn't that she feared them, though she knew enough to respect their threat. It was more the sadness they carried with them, the suffering in their eyes that only faded when the life was snuffed from them, the killing blade slid free and their pain finally extinguished.

'Cortis,' she whispered to herself, spitting the words out.

No. Not Cortis. Others, though.

The cat was above her again, slinking along the rooftops, watching the same sentry shuffle back and forth in front of them. Its ears flickered as it watched, tracking the sound that had led them this far.

Weld song. Listen.

Daemi closed her eyes and felt a lurch as she moved into the cat's mind, its thoughts a jumble of noise that she shied away from, trying to hold herself separate. She felt the tightness of panic rise up, then ease away as she breathed, letting the beat of the cat's heart soothe her. There, the song, coming from the alleyway behind the beast. There was no doubting it.

The cat sat up and peered through the shadows of the alley, its night eyes piercing the darkness easily. There was nothing there, just a single doorway in an empty alley. Only the one sentry to deal with.

Daemi opened her eyes and was back in her own mind. 'Leave the dog to me. Go do what you need to.'

She could feel the thrill of hunger through the connection they shared as the cat padded forward, then pulled herself back from it. The night air suddenly dropped in temperature as the cat disappeared and the wraith floated free.

The dog felt the change, stopping its pacing and raising its eyes for the first time, half its face in darkness and half lit by the moon, its silver light glinting strangely from the single red eye that scanned the street.

Its breath steamed in the cold, and all the noise of the sleeping city seemed to still.

Daemi charged, drawing her weld blade as she ran, its blade glowing blue as she closed the twenty or so feet between them in moments. The beast pulled back, ready to spring, but wasn't prepared for her pure speed and was only halfway into its leap when the shining blade cut across its throat. Daemi twisted and slid up against the wall as the dog's body slumped onto the street, its blood pooling around her boots and draining into multiple little rivulets between the cobbles, flowing down the angle of the hill and away. She watched the carcass fall, her eyes taking in the stretched skin and patched coat of the thing, then put it out of her mind and peered around the corner into the alleyway.

There was no movement.

A breath of chill moved overhead, then a black shadow that she could only just make out sank down in front of her and moved toward the door.

She clenched the hilt of her blade as she watched, fighting back against the urge that reared up in her mind.

Come. Join me.

It was Wilt, his voice clear and strong.

'No,' she closed her eyes, determined not to weaken.

A single thread of regret pulsed back to her, then it was gone. She opened her eyes again, but the alleyway was empty.

A clatter of noise and panic erupted from the other side of the wall as the wraith began its grim work, and she held her position, watching for but not expecting to see any escapees.

Flashes of vision bloomed across her mind, but she resisted falling into them. A panicked rush of fear, scattered movement and chaos as their targets tried to flee the inevitable, then another pulse of pure cold that made her shiver, her fingers suddenly numb on the hilt of her sword, then a sudden yawning emptiness she hadn't known since …

'Wilt?' she whispered through chattering teeth.

He was gone, their connection suddenly and surely severed, a dizzying void opening beneath her like she was a kite loosed in the wind, its string cut.

Daemi peered through the shadows of the alley, the moonlight seeming also to have dimmed suddenly, as though the night had deepened around her. There was nothing, just the closed wooden door and a waiting stillness.

She looked down at her blade. It was glowing, the blue light of the blade shining even brighter than it had been. There was still something there, behind the door.

'Wilt?' she whispered again, though she knew there would be no reply. She hadn't felt this alone since before she had found him in Sontair, before he had saved her from the gloomclaw.

The memory still brought a thrill of fear with it, and she had to concentrate to force it back down.

'Move.' She spun out from the corner and hurried up to the side of the door, placing one hand against its knotted timber as she spread herself against the wall beside it. It was cold, but not unusually so. No ache of loss and silence to it. It was just a door.

She raised her blade to her shoulder as she reached for the handle and pushed it open.

It creaked halfway open, then stopped as something behind it resisted. Daemi waited, then pushed harder against whatever was blocking the door, and it gave another couple of inches before stopping again. She dropped down into a crouch and peered slowly around the corner.

A dim orange light struggled against the darkness of the room, a low fire in the corner covered by something that was damping its coals. She sniffed the air, and the sour scent of burning thread and hair told her what that something was.

She bent inside and saw another body blocking the door from moving any further. She reached out to it and grimaced at the shock of cold it sent back through her fingers.

Daemi waited again, trying to let her eyes adjust to the strange light. There was another shape crumpled on the floor in the centre of the room, unmoving. She watched it intently for any sign of breath, but there was nothing.

Slowly she spun herself around the corner of the opened door to sit crouched in the entranceway, all senses alert for any movement. There was nothing. The very air was still and empty.

Daemi raised herself into a fighting stance and pointed the still-glowing blade at the shadows on the far side of the room. They seemed to resist its light, pulsing strangely as she took a cautious step toward them.

Suddenly the shadows popped, and the gloomclaw was upon her, a nest of sharpened claws striking out toward her at once, only her honed instincts saving her from instant death. She slashed the weld blade out and rolled to the side, legs crashing against a chair that the gloomclaw sent flying at her as it leapt out of the darkness. She twisted into a spin and cut blindly at the space between them, feeling the blade slice through another set of limbs that arrowed out at her. A fire of pain bloomed below her knee as one of the claws hit home, and she almost fell as her entire leg seemed to freeze from the wound.

The gloomclaw didn't seem to react as the blade flashed out again, slicing off another spur that shot toward her chest. She tried to circle it, her right leg dragging on the floor as she shuffled, but another sharpened claw struck out to her side, and she only just managed to slap it away with the flat of her glowing blade.

It was fast. Too fast. Faster even than the ones she and Wilt had fought on the ice. She wasn't going to last long on her own.

The gloomclaw slowed then, as though it too knew the inevitability of her death. Its shifting shadows morphed as she watched it, a growing sense of doom threatening to overwhelm her entirely.

Her breath steamed in the cold and she felt her arms droop with an undeniable exhaustion, her muscles blindly following the silent command despite the best efforts of her mind to shout back in denial. She could feel her will draining out of her, her inner voice sinking beneath the waters, her body completely dominated.

The gloomclaw slowed its movement even further, and a single clawed limb reached out to her as she stood swaying and helpless in front of it.

No.

A door slammed closed in her mind at Wilt's voice, the weld that had controlled her severed and sent flailing free. Too late, the gloomclaw realised its mistake and shot three sharpened darts right at her chest.

Daemi watched as they slid toward her, knowing there was nothing she could do, that there was no possible way for her to react in time, but something else told her it no longer mattered.

The wraith rose up in front of her, its form a twisting nest of serpents, and the limbs of the gloomclaw disappeared into it, pulled down into its heart. The gloomclaw was sucked toward it, the wraith unmoving as the gloomclaw struggled to pull itself free, its claws scratching against the wooden floor, gouging deep ruts into its timber. A moment later it was gone, subsumed by the shadowed form of the wraith.

She stood and watched, her muscles still not responding to her commands, as the wraith turned toward her and she stared into its face.

No.

Once again Wilt's voice cut across her mind, its anger blasting the fear free and snapping her eyes closed. She felt the wraith leave her, the chill of death only inches from her body fading as it moved away and disappeared back into its grey, shadowed world.

The clatter of the weld blade falling to the floor brought her back, and Daemi opened her eyes to see the sword lying still in front of her feet, its blade no longer glowing in warning, all threats now gone.

'Wilt?' She whispered his name for a third time, and soft padded feet answered her as the cat trotted out of the shadows and twined itself around her legs.

Here. I'm here.

His voice was fading again, becoming less recognisably human.

'Where were you?'

A jumbled flash of images washed across her mind, a glowing golden thread, a shimmering tunnel, a cold set of eyes shining out of the dark, staring through her.

Then, just as quickly, the vision was gone.

Come. Home.

Daemi bent to pick up her sword and her knee flashed in pain where the gloomclaw had struck her. She looked down at it, a single bloom of red spreading out across the fabric of her trousers.

Come.

She shuffled into movement and followed the cat out of the room, dragging her wounded leg behind her as she limped into the night.

Chapter 13

Higgs sat with his back against the cold stone wall, legs straight out before him, fingers drumming idly on the rough rock floor. Someone had carved this cell out of the mountain, hewn it and shaped it, but he felt no spark of life in response to his touch. There was only an emptiness, an ache of what once had been. No way to shape it to his will, to call it into focus. He was a prisoner, trapped. No way out.

He closed his eyes again, hoping for the emptiness of sleep to take him, to let him drift free of this numb dread, but it would not come when called. He had already slept for hours, perhaps days, yet no hunger or thirst troubled him. Perhaps he was not truly alive after all. Perhaps this was what lay on the other side of death. A holding cell. A silent, endless purgatory.

His fingers slowed their beat, slipping unconsciously into a rhythm that was instantly familiar, like an early memory that only moves into focus in fleeting glimpses. Then he heard it. Music.

Impossible.

Music. It was music, just on the edge of hearing. Instantly, the memory of another time overwhelmed him, and he was back in Greystone, with Wilt, back before all of this.

Higgs stopped abruptly, and Wilt had to twist out of his way to avoid bumping into him.

'Now what?'

'They're doing it again.'

'What?'

'Listen.'

Wilt looked toward the three men but could no longer see them in the crowd.

'We're losing them!'

'Wilt. Stop and really listen. Can't you hear that? It's like an echo on the stones.'

Higgs's eyes had lost all focus, and he was tilting his head slightly to the side like a dog. Wilt sighed in frustration and closed his eyes, willing himself to hear whatever it was Higgs was talking about. For a second, he almost heard it, a whisper in the distance …

Higgs opened his eyes as the memory dripped away, but the music was still there. He reached up inside his shirt to scratch at the sudden itch on his chest, his fingers drifting over the smooth skin there and coming away confused, not recognising the feel of his own body.

A scar. There should be a scar there.

No. That was Wilt. Wilt had the scar from the medallion Petron had given him. He had something else.

The heartstone.

Higgs sat up straight, his thoughts firing into focus as the idea lit up his mind. The heartstone. The necklace Heather had made him. He was wearing it when—

When he died.

Now it was gone. But that music, that was the same song. The heartstone's song. And it was getting louder.

He shuffled forward to the bars at the front of his cell, leaning his head against the green stone and pushing one ear out as far as he could, trying to track the music. There was no mistaking it; it was growing in volume.

'You, boy. I hear you moving about. What are you up to?'

It was the girl's voice again, cutting across the music, drowning it out. He willed her to be silent, but she was already moving to join him at the front of the cells.

'What is it?' Her voice was closer now, a conspiratorial whisper.

'Quiet!' He croaked out the word, still struggling to form them naturally in his throat. 'Don't you hear it?'

The music was still gaining in volume. There was no way she couldn't—

'I don't hear anything.' Another shift from the adjoining cell and the voice drifted away again. 'You're probably still dreaming, mind still carrying the clutter from your trip. This place can do that to you.'

Higgs had no idea what she was talking about, but he felt more lucid than he had since he had woken up here. It wasn't a dream.

He pushed the thought from his mind and tuned into the music, its familiar tune tugging at his chest. Heather. Heather had given the heartstone to him. Trapped him with it, actually. Though if he was honest, he'd almost started to like it …

'Who's there?' The girl's voice called out clearly now, and Higgs heard what had caught her attention. Footsteps. Shuffled, hurried footsteps approaching their cells. Wet, slapping steps rushing along. It was clear from their sound that whoever made them didn't belong here.

Higgs pushed his head even harder against the bars of his cell, trying to see as far around the corner as he could. Then all at once a figure loomed over him, and the music instantly stopped.

'Higgs?'

It was a boy's voice. Familiar. From the time before. From Redmondis.

Higgs stared up at the face of the boy standing in front of him, eyes squinting in the dim light to try to make sense of what he saw. 'Frankle?'

It was him. Frankle. Somehow here, staring in at him. He was standing unnaturally still, his hair and clothes soaking wet.

Higgs blinked and shook his head, refusing to believe what his eyes were showing him.

'Frankle?' he tried again, but the figure of the boy didn't seem to hear him. He was just standing there, staring at him, dripping. And his eyes, there was something wrong with his eyes.

Then, just as suddenly as he had appeared, he was gone, a vision ripped away. All that was left were two wet footprints on the stone outside Higgs's cell.

'Who's there?' the girl called out again, angry now. 'I can hear you there.'

Hadn't she seen him?

Had he really been there? Or was this just another vision from the past sent to overwhelm him, to break down his mind?

But the footprints. They were real.

Higgs reached one hand out through the bars to the small pool that marked one footprint, the puddle already spreading out and smearing the boot shape away. As soon as he touched the water, he hissed in unexpected pain.

It was cold. Cold beyond ice. Cold that burned deeper than flame.

Higgs jammed his throbbing finger into his mouth without thinking. It tasted of salt water.

'Who was that? I heard something.'

Higgs backed away from the bars and didn't reply, his mind a whirlwind. It had been Frankle, all right. Somehow here, in this place. Eyes filled with ink just as Wilt's used to be.

He pulled his finger out of his mouth and looked at it. A red burn was forming where the pad of his finger had touched the puddle.

What was it the voice has said? The Novus?

Your friend knows you are here, that much is clear. He will come for you.

So, they could find him, somehow. They knew where he was, even if he didn't.

Higgs stared around his cell, at the stone walls that caged him, feeling the first awakening of the spark that was his true self start to spin up to speed.

He wasn't going to just sit here and wait for them. Bait for the Novus's trap.

Time to start helping himself.

It was all well and good deciding to escape, but where to start? Higgs drew his knees up to his chin and peered around the cell, scanning every inch of it in the dim red light that seemed to coat everything in blood. It was one more oppressive detail of this place, designed to keep his mind fuzzy and his will weak. Well, no more.

'No more,' Higgs whispered to himself. His voice was improving, and it felt good to put thoughts into actual words. Each time he spoke, he felt stronger, more present, as though each syllable rooted him more firmly in reality, screwing him down into place, holding him firm and secure.

'So, again, where to start?' Higgs's eyes ceased their circling of his cage and ended up fixed on the front corner where the green stone bars disappeared into the red rock wall. The girl.

'Hey!' Higgs hissed out the word, unable to bring himself to speak any louder than a thick whisper. The enveloping dimness still weighed heavily on him, making even this level of volume seem wildly reckless. 'Hey, are you there?'

He was rewarded with the sound of shuffling from next door, then her voice, much louder than his. A confident, almost regal tone. Daring the world to defy her.

'I'm here. Are you finally coming back to yourself?'

Higgs looked down at his hands, flexing his fingers. They were still slightly numb, tingling as the blood pumped back through them. She was right; he was pulling back into himself. 'Who are you?' It was as good a place to start as any.

'Me?' The girl chuckled, though there was no joy in it. 'I'm nobody, just as you are. A weldfarer, they call us.'

'I'm … Higgs. My name is Higgs.' He stumbled over his own name, his tongue struggling to latch on to it.

'No, that is not your name. Not in this place. What name did they give you, the Incarnate, when they held you in the pit?'

'Stone.' It came to him automatically, much easier than his real name had. 'I am Stone.'

'And I am Flame,' the girl responded, as though answering some pre-rehearsed call and response. 'You see, they know who we really are.'

'You called them Incarnate. The hooded ones?'

'I can tell from your accent you are not from these lands. You are from the west, yes? I have heard your accent before. What do you call them, those who control the welds?'

'Wielders,' Higgs replied, the image of Wilt flashing into his mind. Wilt staring back at him, eyes filled with grey, spilling into black. Face sprayed with blood. 'We call them wielders.'

'Yes. I have heard this name.' Another shuffle of movement, and her voice gained in volume again as she moved to the corner where their cells met. 'You would do well to keep such knowledge secret. They will want you clean. Pure. Unmarked by memory.'

'Where are we? Why are they keeping us prisoner?'

'Do you really not know? How strange. You are a guest of the Novus, Stone. A weldfarer. Sent out to alter the weave of time itself. How you came to be here, I cannot say. We each make our own journeys.'

Weldfarer. The Novus, the voice in the dark that had held him inside its fist—it had called him that too. Using the welds to alter time. Was it possible?

'What do they want with us?' Higgs raised his voice again.

'Want? That is beyond our understanding. They find us, those who can ride the welds. Seek us out and assign us tasks to shape the world to their desire. Then they send us out, like dogs.'

Higgs could hear the hatred in her voice. Hate, and something more. Something he could use. 'We have to get out of here.'

'Ha!' The girl's laughter was a short bark of contempt. 'You think you can simply walk free of this cage? Think these bars will obey your commands, boy?' She punctuated her words with a dull thump against the bars of the cell.

The stone bars. The same stuff the shackles had been made from.

'And before, when you were with Wilt. Vargul had used the same chains to bind him. Bind us. But we had escaped ...'

'What are you muttering about back there? If you want to speak, speak— What is that?' The girl's latter words were louder, her tone suddenly demanding. Another scuff of movement. 'That puddle. You brought something back with you. An artefact. A sliver of time. Do you know how dangerous that could be?'

This time, the movement was in the other direction, as though the girl was scurrying as far away from the small puddle at the front of their cells as possible. 'If they find it, if it finds you—'

She was cut off by the scrape of a key in a lock and the creak of a door swinging open. Marching boots entered the dungeon, and Higgs ducked his head back down between his knees, an irresistible jolt of fear squeezing him into a ball.

'What is this mess, Grell? Look to your duties, basic as they are. Keep the place clean.'

'I don't know what could have—'

'I do not wish to hear excuses. We need the girl. Leave the other one. He is still days away from being any use.'

Another snap and creak and the boots moved into the adjoining cell.

'You there. Flame. Come. We have another task for you.'

There was no reply that Higgs could hear, just more movement and the sudden slam of the cell door closing, then the boots and noise faded down the corridor, leaving Higgs alone in silence.

Chapter 14

'Not as bad as some wounds we've seen at least.'

Daemi opened her eyes at Petron's voice and found herself lying on her bed, head propped up on pillows and her injured leg stretched out in front of her, towels and wraps of cloth draped over the bed to protect it from the blood and whatever else Petron was treating her with.

She blinked her vision clear and stared down at the wound, a lone deep circle of dried blood, about the size of her thumb, and watched as Petron poked around its edges with a strangely scented wet cloth. It didn't hurt, there was no pain at all.

'Petron?'

'Ah, our patient awakes!' Petron smiled up at her briefly before turning back to his work. 'Try to stay still while I do this, will you?'

Why was there no pain? Surely, she should be able to feel something.

As she watched him scrub at the dried blood around the wound, she realised she couldn't feel that either. Not even the briefest touch.

'Petron?' The fear edging her voice gave Petron pause, and he peered up at her more keenly.

'Am I hurting you?'

'No, it's not that. There's nothing. I can't feel anything at all.'

'Oh.' Petron's smile widened, and he turned back to his work. 'Don't worry yourself about that. Our old mutual friend Nurtle taught me a thing or two about medicines.'

He held the cloth up and squeezed some more of the liquid it contained onto the wound, dripping into and around it to soak into the towels below.

'Quite good, isn't it? I just hope I got the measurements right. Wouldn't want you to have a dead leg for too long.'

As if to emphasise his words, he reached out with his other hand and rapped his knuckles on her knee, just above the gash.

Daemi didn't feel a thing. Not even a numb thud.

She looked back and forth from her leg to Petron dumbly, and he let out another chuckle. 'Sit back now. Rest. Let this old man do his work.'

The door to the room swung open and Heather poked her head around it, her face breaking into a wide smile once she saw Daemi was awake. 'Morning! All ready for us?'

Petron looked up briefly from tending the wound and scowled. 'Don't rush me, child. I'm almost done.'

Heather skipped into the room, Frankle wandering in behind her, twin dark circles under his eyes the only sign of his recent troubles.

Daemi smiled at them both, happy to have some company, though her thoughts immediately went to her other, closer companion. 'Where's W—'

The cat darted through the closing door and sprang up onto the bed, leaping clear of Petron's annoyed swat and into the roof beams above.

'Didn't think he'd leave you for long, did you?' Heather grinned and wandered over to peer down at Petron's work. 'Do you think it will need us both?'

Petron glanced up at her as he gave the wound one final swab. 'You're the expert, young lady. You and Frankle seem to have done the job on our patient's other wounds well enough. Better than I ever could. You tell me.'

'Frankle? What do you think?'

Daemi watched Frankle walk over to join the others examining her leg. He looked much better, just tired, though he did still seem to step carefully, as though he wasn't quite certain of his balance.

'Uh-huh.' Frankle coughed as he replied, then went bright red and covered his face. 'Sorry.'

'It does look similar, doesn't it?' Heather said. 'The edges cauterised, as though burnt, but still resisting closing. Gloomclaw, was it?'

Daemi nodded and flinched automatically as Petron patted the wound again and stood up, though she still felt nothing.

'Show me what you can do then, you two,' Petron said, stepping out of their way and turning to Daemi. 'A gloomclaw? In Sontair? You're quite sure?'

'Yes.' Daemi nodded, aware suddenly that her news would cause quite the disturbance among those still trying to maintain some sort of order in the city. 'But different, this time. Bigger. Faster. It almost—'

'Different?' Petron tapped his chin thoughtfully. 'Not like the ones you fought on the ice?'

No.

Daemi winced at the word, the power of the voice seeming to shout across the room. Then she realised all three of the others were staring up at the cat.

'Did you—' Frankle began.

'Yes. I heard that too.' Petron seemed both troubled and curious at this turn of events. He turned back to Daemi. 'So how did it get here?'

Summoned.

The voice was quieter now, still clear, but no longer the powerful shout it had been. Once again, however, all four of them turned to face the cat.

'Did you hear that as well?' Daemi asked.

They each nodded, their eyes not moving from the silent form crouched in the shadows above.

'It's not Wilt's voice though.' Petron finally broke the silence. 'It's different. Less … human.'

'Wilder,' Frankle replied.

'Wildler, perhaps,' Heather whispered, her eyes moving back to watch Daemi.

'So, it wasn't—' Frankle stopped and tried to reword his thoughts. 'I mean, I didn't make this one—'

'Oh no, Frankle. I think you're off the hook this time.' Petron smiled and reached out to pat Frankle's shoulder.

The cat leapt down onto the bed then, and sniffed cautiously at the edge of Daemi's wound, then trotted up to her chest and curled itself into position. Its black eyes stared into Daemi for a moment, then turned back to the others.

Come.

'Um, I'm not sure—' Heather began, but Daemi cut her off.

'Do your work.' Daemi nodded down at her leg. 'You and Frankle. You use the welds somehow, don't you? To heal it? I think Wilt wants to join you. Help you see.'

'Frankle?' Heather looked back at Frankle, and Daemi finally realised what it was that worried her.

'I'll be okay.' Frankle smiled, trying to sound confident. He moved to sit next to Heather and pulled his sleeves back, ready to begin.

'I'll keep an eye on all of you,' Petron said. 'Just make sure you don't sink too deep this time.'

Heather reached out and took Frankle's hands in hers, then moved them both over the wound.

'Ready?'

Frankle nodded and closed his eyes, and immediately Daemi felt the familiar tug in the centre of her guts.

She looked at the cat, staring back into her, calling her onward.

She closed her eyes and fell down into the spiralling void.

The wraith stood alone on the rooftop, cloaked in the shadows of the night, the world below it grey and dim. A flash of life and movement flitted across the street below, joining with another glowing form, then becoming one again as the life of the second form bled out onto the cold cobbles.

That was me. Taking out the sentry. The dog-thing.

Daemi? Where are we? I can feel you and Frankle, but—

Wilt. We're seeing through Wilt's eyes, Heather. Seeing what he saw. What it saw. The wraith.

The wraith shuddered as the strange thoughts ebbed through its mind, shouting out in the whirling storm that spiralled endlessly inside it. Some part of it wanted to find them, search them out and drain them, but this thought, too, was ripped away and forgotten.

It turned back toward its target, the three glowing forms in the room behind the door in the alley. Three men. Two with blades drawn. Waiting for it.

It could sense their fear through the thick wood of the door, their vain faith in the steel they held. And something more, something strange. An impatience.

The wraith dropped out of the sky and stepped onto the street, forcing itself to move past the glowing life force pressed up against the corner of the alley behind it. A different hunger there, a stranger one. Not for now, though. Now it was time to feed.

It passed through the thick stone wall feeling only a momentary kiss of resistance, of a long-forgotten life frozen in time centuries beforehand, and then it was through, reaching out its clawed hand into the chest of its first victim, his dying thoughts a torrent of memory and regret.

It considered the taste of the final moments of life and felt a strange coldness as the second man slid a blade into its form, into and through it, the thousand twisting welds that comprised its body simply allowing the blade through, swallowing it whole and grasping the hand that wielded it in a vice grip of death.

Another rush of memory, more violent this time, less controlled. A more metallic tang. The body fell to the floor and disappeared into the grey fog of shadow that comprised the world beyond life, and the wraith turned to the third figure in the corner.

It paused. There was something strange about this one, something different. A lack of fear. It looked into the face of its next victim and saw that the man was smiling in anticipation.

The wraith only allowed itself a moment's pause before reaching out and into its victim, opening itself as the life force flowed into it, a sudden torrent of it overwhelming it, swamping its mind and pulling it down, into the familiar chill of the waters beneath the ice, where the nightmares waited for it.

Daemi, what's happening? I think we're losing Frankle.

No, it's okay, Heather, I'm here. It's just hard to control the panic. It's pulling at me, trying to drag me back down into it, like the welds do, but stronger, but at the same time there's something holding me separate. I … I think it's Wilt.

The wraith felt the world behind it snap closed, the connection to the one who waited there on the other side of life sever, and knew it had made a mistake. The ice darkened and closed around it, cracking as it locked into place, and a familiar voice overwhelmed its mind.

You. I know you.

The voice closed on him like a fist, squeezing his mind in its unrelenting grip.

You have fallen into my trap once again, wielder. I will not let you slip away.

The wraith felt itself being pulled further below, the black freezing waters rushing through it as it plummeted ever deeper. Then a touch of something else pulled past it, a snapshot of horror that slithered around its form and pulsed up to the ice above.

You still meddle with that which you do not understand. Every crack in the barrier only gives my servants another path to the light. It is beyond saving now.

He felt the wraith form fade in the tightening grip, its shadow wrung free and left to dissolve in the freezing waters of night. All that was left was Wilt. Wilt, and those he carried with him.

I have hunted you across time itself, wielder. You gave me a part of yourself to escape last time. What can you offer me now? What hope can those fragile minds you shelter offer you?

Underneath the voice, beyond its echoing cacophony, a familiar music could just be made out, darting in and out, dancing at the edge of hearing. He recognised that song. Weld song.

Wilt turned his head toward the sound and saw the flicker of a golden weld floating in the distance, reaching toward him with every pulse of time.

Come then, wielder. Ride the welds to where that other part of your mind waits for you. Back to the time beyond this age, before this weakening barrier was built, when nightmares walked free. Come to where we wait. Come and join with us once again.

Wilt reached out for the weld, though he could see nothing in the inky blackness that held him. Nothing but the ever-growing golden light calling him onward. Onward and away.

The weld song was growing louder, moving the waters around him with its rhythm. He felt it take hold of his mind and lead it away.

Daemi! We're losing him!

I know, Heather. Frankle, what can you do?

I … I don't know. It's so cold.

The music, Frankle. The song. Remember what Wilt gave you. What Higgs gave you. The heartstone's song. Remember it.

The golden weld was all that he could see now, curling and writhing in front of him, just out of reach. He only had to pull his arm free and grab on to it, dive into it and ride it back to where Higgs waited for him. He could almost see him, down the end of a long glowing tunnel, sitting alone on the floor of his cage.

The grip on him loosened just enough, and he reached his arm clear. Then Higgs looked up at him and slowly shook his head.

The weld song changed, its haunting melody lightening as he pulled himself free of the grip that had held him. The music was familiar again, but different. It no longer spoke of darkness and horror, of power and glory, of triumph and consequence. Now it was a simple tune, a warming song, something that pulled at the heart and floated him back up toward the surface and those who waited for him.

Argh! Still you resist me. Those others only weaken you, and yet you do not see. Bring them then, bring them all. Bring them with you and see what good these connections can do when faced with death itself.

Wilt felt the voice fall away, sinking into the depths, and he wrapped himself once again in the cloak of his wraith form as the heartsong pulled him up and out, back to the living world and its grey shadows. He felt the other near him once again and blinked back into the room just in time to step between her and the final strike of the gloomclaw that cut toward her struggling form.

The wraith pulled its shining weld blade clear and struck at the massive gloomclaw, shielding the glowing life that sat crouched and bleeding on the ground.

Frankle? Come back now, come away from the wash of memory. Come back to us.

Yes. Yes, Heather. I'm coming.

Daemi opened her eyes and saw Frankle and Heather standing above her, their hands linked and moving over her leg where the gloomclaw wound had been. The skin was already knotted and healed, just the slightest pinkish blush the only sign there had ever been any damage at all.

Frankle and Heather opened their eyes together and stared at each other, their hands still linked.

'Well?' Petron spoke from the other side of the bed, and all three of them started at the sudden sound of his voice. 'Daemi?'

Daemi looked up and smiled. 'I'm okay.'

'Frankle?' Petron turned to the younger wielder, who looked like he had just woken from another long sleep.

'Um. Yes. I'm okay too. I think.' He extracted his fingers from Heather's and wiped them slowly down the front of his shirt, feeling himself as if unsure of his own reality. 'That was … strange.'

'You can say that again,' Heather agreed. She looked better than both of them, the only sign of trouble a slight paling of her skin. 'And Wilt?'

'He's here. He's safe,' Petron answered, pointing up to the ceiling where the black cat sat curled around the nearest roof beam. 'Though for a moment there, I wasn't too sure I was. It suddenly got very cold in here.'

Petron raised his eyebrows but left it at that, reaching out to pat

Daemi on the shoulder. 'Looks like our two young healers have put me to shame once again, at least. Rest now. Everything else can wait.'

Chapter 15

In his dream he was running down a narrow forest trail, one he had moved down many times before, many nights before, but now there was an urgency to his passage, a rush of panic that drove his feet into a trot, then a full run, his heavy plate armour clanking awkwardly as he forced his tiring limbs to keep moving.

Was he chasing something, or fleeing it? He was no longer sure.

The forest path narrowed further, the trees on either side reaching out to him, grasping at his shoulders as he pushed past, trying to halt his movement. But he was stronger than them. Surer in his step. He knew he had to keep going.

He reached up to his shoulder and tugged at the leather strap of his armour, finally managing to pull the knot free and shrug out of the chest plate that fell with a dull thud to the damp forest floor. The sudden freeing of weight gave his legs a new burst of speed, and in the next few steps he managed to shake off the armour that covered both arms as well, leaving it to sink into the dirt as he charged ever onward.

He felt his breath pant in and out of his lungs, his chest whistle as it heaved and strained. Yet still he kept on running.

The trail closed again, causing him to duck down now to pass through, its branches no longer just brushing past. Now they clawed at him with sudden thorns, scraping and gouging at his flesh to try to stop him. But the rush inside his mind wouldn't allow any slowing. He had to run. To move. Ever onward.

Soon he was on all fours, somehow still moving quickly, the

pant of his breath a steady throb now, his long tongue lolling out one side of his mouth as he ran, back legs to front, his snout following the scent that called him on.

Then a howl cut through the forest and he broke through.

Captain Mont sat up in bed, his breath shuddering heavily in and out of his lungs, sending thick clouds of steam out over his bed in the chill of the morning. The window to his chamber had been left open overnight, and a brassy blast of horn echoed into the room from the training grounds outside where his troops were assembling.

The horn, that's what had woken him. That's what that howl had been. Nothing more.

He wiped his hand over his face, brushing the sheen of sweat from his brow and scratching at the long whiskers on his chin. For a moment he was back there, his face covered in hair, the shape of it all wrong, stretch and elongated. Not human. More than human.

He blinked and shook the last remnants of the dream from his mind, swinging his legs out of bed with a grunt and looking around the room. It was a mess; reams of paper pooled in one corner where the wind must have gathered them during the night, discarded clothes scattered across the floor in heaped piles. Not what a commanding officer's bedchamber should look like in the slightest.

He grunted again and let the troubling thought drop from his mind. He was hungry.

Moments later, he was out of the room, pulling his heavy cloak around him as he stalked toward the kitchens, rubbing his hands together in the cold. He had only been able to find one glove, the other having disappeared somewhere in the chaos of his room days ago, and his fingers felt stiff and strange as he tried to rub some heat and life into them.

A servant moved down the corridor toward him, trying to balance a heavy-looking bowl of steaming hot water in his hands as he walked, and for the briefest moment Captain Mont felt an overwhelming urge to bury his face in it, rub his muzzle in the water and lap it up, and he had to slow his walk to regain control of his thoughts as the servant hurried past. The servant nodded quickly as he passed, and Mont could only respond with another grunt, throaty and horse and no longer quite human.

He shook his head again. The visions of night were staying longer now, clinging to his mind and pulling at him, leaving him more exhausted every day.

He could feel himself slipping. Surely, they all could. Yet still, he was here.

Captain Mont shouldered the door to the dining room open and stepped into warmth and the sweet scents of freshly baked bread and roasted meats. All other thoughts dropped away. He hurried to the table and tore at the nearest leg of flesh that came to hand, stuffing it into his mouth. He swallowed without chewing, the large hunks of beef pushing at his throat on the way down, the hot juices searing the roof of his mouth, yet he ignored those too and reached out to the meat once again.

'Hungry, are we?'

Petron's voice called him back into his human mind, and he almost choked on the mouthful of meat he had been about to wolf down. He coughed roughly and finally managed to swallow it, wiping his hands on the nearest cloth and turning to the far end of the table where Petron sat.

'Sorry. I think I missed dinner.'

He reached out for a plate and began stacking bread and fruit and more reasonable serves of beef onto it.

'No, I'm sorry, Captain.' Petron waved as if dismissing his own words. 'I know you've been very busy. Are things beginning to get under some sort of control?'

Captain Mont finally finished arranging his plate and sat down on the nearest chair, picking at his food as he considered his answer. 'No. No, control is not the word I would use.'

Petron smiled and pushed his own plate away. 'I think I know something of how you feel. When I was asked to lead what was left of Redmondis, I don't think I slept properly for weeks. Always something waiting to be done, some task postponed that shouldn't have been, some nagging worry scratching at my mind. It does get better, I can tell you that much.'

'I hope that's true. Right now, I cannot see the end of it.'

'That's part of the reason I need to get back, you know. To bring more help.'

Captain Mont turned to fully face him now, his tired, yellowed eyes both locked onto the older man for the first time. 'You really mean to attempt it, then? What Lodan told me? You mean to try to journey back through the ...'

'Conduit,' Petron prompted.

'Back through the conduit alone? Is that safe?'

Petron frowned and shook his head. 'Not safe, no. But not out of the question either. I've learned much just in the past few days reading what I could find in the queen's study. Besides, with what we've seen from Daemi and the others, I don't think we have the luxury of time. It's worth the risk.'

'They have news then?'

'Nothing you would consider concrete.' Petron smiled at the captain's scowl. 'I know your soldier's mind would prefer solid reports, but unfortunately that's not the world we're dealing with here.'

'No.' Captain Mont barked out a sharp laugh then, his face feeling strange as it stretched into something resembling a smile. 'Though I'm becoming more used to the strange ways of Redmondis and the like. It seems Sontair had its own share of wielders and their doings. They just hid it better.'

'And now they are being forced out of the shadows. This is a good thing, Captain. But it can be dangerous as well. That's why I need to move quickly to bring you reinforcements. The Redmondis guards are well-drilled and well-armed, and they have experience dealing with such things. They should be a great help to you.'

Captain Mont nodded and bent back to his food. With each bite, he felt his strength returning, his troubled dreams sinking further into memory.

'Good. And when do you hope to make the attempt?'

'Tonight.'

That stopped him. Captain Mont stared at Petron, the food on his plate forgotten now. 'So soon?'

'I see no reason for any further delay.'

'And the others?'

'They will stay here for now, though as we said they too will need to move on soon, once they've fully recovered from their ... exertions. It won't take long to organise things at Redmondis. All going well, I should be able to lead a small force back through the conduit in the next day or to. Then you will start to see more control here in Sontair, I'm sure of it.'

Captain Mont felt a flash of panic at the words, though he wasn't at all sure why. Something troubled him, deep within his chest, and a cold spike of pain throbbed behind his eyes. He stood up quickly, pushing his half-finished plate away. 'Then I have much to do to prepare. If you'll excuse me.'

He turned and left the room without waiting for a reply, a sudden urgency driving him onward.

Heather woke as she often did lately—in the still, silent dark before sunrise, her quiet shufflings about the bed chamber seemingly the only sound in the entire castle.

She poked the coals of the hearth back up to a warming glow and carefully opened the single window to allow the morning air in, its chill breath blowing the last shreds of sleep from her mind.

On the small side table beside the window sat a large stone bowl, and she filled it with water from the pitcher beside it, still slightly surprised each morning that she didn't have to crack a layer of ice covering its surface, not accustomed to the simple luxuries of this southern climate. Once the bowl was filled, she sat in front of it, waiting for its ripples to clear, her breath slow and steady in her lungs as she emptied her mind and prepared herself.

A call and answer from the soldiers in the courtyard far below announced the dawn change of guard, but Heather was already far away, chasing down visions seen through other eyes.

At first it had almost been too much for her, a wash of images that threatened to swamp her mind, timelines twisting around themselves, people and places seeming to fight for her attention, strange visions popping to the surface only to be sucked down again by the next one forcing itself upward. It was overwhelming.

Now, though, she was beginning to gain some semblance of control. Part of it was simply practice and familiarity—knowing instinctively which scenes to ignore, which threads to cut free of the tangle that writhed within the viewing bowl. Part, too, was her own frequency of use. It was as though the viewing bowl knew her now, knew what she sought, what she valued, what visions would hold her attention, opening access to her mind.

Petron had warned her about spending too much time in the wash of possibilities contained within its waters, but Heather knew it was worth the risk. They all took similar ones. Frankle with his journeys into the depths, Daemi and her growing connection to Wilt, even Petron and his fascination with the conduits and what use they could be put to. No, she would not worry about what effects her use of this tool was having on her mind. She would do what she could to help.

Heather took a final deep breath and closed her eyes, pulling her chair forward so that she was leaning directly over the viewing bowl. She leaned closer still, so that it filled her vision, and opened her eyes.

A flash of fire scorched across the surface of the water, revealing a long dark tunnel, an orange-lit figure standing ahead, a flame in its hand—her hand—her eyes turning toward you now, reflecting back the flames and burning into you.

A shift. Outside now, under an open sky, standing at the lip of a flat stone ledge, a sea of fire burning far below.

Shift. A closed fist. Your fist. Staring at it and opening your palm slowly to reveal a cooling stone key.

Shift. Running ahead now, away from the figures in the passage, away from the key, further down into the darkness, speeding along corridors, unable to stop the pull.

Something grabbing you, sucking you down, into the vision.

Heather's panting breath pushed against the surface of the water but was unable to break it, unable to wrench her mind free.

Another watcher, staring back at you, recognising you. Waiting for you to come into its presence. It opens its mouth, and you are pulled under.

Through the ice, into the freezing waters below, your skin burning with the sudden cold, your breath stopped, eyes locked open, watching the strands of your hair float past your vision.

'Heather!'

The voice calls to you through the water, muffled and warped. Calling to you. Calling you back.

The nightmare twisted and pulled and finally dropped away as Heather pushed herself back from the viewing bowl with a gasp, her hair flinging out a spray of water from where it had been floating inside the bowl, her breath coming in sudden ragged breaths after being held for so long under the water. She looked around, panting, trying to remember where she was.

'Are you okay?' Frankle was standing at the open door to her chamber, his body half in and half out the door.

Heather brushed her streaming hair back from her face and pushed the viewing bowl back to the centre of the table. 'Yes.' She coughed slightly as she answered, her breath still coming in gasps. 'I was just … washing.'

'Oh. Sorry. I wasn't sure what you were doing with your face in the bowl like that.'

'In the bowl?' Heather looked back at the bowl, its water lower now, most of the rest of it soaking into her hair and dripping down the back of her nightgown. 'Yes. Trying to wake up, you know.'

She stood up and reached for a towel, ending any further discussion on the point. 'And what can I do for you?'

'I was just wondering where you were. You missed breakfast.'

Heather pulled the towel down off her head and looked out the window. The morning sun was clear above the surrounding buildings. How long had she been—

'Petron's hoping to do it today, you know. This morning, I mean. I think we should both—'

'Of course, we should. Sorry, I lost track of time. Just give me a second here.'

Frankle watched her for a moment more before catching himself and slipping back out of the room, closing the door behind him. 'I'll just wait out here then?'

As soon as the door closed, Heather leaned back over the bowl, searching its surface for some glimpse of the vision that had held her, but all she saw was a young girl's reflection staring back at her.

By the time Heather and Frankle got to the queen's study, Petron was pacing back and forth outside the door, head down and muttering to himself. They both slowed their step and watched him silently. He appeared to be having an argument with himself.

Finally, he looked up and noticed his audience. 'Ah! You're finally here. Come on then, let me show you what I've found.'

He ushered them both inside the room and hurried over to the conduit on the far wall. 'Here. Look at this.'

Petron traced his fingers lightly over the strange carvings lining the border of the conduit, his mouth moving silently until his voice seemed to catch up with his thoughts.

'These carvings. At first, I thought they might just be decoration, or even instructions on how to activate the conduit. But this one—' He tapped a symbol just to the left of the centre of the arched frame. 'Recognise it?'

It looked to be a crude representation of a mountain range, with a single building squatting between two triangular peaks.

Frankle and Heather looked at each other, both waiting for the other to jump in.

'It's Redmondis!' Petron finally answered for them. 'And here, this one?'

A star shape on top of another pyramid, much smaller than the others. 'Sontair, of course. The jewel of the south. Now look.'

Petron traced his fingers across the surface of the symbol, then pushed against it, as though it were a button.

Nothing happened.

'You see?' Petron turned to them, an expectant smile on his face.

'Um …' Frankle began to stammer out an excuse, but Petron cut him off.

'It can't activate, because we're already there. Here, I mean. In Sontair. But now look.'

Petron repeated the trick with the symbol representing Redmondis, and as he pushed against it, a bright glow flashed across its surface, as though liquid silver had just been poured into the grooves of its markings. The flash only lasted a moment before vanishing.

'So, the destination is set. Redmondis.'

'You mean it's as simple as that?' Heather spoke up. 'You don't need to bring a wielder with you?'

'I think judging by our last little expedition, bringing Frankle along might lead to some uninvited guests.' Petron smiled and turned back to the conduit. 'Now if only we knew what these other symbols represented, what other destinations there might be.'

'But you're confident you can just go straight to Redmondis like this?'

'Oh yes. It's all in that book over there.' Petron waved vaguely at the desk on the other side of the room, piled high with books and scattered parchment. 'Most useful, once I found it. We really need to do a proper cataloguing of the tomes in here. All the more reason for my little trip, of course. Head back to Redmondis, set the conduit there to return to this one, then start to bring through everything we need. Which reminds me.' He finally pulled his eyes away from the conduit and peered down at them. 'Haven't seen Lodan this morning, have you? I was hoping to talk to him before I left.'

'Uh, no. Haven't seen anyone, really,' Frankle answered.

'Probably busy. I know Captain Mont is struggling with things. Lodan's probably stretched to his limit helping out. Well.' Petron sighed and turned back to the conduit. 'May as well get on with things then.'

'Do be careful, Petron.' Heather reached out and wrapped him in a hug before he could wriggle free.

'Yes, yes, girl. You just make sure you keep an eye on things here for me. Shouldn't take too long to start bringing others back through. With any luck, you'll see me again tonight.'

Petron finally extricated himself from Heather's hug and patted Frankle on the shoulder. 'And look after our budding wielder here. Keep him out of mischief.'

Frankle blushed and ducked his head in acknowledgement.

'And maybe step back a bit.' Petron shooed them both back away from the conduit. He stood directly in front of the doorway, then reached out and pushed against the Redmondis symbol again. There was the briefest flash of silver, then the space inside the door frame billowed into grey mist.

'Here goes nothing,' Petron whispered to himself and stepped through.

Frankle and Heather watched him disappear into the fog and blank stone replace the mist. A moment later, they both exhaled and grinned sheepishly at each other.

'He'll be okay, I'm sure of it.' Heather smiled and turned toward the desk. 'Come on, help me organise this mess.'

'Wait, there's something—'

Frankle's next words were cut off as a horn blared somewhere outside the castle walls, and was immediately joined by another, then another.

'What is it?' Heather asked, pulling Frankle with her out of the room and over to the nearest outside-facing window.

Before they reached it, her question was answered, as a wolf's howl cut through the air, sending a thrill of recognition and fear down both their spines.

Chapter 16

A single bead of sweat tickled the edge of his eyebrow before dropping to the stone floor, its tiny splash distracting him and instantly pulling him back to the now, away from the swirl and pull of the vortex inside his mind he was trying to wrangle, to force into some sort of shape that he could wield.

Higgs sighed and rocked back on his heels, examining the rock surface he'd been struggling with. It was completely unchanged, all his effort and straining no use at all against whatever it was inside of this stone that seemed oblivious to his call.

'Well, it seemed like a good idea at the time,' he muttered, wiping his brow.

The idea had come to him from the past, from the last time he had been locked inside a cell, in Redmondis, by Cortis and his wolves. It had all been so much easier then. Call to the stone, the life within it, the blood, reach into it and pull out the key that was waiting for his hand to find. Like a stone for his sling on the riverbank.

Higgs sighed again and rubbed his palms together, examining his smooth fingers, even pinker than normal in the constant dim red glow of this place. This prison. His fingers looked younger than he felt. Unmarked by time. His mind, though, that felt old. Far too old. Out of time in more ways than one.

He got to his feet with a sigh and stalked back and forth across his cell, trying to pump some blood back into his stiff legs. It felt like he had been at it for hours, but time was impossible to track in this place, where the light never changed and there was nothing but the distant sound of dripping water to accompany his thoughts.

The girl next door had stopped talking to him. Flame, that was her name. Flame. He wasn't sure she was even there. He could hear no movement, not even a sigh of breath. He hadn't heard them return her from the last time they had led her away, but he might have slept through it. Taken her away to the Novus. The one who ruled this place. The one who had been inside his mind.

Higgs shuddered at the memory and shook it away, turning back to the stone ground.

'You know what you need to do. The stone resists; it is linked to the power of this place. The memory of it. You need to separate it, spread it thinner somehow, the connection. Break a chunk free.'

He had stopped questioning this constant chatter to himself that was becoming a habit. He needed the company. Besides, it was almost like talking to Wilt, almost the same, just missing the familiar bloom of warmth that came with each reply. No spark.

'Spark. That's what the Guardian called him. Called us. Spark.'

He grinned suddenly at the memory and arranged himself back on the floor, bending his will to the stone. He closed his eyes and lightly stroked the ridged rock, his fingers capturing every edge and ripple of its form.

'Spark,' he whispered again. There was something important there, in that memory. 'Blood. Blood within the stone. Spark that ignites the flame.'

In his mind, he was inside a long tunnel, four feet padding across the cold ground, a chill wind blowing into his face from the solid darkness in front of him. The void, calling him onward.

'But there was something else that called me, called me back. Wilt, and something more. A spark.'

He remembered it then, floating above him, dipping and swooping in the currents of air, just out of reach of his paws. Teasing him. A hint of music as it danced, grabbing his attention and turning him. Back toward the light.

Higgs's hands pushed down harder on the stone, his fingers

moving in slow circles as a glow of power ignited within his chest. A circle of stone figurines, falling in order. A rolling wave of movement. Never ending.

'The golden weld. The one we caught, that pulled us here. That was the same. The same sound, the same song. Just like the spark, only louder. More pronounced.'

His memory flickered to that moment, his body locked inside the ice, the crack and shift of it threatening to tear him apart, the deep, burning cold. The song that lit up the world around him, the golden weld dancing with it. He saw himself reach for it, part of him joining with it, floating with it, stretching out along it and leaving the rest behind.

'Wilt,' Higgs murmured, a sick tug of separation wrenching his stomach. The weld song took that too and wrapped it in a warming glow of contentment. It was filling his mind now, filling the room, almost spilling out over his lips as his hands moved to the rhythm of it, around and around, then down, into the living stone.

Higgs opened his eyes and saw both his hands inside the stone ground, reaching for something they knew could be found. The song was still there, shouting down his sudden doubt and fear.

He felt the first tug of panic at the base of his skull, and the cold stone began to grip his skin.

Higgs pulled back hard, wrenching his arms free as the rock closed around them, the backs of his hands stinging suddenly as the skin was scraped and ripped, the weld song abruptly cut off as he fell backward, leaving him staring at the ceiling of his cell, listening to the slow drip of water that was once again the only sound he could hear.

He sat back up and raised one fist to his face, slowly uncurling his fingers to confirm with his eyes what he already knew was there. A stone key sat on his palm, slightly warm but cooling quickly.

'See? I told you so.'

Higgs scrambled to his feet and hurried to the locked door, reaching out through the bars to slot the key into the keyhole on the outer side of the gate. He closed his eyes and breathed.

'Here goes nothing.'

He tried to turn the key, but it didn't shift in the slightest. He tried again, harder now, wrenching at the key in both directions, but it remained locked in place.

'Well, I guess nothing's ever that easy.'

He left the key in the lock and felt around the edges of the keyhole with his fingers. The key fit well enough, but it wasn't shaped to fit the inside of the lock itself, to drop the tumblers required to open the door.

'Let's try something else.'

Higgs closed his eyes again, his fingers touching the outer side of the key, trying to will the vision of the golden weld back into his mind. The heat and spark floating in the air, the song of it calling him onward.

It came much easier this time. It was as though the stone was no longer actively resisting him, pulling him back up to the surface. It was as he had thought; he had wrestled it out of the living whole of the rock chamber and now it was weaker. Separated. Easier to craft.

He left that thought behind and dropped deeper into the flame of song.

The key warped again, warming and melting, spreading itself into the spaces inside the lock. Then the spark drifted clear, and he opened his eyes, the key once again cooling quickly in his fingers.

'This time.' He turned the key, and the lock opened with a clean snap.

Higgs just had time to grin to himself in victory before another sound rang out from the shadows of the corridor. Another door swinging open.

They were coming.

He hurriedly locked the door again and pulled the stone key free, almost fumbling it in his rush. He wrapped it tight inside his fist and scurried back to the far wall of his cell, pulling his cloak around his shoulders and dropping his head into feigned sleep.

There was more than one set of feet. And something more, a scraping across the stone.

'Here.' It was Grell's harsh voice again. A jingle as a chain of keys was picked through, and another snap of a lock opening, the door swinging wide with squeaking complaint. More scraping as something heavy was dragged inside the cell and dumped unceremoniously on the floor.

'Careful now. The Novus won't want her damaged.'

'Did she return with the offerings?' The second voice was different from before. Softer, yet somehow much more menacing. It carried the edge of danger, as if the speaker was always only moments away from lashing out.

'Of course. Here.'

'I will not touch them. You have already soiled them enough. Keep them wrapped. What did she recover?'

'Hair. A glove. Some sort of mush that used to be food, I imagine.'

'Yes. It would be just like those fools to try to pass food through. No matter, it will be enough. Come, leave her to recover.'

The door swung closed, and the boots moved away, back down the corridor. Higgs raised his head as another slam further down told him his captors had once again gone.

He waited a full five minutes of silence before moving, slipping the stone key into the lock and turning it smoothly, pulling it free as he slowly pushed the gate open, eyes scanning the dim light for movement, ears straining for any noise other than the distant slow drip that accompanied him.

There was nothing.

'I guess sometimes it is that easy,' he whispered, a tight grin twisting across his features and lighting the centre of his chest, as though a grey cloak of shadow had been shrugged off and left behind on the floor.

Higgs stayed in a low crouch as he waddled out of the cell, trying to stay as low to the ground as possible. He paused in the corridor, looking left and right, neither direction seeming very appealing. Both ways led to shadow, his captors having gone left, the drip of water coming from somewhere to the right.

That was the way Frankle had gone, too. If it had been Frankle at all and not some mad vision.

'You're not mad. Not yet. Just ... a little disorientated.'

He squinted down both directions again, unsure of his next move.

A small cough interrupted his mulling, and he scurried over to the next cell. Peering through the bars, he could see a bundle of rags piled in the centre of the floor, shifting slowly as whoever was huddled underneath them breathed. Flame, if it was still her. Obviously fast asleep.

'She did seem to know a bit about this place,' he reasoned, and instantly made up his mind. He slid his key into the lock, once again holding two fingers on it and closing his eyes as he dropped into the song, feeling the stone warm and melt into the spaces inside the lock. Then he turned it and opened the door.

Chapter 17

For the briefest moment, Daemi thought she was back in her nightmare—the wolf's howl cutting through the crowd in Redmondis, the enormous four-legged body leaping over the heads of the nearest faces in the chaos and crashing into another knot of people, sending bodies sprawling across the field as Daemi turned toward it and it dropped its head in some sort of salute.

The glisten of drool dripping from its jaws, already stained pink with conquest, the golden gleam of its eyes as it stared at her and readied itself to spring.

Wake up!

Daemi sat up with a gasp, as though she had forgotten to breathe in her sleep, and looked up to see the black cat sitting on her legs, staring up at her. Another howl echoed from the courtyard below, and she sprang into action.

Moments later, she was running down the corridor toward Heather and Frankle, still buckling her leather armour across her chest as she moved.

Heather was leaning out a window trying to get a view of what was causing all the commotion outside, and Frankle was standing behind her, as if unsure he wanted to confirm what his ears told him. He looked green with fear.

'Frankle! Heather! Step back from the window!'

Heather almost fell out as she spun on the spot, looking like she had been caught doing something she shouldn't. 'Daemi!'

'No time now. Get into your chambers and bar the door.'

Daemi didn't pause to see her command followed, still charging down the corridor toward the stairs.

'But we can help—' Heather began to protest.

'Now!' Daemi's bark was even louder than before, and both of them followed the order immediately.

As she ran, Daemi caught a glimpse of fighting in the courtyard below, seemingly two sets of soldiers from the same army milling about and fighting each other. What was going on?

They come. Gloomclaws.

The cat was running beside her, easily keeping up as she finally finished buckling on her armour and bent her head into a full sprint. She pulled her weld blade free as she ran, and the blue glow of the blade gave truth to the cat's prediction.

By the time they finally burst out the door into the courtyard, there were already men down. Daemi counted at least ten figures lying still, blood pooling in the dirt. Scattered around them were various soldiers, pushing each other in their confusion as to who exactly was attacking them. Then a flash of steel and a cry and another body dropped.

Daemi dashed toward them, only to glimpse a silver blade disappearing again into the crowd of soldiers. She grabbed the nearest body and spun it around to face her. 'You! What is happening here?'

She recognised the face—a young soldier, only recently out of training, his face pale with panic.

'I ... I don't know. There was a howl, then panic—' He gestured helplessly.

'Gather your wits, man!' Daemi shook him roughly and he snapped his eyes back to hers. 'We're under attack. Take your position. You know what to do.'

She almost threw him away and turned to the next man, determined to try to impose some sort of order on the chaos.

No time. They come.

A black flash of movement shot across her vision as the cat darted away. As she followed it, another, much larger shadow appeared at the top of the wall.

'Gloomclaws!' Daemi cried out. 'Form your defences!'

Once again, she didn't wait to see her order obeyed, rushing after the cat heading straight for the nightmare atop the castle walls.

Lodan was halfway out the door, carrying his long sword still in its sheath, when Griggs cannoned into him, sprinting full pelt down the hallway in answer to the horn blast that had trumpeted out moments before. Lodan managed to grab his shoulder and spin him in place as he charged past.

'What is it?' he asked, almost dropping his sword as he held Griggs's shoulder.

'Gloomclaws. The castle is under attack.'

'And the lower city?' Lodan's thoughts immediately went to the masses of unprotected people crammed inside the city's walls.

'No idea. They're at the walls, heading this way, so—'

'Go!' Lodan interrupted him and shoved him on his way. 'Take the first patrol you find and make sure. There's no point defending the castle if they're going after the townsfolk.'

'What are you going to do?' Griggs called over his shoulder as he stumbled into a run.

'I'll find Captain Mont. He must know something. Go! I'll be with you at the walls as soon as I can.'

With that, he turned and charged the opposite way, glancing quickly out of every window he passed to try to make sense of the scenes below.

There were soldiers moving everywhere out there, not in any sort of order or system.

A wolf's howl cut through the air and the crowd of soldiers seemed to surge in response, a wave of movement shifting across them as they reacted.

Lodan turned a corner away from the outside windows and charged deeper into the castle, headed for Captain Mont's chambers.

Moments later, he skidded to a stop at the open doorway to Captain Mont's room, bending his head inside to confirm it was empty. Scattered papers lined the floor, and the desk at the side of the room had been thrown over, lying awkwardly on its side against the wall.

Lodan didn't stop to try to make sense of it. A servant rushed past him and he thought about reaching out to stop him, but something in the man's eyes held his hand. The man was more than panicked. He was terrified.

Lodan buckled his sword onto his hip and ran down the corridor, headed in the direction the servant had been fleeing from, his mind a rush of questions.

How had this happened? How had his spies not warned them? Hadn't Wilt and Daemi been hunting down these enemies for them? Had they missed something?

He rounded another corner and stopped. There was another servant, this one no longer moving, lying half-propped against the wall, a red splash of blood streaked behind his head. A matching bloom of crimson slowly spread out from his chest where the sword had entered.

There was nothing he could do for this man.

Another cry of panic and the crash of a door giving way further inside the castle got him moving again. Who had killed that man? How were they already this far inside?

Where was Captain Mont?

Another, deeper thump led him onward. It sounded like something striking stone. Then another, and an ugly ring of steel against rock.

Lodan slowed as he got to the doorway that seemed to lead toward the noise, and drew his sword as he peered around its edge.

Inside the room was another mess of papers and books. It was the study—the queen's study. And standing against the far wall, sword held high to strike at the conduit, was Captain Mont.

Lodan lowered his sword, but didn't sheath it. 'Captain?'

Captain Mont didn't respond to his voice, and his sword cut down to strike at the stone of the conduit, sending sparks and shards of rock flying out from it.

'Captain! What are you doing, man?'

The captain stopped and slowly turned to face him.

For a moment, Lodan was transported back in time, to another place, another scene of battle and confusion. He was standing on the flagball field in Greystone, one hand clasped on his teammate's shoulder in victory, watching as a guard stumbled toward Wilt, a silver blade in his hand.

It was his eyes, his shining, golden, dead eyes that were the same. As the guard was tackled to the ground, he had looked straight at Lodan. Then the voice, forced out of him, not sounding human at all.

The blood within the stone.

Captain Mont took a step toward him, his golden eyes shining.

'Mont! What's happened to you?'

The only answer was a dead eyed grin and the sudden thrust of a sword that Lodan barely parried before the captain rushed at him and knocked him to the ground, the weight of his heavy armour pinning Lodan to the floor.

Lodan gasped for breath as the wind was blasted out of his lungs, and tried desperately to twist clear of the weight holding him down, but it was no good; he simply wasn't strong enough to shift it.

Captain Mont's head was turned sideways, his ear squashing into Lodan's nose, but now he raised his head up, and Lodan could once again see the man's strangely shining eyes. It wasn't Mont, not anymore. Something else was behind those eyes; some other power now held the reins.

The creature that had been Captain Mont grinned down at him, his sharpened teeth leering in the face of Lodan's struggles to free himself. Then it snapped down onto him, a sharp, fierce headbutt that cracked into Lodan's nose, shattering the bone and sending a spray of blood across both their faces.

Lodan fought to stay conscious, a red wash of pain threatening to pull his mind out of the present, sink it into the comforting numbness of anaesthesia. He shook his head, trying to resist the blurring at the edges of his vision, willing his mind to stay on the surface.

It was no good. Another crack of a headbutt pushed him deeper, and he saw himself sink toward death.

'Lodan!' It was Heather's voice. So familiar, yet so distant. Calling from so far away.

He struggled to open his eyes but his face was covered in blood. His own blood. It bubbled in his nostrils as he tried to suck in another breath.

Then darkness took him in hand and led him away.

Heather had finally managed to get Frankle to leave the door alone and sit on the bed, his face drained of blood entirely and his movements stiff and distracted. It had been that way since the first howl of a wolf had rung out from the courtyard below, the memories of the last time Frankle had encountered such creatures almost too much for him to bear. Heather took his hand and led him here to her chamber, but he was so scared, so terrified of what might be coming for them that it was all she could do to stop him from trying to bar the door with every movable piece of furniture in the room.

'Frankle!' she tried again. 'It's okay, Frankle. We're safe here.'

'Safe.' He nodded, uncomprehending, then turned to the door again, as though convinced it was about to slam open.

'Just … try to sit still.' Heather hurried to the window, determined to see what she could of the chaos in the courtyard below.

She flung the window open and leaned out, but the ground below her window was empty. Shouts and the cries of fighting echoed out from somewhere around the corner of the castle, but there was nothing to see from her vantage point.

'We should be out there. Helping.' Heather spoke mostly to herself, though she had no idea what she could actually do to help. Daemi had been so stern, so clear in her orders that she had followed them automatically.

'Safe,' Frankle murmured again, and she turned to watch him, suddenly aware that he was more damaged than she had realised.

His face was almost white, all blood drained from it, and his hands twisted and knotted in his lap, his fingers wrapping around each other as though he were trying to wash some stain free.

He turned to face a pile of clothing crumpled in the corner of the room. 'Safe.'

'Frankle?' Heather moved toward him slowly. 'Are you okay?'

'Safe. I'm safe.' His voice was stronger now, more present. He tore his eyes away from the clothes and stared straight at her. 'We can't … we can't just hide.'

With an obvious effort, he stilled his hands and pushed himself to his feet, turning to the door. 'I'm not going to hide anymore.'

'Frankle?' Heather watched as he pulled his shoulders back and took a deep breath.

He turned to her, his face no longer pale, his eyes shining with determination.

'C'mon, Heather.'

She nodded as he reached for her hand and pulled her along.

Outside, the corridor was deserted, but the sound of steel on steel could still be heard from somewhere further on.

'That's not—' Heather started, turning her head to listen. 'That's not outside. It's coming from inside the castle.'

Frankle strode forward, his hands flexing at his sides as though readying himself.

It didn't take long for them to catch up to the fighting. A panicked servant almost knocked them over as she threw herself around the corner of a doorway into their path, not stopping to warn them as she crashed past them and fled, her sandalled feet slapping on the stone floor. A second later, a soldier appeared, blade drawn and a hungry, mad scowl on his face.

Frankle took a moment to size up the threat before pointing at the man and sending a thick black weld striking down on him, a furious hammer blow that shattered the man's defences and instantly blasted all consciousness from him, dropping him in his tracks.

Heather hurried up to him and rolled the soldier over from where he had landed face first on the floor. His eyes were still open, their golden shine slowly dimming as she watched. In moments, they were clear and blue again, and she reached out to lower his eyelids.

'Is he—' Frankle began, his voice no longer strong and sure.

'He's fine, Frankle. He's just unconscious. You did well.' Heather smiled grimly back at him and stood up. 'Come on. There will be others we can stop.'

Frankle nodded and strode forward again, leading the way further inside the castle.

The sounds of fighting and crashing furniture led them on, through room after room, sometimes arriving too late to help, their eyes shifting past the bodies slumped on the floor, sometimes arriving in time to stop a crazed soldier and drop them with a weld. Heather made a point of checking each body they found, each time waiting for the golden gleam in the soldier's eyes to fade away before closing them.

After they left their third victim breathing shallowly in unconsciousness, they heard a familiar voice call out.

'Lodan,' Heather whispered. 'That was Lodan.'

'Look where we are,' Frankle said. 'The queen's study. C'mon!'

He broke into a run, grabbing Heather's hand again to pull her along, no longer worrying about what lay ahead.

They slid to a stop outside the study, the door hanging from a single hinge as though it had been kicked open. Inside, there were two bodies writhing on the floor, both faces covered in blood.

'Lodan!' Heather cried out, and the man on top raised his face to look at them.

It was Captain Mont, yet not. His face was twisted into a grimace of insanity, and his dead eyes stared through them. Then he smiled cruelly and smashed his forehead back down on Lodan's broken face.

Frankle didn't hesitate, sending another black weld smashing into the madman's mind.

This time was different though; as soon as the weld struck, Frankle seemed to jerk in place, some magic Heather couldn't see blasting back at him and fighting to take control.

Heather watched, waiting for the moment when Frankle's victim collapsed into unconsciousness, but it never came. Instead, Captain Mont seemed to freeze, his eyes wide open, their golden light still glowing bright as he locked eyes with Frankle.

'Frankle?' She turned to her friend, only to find him locked in place too, as though both of them had been frozen in time.

The body underneath Captain Mont coughed and spluttered, and she put all doubt from her mind. Lodan needed her help.

She crawled up beside the prone figure, careful to keep as much distance from the man on top of him as she could. She reached out and touched the blood-slick forehead, and Lodan seemed to react, coughing once more and sending another spray of blood into the face of his attacker.

'Lodan!' she whispered urgently, though Captain Mont seemed oblivious to her presence. 'Lodan! Can you hear me?'

There was no further response from Lodan, and Heather reached out with both hands to try to free him. She hesitated as she placed her hands on Captain Mont's armour, but he was still frozen in place. She took a deep breath and leaned all her weight into trying to roll him off.

With a surge of adrenaline, she managed to roll Captain Mont away, his body twisting as it moved so that his shining eyes stayed locked on Frankle, his head turning strangely on his neck as he ended up lying on his back, head tilted unnaturally backward, chin high in the air.

Heather attempted to drag Lodan clear, but he was too heavy. Instead, she cradled his head in her arms and tried to get some response from him.

His face was a crumpled mess, his nose flattened and smeared to one side, and blood bubbled from his lips.

'Lodan! Breathe!'

She looked back up at Frankle, but he was somewhere else, his eyes filled with black and his face still, locked in some unseen battle of wills with Captain Mont. It was up to her.

Heather ripped at her sleeve, finally tearing a length of cloth free and using it to wipe at Lodan's face, cleaning what she could of the mess. She tilted his head to the side and reached into his mouth to clear his airway.

With a sudden heave, a thick glob of blood and phlegm came clear and Lodan coughed, his head moving in her hands finally as he regained consciousness.

'Lodan! Can you hear me?' She wiped at his face again, attempting to clear the blood from his eyes.

He looked up at her from her lap and smiled, his cracked lips stretching over the gap where his front teeth had been. 'Heather?' He peered up at her, as though trying to place where he knew her from. 'You look a mess.'

She smiled back at him, relief washing over her at the sight of his smile.

'It's me.'

'I think—' Lodan started, then coughed again. 'I think I'm going to pass out.'

His eyes rolled back in his head and finally closed as his body relaxed into unconsciousness.

Chapter 18

Daemi felt Wilt change as she rushed toward the wall, a deep chill falling over the area and a surge of hunger blooming in her belly.

'Are you sure you can control it? There are men everywhere!' She shouted the question as she ran, not worrying about the confused looks of those who heard her on her way through.

Yes. It's okay. It's … natural for me now.

Wilt's voice was once again much clearer and stronger in her mind, and there was something more—an edge lacing the words, as though she could sense more of the person behind the voice, feel what he felt. Behind the hunger, the craving for life, was a wave of regret at what had been lost.

Daemi pushed the thought from her mind as she saw another flash of silver in the small crowd of soldiers at the base of the stairs leading up the outer wall of the courtyard. Another cry, and the bodies surged outward as one of them fell.

'There! Stop that man!'

The soldiers immediately surrounding the fallen figure milled about in confusion, not sure where the attack had come from, but Daemi saw one break free and sprint away from the staircase. She raced after him, determined not to lose sight of him this time.

Another bloom of heat inside her belly told her Wilt had taken his first victim.

Just a soldier. Golden eyes, but human. I'm going to stop the gloomclaw. Meet me at the top of the wall.

Daemi danced around another knot of soldiers hurrying into

position, keeping her eyes locked on the legs of the man she was chasing. He was twenty metres ahead of her, and as he turned, she caught another glimpse of shining, golden eyes.

She bent into a full sprint. Two men loomed in her path and she knocked them sprawling. She was gaining on him.

Another howl cut across the courtyard, and every man around them paused and looked to the sky, their eyes wide with panic.

The soldier she was chasing disappeared around a corner, and Daemi hurried toward it, sliding into a skid as she turned it. She felt rather than saw the blade cutting at her and fell to her knees, bending back under the strike that threatened to take her head off.

Daemi raised her blade into a thrust, but stopped at the last second. In front of her was the soldier she had been chasing, his golden eyes wide with shock, the red point of a long sword jutting out of the centre of his chest.

With a final sigh the man fell to his knees and toppled forward, Griggs pulling his blade free as the body fell.

'That's three,' he muttered and stepped forward to help Daemi to her feet. 'Any others?'

'Gloomclaws. On top of the wall.' Daemi clapped him once on the shoulder and started back toward the staircase, calling over her shoulder as she ran, 'You stay down here. Let us handle them.'

'Wilt?' She turned her attention back to the cold vortex spinning inside her mind.

One down. Two to go.

She caught a flash of vision from the wraith's eyes, a clawed black shape spinning around a glowing weld blade, banished back into the depths. 'I'm on my way.'

Daemi finally reached the stairs and bounded up them, two at a time. As she reached the top, another breath of ice misted out from her left, and she watched as the shimmering form of the wraith struck another gloomclaw down. 'Where's the last—'

Before she could finish the question, she fell backward and a black wave crashed over the edge of the wall, striking two sharp claws into the stone at the space where she had stood.

Daemi raised her blade and slapped away three quick strikes, pulling herself back to her feet as she danced clear.

The gloomclaw was enormous, just as big as the one that had almost killed her the other night. Just as fast.

She didn't have any time for further thought as the gloomclaw pressed its attack, moving forward with each strike, getting closer and closer to breaching Daemi's frantic defences.

I'm coming.

The voice echoed through her mind, but she had no time to make sense of it, her back foot stumbling as it caught in a gap in the stone, almost costing Daemi her footing and her life.

She was at the corner of the wall, at the guard tower. She had run out of room to retreat.

The gloomclaw loomed larger still, drawing itself up into another strike as though rearing on its hind legs.

Without thinking, Daemi jumped backward, one leg reaching for and finding the wall of the tower behind her, springing again from that point to launch herself up and over the nightmare form, blade cutting down as she flipped over it to land on its other side.

The gloomclaw only paused a moment, its form shifting in on itself to face her without turning. Daemi raised her blade again, ready to defend herself.

Then a black shadow dropped between them, and she knew she was safe. She felt another surge of heat and fury as the wraith reached into the gloomclaw, ignoring the claws that struck down at it, merely slicing through the shadow as though cutting through smoke.

A pull, an urgent calling within her chest.

Come. Come with me.

Daemi had no choice but to obey, letting herself be pulled into the mind of the wraith, into Wilt and beyond, into the gloomclaw itself.

A rush of movement, a snaking curve of blurred shapes that broke into the centre of darkness, then sudden stillness, as though the world itself had frozen in time, holding its breath and watching for what would come next.

Daemi was standing on a flat black landscape, the only sensation that of a warmth in her hand from the other one gripping it. Wilt. It was Wilt.

Come.

Movement again, racing over the still expanse, arrowing toward the dim horizon where dark grey sky met black ground.

She wanted to turn her head, turn and face Wilt. See him truly once again as he was. As he still must be, somewhere.

A faint golden glow bloomed on the edge of her vision, and they altered their path.

There. The golden weld.

It was a weld. Shining and floating in space, getting larger as they skimmed toward it, then seeming to shrink again as it recognised them and pulled away.

Not this time.

Daemi heard the concentrated fury behind his words, seeming to triple in speed suddenly, the blank mindscape around them blurring as they cut across it. Once again, the weld grew in size, until it filled the sky, dancing above them, teasing them with its song.

Song. Yes, she recognised it now. Weld song. Filling her mind, forcing her to close her eyes to try to keep herself from drowning inside of it.

Hold on.

The hand that gripped hers pulled her arm forward, and she saw them both reach into the golden weld, their fingers intertwined as they merged with it, sucked into its light and song.

Then it was too much for her mind to understand and it retreated into darkness.

When she opened her eyes again, she gasped for breath, breaking to the surface after too long under, her lungs on fire. The world around them was changed. Alive now, filled with chambers and pathways that snaked away in every direction. Red-tinged and somehow liquid, the entire world seeming to breathe with them, surging back and forth with each passing moment.

The hand still held hers and squeezed once again.

Be silent. Be still. We are not safe here.

An opening appeared in the nearest wall, the damp, almost flesh-like covering peeling back on itself to reveal a single faceless figure. She sensed movement again and saw the wraith's hand reach for it. A tumble of memory swamped them.

Holding the offerings in two clawed hands. Turning them over and over, sucking in every last drop of life and memory. A soldier. A leader. Tired. Weakened. Ready to be taken. Yes. These would do nicely.

'*Go. Send them. Send all we can. We must not allow them to recapture the city.*'

'*But they are already inside. Our agents are few and failing. Their power is greater than we imagined.*'

A blaze of anger at the words. Then malice. Then satisfaction.

'*We do not need to take control. We only need a distraction. The weldfarer will do the rest.*'

'*Are you so sure?*'

Another flash of fury that burned like agony. So hard to resist lashing out, but it could not be afforded. Not yet.

'*Send all you can. Close the pathways. Ensure they cannot breach the Spine.*'

A pause then, which almost cost the man his life.

'*As you command.*'

Daemi stumbled as she fell back into herself, the figure in front of her collapsing in on itself as it was drained of all memory.

Come. We must know more.

'Wilt? Where are we?'

She wasn't sure she spoke the words aloud, but their meaning seemed to be made clear.

We are inside the mind of the one who sent the gloomclaw. The one who controlled it through the golden weld. We do not have much time until he realises his mistake.

They surged forward again, to another open chamber and another silent, faceless figure. It turned toward them, but the wraith reached into it and the world dropped away.

'We must do as the Novus commands. Send the gloomclaws. Send the weldfarers. Take what we can.'

'But the others. The ones who escaped. Does he know?'

'He does not. Nor will he. They will be found before it matters.'

'But without them we only have three ready. And the few dogs who remain there. It will not be enough.'

'It will have to be. Come. We do not have time for squabbling.'

They pause in front of a cell door, and it swings open. A huddled figure peers up at them from the dark.

Daemi stumbled to her knees as she returned. It had been different this time. As though they had been spat back from the memory. Recognised and rejected.

Come. We must leave. He has found us.

Another gap tore open beside them and a hand shot into the space where she had stood moments before. They arrowed backward, racing away from the scene as more and more faceless figures appeared where they had been, turning their heads in the air as though sniffing for their scent.

The red tinge around them grew brighter as they moved, ever faster, the world blurring into smears of colours as she was pulled away from it, the weld song growing once again in her mind as the golden weld lit up and burned away the scene.

She was on her knees, the rock of the castle walls underneath her, the sounds of battle and confusion echoing out from the courtyard below. A black shape darted across the edge of her vision and she raised her blade in panic, ready to fight the gloomclaw, only to see the black cat waiting for her, its tail curving back and forth in the air.

Come. The gloomclaws are no more. The soldiers can handle the rest.

It sprinted toward the stairs, dancing in and out of the legs of soldiers who hurried to take their defensive positions on the wall.

Daemi pushed herself to her feet and followed the cat. Back to the castle. Back to the conduit.

Frankle was falling, the darkness washing past him, tearing at his hair and whipping it around his face. Then he pulled free of the chaos and opened his eyes.

He was standing on a flat, broken landscape, the sky above him roiling with dark grey clouds, familiar shapes forming and melting away, never locking into place. Beneath the clouds the sky dripped down toward the black surface, as though he was watching a painting smudge and smear as it was washed clear.

He was inside Captain Mont's mind. What was left of it.

Beneath his feet, the ground shifted, and he lifted his boots clear as they sank into the dirt, the mud sucking at them as he moved.

What was this? What had happened to him?

At the edge of hearing, the familiar weld song called to him, leading him onward, and he walked, the world around him speeding past much faster than he moved, as though he were falling through a dream. Which, he supposed, he was.

A glowing light appeared on the horizon, then a few steps later, the golden weld floating in the air became clear. It was the only living thing left in this blasted landscape, the only thing giving Captain Mont's body life. The man he had been was gone.

Frankle reached toward the weld, with both his hand and his mind, sensing it writhe and twist away from his grip, resisting his pull. Whatever controlled it, controlled Mont, didn't want anything to do with him.

He gritted his teeth and bore down on it, determined to coral it, to pin it down.

With a lash of movement, the golden weld struck out at him, his vision shocked with a detonation of light and a roar of song, then he was falling again, blasted away from what had been Captain Mont.

When he opened his eyes again, he was standing on the shifting ice. Ahead of him, twin columns of steam shot into the clouds above, black shapes darting through it, the ice under his feet rolling as it cracked and broke apart.

Frankle. Come back.

He looked up toward the voice that called to him, and a familiar face formed in the clouds, warping in and out as the winds shaped it in turn. It was Wilt. Then Higgs. Then Heather.

The world shook and tilted suddenly, the entire ice sheet he was standing on ready to flip completely over.

A hand reached out and grabbed his shoulder, and he was pulled free.

He was back in the queen's study, standing in the middle of the room. In front of him, the twisted and broken body of what had been Captain Mont collapsed from its strained, warped position and relaxed into death.

He stared at the golden eyes as they faded back to brown, aware that he was watching someone else, something else that had taken control of the man abandon him and flee.

'Frankle?'

He finally wrenched his eyes from the slumped body on the floor and turned to Heather.

For an instant, he panicked—she was sitting on the ground, covered in blood. Then he saw Lodan lying beside her and he realised where the blood had come from.

'Heather?'

'It's okay—he's alive.'

A sudden spark of blue light lit the room as a crack of noise erupted from the conduit on the back wall. The carvings around its stone border were scratched with deep cuts, some shattered completely, and a lightning bolt of energy danced around them, shorting back on itself as it ran into the flaws that now marked its surface.

'But I think we need to get him out of here.'

Frankle nodded, flinching as another shot of noise cracked out from the broken conduit.

'Help me. He's heavy.'

Frankle hurried over and reached down to grab Lodan's shoulders, trying to grip his cloak through the blood. Lodan's head lurched to the side as he pulled, and he averted his eyes from the sight of his broken features.

Together Heather and Frankle managed to drag his body up and out of the room, pulling him through the door and around the corner, then propped him against the corridor wall. Lodan's head lolled again, but his breathing seemed steady and regular.

'What happened?' Heather finally looked up at Frankle. 'What was Captain Mont doing? Why did he—'

'It wasn't him. It wasn't Mont,' Frankle answered, looking back at Heather's blood-streaked face. He held back a sudden urge to reach out and wipe her face clear.

'What—'

'It was them.'

They both turned to the new voice. It was Daemi, her weld blade drawn and glowing blue—the same blue light that the broken conduit had been emitting. A black shape darted between her legs and past them as the cat ran into the study.

'Them?' Frankle asked, uncomprehending.

Daemi reached them and bent down to Lodan, her face a mask of control as she lifted his chin to examine the damage. 'He'll live. Though he won't be quite as handsome as he was.'

Come. There is no time.

It was Wilt, his voice distant yet still echoing in each of their minds.

Daemi stood up and sheathed her blade. 'We have to go now.'

'Go?' Heather asked. 'Go where?'

Through.

Wilt's voice was followed by another crack of lightning and a blaze of blue light that left stars dancing in their eyes.

'But it's broken.' Frankle gestured back toward the door. 'Captain Mont—I mean, whatever controlled him. He shattered it.'

Come. Now.

Daemi didn't stop to argue, just gripped Lodan's shoulder once in farewell and marched into the study. 'We have to go now,' she repeated. 'Come on.'

Frankle watched her disappear through the doorway and looked at Heather. She shrugged once, then took his hand in hers. 'She's the boss, right?'

He looked down at Lodan. The wounded man's breathing was stronger now, and the sound of hurrying footsteps told him help was only moments away. He nodded and followed as Heather led him into the room.

The cat was waiting for them, its body a black shadow against the constant blue glow of the conduit. The sparks and crackles of noise were getting louder now, and chunks of rock began to fall and crumble from its border.

Now. Together.

Daemi took both their hands in hers and pulled them forward as the space inside the border of the conduit turned to a roiling mist.

Heather closed her eyes, and with a final squeeze of their hands, they stepped through.

Chapter 19

The door of the cell opened with a slow groan and Higgs hesitated at the threshold, suddenly wary, watching the bundle of rags on the floor.

'She didn't sound dangerous. Cocky, maybe.'

He peered back up the dark corridor in the direction the guards had gone, then crawled inside. 'May as well get on with it.'

Now that his mind was made up, he moved quickly, hurrying over to the feet of the figure sprawled out on the ground and poking gingerly at it.

'Uh … hello?'

Nothing. His fingers might have touched a thigh or calf, but it was hard to be sure inside the rough bundle of cloth covering her. He grabbed the edge of the covering, slowly sliding it free.

As her head came free of the coverings, a wave of vertigo washed over him and he reared backward, almost falling over onto the stone floor. Her hair was a bright, deep red. Just like the queen. Just like the Sister.

The dizziness only lasted a moment, and he shook his head to banish the thought from his mind. 'Nonsense. Look at her, she's your age.'

He was right. Even in this dim light, it was clear the girl was far too young to be one of the Sisters. Her hair was red, and underneath the grime she might be quite attractive, but that was it.

'Silly,' he scolded himself, and reached out to the girl's shoulder to shake her awake.

As soon as his fingers touched her, she sat bolt upright, one hand snatching his wrist in a vice grip, the other pinching at the centre of his throat, pushing him back down to the floor and choking the air out of him.

He stared at the wild eyes burning into him, blazing with anger, the darkness of the world closing in on him, his vision stretching into an ever-receding tunnel as he struggled and gasped for air.

Her grip on his larynx loosened as she spoke. 'You talk too much, boy.'

It was definitely her, the same voice from before, the same condescending tone.

Higgs stayed frozen on the floor, trying to swallow and suck for breath as she looked up from him to see the cell door wide open. She released him completely, springing up and out into the corridor in a flash of movement.

'Wait.' He coughed and rubbed at his bruised throat as he rolled to his feet to follow her. 'Do you know where—'

She was already away, heading right, disappearing instantly into the shadows. Higgs stumbled after her, only just remembering to retrieve the stone key from the lock before moving into a trot, willing his eyes to hurry up and adjust to the darkness before he ran face first into a wall.

'I guess she does,' he croaked.

Higgs shuffled on through the dark, one hand held out in front of his face. He was just beginning to be able to make out the shape of his fingers against the blackness when a hacking cough echoed out from somewhere in front of him, and a sudden bright flare of light burned the shadows away, blinding him completely.

He ducked his head away from the light, blinking the stars out of his eyes before raising them again to see the girl waiting for him for him further down the corridor, an iron gate barring any progress.

She was staring back at him, one hand held high in the air, a dancing ball of flame hovering over her palm. Her red hair shone even brighter in its light, seeming to reflect bright licks of colour to the flame, almost as if it was calling it onward, teasing it ever higher and brighter.

Higgs found his step slowing as the strange vision hypnotised him. She bent over and hawked out another rough cough of phlegm, shattering the magic.

'Are you coming?' she demanded, wiping her chin with her free hand.

As he stepped closer to the circle of light thrown by the captive flame, he could see her face more clearly, the deep dark circles under her eyes and the stretched, worried pinch of her lips.

'Uh … hello again?' Higgs began as he moved toward her, one hand still held out in front of him in something between greeting and surrender.

The girl stared down at his offered palm and back to his face, her frown deepening. 'Can you open this?' She nodded at the locked gate.

Higgs dropped his hand and bent toward the lock. It seemed the same as the others, the bars dull iron instead of stone but a similar keyhole marking its lock.

'I think so.'

He brushed past her carefully, pulling his stone key free and slotting it into the gate. The girl bent over his shoulder curiously, holding her flame higher to better light his work. He tried turning the key, but it didn't move.

'Nice trick you have there,' he mumbled, pointing his other hand up at the shifting ball of flame.

She ignored him, and he sighed and turned back to the lock. He held two fingers on the key and closed his eyes, the weld song washing over him instantly, louder and stronger than before, threatening to drown him in its rush and pull.

He fell away from the gate, the fingers that had held the key tingling with quickly cooling heat. 'Whoa.' The power had been too much for him this time, forcing his head under, swamping him completely.

'Are you—' The girl caught herself and turned back to the gate.

She reached for the key and hesitated, obviously having second thoughts about touching it.

Higgs scrambled to his feet and grabbed the key, turning it easily now and pushing the gate open. 'There you go.'

She was already moving again, pushing past him and hurrying down the passage, the glow from her flame sending gleeful shadows writhing across the walls before she closed her fist and all light was extinguished.

Higgs stared into the sudden darkness, listening to her footsteps fade into silence.

'You're welcome.'

He reached down to retrieve the key before moving after her, once again raising one hand to ward off any unseen obstacles in the darkness.

It may have only been a couple of minutes before he heard her again—it was impossible to mark the passage of time in this dark, silent place—another cough and the wet smack of something unpleasant hitting the stone floor reaching back to him from the shadows further ahead.

The tunnel had begun to curve, the wall to his left pushing in at his shoulder, before he realised what was happening and adjusted his path. A bright orange light flared out again, further around the bend ahead.

'Stuck again, are we?' he whispered to himself as he moved into a trot.

The girl was waiting for him, but no gate was halting her progress. Now she was leaning through a large crack in the stone wall, one hand holding the ball of fire, reaching into the space to try to light whatever she had discovered.

His step slowed as he watched her, once again the similarity to the Sister from Redmondis causing a shard of doubt to lance into him. Perhaps it wasn't such a good idea to charge straight up to her. She hadn't exactly been friendly so far.

She seemed to sense his hesitation, leaning back from the wall and peering down the passage toward him. 'Are you still there?' she called out impatiently.

'Yes,' Higgs found himself answering immediately. 'Idiot,' he admonished himself under his breath as he stepped forward.

'What was that?'

'Nothing, I'm … hang on a second.' Higgs walked into the circle of light thrown by the captured flame, blinking quickly to banish the stars in his eyes and trying his hardest not to look intimidated.

It wasn't easy. The girl standing in front of him seemed transformed from the huddled figure he had freed from her cell only minutes earlier. She stood tall, at least a head taller than him, her spine straight and shoulders pushed back, eyes blazing with the same fire she held in her palm.

She looked him up and down, her eyes finally falling upon the stone key he still held in his hand. 'Show me,' she commanded.

Higgs raised his hand immediately, once again his body reacting before his mind gave it permission, the stone key held upright in his palm. The girl bent her head toward it but didn't attempt to touch it.

She looked back up at him, her eyes curious now. 'That's living stone. Weld stone, from the mountain itself.'

Higgs waited, unsure what he was supposed to take from that.

'You shouldn't be able to do that,' she explained. 'It's kind of the reason they formed those cells out of this stone. To contain those such as us.'

She turned to the crack in the wall again, seeming to lose interest in both the key and Higgs at the same time.

'Us?' Higgs prompted, dropping his hand to his side and sliding the key into his cloak. 'You mean crafters?'

The girl ignored him, leaning further through the gap in the rock wall, so that only her lower half was still inside the tunnel with Higgs.

Higgs waited for a few seconds before trying again. 'Uh, Flame?'

She pulled back into the passage and turned to him.

'That's your name? Flame?' Higgs found himself suddenly wilting under her gaze again.

'It is what I wield, so it is me,' she stated matter-of-factly, bringing her hand down between them, the dancing ball of flame shrinking in size and brightness so as not to blind them both entirely. 'All are so named here. I am Flame. You are Stone.'

'I'm Higgs,' he countered, unsure why he felt the need to argue. 'I mean … Where is *here*?'

She stared at his face, seemingly unsure whether she was being tested. '*Here* is Pankesh. The mountain of the Novus. The beating heart of the world. Where all paths meet.'

'Um.. okay.' Higgs nodded, as though all of that made perfect sense. 'So much for where. How about *what*? As in, what are we doing here? Why are they keeping us in cages? And most importantly, how do we get out?'

Flame waved her free hand back toward the crack in the wall. 'The Pit. You have seen this, all who arrive here have. It is further down, inside the mountain.' She took a deep breath. 'I can taste its fire in the air. I have … friends there. They will help us.' A sudden wave of coughing broke over her, and she bent to the floor.

Higgs waited for the spell to pass. 'Are you okay?'

'I only recently returned.' She stood back up, wiping her chin with her sleeve. 'The ice is still in my lungs.'

Higgs remembered his first moments in this place, the freezing water that he coughed up, the feeling of drowning and being wrenched toward the light.

'Come.' Flame turned away, holding the light out in front of her as she started off down the tunnel. 'You may travel with me. We must find the Pit, before they realise we are no longer captive.'

She didn't wait for him, and Higgs hurried to catch up, still muttering to himself. 'They? Who're *they*?'

Higgs was walking in a daze of fog, his mind floating and drifting as a ship unmoored, the currents pulling his thoughts this way and that, yet not allowing any purchase or clarity. His stomach rumbled, and he realised he was probably simply weak from hunger.

How long had it been since he had last eaten?

'Too long,' he answered himself, unable to stop the thought being voiced.

'What was that?'

The girl—Flame—pulled him to a stop. They were still trudging down the long, dim tunnel, seemingly making no progress at all. She had shrunk the ball of fire in her hand to a small point, little more than the flicker of a candle that threw only the weakest of shadows against the rough-hewn walls. Strange shapes blurred and smudged across the stone, forming themselves into faces before sliding away again.

Higgs shook his head, reeling his thoughts back in. 'Sorry. Talking to myself.'

'No, listen.' She grabbed his shoulder with one hand to stop him, and a rush of heat bloomed through his cloak. 'That music.'

'Music?' Higgs closed his eyes and concentrated, demanding his mind obey. She was right, there was something … very faint. Weld song.

Faint, but growing in volume.

'Come, we must hide. I am not strong enough to face them on my own.'

Flame pulled him down the tunnel back the way they had come, toward the fork in the passage they had passed moments before.

'*Them. They.* Who exactly are you talking about?'

'The Incarnate. Our captors.'

Higgs waited for more, but that seemed to be all he was going to get out of her unless he kept prodding. 'The hooded ones, you mean? The ones who took me to the Pit?'

'Yes. Incarnate. Wielders, in your lands. Echoes of the greater song. Ripples in the—' Another bout of coughing interrupted her, and she covered her mouth with her hand to try to smother the noise. 'In the waters beneath. Reflections of their master.'

'The Novus.'

'You've met him too, haven't you?' She spat the product of her cough to the side and pulled him along again. 'The Novus, the first of them. If they are the ripples, he is the stone that fell. Stone, like you. He must have been very interested in you.'

Higgs remembered. The voice inside his mind that seemed to know everything about him, cradling his consciousness like a bauble inside a fist.

He shuddered at the memory, forcing it out and away. 'I've met him.'

'This place, this mountain. This prison. This is his place. We weldfarers are his servants, his tools, his playthings. He will not let us go so easily. Here.'

They had come to the fork in the tunnel, and turned down the path they had ignored earlier, this one not angling down but seeming to rise slightly as they walked. Flame was still gripping his shoulder with one hand and pulled him to a sliding stop after only a few steps.

'No,' she whispered, her voice desperate and seemingly close to tears.

Higgs heard it again, the weld song, emanating out from further down this new tunnel. If anything, it was even louder than before.

'They must have discovered our escape.'

The flame in her fist flared brighter, and Higgs could see her panicked face, eyes wide and scanning back and forth down the tunnel, searching for some way out. Finally, they lit on the rock wall beside them and she gave his shoulder a rough shake.

'Of course! Stone. You are Stone. You must do something!'

'Something?' Higgs replied, dumbfounded.

'Open a gate. Speak to the rock. These tunnels were formed by ones such as you long ago. Try!' She pushed him toward the wall, almost smashing his face into it. 'I cannot go back!'

Higgs squirmed free of her grip and stood facing the wall. It was the same red stone as in his cell, and he had managed to retrieve the key from it there. Maybe she was right.

He closed his eyes and reached out to touch it, mapping its

coarse surface with his fingertips, listening for the song. The life. The blood.

It was no good. The music was there, but muddled, washed over by the notes echoing out to them from further down the tunnel. Getting ever louder.

'I can't.'

'You must! You did it once!'

'That was different. I had the—' He stopped. *The key. You had the key.*

He reached into his cloak and brought out the key, the stone slightly warm again in his palm. 'Perhaps if I—'

Higgs dropped all thought from his mind, emptying it completely and letting the song wash over him and fill the space. He pushed the key against the wall of the tunnel. Against it and into it and through it.

Then he was elsewhere, another place and time, another set of eyes, another mind entirely, standing in front of a shimmering weld wall, watching as the light rippled along its surface. Reaching out to it with a moonsteel blade, a weld blade, flailing as it pulled him into it. Down into the roaring depths.

You see? Like this.

It was Rawick. Rawick and Delco. Two brothers, other minds he had shared inside Wilt. Other powers that remained within the welds. Speaking to him.

He was sitting huddled by the side of a river, a thin blanket around his shoulders, trying to catch the heat from the fire to warm himself. His dripping clothes were staked close to the fire to dry, and he watched sparks rise from the flames and float over them, into the darkness beyond.

Rawick strode suddenly into the light, his skin still dripping with water. He smiled as he reached out and grabbed Delco's hands, pulled them out so the blanket billowed behind him like a great sail. Instantly, Delco could feel more heat become trapped in it, and his shivering began to subside.

You see? Like this.

Now go, little brother.

He almost saw them, twin sparks dancing in the air, spinning up toward the night sky.

Higgs was shocked back into the world as Flame pulled him through the gap that had torn open in the rock wall, stumbling and only just clinging on to the key, the echoes of weld song fading as he wrenched his hand out of the rock and the gap slid closed behind them, leaving them once again in silent darkness.

He bent, panting, with his hands on his knees, mind reeling from the chaos. Her flame bloomed back into life, dazing him further, lighting the edges of this new tunnel.

'There. Listen.'

Higgs was too busy trying to catch his breath and stop the world spinning in place to obey.

'The song has faded. They are gone.'

Flame looked down at him, then back along the tunnel. 'This will do. Come. We must hurry before they discover us once more.'

She turned away and continued down the shaft, following its slope deeper into the mountain, the light fading as she moved further and further away.

Higgs finally managed to stand up straight and watched her go, still panting for breath. 'You're welcome.'

Chapter 20

Frankle held Daemi's gauntleted hand in his as he fell ever faster down the shimmering blue tunnel, lightning flashes blinding him as the storm crackled and roiled around them, reaching for them, pulling at their hair as they plummeted past.

With each flash of energy, the coiling storm inside his chest reacted, answering the call, the weld song that filled his mind trying desperately to fight back against the thunder but being slowly drowned. The grip on his fist was fading, he was falling too fast, faster than the others, the storm calling him irresistibly onward.

Calm, Frankle. Calm the storm. Stay with me.

It was Wilt, the voice inside his mind, but it, too, was losing the battle with the chaos, and he felt something cut free as another flash of lightning shook them, bright blue energy arcing across the tunnel and forking toward him, straight at his chest.

He closed his eyes as it struck and tumbled free. Cold stone grazed his knees as he was thrown clear of the conduit, rolling across the rough ground and coming to a halt upside down against the rock wall of a cave. He kept his eyes closed, breathing deeply, trying to pin down his spinning mind before he opened them, afraid that the churning world would cause him to be sick all over himself.

'Is everybody okay?' Daemi's voice called out from somewhere to his side. 'Heather?'

'I'm here.' He could hear Heather shift and pull herself to her feet on his other side.

'Frankle?'

Give him time.

Wilt's voice was impossibly loud, and he flinched away from the power of it.

The storm, the weld storm. It was called to him.

A warm palm rested on his forehead, and Frankle felt some part of his mind return from its shivering daze.

Give him time.

'Here.' Heather's voice was calm and soothing. 'Turn yourself around, Frankle. You're upside down.'

His legs fell to the side, and the world lurched nauseatingly to the left. He kept his eyes locked closed and tried to breathe slowly.

'Heather?' Daemi asked.

'He's okay, I think.' Heather's voice sounded as though it was coming from the end of a long tunnel, and Frankle realised he was falling into unconsciousness. He sucked in another breath, determined to hold on.

'Wilt's right. Give him a few minutes.'

'If we have them,' Daemi muttered, her boots shuffling away from Frankle. 'What is this place? Are we where Higgs is, where we saw those ... others?'

No. We are closer, but not there. Not yet.

'Look at this cave. The green and red rock, intermingled. It's like the stone in Redmondis mixed with that other place we saw.'

'The conduit. It's breaking up.'

As if in answer to Daemi's words, another bright flash of lightning lit the backs of his eyelids, sending stars streaking across the orange horizon.

Heather's palm brushed cold sweat from his forehead and a deep, feverish shiver ran up his spine. 'Frankle?' she whispered, her lips next to his ear, her breath warm against his skin.

He opened his eyes, and the world reluctantly blurred into focus.

Frankle was lying against the rock wall of a cave, a dim red glow from the stone walls lighting the scene strangely, and he had to blink his eyes clear to force them to make sense of it. Heather was crouched beside him, her hand still on his forehead, her sudden smile bringing him further back into himself.

'There you are.'

He tried to answer, but thought better of it as hot bile filled his mouth. He forced himself to swallow.

The black cat trotted toward him from the shadows to one side, its ink-filled eyes scanning his face as though looking through him into the storm that still twisted inside.

You did well, Frankle.

A sudden quake shook the cave, sending Heather sprawling on top of him. Frankle found himself clutching Heather closely to his chest, not sure if he was trying to protect her or cling on for his own safety.

Dust and small rocks rained down from the low stone ceiling, and Daemi was suddenly standing over them both, her body shielding them from the cascade.

It was over in moments, and the world suddenly seemed impossibly silent.

'Well,' Daemi stood up and brushed herself down, 'I think we need to get moving as quickly as we can.'

A strange low groan echoed out from the surrounding walls, as though two mountains were rubbing against each other, wrestling for control.

'Agreed.' Heather pulled herself free from his arms and stood up. 'Come on, Frankle. It's not safe here.'

Daemi reached down and pulled him to his feet, catching him as he lurched suddenly to the left, the world refusing to keep pace with the movement of his body.

'Steady, Frankle.' Daemi hooked her hand under his arm, holding him up. 'We have to go. Which way?'

This last was aimed at the cat, still standing silently in the centre of the room as though nothing was wrong.

Follow me.

It darted off down the tunnel Frankle only now noticed, its voice speaking to each of them in their minds, calling them onward.

Heather stumbled and had to catch herself on the stone wall of the passage as another quake rumbled through the mountain, throwing her off balance. Further ahead, Daemi marched on, Frankle's weight still taking up one arm, the other pushing against the wall to hold herself upright. She hardly broke stride, her long legs continuing to hurry down the tunnel.

The mountain. They had to be inside of it, the green and red rock that tingled slightly under her fingertips as they brushed over it, groaning and twisting with each shift of movement. At first, she had hoped they were back in Redmondis, back with Petron, but there was nothing like this there. Nothing as foreign and … ancient as this stone. And Wilt had said they were closer to their goal. Closer to Higgs.

The Spine. That's what the maps in the queen's study in Sontair had named it, the great mountain range that stretched across the continent along the edge of the Tangle, blockading its spread any further east. That's where they must be. Inside it, somehow.

Stop! Watch your footing.

Wilt's shouted warning pushed any further thought from her mind and she almost crashed into Daemi's back before she could make her feet obey the order.

Another groan of rock against rock echoed down the tunnel, much louder now, and she reached out to grab Frankle's shoulder and peer past it, just in time to see a large crack yawn open in the stone ground in front of them, shadows spilling out of it as it twisted into something like a great grinning mouth, readying itself to swallow them whole.

Daemi lurched to the side, pulling Frankle and Heather with her as the cat danced ahead, leading them off the now closed path and down a side tunnel, angling down and shaking with the continuing quakes that rocked the mountain.

'What's causing this?' Heather cried out, coughing as more dust rained down on them. 'Is it the conduit?'

No. Something else. Something more.

With Wilt's words came a rush of images, visions projected straight into her mind from other eyes. The Tangle. Great shifting trees lurching as their roots pulled deeper into the soil, opening and closing off possibilities in their impossible reach backward in time. Massive elder trees giving in and falling, knocking out entire swathes of forest as they came crashing down. A rushing, silver river cutting through it all, and something dark beneath its waters, answering an ancient call. Rising closer to the surface.

Come. This way.

She was back in her own mind again, stumbling onward as another, smaller quake rumbled beneath her feet, gasping suddenly for the breath she only now realised she had been holding.

'What ... what was that?'

'Not now.' Daemi's angry answer shut down any further questioning. 'This is not the time. Wilt! This tunnel is shrinking! Are you sure you know where you're going?'

The cat didn't answer. Heather could just make out its shape bouncing back and forth from the encroaching walls on either side of them as it bounded ahead.

The walls were close enough to touch on each side now, squeezing in on them with each shake and movement. Daemi was right; they were moving closer. They were in danger of being crushed.

Daemi pushed Frankle behind her and charged ahead, one hand bent in front of her face, the other still grasping Frankle's hand to pull him along. Heather reached out and pushed Frankle's back, trying to help move him. He was still dazed from whatever the trip through the conduit had done to him.

'Wilt!'

Daemi's voice had the edge of panic to it now, and another crack and shift brought the left wall suddenly in toward them, shoving Heather to the side and grazing her shoulder as it squeezed.

For the first time in her life, Heather suddenly knew the

looming possibility of death. A part of her mind held itself separate from her panic, studying it, watching as the tears formed in her eyes and her chest tightened.

So sudden. So … silly. To no real end at all. Crushed inside a mountain by forces beyond control or reason. Forces that didn't even know what they were taking away.

The rock on either side touched her shoulders now, squashing her. This was it.

For an endless moment, she saw him. Higgs. Standing in front of her, a dim red glow lighting his face, his lips forming her name, calling to her, calling her onward as he reached out to the stone wall and *pushed*.

'Here!'

Sudden grey light lit the back of Frankle's robe as a gap was ripped open in the stone wall beside them, and Heather tumbled into the chill air of the outdoors, falling forward as Frankle was pulled to the side and crashing down on top of him. She gripped tighter as his body seemed to slide beneath her, dust and rock blooming up and blinding her as they somersaulted clear of the tunnel they had been spat out of.

Heather squeezed her eyes shut against the dust and dirt as they slid, the loose rock surface slipping away like water, her body no longer sliding across it but with it as the entire slope around them broke free and started to shear off down the mountain.

The back of her robe tightened as it was gripped by a strong fist, and her momentum slowed, the loose stone beneath her slipping onward as she was wrenched to a stop.

Moments later, she managed to blink her eyes open through the dust, and looked up to see Daemi lying on the ground above her, one hand twisted in Heather's cloak, the other clinging to a sharp stone protrusion that angled out of the rock above her.

'Don't let go,' Daemi grunted.

Heather looked down and realised Frankle was still beneath her, their cloaks wrapped around each other, her fists still gripping him below his arms.

She tried to push against the ground with her leg, but it sank into the loose dirt and sent another small avalanche of rock and dust sliding further down the slope.

'Try to keep still,' Daemi spoke through gritted teeth, the effort of holding both of them obvious.

Another spray of rock kicked up across them as the black cat danced around them, its four light feet seeming to float on the treacherous stone surface. It bounded past and peered further down the slope, its tail twisting slowly back and forth.

There. Two metres to the left. The surface is solid.

It crossed the gap to the spot in a single leap and turned back to them expectantly.

Daemi grunted again, and Heather could feel the tug on her robe as she tried to shift them over.

'No good,' she muttered moments later. Heather and Frankle had barely moved. 'I don't suppose you have any bright ideas?'

Heather assumed this last was addressed to the cat, but it continued to sit silently, staring at them.

Frankle shifted beneath her and sent another cascade of dirt and rock sliding down the hill, and Heather felt them both sink a little deeper into the dirt.

'Frankle, stay still.'

'What … where are we?' Frankle's voice was muffled by the dirt he lay face down in, but Heather could sense his body tense into stillness.

'Stuck.' Heather looked up at Daemi, still straining to hold them in place. 'Daemi? I think I have an idea.'

'Great,' Daemi grunted. 'I'm all ears.'

'You have to let us go.'

'Um.'

'You can't pull us both over. Let us go and we'll roll to the side. Shouldn't get more than a few bruises.'

Daemi took a few moments to consider Heather's words and Heather felt another tug on her back as she once again tested her ability to move them.

Eventually, the grip loosened as Daemi surrendered. 'Okay. On three. I'll try to help you over.'

'Okay.'

Heather ducked her head down to Frankle's back and gripped him tighter. 'On three, Frankle. We have to roll as fast as we can to the left. Keep your eyes closed. This entire slope is going to slip beneath us.'

'Right.'

Frankle's body tensed as he drew his arms in against Heather's hands, locking them in place against his body.

'Ready?' Daemi called.

'As we'll ever be,' Heather muttered, then called back louder. 'Yes. Ready.'

'One.'

Her cloak tightened again as Daemi tried to rock them to the right, then left.

'Two.'

The surface beneath them slipped again as their weight shifted, and Heather took a deep breath.

'Three!'

With a final shove from Daemi, Heather started to fall, and she pulled herself and Frankle to the left, sending them both twisting into a roll as the ground beneath them gave way. Frankle rolled with her, their bodies pressing against each other within the roil of dirt and rock that washed over them. They rolled over three times in total before her shoulder dug into solid ground, sending a sharp pulse of pain stinging up her arm, numbing it completely.

She felt Frankle roll free, and let go of her grip with her one good hand, keeping her eyes closed against the dust that filled the air.

Suddenly, her legs dropped away beneath her and she started to slide again. She tried desperately to cling to the stone ground that still held her upper body, but it was no good; she couldn't stop the slide of her weight pulling herself out and over.

Her hand scratched against the sharp edge of rock, then fell into open air as she went over the edge.

Her momentum slammed to a stop as a strong hand slapped into hers, gripping it tight, refusing to let her fall. Heather looked up, blinking against the cloud of dust that surrounded her, to see Daemi standing above her, holding her hand in hers.

'I've got you.'

Daemi smiled, for the first time in Heather wasn't sure how long, and pulled her back up to the safety of the rock.

Daemi hoisted Heather up with ease and set her on her feet, holding both hands on her shoulder for a moment as if to plant her firmly into the ground. 'You okay?'

Heather nodded, her faced still drained of blood from the shock.

Daemi patted her once on the shoulder and turned back to the others. Frankle was still lying face down on the large flat rock they were perched upon, but she could see his chest moving up and down with each deep breath.

Look where we are.

Wilt's voice in her mind brought her eyes up to scan the surrounding scene. They were still quite high up the mountain they had only recently been inside, the steep, treacherous slope they had scurried out from falling away beneath them, a loose cascade of rock and dust still slowly moving below them, like a great tide of earth washing out from the shore.

Above them there was no sign of the tunnel they had broken from, though it was impossible to tell how far they had slipped before Daemi had managed to stop their slide. The platform they had landed on was the edge of a seemingly solid stone path that curved around the mountain, angling down its slope slightly, broken here and there by channels of loose rock and dirt that cut through it. It seemed an obvious path down the mountain.

The black cat was perched on a small rock above Frankle's head.

'You recognise this place?' she asked.

Almost. There's something…

The cat jumped off the rock and trotted further down the path, obviously expecting them to follow.

Daemi sighed and reached down to pull Frankle to his feet. 'Come on, Frankle. Rest time is over.'

Heather slipped past her and wrapped an arm around Frankle to help him walk. They both moved on ahead of her without further protest. Daemi watched them move as she brushed dirt and dust from her armour. Within a few steps, they had fallen into a comfortable enough rhythm.

They're getting stronger. Growing up.

Come.

The word was wrapped in a cascade of vision that flooded her mind, and she grasped the hilt of her weld blade to try to still the rush of it. As soon as her fingers touched the hilt, the chaos slowed into a recognisable series of images. A stone pathway. A break in the mists below them revealing a great green sea, moving strangely in the wind. Just like—

The Tangle.

'Yes, but there's something … It's too uniform. Almost like water. An ocean?'

No. Something more.

Daemi shook her head clear and hurried onward, trotting ahead of Heather and Frankle to ensure they didn't stumble into any further trouble on the path.

The breaks in the rock she had noticed turned out to be only a minor inconvenience, the longest gap less than five feet wide, narrow enough for her to leap and help the others across. Within the hour, they had moved more than halfway down the slope, the trail twisting around itself as it fell toward the base of the mountain.

'Weld song,' Frankle muttered, lifting his nose suddenly as if smelling something on the wind.

'What's that?' Daemi asked. She was a few metres ahead of them.

'Listen. Don't you hear it?' Frankle's eyes were closed, his head angled up to the sky as he listened.

'There's … something.' Heather nodded, though she looked unsure of what exactly it was she heard. She reached into her cloak and grasped the necklace around her throat, but didn't say anything more.

Daemi looked to where the black cat sat perched above them on a rock, and a sudden wave of memory washed over her.

She slung her pack over her shoulder and caught Frankle's hand as he slid down the steep, rocky incline. He was still dazed, his eyes glazed and shadowed, his legs weak. The skies above were already darkening …

Daemi stumbled as the vision took her, the world warping around her as the memory shifted and scratched across her mind. This was a memory, a vision, seen through other eyes. Heather's eyes.

Ahead of them, Daemi waited at the base of the slope, watching them stumble their way toward her with barely disguised impatience. They were only halfway down the mountain, and she didn't want—

Again, the memory seemed to slip free of its hold, losing traction on her mind, then washing back over her again.

Above Daemi's head, perched on a tall boulder, sat a large black cat, its silver claws digging into the stone, its eyes turned to the east, toward their destination.

Daemi fell to her knees as the weld song broke over her, the vision replaced by a blinding golden light that danced just out of reach. Then a searing pain as scars that no longer existed tore open across her back.

Daemi! Come back to me.

A deep chill of cold froze the air around her as the wraith reached for her.

'Daemi!'

She opened her eyes to see the rock path beneath her knee, her breath panting in and out of her lungs.

'Daemi!' Heather continued. 'Are you okay?'

Heather's hand gripped her shoulder, and she pulled herself to her feet.

She was back in the present, the wash of memory gone. 'What—what was that?' Daemi asked, turning her words to the black cat that still sat perched above her head.

Welds. Visions. Memory bleeding into memory. It is how I escaped from the place below.

'The weld. The golden weld,' Frankle spoke up. 'I've seen that before, but never so close, so bright.'

We should move on. This place is a junction of sorts, a meeting of conflicting pathways. It is not safe for us.

'The music,' Heather said. 'I think I heard it for a moment. It sounded like the heartstone song.'

'Heartstone?' Frankle asked.

'The music back in Sontair.' Heather flushed. 'Like in the queen's study, with the conduit.'

'That's right.' Frankle nodded, all tiredness seeming to have dropped away now in his eagerness to understand this strange new phenomenon. 'It was so clear. Then it stopped, suddenly. Like a door had slammed closed.'

Come. It is not safe.

The cat moved on down the path, obviously not wanting to continue the conversation.

Daemi watched it go, a chill breath tickling up her spine at the memory of the touch of ice that had reached into her. 'Come on, you two. Not long to go.'

She rolled her shoulders as she walked, as though trying to arrange some heavy weight better across her back. Her scars were healed; there was no trauma. But the pain had been so real, so present. Not like a memory at all.

Then they saw it, as they rounded another corner of jutting rock. The mists that had been below them now parted, blown away as from a great breath to reveal a wide, endless sea of green stretching out from the base of the mountain only a few hundred feet below.

'The Eternal Sea,' Heather whispered, awed by the sight of it.

'A sea? Here?' Frankle asked.

'Honestly, what did you spend all that time in the queen's study doing? Didn't you see the maps?'

'I saw lots of maps, but they were all so old. They didn't make much sense. For one thing, the Tangle was marked on most of them as spanning the entire world. I guess I assumed no one had ever reached the end of it.'

'Those were old maps, from when the Tangle did stretch across the land. But something happened, long ago now. I couldn't find any accurate, clear information as to what it was, exactly. Just something big.'

They each stood perfectly still, hypnotised by the strange rippling movement that sighed over the green blanket below.

'So … there was a flood?' Frankle finally broke the silence.

'No, not a flood.' Heather smiled. 'Look closer.'

'It's not water,' Daemi answered, once again the chill running down her spine as she realised what they were looking at. Miles and miles and miles of it, stretching unbroken to the horizon. A barrier as effective as an ocean would have been. More so. Now what were they going to do?

'What do you mean it's not water?' Frankle protested as Daemi started to march away.

Finally, she called back over her shoulder, her voice echoing strangely against the stone of the mountain. 'It's not water. It's grass.'

Chapter 21

Petron's first step through the conduit landed him on solid stone ground, and he almost tripped over himself as his boot hit, his body expecting the sensation of falling like the last time he had travelled this way. But there was no free-fall, no ice surface to skid across, searching for the next conduit to enter, just a dimly lit stone hallway, no wider than a metre or so, stretching straight out in front of him.

Perhaps this was a result of him using the conduit correctly this time, activating it and giving it a clear destination instead of simply stepping through and relying on Frankle to guide them. Whatever the reason, Petron was sure he preferred this mode of travel. A plain, simple corridor. Solid stone under his feet. Much more sensible.

He started to walk, then stopped immediately as something disturbed him, some movement in the air that felt unnatural. Then he realised it was the sound. He looked down and scuffed his boot across the dusty floor. There was just the slightest dull scrape of sound, as though he were listening while underwater, the noise of the world filtered and dulled. He jiggled his ears to unblock them, but there was no change. Sound simply didn't seem to work properly here.

That wasn't all. As he looked further down the corridor, he could make out footprints in the thick dust, a single set that stretched on ahead of him. Someone else had passed this way before. Long before, to judge by the layers of dust.

Well, this was all very interesting, but it wasn't getting him anywhere. He stepped forward, his boot fitting perfectly into the footprint in front of him, then continued on, studying the cut stone walls on either side of him as he walked. They glowed faintly green, and he was reminded of the stone walls beneath Redmondis, where the Nine Sisters had made their home.

After only a few moments of walking, he could make out another conduit at the end of the corridor, its centre a grey boiling mist of cloud. That had to be the conduit in Redmondis, his destination. Waiting for him. It was almost too easy.

As soon as the thought occurred to him, a deep crack echoed through the tunnel, and the floor seemed to drop two feet, plumes of dust blasting into the air as the stone beneath dropped away.

Petron stumbled to his knees, one hand resting on the wall of the tunnel, the green glow of the rock seeming to grow brighter as he stared at it, until it became so bright that he had to look away and cover his eyes entirely. The light became blinding white, and a low roar started to build somewhere beneath the rock floor.

He lurched to his feet and crashed against the other side of the corridor as the floor shook again, peering through his fingers at the conduit ahead of him, still open, seeming to twist in the air. He felt himself pressed against the rock wall and realised the entire corridor was tilting, angling to the side and down toward the conduit, and his feet started to slip against the ground.

Another crack, louder than the last, shaking the world itself, like a bolt of lightning had struck beside him, and the blinding white light blurred into blue.

Petron's fingers slipped across the rock wall, and it seemed to lean away from him, pulling clear and sending him into a fall, the floor tilting further until he could do nothing but try to roll into a ball as he was sent crashing toward the conduit at the end of the corridor.

The wall slammed back into him as another quake struck, and it was all he could do to cover his head as he rolled helplessly along it. The blue light was all around him now, a shimmering tunnel that he was falling through, and his final vivid thought was that it was like a weld, just like the weld he had seen with Wilt, when they had first stood up against the Sisters. Then his head cracked against the rough stone ceiling and he knew no more.

Wind. Wind pulling through the tips of your wings, urging back the feathers that edge them, whispering gently as you bank into the turn and gain speed, the air buffeting your body now, bouncing you up then dropping out from under you as the turbulence at the top edge of the ridge you are riding washes around you.

You scan the land beneath you, the rocky outcrop dropping away to a thick forest that calls you onward, the treetops waving up at you, reaching hopelessly for you as you skim over them, skating the cloud of warmer air that blankets them.

You raise your eyes to the sky and see another shape, another bird, flying high above you, its shadow growing ever larger as it dives toward you. You pull upward in reply, trying to gain altitude, but it has the drop on you, angling in from above, its speed much greater than yours.

A twist of recognition then as it comes fully into sight, its size and shape unmistakable. You know this one.

Stax. The name floats across your mind and away, leaving only a ripple on the surface.

It banks now, headed north, and you know to follow it, beating your wings hard to try to keep pace, the wind roaring as it rushes past. You level off, finding a chute of clear air to coast within, the deep blue sky filling your vision.

—Petron.—

The voice carries with it a thought that you instantly shy away from, your body physically reacting as though struck, dropping into a spiralling dive that costs you half your altitude before you can recover and pull yourself back into the slipstream.

No. That way is … other. A foreign world of pain and regret. Much better to stay here, in the sky, without thought or consequence.

—Petron. Come back. Come back to your mind.—

You control yourself better this time and only flinch at the flare the words cause. The blue of the sky darkens, and a flash of angry lightning sparks on the horizon, warning of the storm to come. You must hurry. You must find shelter soon.

—Petron. This is not the way. Return. Remember who you are.—

You lose altitude again, your wings heavy now, your bones full of weight. You struggle to hold yourself level as the wind picks up again and you plummet toward the waiting forest.

They reach for you, waiting for you. Watching you fall.

—Petron. You cannot stay here. I'm sorry.—

A flash of lightning cracks across the sky, stunning you into a stall, your wings wrapped close around your body as you plummet, your eyes blinded by stars that flicker and dance across your vision. They coil around you, leading your mind away, sparks dancing in the breeze, and you feel yourself lose contact with the body that drops into the trees below.

—Come now, back into yourself. Away from dreams. Away from the chaos of the welds and the wash of the depths. You do not belong in this world. Not yet. It is time to return. They need you.—

Biore. Another name that pops into place.

—We are here, Petron. When you call us, we will answer. Now go.—

Petron coughed into consciousness on the rough stone floor, his fingers clawing at the rock as though trying to gain purchase, but the ground stayed steady and firm and unmoving, right where it was supposed to be, and the world finally stopped spinning as he sucked in breath after breath.

Just as the ground settled into one place underneath his chest, it dropped away again as he was lifted bodily into the air, two soldiers reaching under his arms and dragging him out of the dust-filled room, the toes of his boots leaving twin trails in the dirt as he was pulled free.

He tried to blink his eyes clear, but all he could make out as they moved was dirt and a strangely familiar blue glow; the light flashing brighter as a crack of rock echoed around them and the air seemed to tingle with energy.

The guards carrying him moved out of the chamber and passed his body on to another pair of soldiers, then turned back toward the room.

'No!' Petron coughed as he tried to speak, then managed to make his meaning clear. 'Get everyone out of there! There's nothing you can do.'

The soldiers holding him didn't stop to acknowledge his order, and he was half carried, half led up and out of the tunnels as he coughed his lungs clear of the dirt and dust. Another crack chased them out of the tunnel, and he could hear heavy boots trot along behind them where the other soldiers had hopefully decided to listen to him and follow them out.

Halfway up the passage, he managed to catch his feet under him and tried to shrug the soldier's hands free from where they gripped him under his arms, but they were insistent and forced him onward, away from the growing cacophony behind them.

'How—' Petron started to ask, but his voice was drowned out by another ground-shaking quake and a loud explosion of noise from the chamber behind and beneath them now, the path under their feet dropping away and almost sending the entire party sprawling.

The noise added even more urgency to the soldiers leading him out, and when they finally did reach the heavy stone door to the catacombs they were fleeing from, Petron was practically thrown clear of the doorway, only managing to keep his feet because he was caught by yet another pair of waiting arms.

He looked back at the tunnel as four soldiers came flying out of it, their faces streaked with dirt and the tracks of tears, arms held across their faces to shield their eyes from the blinding blue light. Another boom sent a thick cloud of dust spewing out behind them, and the ground shook again as the entire facade of the entrance collapsed in on itself.

Hands began patting the dirt from his shoulders and he finally managed to shake himself free of their attentions and stand on his own two feet as the blue light faded and the dust slowly settled around the mound of broken rock and dirt that moments before had been the entrance to the catacombs beneath Redmondis. The tunnels of stone and shadow that the nine Sisters had all too recently called home.

'Sir, are you injured at all?'

Petron pulled his eyes away from the wreckage to peer at the young soldier standing in front of him. A sergeant, to judge by his markings, but not one he recognised.

'I'm all right. Did everyone get out?'

'Yes, sir. There was only our patrol. There wasn't time to—'

'And how did your patrol manage to find me down there in the first place? Not that I'm not grateful.' Petron smiled.

'We were sent word, sir. A messenger.'

'A messenger? From Sontair?'

'From the forest, sir. From the Tangle. A bird.'

'A bird?'

For an instant, he saw it again, the vision from inside the conduit, his body soaring over the tips of the trees, chasing the figure in front of him. Stax.

Petron brushed himself down and coughed again, reaching for the waterskin one of the soldiers was passing around. He rinsed his mouth clear of dirt and took three long swallows.

'Ah. That's better.' He wiped his chin and handed the skin back. 'Now then, Sergeant. Perhaps you could show me this messenger.'

'Of course, sir. At once. He's—I mean it's waiting for you. In your tower.'

'Lead on, Sergeant. And send word to your superiors. I want the heads of each of the schools in my chamber within the hour. We have a lot of planning to do.'

Petron needn't have bothered with the order. By the time he had made his way up the spiralling stone staircase of the tower to his chamber on the top floor, each of the masters he had asked to be summoned were already waiting for him, a group of four men and two women huddled on one side of the room, heads bowed in conspiratorial whispers.

In front of them, the outside-facing wall yawned open where Petron had had it removed to allow the wind and air in, and give direct access to some of his more interesting acquaintances, one of which was perched on the edge of the opening, peering back at the humans, who looked as though they were trying to put as much space between it and them as possible.

'Stax.' Petron smiled as he opened the chamber door and saw his friend. 'You know, I was just thinking about you.'

'Sir!' The master sergeant stepped in front of the others and snapped into a salute. 'You have returned.'

'Yes, yes, I have returned.' Petron waved the salute away wearily. 'I wasn't gone that long, was I?'

'Sir? No, sir. It's—'

'You have a visitor, Petron.' The aged head of the crafter school spoke up, waving her walking stick at the great eagle across the room.

'Stax. You've seen him here before, surely, Justinia.'

Petron finally noticed the hesitation and nervousness in the group and tilted his head questioningly at them.

'Yes, Petron. But he's brought someone else along this time.'

Petron turned toward Stax, who took that as his cue to raise one wing and reveal the other visitor standing behind him. It was a boy, younger than most of the students in Redmondis, his face and clothing streaked with mud and dirt.

'Hello?'

Petron stepped toward him, then froze as the boy raised his eyes. They were black. Pure black. Not a glint of light or life within them.

Petron.

The name echoed inside his mind, a chorus of voices bouncing around his head, resisting any attempt to arrange them into separate individuals.

'It … I mean … He's not—' Justinia stumbled to explain herself.

'Are you sure it's safe?' the master sergeant interrupted, his eyes snapping back and forth between the strange forest creature and Petron.

Safe?

The boy turned to face the soldier who had spoken. For a brief moment, his face seemed to shift, and Petron glimpsed something dark and terrifying scuttle across his visage, a horned, malevolent sneer that sent a cold chill of terror down Petron's spine.

Then, just as quickly, it was gone, and once again the strange young boy stared at him.

Never safe. But I bring no danger to you.

Petron waved the sergeant back to the others and stepped in front of them. He recognised that face. He had seen it before.

'The Guardian. You're the Guardian of the Tangle.'

The boy smiled, a strangely unnerving expression given the twin pools of shadow that were his eyes.

I am one form of it.

'Why … What are you doing here?'

In answer to his question, the boy tilted his head and a series of images forced their way into Petron's mind. He saw himself in Sontair, standing in front of the conduit, stepping through, then the strange blue-lit tunnel he had found himself falling through, the choking dust and debris of the collapsing tunnel here in Redmondis that the guards had pulled him from.

Your way is closed.

Another set of images washed across Petron's mind, this time of Sontair itself, after he had stepped through the conduit. He saw the queen's study, Captain Mont stepping up to the conduit and bringing the hilt of his sword cracking into its stone border, Lodan entering the room and trying to stop him, the strange expression on Captain Mont's face as he turned to face him.

They have tried to take control. They fear you.

He saw Daemi standing on top of the castle wall, her weld blade glowing blue in her hand as a massive gloomclaw stalked toward her.

Do not worry. They have failed. For now.

A shift and he watched as Daemi, Heather, and Frankle were led through the conduit by Wilt.

Your friends walk their own path now. You cannot help them.

A final vision, much harder to make out, as though trying to peer through a thick fog. A cliff face, a narrow path, and a great green sea stretched out in front of them.

The image faded, unable to be held in place.

They have passed out of even my sight.

'But they're safe?' Petron waited for another set of images to answer him, but none came. Instead, the face of the boy shifted again, and for an instant he saw Biore staring out at him, a knowing grin twisting his lips.

Safe? You know better than that, Petron. But you have other tasks.

'Sontair,' Petron answered. They had to get soldiers and wielders to Sontair.

Those who seek to topple the city have failed, but they will return. You must send aid.

'But how? Now that the conduit is gone, how are we to move a force of any size that far south? The Tangle would take weeks to cross, if we even could.'

Biore's face was gone, and the boy was back, grinning at him.

That is why I am here.

The boy turned away, facing the opening in the wall, his hands held out on either side of his body and fingers twitching in the breeze. For a moment, he stood silently, the wind tugging at his hair, and from behind he looked all too human. Then he glanced over his shoulder and gestured for Petron to join him.

Come. See what no human has witnessed in generations.

Petron stepped up to the edge beside the boy as he raised his hands out in front of him and held them together. He felt a surge then, not unlike the shift of a weld, but different. Deeper. As though the world itself were sucking in a breath, ready to shout.

A low rumble echoed to them from the Tangle far below, and a change in the movement of the trees caught Petron's eye. The noise grew in volume, filling the room now, and Petron had to resist the temptation to cover his ears. There was something ...

Petron stood frozen in awe as the great sea of trees below them parted, a narrow straight path of dirt tearing through the centre of the Tangle, widening with each moment, continuing over the horizon past the limits of his vision. He blinked and fought back the wash of vertigo that threatened to overwhelm him at the sight and found his hand gripping the shoulder of the small boy beside him to keep his balance.

Finally, the wave of sound seemed to crest and fade, and the boy dropped his hands to his sides and looked up at Petron, who was still frozen in place, staring down at the impossible. A wide, straight path now lay out in front of him, wide enough for an entire company to march through, cutting the Tangle in two.

One path closes. Another opens.

Petron heard a shift behind him, and the master sergeant choked out a cry of incredulity. It snapped Petron out of his daze, and he dropped his hand from the boy beside him guiltily. 'It's—'

Old ways. Silent ways.

Biore's familiar voice answered him, then faded into the chorus.

This path leads to Sontair. Your men will be safe, but do not dawdle.

The boy grinned again, then turned away and pulled himself onto the back of the great eagle.

Even I cannot hold the trees for long.

With that, Stax launched into the air, its great wings buffeting Petron back from the edge as they launched it and its passenger into the sky, leaving Petron and his guests to stare wonderingly at the changed landscape beneath them.

Chapter 22

Lodan lay very still, his eyes closed, the red throb of his pulse beating against the backs of his eyelids, sending slithering worms of dust scurrying out of focus and away. With each beat, the pain grew, his mind pulling up out of the thick, warm mud of unconsciousness that held him safe, but there was nothing he could do to resist it. The pain would grow, and he would wake, and the world would be waiting for him.

He opened his eyes to find the thump that shook the world was just Griggs, standing over him, patting haltingly at his forehead with a pink-tinged cloth. He winced and closed his eyes against the bright light that blinded him, but it was too late to go back to where he had been. That way was shut.

'So, you're not dead yet then,' Griggs muttered as he worked, trying to clear the dried blood from Lodan's face, but only managing to smear it around more.

Lodan tried to open his mouth to speak, but something was wrong with his face and nothing below his eyes seemed to want to follow orders.

'Don't try to talk. Probably just swallow more teeth.' Griggs gave Lodan's face a final wipe and sat back on his haunches to view the damage. 'Well, he certainly did a number on you. Not sure you're going to find it quite as easy to get a date to the ball this year.'

Lodan grunted and tried to move his head, but that too seemed locked in place.

'The city is safe,' Griggs continued, knowing that Lodan would want a report before anything else. 'There were only a handful of those creatures, and Daemi took care of them. The wolf howls were trying to sow panic—and it worked—but the soldiers here are better trained than the guards we remember from Greystone. There were five or six traitors who managed to cause a bit of damage themselves, ten dead all up, but it's under control now. It was all a distraction.'

Finally, Lodan wrenched his shoulder to the side and twisted around, almost falling face first to the ground before Griggs caught him.

'Whoa there!' Griggs pushed his shoulders back against the wall and helped turn his chin in the right direction. 'And there's the reason. Dead.'

They both stared across at the broken body of Captain Mont, discarded on the floor.

Lodan squinted at his face, trying to match his memory of the man he knew to the bloody mess in front of him. Then a flash of vision gripped him, an evil grin topped by glowing golden eyes, as the captain smashed his forehead down into his face. Lodan looked away with a shudder.

That hadn't been Mont. That had been someone else. Something else.

'He broke the doorway there, the magic gate or whatever it is,' Griggs continued, pointing vaguely at the far wall of the queen's study, where what remained of the conduit still stood. Half of its border was cracked and broken, the rubble scattered across the floor. 'But you stopped him in time.'

Lodan grunted, forcing the air out of his lungs and spilling over his split lips. It was a question, and Griggs knew right away what its meaning was.

'They went through, the others. Daemi and Heather and Frankle. Went to wherever that doorway used to lead.'

Lodan continued to stare at it, a strange longing pulling at him as he traced the frame of the doorway. Then he closed his eyes and pulled his face back to Griggs.

'Up,' he managed to croak.

Griggs shook his head, but stepped up and grasped Lodan's shoulders. 'You're sure?' he asked, not liking the way Lodan's eyes seemed to slide to the side instead of holding in one place.

'Up!' Lodan grunted again, spitting blood at the effort.

Griggs leaned back and pulled, and Lodan felt himself lift into the air and keep going, his mind launching up and out and leaving his body behind to collapse against Griggs in unconsciousness.

Days later, Lodan still felt some part of his mind was floating above him, looking down and watching him shuffle into what had been Captain Mont's office, his body leaning into the cane he now used on his left as he struggled around the large desk to collapse into the chair behind it with an exhausted grunt. A simple trip between rooms left him gasping now, and he practically threw the cane onto the floor beside him in frustration.

He leaned both hands forward onto the desk and tried to catch his breath, his eyes stealing across the papers and reports still scattered across its surface. He wasn't sure what he was looking for, but there had to be something. Some clue, some key to unlocking the mystery of what had happened to the man who once commanded the entire city.

After a few moments, Lodan sat back again with a sigh, one hand rubbing his eyes and trying not to aggravate the yellowing bruises that still covered more than half his face. His fingers prodded at them gingerly, testing their shrinking edges of pain. They were healing. He was healing. But he would never be the same.

He kicked his legs out at the cane on the floor, sending it clattering against the far wall, then immediately regretted it. Now he was stuck here in this chair. He wouldn't be able to get to his feet, let alone shuffle over to where it now lay.

Lodan blew out his growing rage at the world and his predicament and tried to rein his mind back in. There was no time for self-pity. There was work to be done. People relied upon him.

He sat up straighter and pulled the chair closer to the desk, determined to get started. The papers immediately in front of him were all days old, their reports no longer worth bothering with, so he sent them to the floor in one sweep of his arm and reached for the more organised looking pile of pages stacked just beyond his right hand, the papers held in place by a stone paperweight in the shape of a cat's paw. As soon as his fingers brushed the surface of the stone, his mind sparked with a rush of memory, and he was elsewhere.

He calmly rolled the ball between the posts marking the guard's goal, then felt the guard defender tackle him to the ground, too late to stop it. He twisted to the side as he landed, kicking his feet free from the guard's arms, and watched as Wilt leapt into the air, his hand grasping the flag at the top of his arc.

They'd done it. They'd won.

'Blade!' someone yelled out in a high voice.

Higgs. That was Higgs's voice.

Lodan pushed himself to his feet as the guard Wilt had tricked his way past stumbled out from the crowd back onto the field of play, a shining dagger in his hand, his eyes wild.

He watched helplessly as Wilt spun to face the man, then the guard stumbled as Higgs's small body crashed onto his shoulders from behind, one hand wielding a rock and battering the guard's head with it. The guard bent over double to dislodge him, and Higgs rolled off, landing in the dirt at Wilt's feet.

Lodan broke into a run, not sure what he hoped to do, but determined to intervene in whatever treachery was about to occur. But he saw Higgs toss the small stone to Wilt, saw Wilt twist the flag in his hand into a makeshift sling, and saw the rock fly straight and true directly into the charging guard's face, dropping him instantly.

'What mischief is this?' Lodan's clear voice cut across the confused babble of the crowd as members of both guard and guild teams raced forward to hold the struggling guard down.

'Dawson! What are you doing, man?' It was the guard captain now, shocked at the actions of one of his players.

Lodan watched as the guard lifted his head, blood covering his face now, and stared directly at him.

'The blood within the stone!' His voice was deep and rasping, only half human. And behind it, riding underneath its cry, was the howl of a wolf.

'Lodan!'

Lodan snapped back into the present with a start and dropped the paperweight he had been holding onto his lap, where it bounced off his leg and rolled somewhere underneath the desk. He blinked furiously, trying to clear the strange vision from his mind.

'Lodan?' Griggs's voice held more than a note of worry now. 'Are you sure you're up to this?'

Lodan shook the last shreds of vision away and stared at Griggs, who was standing on the other side of the desk, his face a mask of concern. 'Yes.' Lodan coughed. 'Yes, yes, I'm okay. Just … daydreaming.'

'Daydreaming,' Griggs repeated, the excuse sounding even more limp on his tongue. 'Well, have you found anything useful in this mess?'

'No, nothing yet.' Lodan sighed again as he surveyed the room. It all seemed so hopeless. 'Here, pass me my cane, will you?'

Griggs stepped across to the wall where the cane had ended up and returned it to Lodan's hands, watching silently as Lodan struggled out of the chair and to his feet. He looked so weak still, so damaged. It was far too soon for him to be up and about. 'Take it slowly, Lodan. We can't afford to lose you too.'

Lodan scowled at him, but nodded his head as he shuffled back around the desk. 'I know, I know. But there is so much we need to do. We're nowhere near secure enough. The attack taught us that much, at least.'

'Well,' Griggs smiled, 'I do have some good news on that front. A messenger arrived this morning from the north.'

'The north?' Lodan stopped and gazed at Griggs. 'You mean—'

'Redmondis,' Griggs confirmed. 'Petron wrote it himself. So at least we know he's safe.'

'Good. Good man.'

'And he's sending aid. Lots of aid, if the message is to be believed. An army of soldiers and wielders are already on their way to us, he says. Though how exactly they hope to get through the Tangle is anyone's guess.'

'Don't worry about Petron,' Lodan said, smiling. 'He's got more than a few tricks up his sleeve.'

'There was something else too—he said you'd know what he meant. That the others are on their own path now.'

Lodan paused and clapped Griggs on his shoulder, almost losing his balance as he did so. 'That is good news. Thank you, Griggs.'

Griggs watched as Lodan gathered himself and stepped toward the door. He looked stronger, suddenly, as though a weight had been lifted from his shoulders.

'Get this room cleaned up, will you? Everything in it is to be destroyed. Strip it completely. I'll be in my chamber, making a start.' Lodan turned and smiled, and for the first time since the attack, Griggs saw the smile reach the man's eyes. 'Best start with a clean slate. We have a lot of work to do.'

Chapter 23

The air inside the tunnel had been growing steadily warmer as they trudged along, their path always angling down as they travelled deeper into the mountain fortress. Pankesh, she had called it. The heart of the world. Higgs could believe it. In his peripheral vision, the walls themselves seemed to pulse with life as they walked on, travelling down this wide vein in the rock.

He wiped the sweat from his eyebrows, flicking drops of salt water away and rubbing his wet fingers together, the thought once again striking him that he was alive. He was human. He was back in the world, somehow.

They'd had no more encounters with their pursuers, no more snatches of weld song drifting up the tunnel like a breath to warn them of the coming Incarnate. They seemed to have lost them, left them far behind in the twisting network of tunnels. Still they walked on, the temperature getting more and more uncomfortable.

'How much further?' Higgs spoke up finally, squirming in his cloak. It felt hot and heavy now, but he dared not discard it.

'I think …' Flame slowed and raised her head, as if listening, though Higgs could hear nothing. 'Not much further. We should see the river soon.'

'The river?' Higgs asked, but Flame had already resumed her pace. 'What sort of river runs through this place?'

He trotted to catch up to Flame as she turned another corner, and a bright reddish glow lit her features. Once again, he was struck by her similarity to the Sister from Redmondis.

'There,' Flame whispered, waving Higgs closer. 'The river.'

Higgs peered around the corner and stopped as a fresh blast of heat hit him. They were standing on a ledge about twenty feet above what looked like a long, wide road beneath them. Then the road shifted and cracked, one long section of it breaking away to slide faster than the rest, a deep orange glow of light and heat opening between the plates. It was a river of thick, hot mud, the surface cooling and hardening and then being wrenched apart once more by the faster flowing liquid underneath.

'They say it starts as a normal river, in the lands to the west, far from here. It mixes with the silt and rock of these lands, of this mountain, and forms this … sludge.'

As Higgs stared at the strangely shifting surface, his eye was caught by movement on the far bank of the river. People. There were people there, moving about in the shimmering air.

'How …?'

'More servants of the Incarnate. Mules. Tasked with dredging up the hot mud and taking it to the Pit. Little more than animals, though they look human enough from this distance. They are protected from the worst of the heat. Their skin toughened, their minds dulled. Do not concern yourself with them.'

Higgs watched, fascinated, as what seemed like a hunched old man reached the bank of the river and leaned out to fill a bucket and heave it dripping up and over his shoulder, his legs buckling under the weight of the load. The shimmer and steam of the air made it hard to be sure, but the man's face did look lined and cracked like old leather.

The man stumbled into some hidden passage in the rock on the far side of the river and disappeared.

'It is good that we found this group. We can follow them back to the Pit. Back to the others.'

'The others?' Higgs looked at Flame as a horrible thought forced its way into his mind. 'These friends of yours, they're not … sisters by any chance?'

'What? No.' Flame shook her head, confused by the question. 'I have no sisters. No brothers. It would not be possible.' She moved on, examining the ledge they were standing on to find some pathway down.

'Well, now I just have more questions.'

'There is a path, a simple enough climb,' she called back, oblivious to his words. 'But we cannot get too close to the surface. Not without protection.'

She stared down at the river, pondering her options. 'I can help with that, but we will need to find a way to cross. Stone.' She looked at him and smiled. 'You are Stone. You will make a pathway for us.'

'I will?'

'Yes.' Flame nodded and started to lower herself over the edge, the issue decided.

Higgs hurried over, but she was already gone, her head and hands dropping out of sight as she scaled down the rock face. 'Are you sure about this?'

There was no answer, and all he could do was follow.

The climb down was easier than it looked. The rock wall was jutted all over with small ledges of stone to use as hand and footholds, and it only took a few moments for Higgs to join Flame on the bank of the river, both of them having to shy their faces away from the fresh heat baking them, radiating from the slowly moving mud.

'Here, take my hand.' Flame reached out and grabbed Higgs's hand, not waiting for him to respond.

She muttered something under her breath, and Higgs heard the briefest whisper of weld song echo to him, his skin prickling at the sound. Instantly, all heat seemed to leave the chamber, and he stood straight, shocked at the sudden change in the air.

'The heat, it's—' The words died in his throat as he stared down at his arm. All around him, seeming to float just above his skin, a flickering layer of bright blue flame danced, not touching him, not burning him in any way. If anything, he felt cool, almost cold.

'What—' He stuttered to a stop once again as he saw the same blue flame covering Flame's body as well, the incandescence lighting her eyes as she grinned at his dumbstruck face.

'Do not fear the flames, they will not hurt you. Think of them as a shield from the heat of the river, feeding on it, burning it away before it reaches your skin.'

'How?'

'I am Flame. You are Stone. Now it is your turn.'

She pushed him toward the edge of the river. He stumbled and just caught his footing before he fell face first into the flowing mud.

'She wants a pathway,' he muttered under his breath. 'Stone. You are Stone. Whatever that means.'

He reached the bank and crouched, the mud only a couple of feet from his face. Still, he felt no heat from it. 'Whatever she did, it's working.'

Higgs stared at the slowly twisting surface of the river, holding the weight of it inside his mind, its movement hypnotising him. Lulling him down into the depths.

'I've seen this river before.'

As soon as he said the words, he knew the truth of them. The Boroni. This was the Boroni. Much further downstream than the last time he had seen it. 'Wilt saw it. You were just with him.'

He remembered it clearly. Its silver surface swirling and twisting in the sunlight. Then Wilt sending out a weld and dropping into it.

A rushing tide, a swirling chaos. A deep coldness, an ache, reaching for warmth, for life. Dark depths, watching the lights far above, waiting to rise.

Higgs pulled himself out of the memory, suddenly uneasy about being this close to the edge. He shook his head, trying to will the fear away.

'Don't be silly. Just get this done.'

He reached out tentatively to the nearest spinning circle of mud and gently rested his hand on its ridged surface. There was no heat at all. There was something, though, a weight to it, a deep pull of gravity inside his stomach as his fingers caressed the surface.

It felt familiar; that was it. Like wrapping his hand around a perfectly weighted stone, ready for the sling …

Higgs snatched his hand back and shook his head, clearing the memory before it could take hold. It was so easy to be led astray here. 'Focus. Concentrate.' He took a deep breath and reached out once more. 'Stone. You are Stone.'

As his fingers touched the surface this time, he was ready for the pull on his mind. He was leaning over the edge of a high cliff, the void calling him onward, sucking him out from the ledge and away, into infinity.

Higgs felt the pull and resisted, holding himself tightly inside his mind, wrapping it closed and allowing the chaos to wash over him and pass him by. Stone. A pebble on the floor of a rushing river. Untroubled.

He heard the weld song then, filtered and warped but recognisable, its tones altered by the weight of the river, like he was listening to it underwater, the sounds smudged and dream-like.

Higgs took another breath and pushed his hand into the mud, the surface cracking easily and soft, wet silt swallowing his fingers. Stone.

He closed his fist, and the sludge froze, the mud hardening into solid rock. Higgs opened his eyes and pulled his hand free.

The river was changed. The surface still slid and twisted in relentless movement, but now a single straight pathway of stone lay in front of him, stretching all the way across to the far bank.

'Good.' Flame was already beside him, ready to cross. 'Come.'

Higgs rocked back on his heels, almost falling over completely as a wave of exhaustion washed over him.

Flame didn't wait. She walked across the narrow path he had formed, her step quick and sure. He watched her cross, feeling the resistance of the river underneath the path tug at his mind, the hot swirling mud push against this new obstacle in its path with something very like frustration.

He pulled himself to his feet, suddenly anxious. 'Hurry,' he whispered. 'You should hurry.'

Flame was already at the far bank as he started across, feet shuffling into a short, quick trot. He could feel the path beneath him shift and start to fail, the stone softening into the sludge from which it was formed.

The weld song was louder now, the music quickening with urgency. He felt another crack in the path, then the unmistakable groan of something other than mud. Something alive.

Something angry.

'Move!' Higgs called to himself. He was halfway across. Flame was on the far bank, but standing right at the edge of the mud. Too close.

He was running now, his feet sinking deeper with each heavy step, his mind reeling with song. Weld song, and something else.

Fear.

There's something there, in the depths. Something ancient.

Something not to be disturbed.

Higgs's left foot slipped from under him as he finally reached the bank of the river, and he flailed out a hand to catch the edge. Flame grasped it, hauling him up and over the last couple of feet, but not before his other hand sunk into the warm, waiting mud.

Wrapping around him, pulling him down, into the depths of memory.

They are already among us. You have another form, Wilt. Give it full rein.

He blinked across the campsite, arriving just as the last of the light from the human form seemed to melt into the grey of the landscape. From the direction of the river, what looked like enormous black crabs were scuttling over each other, pouring out of the water to flow over their waiting victims. They were about the same size as the wild boars Wilt had hunted in the Tangle, though now and then one reared up on its hind legs and became large enough to strike a man in his chest.

The first few travellers didn't know what hit them. They were swamped in moments, flailing under the swarm of creatures, their cries of terror smothered by the evil things that ended them so effortlessly.

Wilt reached out his hand to the closest creature, his fingers a twisting nest of black welds that shot out toward it. As they struck, they seemed to fuse into the thing, not slowing it for a second, and Wilt felt only the briefest glimpse of a connection, a yawning cavern of silence where the creature's mind should have been.

Flame pulled, and his hand came free of the mud with a rush and a pop as the memory sank into the river, releasing its hold on his mind.

'Move!' Higgs gasped as he struggled to his feet, aware they were still too close. Still within reach.

Behind him, a deep crack shook the cavern and another groan of protest echoed out as the last of the stone path melted into the mud.

Flame helped him up, and they both turned to watch the shifting river as they backed away from it, the weld song slowly dying into silence as they moved further from its edge. Finally, it was gone completely, and Higgs felt a sudden shock of heat as Flame banished the magic she had conjured to shield them.

'Come. We should not tarry here.'

'I strongly agree.'

Higgs stared at the hand that had sunk into the river, his fingers tingling at the memory of the muck squeezing between them, melting his hand completely away. He flexed it open and closed, trying to reassure himself of its reality.

'The passage is this way. Come.'

Higgs paused for a moment to stare back at the slowly moving river, the shifting sludge of it, a shudder of disgust tickling down his spine. Then he turned and followed Flame out of the chamber and away.

Chapter 24

Daemi's mood only worsened as they got closer and closer to the edge of the great sea of green. The Eternal Sea, Heather had called it. At least the name made obvious sense. There seemed to be no end to it. It was hypnotic in its movement, the green colour rippling and waving in front of them.

Almost like it's laughing at you. Well, it might.

As they reached the foot of the mountain, the slope of the ground eased into a more gradual curve, and walking was made much easier, but now the full extent of the problem only became clearer.

'Look at the size of it,' Frankle whispered.

It wasn't just grass, at least, not like any they were used to. Each individual stalk towered over even Daemi's head, easily seven feet high at the edge, and taller still further in, the blades clustered together to form an almost solid barrier to any hoping to pass.

Heather pushed past Daemi to inch closer to the grass and tentatively reached her hand out to touch the closest blades. Instantly, she snatched it back, sucking on her finger.

'It's razor sharp.' She looked back at Daemi still standing staring with her hands on her hips, as though waiting for a solution to make itself apparent. 'We can't pass through.'

'We wouldn't try.' Daemi sighed. 'We'd be lost within a few feet. It's worse than the Tangle.'

'That's it!' Frankle exclaimed. 'The Tangle. It sounds just like the Tangle.'

'Sounds?' Heather asked. 'I don't hear—'

'Like the weld song earlier, like the heartstone's song. Much quieter, though. Just at the edge of hearing.'

Heather stopped and held her breath as she listened, but all she heard was the constant rustle and flow of the stalks moving in the wind. Eventually, she gave up. 'It's times like these I remember the wise words of the crafters back in Redmondis. Wielders are weird.'

Come. This way.

Wilt's voice echoed through each of their minds, and Daemi turned to see the black cat waiting for them. 'You can't mean for us to go through there.'

Not through. Come.

Without another word, it trotted away, headed south, skirting along the edge of the sea, keeping to the loose rock path along the base of the mountain.

'Around then,' Daemi grumbled. 'Should only take us a few years.'

Nevertheless, she followed, one hand flexing on the handle of the weld blade on her hip. Frankle was right; there was something about the grass that reminded her of the Tangle. That meant danger.

Heather looked at Frankle and shrugged. 'Maybe there's a path through, further down.'

'Maybe,' Daemi muttered. 'What did your maps show?'

'Nothing good. But I mean, they were old maps. Very old.'

'I don't think there's a pathway,' Frankle said. 'It feels very … solid.'

Not through.

'Enough.' Daemi shut down any further conversation. 'Let's just try to put some distance between us and whatever it was inside that mountain before we run out of sunlight. I'm not keen on spending the night anywhere near here.'

Two hours later they were still marching, the late afternoon light fading fast as the sun disappeared over the mountain range to their right, and the wide sea of grass to their left slowly morphed from green to black.

Daemi had set as fast a pace as she could—still much slower than she would have liked—and Heather and Frankle had done well to keep up so far, but as the light dimmed, they were losing their footing on the loose rock path more and more, until Frankle finally lost his balance completely and almost took Heather down with him as he sprawled face first in the dirt.

'Come on, Frankle.' Daemi reached down to pull him to his feet. 'We'll stop and make camp soon. Just a little further.'

In truth, Daemi wasn't sure how much further they could go. The black cat still led the way a few metres ahead, trotting from rock to rock and always glancing back impatiently at them, but it was getting harder to make out against the darkening background.

The Eternal Sea was changing, too, as the light left it, the vague feeling of unease emanating from it growing stronger every minute. Daemi found herself constantly scanning its edge, watching for light or glints of steel from among its constantly moving blades. A couple of times she thought she caught a flash from eyes staring out at them, but each time she blinked the image faded, and she managed to convince herself it was just her imagination.

Finally, the daylight left them completely, and Daemi called a halt, knowing that to keep on trudging through the darkness was inviting accident or injury. 'We'll stop here for the night. Looks as good a spot as any.'

As soon as she said the words, Frankle collapsed in a heap, head bowed between his knees.

'Is it safe?' Heather whispered.

'It will have to be,' Daemi replied, scuffing the ground around her free of rocks with her feet. 'I'll keep watch. You rest while you can.'

Both of you rest.

The cat was beside her, rubbing itself across the edge of her boot.

I will stand guard better than you are able.

Daemi was about to protest, but one look out at the black wall beside them convinced her of the truth of it. She couldn't see a thing anyway.

'Should we make a fire?' Heather asked.

'With what? Besides, I don't think we want to announce our presence even if we could.'

So, they each wrapped themselves in their cloaks and made themselves as comfortable as possible on the rough ground, trying to make the best of the circumstances.

Daemi felt the warmth of the cat next to her, and reached out idly to pat its back, closing her eyes as she did so. Heather's breathing soon dropped into the regular rhythm of sleep, and Frankle was already snoring. Perhaps she would be able to sleep, if she just …

Wake up.

Daemi's head jerked up and her eyes snapped open, though the world around her was a sea of black. The air was cold on her face, and she shivered as she straightened, her muscles aching and stiff from sleep.

'What is it?' she whispered, not wanting to wake the others.

She froze then, twin lights blinking out at her from the darkness. Eyes. A pair of eyes. There was something there.

Daemi slowly drew her sword and pulled one leg underneath her, ready to spring.

No. Not eyes. Look again.

Daemi rubbed her face and tried to focus on the lights. There were three of them now. No, four. She stood up slowly as more lights blinked into existence.

They were moving, the lights slowly gaining in size as they grew closer. They each moved together, a set distance apart, the white lights turning orange as they came closer.

'Lanterns?'

They did look like flames, but floating on the surface of the grass sea. Flying, somehow.

As she stared out at them, the lights moved away again, angling across the sea toward the edge further south of their rough camp. Then the wind changed, and she thought she heard a voice call out, its words lost in the tumult.

'Is that'—Heather was beside her suddenly, her voice seeming far too loud in the night—'a ship?'

A ship. That was what it looked like. But how was that possible? Floating on top of the grass sea as though it were sailing across an ocean.

Not through.

Wilt's voice echoed through Daemi's mind, confirming what she saw. It was a ship. Somehow.

Not through. Over.

Chapter 25

By the time dawn broke over the far edge of the Eternal Sea, Daemi
was eager to move. She hadn't been able to get back to sleep, the
pure impossibility of what she had seen sending her mind into a
tumult of chaotic thoughts that refused to slow down no matter
how tired her body felt. Heather had had no such problems,
seeming to accept the miracle as just another wonder in a long
string of them, shrugging herself into her cloak and collapsing into
sleep as soon as the strange lights faded back into the darkness.
Frankle had never stirred at all.

Daemi sat now, staring out at the strange expanse in front of
them as it slowly changed from black to grey to green as the sun
crept over the horizon. There was no sign of the ship that had
passed near their position in the night, just a flat, unchanging
stretch of grass waving slowly in the wind.

She looked down at her two younger companions as they slept,
aware of the rumble of hunger in her stomach. If she was hungry, they must be starving. They weren't as hardened as her. They
would have to find food and water somewhere today; the meagre provisions she had snatched on their way out of Sontair were
already gone.

Not far.

She looked over at the cat, sitting on its haunches staring out at
the grass sea, its tail slowly waving back and forth in the dirt.

'How do you know?'

The cat turned to face her, its black eyes staring through her.

I … remember.

'Remember? But you've never been—'

Wilt hasn't. But the other part of me. The wraith. It knows this place. What it once was.

Daemi sat up, suddenly intrigued. 'You have … other memories?'

Many.

Daemi felt a surge of warmth then, as though something was passing from the cat's eyes to hers, and a vision swamped her.

She stood very still between her parents, peering at the enormous armoured foot of the man in front of them, the man who towered even over her father, her father who was the second tallest man in the village behind Fern's, and Fern's father wasn't half as handsome.

Her father gripped her hand as he spoke to the strange man, quickly and urgently, squeezing her hand harder as he went, until she squirmed against the painful grip. He ignored her, lost in whatever it was he was trying to make the strange man understand.

Her mother stood silently, reaching out at one point and placing a hand on her hair, brushing it back from her face.

The strange man finally shook his head and reached out to take her hand from her father's. Her father resisted at first, then seemed to collapse into himself as he admitted defeat. Her hand was engulfed in the mailed gauntlet of the stranger, and he led her away.

She looked back and saw her father, tears running down his cheeks. He seemed so much smaller now, not tall at all.

Daemi fell backward as the vision left her, and scrambled back into a sitting position, hurriedly wiping at the tears that had sprung up in the corners of her eyes.

'That … that was my memory.'

Yes.

'You took that from me when we were training. On the road to Redmondis.'

I took nothing. It is still yours.

'It's private.' Daemi found herself suddenly angry at the violation, her jaw clenched.

The cat didn't reply, simply turned away to stare out at the Eternal Sea.

Daemi stood up and stretched, purposefully banishing the memory from her mind. It was time to move. 'Come on, you two.' She raised her voice loud enough to wake Heather and Frankle from their sleep. 'Time to go.'

Frankle was more than just hungry, his stomach had gone past grumbling into actual cramps, and he felt dizzy, his vision blurring at the edges if he turned his head too fast, but he was determined not to mention it.

They'd been walking for most of the morning along the edge of the seemingly impenetrable grass sea, heading toward some point Daemi seemed confident was up ahead, and neither Daemi nor Heather had said a word of complaint. He'd be damned if he was going to be the first to break. Even if he was the youngest.

Besides, every time his thoughts started to sink into the dark depression that threatened to snatch all hope away, something would catch his attention, some movement in the grass, or more often some fragment of music on the wind. Weld music, just like he'd heard in the conduit, and inside the welds when he'd unleashed them on whatever had taken control of Captain Mont in Sontair.

Now that he thought about it, he'd been hearing it on and off ever since he and Heather had healed Daemi, when he'd found himself much deeper than he'd ever gone before, below the rush and chaos that he'd always been taught to fear within the depths, down onto the strange ice barrier, and the cat, waiting for him.

Ever since Wilt had done whatever it was he'd done to him there. Given him something. Infected him.

'Can't be much further now.' Heather panted, the pace of their march obviously tiring her as well.

'What can't be much further? Where are we going?'

'To wherever that ship was headed.'

The ship. The mysterious lights both Heather and Daemi were

so certain they'd seen shining in the dark of the night, when he was lost to the world in the blank sleep of exhaustion.

He was beginning to doubt they'd seen anything at all. More tricks of the mind. More mischief—just like the Tangle.

Frankle raised his head and stared over the grass again, letting the slow waves of movement push at his mind. Pulsing in and out, like the tide.

'There, listen!' Daemi held her fist up. 'Voices.'

All three of them froze. Frankle held his breath, trying to hear what Daemi was talking about, but there was nothing.

Ahead of them, the base of the mountain range curved to the right, so they could only see a stretch of path a few hundred yards long before it disappeared around the sloping rock. It was completely empty.

'Daemi, I—'

'Shush!' Daemi glared back at him.

He closed his mouth and waited, blinking back a sudden wave of dizziness.

Come.

The black cat appeared from around the corner and bounded on top of a rock column.

Come see.

Daemi broke into a run, charging away from them, and Heather hurried after her only moments later.

Frankle watched them run, unable to bring himself to join them.

Come, Frankle. Come see what wonders the folk of the Eastern Dales have hidden from us for so long.

Wilt's voice spoke only to him now, the strange echo of the cat's normal voice fading into the background. It really was Wilt. Somewhere in there.

Frankle heaved his legs into a trot and tried to catch up with the others. Daemi had already reached the corner where the cat waited, and Heather dropped her pack with a sigh as she joined her.

'How?' Heather gasped, still trying to catch her breath. 'How is it possible?'

Frankle finally rounded the corner, almost tangling his feet in his robe as he skidded to a halt.

'That's … moonsteel.' His mind was struggling to comprehend exactly what he was looking at, but of that much he was sure. Moonsteel, glowing bright blue in the sunlight. More than he had ever thought possible. He sank to the ground, eyes locked on the strange sight in front of him.

It was a ship—or at least, the top half looked like a sailing ship. It was made of dark timber, and two tall masts rose from its hull, white sails furled around them. The hull itself was one long sweeping curve, raised at both ends, and Frankle could make out at least five figures scurrying about on the deck, loading crates and containers from the short pier that jutted out over the grass from the base of the mountains.

But the real wonder was the bottom half. There, rising just above the tips of the tall grass, two long sweeps of moonsteel glowed blue against the green, seeming to hover on top of the grass, the boat rocking slowly in place as the sailors above moved about and the weight of the craft shifted back and forth. Each moonsteel rail was at least thirty feet long and almost three feet wide, the base of them rounded and polished, shining bright in the sunlight.

'Daemi,' Heather whispered, pulling at her sleeve. 'Your sword.'

Frankle finally pulled his eyes away from the impossibility to watch Daemi draw her blade and hold it out in front of her. It, too, was glowing, the blue matching the glow of the railings under the ship, and Frankle felt a tingle of recognition tickle the back of his mind as he watched the light play off it.

He took a breath and let himself drop into the depths, recognising the eagerness of it, the weld music rising as he did so, until it seemed loud enough to announce their presence to the sailors in the distance, as though Daemi's blade was joining the song of the ship, the moonsteel recognising its kind and reacting like a lost friend reunited.

'Do you hear it?' Frankle asked.

'Yes.' Heather nodded, her hand reaching up to clasp the stone hanging from around her neck. 'The heartstone's song.'

'Weld music,' Frankle corrected.

Daemi grunted and thrust her long knife back into the scabbard on her hip. 'C'mon then. May as well see if they're friendly.'

She started to march toward the ship, her chin high and her cloak flapping back in the wind, as though she were leading an official delegation.

Just like she had in Sontair, thought Frankle.

'And what if they're not?' he asked. 'Friendly, I mean.'

Daemi didn't reply, but reached out one arm as she passed the cat to allow it to leap onto her shoulder and curl around her neck.

'I think they need to be more worried about us, Frankle.' Heather smiled and skipped after Daemi, falling into step behind her.

Frankle sighed and pulled himself to his feet. He was the wielder here. He was supposed to be the expert on all of this. So why did he feel so lost? Like a cork bobbing in the sea, slave to the push and pull of powers he would never understand.

'You coming?' Heather grinned back at him, and once again the rush of heat filled his chest.

'I'm coming,' Frankle grunted, hurrying to catch up.

Heather felt more than a little sorry for Frankle. He was obviously close to exhaustion, and she could tell he was doing his best not to show it. But one glance back at the strange ship floating on the grass in front of them and she couldn't help but get excited. Moonsteel, sailing on grass as though it were water. Just wait till the other crafters heard about this.

She'd have to try to get a closer look as soon as she could.

Daemi was still marching ahead, her hair blowing back from her face in the breeze, looking just as regal and confident as could be. The sight made Heather feel very young indeed.

'Katha!' One of the sailors had stood up and was pointing toward them, obviously announcing their presence to the rest of the men.

They were all men, Heather noticed now that they were closer. All dark-haired and swarthy, almost too similar in appearance to each other. Perhaps they were related.

All work on the ship ceased, and the sailors formed in front of the crates still stacked on the shore. More than one of them reached behind their backs to grasp what Heather could only assume were weapons.

'Um, Daemi?'

'I see them,' Daemi muttered, sweeping her cloak back to free her own sword.

The sight of the shining blue blade on her hip had an immediate effect on the men. A burst of argument broke out, four or five of them talking at once, their foreign language a babble of incomprehensibility to Heather's ears.

Daemi stopped a few metres in front of the group, holding one arm out to push Heather behind her as Frankle caught up to them.

The sailors continued arguing, waving their arms about and pointing at Daemi's sword. Finally, one of the men was shoved to the front by the others and stepped forward, obviously their spokesman.

He smiled suddenly, a fawning, ingratiating grin complete with wringing hands that Heather at once recognised from her days dealing with traders.

'Redmondis.' The man motioned with his chin toward the colours Daemi still wore on her shoulder.

'Yes, Redmondis.' Daemi nodded, slightly taken aback. 'You know of it?'

'We know. We trade.' The man smiled again, his words heavily accented but perfectly understandable.

'You have been to Redmondis?'

'No. Not me. But others. My brothers. We trade.' He waved his hand at the various crates on the shore.

Heather peered around Daemi to get a better look at the men.

They did all look remarkably similar, but she had only ever met one other man from the Eastern Dales. Perhaps they all looked like that.

'Moonsteel.' The man was pointing at Daemi's blade now, and the smile faded from his face. 'You should not have this.'

'No?' Daemi looked at her blade, then back at the spokesman. 'You think you can take it from me?'

The man raised both hands as if in surrender. 'We no fight. We trade. But this, you should not have. It is not for sale.'

A sudden memory shook Heather. The trader. The one in Redmondis who had sold the moonsteel blade to Higgs. He had looked just like this man. More so even than the others here. He could have been his twin. She reached out to tug at Daemi's cloak, but Daemi was already talking.

'Your ship. We require passage across this … sea.' Daemi stumbled over the words.

The man still had his hands raised, but now he shook his head and frowned.

'This is not possible.'

'Daemi—' Heather began, but Daemi shooed her back.

'And if we make you?'

Daemi's tone was unmistakable, and the men behind the spokesman muttered to themselves, obviously understanding her meaning perfectly.

'You are strong, yes.' The sailor smiled again. 'Great warrior. We? We no fight. We trade. But the ship will not sail without us. Your strength cannot make that so.'

Daemi rested her hand on the hilt of her sword but didn't draw it.

'He's right, Daemi,' Frankle spoke up. 'There's weld magic here. I can feel it. Hear it. But it's different to anything I've seen before. I don't think I can—'

'Daemi, that man,' Heather interrupted. 'I've met someone very like him before.'

Mallow. His name was Mallow. Wilt's voice echoed in her mind.

'Mallow,' Heather repeated, and the effect was immediate. Instantly, the spokesman moved to step forward, his eyes blazing with anger, and two of the others reached out to clasp his shoulders, holding him back.

'That name!' he shouted. 'How do you know that name?'

Heather stepped out from behind Daemi, trying to look as honest and innocent as possible. 'I met him. Mallow. In Redmondis. He sold a moonsteel blade to … my friend. Not that one though.' Heather motioned to Daemi's blade. 'Another. He … he was your brother, wasn't he?'

The spokesman stopped writhing against the men holding him back and nodded, his eyes dark. 'My brother. Yes.' He stared at Heather, seeming to wilt suddenly as he spoke. 'Was. You said he was. I have not seen him for many months. He did not return when he should have from last trade. He is—'

Dead. Cortis killed him. Broke his mind looking for me. For us.

'Dead.' Heather nodded, dropping her gaze. 'He was killed by a very bad man. One who serves those we hope to find.'

The spokesman almost collapsed at the words, the men who had been holding him back now propping him up as his legs gave way.

'Dead.' Tears filled his eyes and he wiped at them angrily. 'You speak truth. I can see. I knew. We knew. He should never have tried. I told him—'

He was bringing the weld blade to Cortis. But he gave it to Higgs instead.

'He helped us. Mallow. Your brother. He was a good man.'

The spokesman nodded quickly and blinked his eyes clear, staring at each of them in turn. 'Come. Rest here. We have food. We leave tonight. You will come.'

With that, he turned away and began barking orders in their strange tongue, waving his arms, and the group broke into movement.

Daemi looked at her, face filled with wonder. 'How did you—'

'Wilt. It was Wilt. Couldn't you hear him?' Heather answered.

Daemi shook her head and pulled the black cat down from her shoulder, troubled. Then she seemed to force the thought away. 'Well, it worked. Now we rest.'

'And eat?' Frankle piped in hopefully, one hand rubbing his empty stomach.

A sailor was already walking toward them, carrying a platter of food and water, nodding and smiling as he did so.

For the rest of the daylight hours, they sat and watched the sailors load their ship. Crates and sacks of goods moved back and forth from the ship to a cart that appeared later in the afternoon, two large horses drawing it along from the south driven by another dark-haired man. His eyes scanned the three of them suspiciously until another man explained things to him in their foreign tongue.

'I've never heard that language before,' Heather mentioned.

'I have, but only in snatches,' Frankle answered, lazing back in a haze of comfortable sleepiness now that his stomach was full. 'In the markets and such. I don't think they like to speak it much in front of others.'

'More secrets,' Daemi muttered, poking at the dirt with a stick as she waited. 'Why does that not surprise me?'

'The Eastern Dales. Do you think it's far?' Heather asked, obviously enjoying the adventure and its discoveries far more than either of the other two.

'We'll find out soon enough.' Daemi threw the stick down and stood up, brushing the dust from her cloak as the spokesman from earlier strode over toward them.

'Come,' The man said, his smile open and a little too ingratiating. 'Come, we board now. When the sun sets, we go.'

Heather sprang to her feet, eager to learn more about how the ship worked. 'There's no wind. Do you think they have some other way of propelling the ship other than the sails?'

'Let's just get moving,' Daemi grunted, the black cat springing up to wrap itself around her shoulders and neck once again.

The spokesman watched the cat curiously. 'My name is Haddar.' He bowed his head in introduction, then waited.

'Heather.' Heather stepped forward and offered her hand in greeting. Haddar smiled and shook it.

'Daemi. Frankle.' Daemi pointed to them both in turn and returned her hands firmly to her hips.

Her lack of manners didn't seem to faze Haddar in the slightest. 'Very good. And your friend?' He motioned to the cat peering back at him from beneath Daemi's dark curls.

'He—'

'Doesn't have a name,' Daemi interrupted before Heather could say any more.

Haddar looked back and forth between them. 'Come, come.' He ushered them forward. 'We speak more on the journey. I wish to hear more about my brother.'

'Of course.' Heather smiled again and skipped forward, her eyes locked on the strangely glowing rails underneath the ship.

Daemi grunted and waited for Frankle to move ahead of her, her hands never straying far from the hilt of her sword.

'And your blade.' Haddar nodded toward it. 'This I wish to hear of as well. Come. The sun leaves us.' He waved them in front of him and down the short pier to the gangplank, the shadows of the mountain range pulling over the ship and the grass sea like a blanket drawn up to the chin.

Chapter 26

As they proceeded down the narrow tunnel and away from the large river chamber, the heat slowly faded to a warming glow, no longer prickling Higgs's skin and making his eyeballs feel dry and swollen. Once again, he had the uncomfortable sensation of the mountain being some living creature they moved within, ever deeper, down inside its heaving chest toward its heart.

'Here. We are closer than I thought.' Flame's words shook him from his grim musings. She was standing a few feet ahead, eyes wide and eager, face sweat slick and gleaming in the orange light.

'Closer to the Pit?'

'Yes.' She nodded, turning from him. 'Come.'

Higgs followed behind her as she crept, slower and more carefully now. He tried to remember what he had seen when he had been in the Pit, but he could only glimpse flashes of it. He remembered fire, and stone, and forming shapes from memories that were somehow more than memories, that took hold of his mind completely and led it away.

'Why—' Higgs began, then stopped himself and tried a different tack. 'What are you hoping to …'

His words dropped away as they turned a corner and the tunnel opened out into another wide chamber, the sudden chaos of shapes and movement overwhelming him. And the noise! It was as though some plug within his ears had suddenly been pulled free, and he was swamped by the clatter of rock, the clink of heavy chains, and the low roar and suck of fire.

'The Pit.' Flame stood perfectly still, taken aback by the sight of it.

The rock floor sloped downward for about thirty feet to a slowly shuffling queue of those same strangely deformed creatures, heavy buckets of hot mud on their shoulders, one by one emptying their loads into a large circular pool in which other figures moved, stirring the mud with their bodies, their faces dull and empty as they trudged in wide slow circles. The mud within the pool gleamed with orange light, throwing the faces of the mutated forms into startling relief and sending tall black shadows leaping up the high walls of the chamber beside them. Beyond the pool, another line of figures moved, hooded and linked together by green stone chains. Prisoners. Another memory flooded in, unable to be held at bay.

He felt himself be pulled up and out of sleep, hands first, the heavy shackles around his wrists cutting into his skin to send a scream of consciousness tearing through his mind, blowing all shreds of the dream clear.

He looked down at the source of the pain, blinking his eyes free of tears to stare at the single large clasp locked around both wrists, forcing his hands together in supplication. The bindings were formed from green stone that sent a thrill of memory through him. He had seen these before, through other eyes. Some other place. Some other time.

Higgs stumbled against Flame as the vision deserted him. Here. This is where he had been. The Pit.

'Weldfarers, captives as we were.' Flame kept her eyes locked on the queue, her mouth set. 'You remember.'

Higgs clutched his forehead, his mind thrumming like the skin of a beaten drum. 'Why does the memory feel so …'

'Overwhelming?' Flame grimaced, eyes flashing as she scanned the slowly moving forms. 'This place is made from memory. It feeds on it, on what once was. Everything about it calls up visions from the past, and we shape them. Form the mud and flame and stone into shapes that the Novus finds pleasing. Only then can we ascend. You see?' She raised her chin to the front of the line of prisoners, where a tall hooded figure stood guard. 'The Incarnate watch. Watch and judge.'

Higgs felt a rush of fear as he recognised the tall Incarnate, the shadows of its hood turning toward them.

Flame pulled them both down into a crouch, away from sight. 'Do not fear. They cannot sense us yet. When they do, it will be too late.'

She moved, hurrying over toward the line of mud carrying servants, keeping their shuffling forms between her and the Incarnate at the rear of the chamber. As she reached the creatures, she shoved through them, two almost losing their balance entirely as she knocked them aside, but seeming to take no interest at all in what had occurred. They stumbled, then regained their footing, their eyes never leaving the back of the one in front of them.

At once, another image from the past took hold of Higgs, refusing to be ignored.

He didn't know how long he had been in Redmondis. Time seemed to have faded from importance. All he knew was the routine: up early each morning to trudge to the massive dining room on the ground floor of the dorm, forcing the tasteless porridge down his throat, and following his fellow first years out to begin their classes. Standing in bare stone rooms before various cantors and lesser masters as they droned on, all of them somehow merging into a single grey-faced figure in his memory. Always keeping a fixed, neutral expression on his face. Moving back through long enclosed corridors to the dining hall for another lukewarm meal of vegetable mush, then following the boy in front of him to attend afternoon classes. Never remembering exactly what was taught, simply soaking in the drone of words that washed over him. Back to the dorm before dark, to eat again and then trudge back up the stairs, watching his feet to avoid stumbling on the irregular stone steps, worn down by centuries of feet just like his. Collapsing into a dark, dreamless sleep before starting it all over again as the sun rose.

'Wilt.' The sound of the word on his lips banished the dream, sending it down into the wash and swirl of the depths. 'Just like that mud,' Higgs whispered, still staring at the twisting pool.

He had lost sight of Flame, a gush of smoke and steam rising up from some hidden crack in the rock floor, and the thought occurred to him that she might leave him here, that his use was ended and she would discard him as easily as …

'As what? An unwanted memory? Control yourself.'

He bent as low as he could and scurried across to the queue of mud carriers, trying his best to slip between them without touching them, the sudden stench of their bodies up close turning his stomach. They smelled worse than animals, worse than the stables back in Greystone after a summer shower. He risked a glimpse up into the nearest one's face and was rewarded with the blank, uncurious stare of a cow. He felt a wrench of nausea at the sight, and suddenly another memory leapt at him, almost knocking him to the floor as it overwhelmed him.

The sense of wrongness was almost overpowering. The cat's body shook as his senses screamed to flee. Something deeper, something foreign yet understood, held it in place. A man stood amongst the guard. Cortis. His eyes were alive with power and madness, scanning the room in triumph. He was flanked by two enormous wolves, glaring coldly out at the men. Waiting …

The cat followed the guard's glance to the far side of the bonfire where the light broke over a pile of strange, shifting forms—those who hadn't been able to accept the full transformation thrust upon them, half-formed bodies writhing in agony, screaming through mouths and throats that no longer worked—

Higgs shuddered and swallowed and shook the memory free, pushing through the mules and hurrying around the rock column that he had last seen Flame disappear behind.

He had been back there, in Redmondis, in cat form. Watching Cantor Cortis and the horrors he wrought on the wielders there.

But they had won. They had beaten him. That was only a memory now.

Wasn't it?

He almost crashed into Flame, who was crouched in front of him, peering around the stone column at the line of shackled prisoners.

'There they are,' she whispered.

'Who? Who are you looking for?'

Flame reached backward and pulled him alongside, their cheeks almost touching. 'The others. My others.'

She pointed, and Higgs's breath caught in his throat as his eyes followed her finger to one particular figure in the queue. It was hooded, but the hood was pulled high on the head and in the orange glow, Higgs could make out a regal, coldly handsome face, her eyes knowing and cruel.

She stepped forward and threw back her hood, and all the air seemed to leave the room.

Wilt found himself floating in a deep stillness, his eyes locked onto her beautiful face, unable to even think. Her deep red hair curled down over her shoulders and was lost in the fold of her robes, and her alabaster skin seemed to glow in the sunlight shining down from the ceiling high above. But even more intense were her eyes: deep green pools lined with black, scanning the line of mere men in front of her with contempt.

Wilt watched her eyes move along down the line and wondered how he would survive their glare.

Higgs blinked, dispelling the memory. He stared at Flame, then at the figure, then back at Flame again, his mind reeling in silent shock.

They were the same. They were exactly the same.

Chapter 27

The strange ship cut silently through the darkness, the only sound that of muttered conversation between the sailors in their foreign tongue as they moved about their tasks. Daemi stood on the bridge, wrapped in her cloak, furiously ignoring the chill of the night air. Frankle was already asleep, the workers having guided him to a chamber of his own in the hull, bowing and waving obsequiously as they did so in a manner he had found quite unnerving. Heather was at the bow, leaning as far over the rail as she could to try to make sense of whatever magic was powering their movement.

There was no wind. The sails stayed furled against the masts, yet still the ship moved quite quickly, gauging by the push of the air against Daemi's cheeks. There was no other way to judge, no landmarks to be made out in the sea of ink outside the bubble of lamplight they floated in.

It all made Daemi very nervous.

'You should sleep.' Haddar was standing at the wheel, one hand rocking it back and forth to follow some secret path of his own over the grass sea, the other placed proudly on his hip, obviously enjoying the motion of the ship underneath his feet.

Daemi scowled at him and turned back to the darkness.

'Your friend, he sleeps,' Hadder continued.

'He's not used to guard duty.'

'Ah.' Haddar smiled, as though her words had said more than she meant to. 'He is one of them, yes? One who wears the robes.'

'A wielder.'

'Wielder, yes. My brother told me of this word. It is not one we use.'

'What do you call them?' Heather was beside them suddenly, having given up on trying to satisfy her curiosity about the ship in the darkness.

Haddar peered at her with one raised eyebrow. 'We know them as Incarnate. Those who ride the welds.'

'Really?' Heather plonked down on the rail beside Daemi, obviously ready to pepper Haddar with a whole stream of questions. 'What does "ride the welds" mean? Oh! Is it like this ship?'

'Ha ha!' Haddar chuckled. 'You are a bright one. Yes, it is like this. In a way.'

'How does the ship float on the grass like this? It's the moonsteel, isn't it? Some reaction it creates.'

'In a way. Tell me, bright one, what do you know of this great sea we sail upon?'

'We call it the Eternal Sea, though it isn't marked on any of the maps I've seen. There isn't really a lot of information about this in Redmondis. At least, nothing I could find. I doubt even Petron knows much.'

'Heather!' Daemi snapped a warning through clenched lips.

Haddar's grin only widened. 'You have secrets. We have secrets. The world is full of secrets. It was not always so, I think.'

Heather peered up at Daemi, wondering what topics she could broach that wouldn't cause her to lose her temper, but Haddar continued.

'You say that this was not marked on your maps. That is because it was not always here. This, all of this, was once a great forest.'

'Like the Tangle!' Heather exclaimed.

'Yes, like your Tangle. The same, I think. I have not seen, but my brother—'

'I'm very sorry about your brother,' Heather offered, seeing the shadow of grief cross Haddar's face. 'I only met him very briefly. He sold a moonsteel blade to'—she glanced up at Daemi again—'my friend.'

'Yes. Moonsteel. He was foolish. He was always foolish.' Haddar looked away, lost in some memory. 'It is very valuable, this blade. This ship. It is said that long ago our people forged moonsteel from the fires of the great mountain, but this skill has been lost. So much is lost now.'

Heather felt Daemi's hand clench tight on her shoulder, silencing her before she could reply.

'The great forest was lost. Burned. Now there is only this sea.' Haddar gestured to the silent darkness. 'And we sail upon it through power we do not understand. This ship is old. Very old.'

Haddar seemed to physically pull himself back from his thoughts and smiled again at Heather. 'But you knew my brother's name. His secret name. How is this?'

Heather stared back at him silently, not sure how to reply.

'It wasn't she who knew his name.' Daemi turned from the rail and faced Haddar fully, her mind made up. 'It was him.'

She pointed at the black cat perched on the rail at the rear of the ship, almost invisible against the darkness. At her words, it turned to face Haddar, its eyes locking onto his.

Haddar stood silently staring, unable to look away, and a single tear slowly rolled down his cheek.

A moment later, the spell was broken, and the cat bounded off, disappearing into the hull of the ship.

Haddar stared after it, his face changed. 'Thank you,' he whispered. Then he seemed to realise where he was and pulled himself together, wiping the tear away and turning back to the wheel.

'Come on, Heather,' Daemi whispered, pulling her to her feet. 'We should rest.'

Heather wanted to protest but relented, allowing Daemi to guide her below and leave Haddar to his grief and memories.

'But we still have so many questions for him!' Heather began protesting as soon as they stepped down the short stairwell into the below decks. 'How does the ship work? Where is he taking us, exactly? Why don't they know how to forge moonsteel anymore? What happened to the forest? He said it burned, but—'

'Enough, Heather,' Daemi interrupted as she pushed open the door to the small chamber Haddar had offered for their use. 'Can't you see he doesn't have any answers for us?'

'What—' Heather had been about to continue, but Daemi's words finally broke into her train of thought. 'What do you mean he doesn't have the answers?'

'The ship—didn't you notice anything strange about it once we got going? The sailors were running about on the deck, but none of them actually seemed to be doing anything productive. And Haddar, he had his hand on the wheel, but he wasn't steering. I don't think he knows any more about how the ship works than we do. Probably less.'

Daemi slumped down on an empty pallet and began tugging at her boots. In the corner of the room, Frankle was snoring away, the black cat curled up at his feet, staring coldly back at them.

'And you—been up to your mischief again, haven't you?' Daemi addressed the cat. 'Probably forced him to take us on board in the first place. With your worms.'

The cat didn't reply.

'You mean welds? Did you use a weld on him?' Heather asked.

He only needed the slightest push.

'I'm sure,' Daemi spat back, her distaste obvious. 'And just then, what did you do to him to affect him so?'

I showed him his brother. I showed him how he died.

'You show too much sometimes,' Daemi muttered, rolling onto the bed and turning her back on them both. 'It isn't right to meddle with people's memories like that.'

Heather could hear the hurt in Daemi's words, and for once kept her questions to herself.

The cat stared at her, watching as she too readied herself for bed, its eyes still and unblinking.

She lay back on the rough cloth pallet, pulling her cloak around herself as a makeshift blanket, and stared up at the dark timber ceiling, feeling the strange rock of the ship move beneath her. It wasn't quite like being on water, now that she really thought about it. The ship didn't roll and pitch side to side. It was more of a tremor across all three axes, as though a thousand small hands were passing the ship along on top of them.

After a few minutes, Heather could hear Daemi's breath drop into the deeper rhythm of sleep, and she rolled onto her shoulder to face the cat.

'What did you show him?' she whispered. 'What did you show Haddar?'

The cat didn't move from its position, but Heather heard the briefest snatch of song on the wind before she fell into its eyes and the vision swamped her.

He was standing at the entrance to his tent. Coin was heavy in his hand, and he felt the slightest twinge of regret as the young boy walked outside into the waiting guards. It had been a good trade. Rare to enjoy such trading skill here, where the crafters and Black Robes were often so desperate for goods. He preferred it this way. Yes, he had liked trading with the boy. Now, though, now it looked as though the boy had made some powerful enemies. He stepped behind the tent flap of his stall to view the scene, making sure to stay out of the guards' sight. One never knew what those dogs could do. Best to stay out of their way.

He watched the guards question the boy, saw them strike the young girl standing with him. The boy lashed back, reaching into his tunic to pull out the glowing moonsteel blade. Recognised the sharp pain flash across the large guard's face as the blade cut across him. The moonsteel had hurt him badly. That meant he was one of them. At least he was on his way.

Heather's breath steamed in the chill as she exhaled, suddenly back in her own body, her own mind. That had been her. Her and Higgs. Before—

'Is he …' she began, then stopped, not at all sure she wanted to know the answer. 'Higgs. Is he still there with you? Somewhere in the welds?'

The cat dropped its head down onto its crossed paws, but kept its eyes locked on hers.

It's ... difficult to explain.

The voice had changed. It sounded more like Wilt. Much more human.

Higgs was killed. He died. But I held on to some part of him within the welds. And now, that part has pulled away from me. I think that's the reason I'm stuck in this form. This or ... the other one.

'The wraith. You mean the wraith.'

It calls to me. Pulls at me more and more. This cat form helps hold it back, but it is getting harder every day. Higgs took me with him, my human form. We have to find him so I can get it back.

Heather shivered under her cloak. 'And where will that leave Higgs?'

The cat closed its eyes, unable—or unwilling—to answer.

Frankle slept deeply, the rocking of the ship lulling his mind, the whisper of the grass murmuring in his ears, morphing his dreams as it washed over him.

Words of longing, words of pain and patience, and an inhuman yearning for eternity. Words of warning. Words of fear.

—Come back, Frankle. This is not for you. These visions are not yours.—

The voice was ignored, pushed out and away by something deep and cold and impossible to deny.

The words brought with them visions that slid across his mind, not leaving any trace in his memory as he slept on, the Tangle murmuring its dark lullaby into his ears.

Stop! Thief!

He ducked under the guard's swinging arm and swerved into the alley, dropping half his haul as he went, not thinking for a moment about stopping to recover any of it. A loud crash behind him told him the guard hadn't been quick enough to change direction and had crashed into the fruit stall that lined one wall.

He grinned, tucking the two loaves he still held into his shirt as he ran, turning again as the next opening reared up, not slowing until he could no longer hear the heavy boots of the guards stomping after him. Even then, he took two more twists deeper into the nest of alleys behind the market square before he slowed and risked a look back.

Safe. He was safe.

—No, Frankle! Don't let the voices lead you! Don't let them.—

It was no use. The voices, the siren song of what once was the forest, were too strong. It had waited for one such as this to come. Waited and watched and nursed its wounds. Staring up at the lights far above. Waiting to rise.

He shook the water from his hair and wiped his eyes. He squatted on a rooftop; the rain streamed down upon him, a heavy rain that had set in hours ago and showed no sign of easing. It cut visibility to only a few feet, but that was all he needed. Below him, huddled under a poor excuse for a shelter, lay his father.

He twisted the knife in his hands, the point digging into the callus of his index finger.

It would be so easy to—

The sudden pain of the knife slicing into his flesh cut through the dream, searing it away and pulling him up and out of its spell.

Frankle sat up with a gasp, his heart racing and lungs burning, as though he had surfaced from being too long under water.

The cat was on his chest, staring down at his face, and he pushed it off him as he sat up, his finger still stinging.

He lifted his hand to his face and saw a single drop of blood expand and pool on his fingertip.

Sorry about that. It was the only thing I could think of.

Frankle watched the blood, unable to get his mind to understand what he was looking at.

'The knife,' he finally whispered. 'It was—'

My claw.

The cat held up a single paw and long silver claws slowly slid out from its tips.

'You … cut me?' Frankle pushed himself fully into a sitting

position and stuck the bleeding finger in his mouth, speaking around it as he continued. 'I was having the strangest dream about a knife.'

That was a memory. Not your own. Not something you should dwell on.

'Huh.' Frankle considered the words, knowing the truth of them. He didn't want to have that dream again. It had felt so real, so ... sticky.

He looked around the small chamber. Heather and Daemi were both sleeping, the room lit by a dull orange glow. 'Dawn already? I guess that's enough sleep for me anyway.'

Frankle pulled his boots on and quietly crept from the room, leaving the others to their sleep. Hopefully they weren't troubled by similar dreams. They looked contented enough.

He closed the door behind him and tip-toed up the stairs to the deck, the cat darting between his legs and trotting ahead.

The orange glow was brighter now, but a wave of dizziness hit him as he struggled to understand that something was wrong. It wasn't the sunrise. The wide sea of grass around the ship was still dark, the orange light focused on a single point to the east, not lighting the world correctly at all.

He caught himself as he felt the dip and pull of his dreams clinging to his mind again, then shook them off as he stepped onto the ships' deck.

'You see,' Haddar called to him from the bridge just above his head. 'It calls to you, Incarnate. It calls to all who ride the welds.'

Frankle blinked as he stared at the strange light, trying to understand what he was looking at.

It was a mountain. A mountain of fire. Glowing bright and hot and dancing in the distance like a candle's flame in the darkness of a bedroom, chasing the nightmares away.

'Pankesh, we call it.' Haddar's voice dropped into a whisper. 'The beating heart of the world.'

Chapter 28

As the black sea of grass stretching out beyond sight in all directions slowly warmed to grey, then green, Frankle sat perfectly still, unable to take his eyes off the glowing mountain of flame in the distance. It dominated the horizon, outshining even the sun that rose behind and above it now, lighting the Eternal Sea.

Frankle shivered in his cloak, the chill of the morning tickling where it wormed its way between the folds of cloth, as though trying to wrest his attention away from the sight. But it was hopeless. He was enthralled, eyes locked on the impossible, breath sighing in and out of his lungs in time with the pulse of the vision.

'Frankle?' Heather's voice cut across his thoughts, but didn't find any purchase.

He felt a hand brush his shoulder, his forehead, then pull away.

'Daemi! Something's wrong with Frankle! He's burning up.'

'It is the fever. Pankesh's Kiss,' Haddar answered her, and Frankle lost interest in the rest of the conversation, his mind swelling and pushing against his skull, his thoughts hot and flowing like lava through his fevered brain.

'What do you mean?' Daemi cut in. 'What is Pankesh?'

'That is.' Haddar pointed. 'The heart of the world. All Incarnate know its pull. Your young friend especially, it seems.'

Another shift of movement, and the soft fur of the black cat pulled across him, curling around his skin and demanding he open his hands to pet him. His hands obeyed, though he felt no connection to them. They were somewhere else. Someone else.

A high buzz echoed in the back of his skull, and his eyeballs felt dry and too large for his head, so that when he managed to blink them, they scraped painfully against his lids.

'Here, Frankle.' He heard Heather's voice again, and a touch on his shoulder. 'Drink.'

The water was cold beyond bearing on his lips, but it surged into his mouth and he managed to gulp some of it down.

'What should we do?' Daemi asked.

'I have seen this before, many times,' Haddar said. 'Your friend will recover. Something about those who ride the welds lose themselves in Pankesh. Its glow calls to them, from the depths, from the place where they call their powers. He answers that call, but he will return before we arrive.'

'How long?'

'Not far now. There, you see?'

Frankle considered turning his head to see what Haddar was indicating, but his neck was locked in place, the muscles of his back and chest creaking with stiffness and pain. He would stay still. Stay still and watch.

'That gap, to the south, the black line in the sea.'

'Yes. I see it,' Daemi answered.

'That is the river. What once was the river. Now choked with silt and dirt and little more than a mud flow. It, too, leads to Pankesh. Feeds it. Answers its call.'

'The Boroni!' Heather exclaimed. 'It was marked on the maps in Sontair. Flowing into the Eternal Sea.'

'Into and through,' Haddar replied. 'It is said that long ago, before this sea of grass, when the forest still claimed this land, the river flowed fast and bright and silver. Some believe it is the reason this ship has these masts and sails we no longer use. I am not so sure.'

The cat moved beneath his numb fingers, its silver claws sliding out to tickle the palm of his hand. As soon as they touched him, he felt a flash of threat light up his mind like a shout.

Frankle coughed and raised one hand to his forehead, feeling the heat and sweat of it.

'Frankle.' Heather was beside him in a moment. 'Come on back down to bed. You need to sleep.'

There was no way he was going to obey her, no way he was going to leave this sight that pulled at his chest, spoke through him—no way at all. But suddenly he was walking, one arm thrown across Heather's shoulders, and his eyes were pulled away and released.

'You see?' Haddar said. 'He comes back already. Yes, let him sleep some more. We will be landing in two hours or so, before the sun gets too high in the sky. Come. Let your young friend rest, then join me to break our fast before we arrive.'

Frankle closed his eyes as he was led away, and felt his mind release and fly free, his body moving automatically as his consciousness fled into the safety of sleep.

Heather barely got Frankle to his bed before he collapsed onto it, his eyes closed and his breathing deep and regular. She arranged his feet on the cot and brushed the hair from his face, feeling his forehead and noting that whatever fever had taken hold of him up on deck already seemed to have broken. The skin was cooling, the sweat drying on the skin, and he no longer seemed troubled.

'Well, at least we don't need to worry about that,' Heather whispered to herself, then glanced at the doorway to see she had an audience. 'I don't suppose you want to shed any light on things?' she asked the cat, who stared blankly back at her.

'No.' Heather stood up and stretched. She was sore from the short sleep she'd had on the hard cot. 'Thought not.'

The cat darted between her legs and leapt up onto Frankle, settling itself down around his knees.

Heather noted the growing red glow in the room, the light seeming to leach in through the timber of the ship itself, as though bleeding through it. 'Do you feel it? The mountain? Anything different?'

The cat seemed to ponder her words before answering, its black eyes never shifting from Frankle's face.

I feel … something. A hunger, perhaps. An impatience.

'Well, whatever it is, it's affecting all of us. Daemi seems even grumpier than normal.'

We are linked, she and I. Deeply linked. It is hard for her to deal with such forces pulling at her and no knowledge with which to control them.

'Just sounds like she's in love.' Heather smiled, reaching out to pat the cat's back. It scowled and flashed its fangs at her, but she ignored it and went ahead anyway. 'Come now, you know it's true. Perhaps that's what causes all this trouble. Love.'

Heather had been teasing, but now that she put the thought into words, it seemed worth pursuing. 'Perhaps that's part of what you wielders can never quite grasp. The welds are connections between minds that you can bend to your will. But making the connections in the first place is what matters.'

She reached into her shirt and pulled out the heartstone. Her half of the heartstone, at least. Both Heather and the cat stared at it as it turned slowly, glinting in the red light.

'We crafters have a deeper understanding of such stuff, or at least, more respect for it. The life within all things.'

The blood within the stone.

'Yes, but not just that. You see, you wielders take that line and build a prophecy and a whole school about control and domination and power. But that misses something, I think. Something important.'

Heather poked the heartstone, setting it spinning faster. 'Higgs still holds the other half of this, doesn't he? Somehow. Like you carry the weld blade with you in those shiny claws of yours. Yet somehow this reacts to Frankle now as well.'

We gave it to Frankle, that part of Higgs. To help grow his power. To help protect him. And … for other reasons.

Heather tucked the heartstone back into her shirt. 'You do so enjoy your mysteries, don't you?'

Perhaps the reason the heartstone reacts to Frankle is not our doing at all. Perhaps the change is in you.

Heather sat back, one eyebrow raised at the cat staring back at her. 'Oh, I see. Now you're teasing me. Well, at least that's an improvement of sorts, I suppose.'

She stood up and looked down at Frankle again, his face clear and worry-free in the silence of sleep.

Heather leaned forward and planted a soft kiss on his forehead before turning to go.

'And you can keep that to yourself.' She smiled as she left the room, the cat still staring silently after her.

'Your colours, they will need to be covered.'

Daemi glanced back at Haddar, one hand still nonchalantly resting on the wheel of the ship.

'My colours?'

'Redmondis.' Haddar waved at the markings on Daemi's shoulder. 'Those colours are known here. They will not be welcome.'

'What do your people know of Redmondis?'

'It is what will be. It is what they seek to change. Control.'

'They?' Daemi frowned. 'You mean the Incarnate.'

'Yes. Like your friend. But … different.'

Daemi turned away to stare at the glowing mountain gaining in size, seemingly growing up and out of the horizon. There was something about it that drew the eye. Something beyond the scale and colour of it. Something … deeper.

'You do not yet understand this place. Take your hand.'

'My hand?'

'You are marked, yes? One of the Nine.'

Daemi held up her hand to show the four remaining digits and the scar where her little finger used to be. 'You know of our traditions. Thankfully, these have changed now.' She flexed her fingers in front of her face, frowning as she did so. 'We no longer require such a sacrifice.'

'Put it in the grass.'

'What?'

'Your hand, reach overboard into the grass we sail upon. You will have to lean, but you will reach.'

Daemi peered back at Haddar, wondering what sort of fool he took her for. 'The grass is sharp, we felt it on the shore. Razor sharp.'

'Do not worry about that. This grass, it cuts beyond flesh. Trust me.'

She stared into Haddar's eyes, looking for the slightest flash of cunning or trickery, but there was nothing. She knew she could trust this man, on this point at least.

'Very well.' Daemi stepped up to the side of the ship and leaned over, reaching her hand out over the railing.

'Use your scarred hand,' Haddar called. 'Be careful not to lean too far. You will not survive if you fall.'

She reached out, her entire upper body dangling over the rail now, and let her hand dip into the tips of the grass. She clenched her teeth, waiting for the first flash of pain.

Nothing. There was …

No. A scratching. A tingle. A hint of song.

'Now. Come up and look at your hand.'

Daemi pulled herself back onto the deck and held her hand up, flexing her tingling fingers. They were unharmed; no cuts or marks on them at all. One, two, three, four, five. She looked back at Haddar, who had a wide grin plastered over his face.

'You forget so quickly.' He smiled.

'Forget?' Daemi asked, still flexing her hand. She felt dizzy, as though the world around her had stepped suddenly sideways, leaving her behind.

'This sea we travel upon you know as the Eternal Sea. This is not because of its size.'

Five. Five fingers. There was something wrong with that.

'You forget. We forget. All forget in the face of eternity. It is the way.'

A sudden vision took hold of her. Another time. Another set of eyes.

When the axe fell, he felt no pain, just a sudden cold fire as he moved his hand, leaving his finger behind on the block. A cheer went up from the troop, but he ignored them. The captain clapped him on the shoulder and he turned away.

'My hand,' Daemi stammered, her mind unwilling to form the thought. 'It healed me.'

'Healed you, or simply changed your memory,' Haddar continued. 'Have you not always had all your fingers on that hand? I do not remember anything else.'

'No.' Daemi shook her head. 'It healed me. I remember.'

But she didn't, not really. She blinked as she tried to force her mind back to her own memory of the ceremony, but nothing was coming to the surface.

'You are strong, stronger than most.' Haddar nodded approvingly, but the grin didn't leave his face. 'Stronger than me. But none of us are strong enough to resist the tide.'

Daemi continued flexing her hand, the tingle slowly leaving her skin, the burn fading back into the past. Finally, she stopped, wondering why she was holding her hand up to her face in the first place.

'Come.' Haddar's voice cut through her musing. 'We arrive soon. We should break our fast. Come.' He was beside her now and clapped her on the shoulder. 'I would hear more about Redmondis, and your blade.' He walked ahead of her, leading her back down below decks. 'And we should talk about what to do when we arrive. Not all will be so welcoming.'

Chapter 29

'Come.'

Flame was already moving, once again not waiting for Higgs to respond. She hurried along, bent almost double, shielded from the sight of the Incarnate at the far side of the room by the long shuffling queue of hooded figures.

Higgs sat stunned, unable to wrap his mind around what he had just seen. The one Flame was arrowing toward looked exactly like her. More than just a familial resemblance, she was an exact copy.

He shook his head and hurried after her, reaching out to tug at her cloak as she paused once again. 'A Sister?'

'No, I told you that would be impossible,' she scowled, ducking behind another fat stone column. 'Do you remember nothing of this place?'

Higgs peered around the chamber, only just holding himself above the suck and pull of memory and vision that clawed at his mind. Orange glowing light, baking heat, a cacophony of noise that seemed to only half exist in the real world, as though what he was hearing was only the blood roaring inside his head. He felt dazed and vulnerable, at the tipping point of a dream.

'The Pit.'

'Part of it,' Flame replied. 'This is one of the antechambers. The mules bring the mud from the river, and it is prepared here.' She nodded back toward the large pool of swirling mud that the cow-like workers moved through. 'Then these others are given shape and form and led into the Pit itself to be sent on their way.'

She started off again, bent low, keeping her eyes locked on the Incarnate. The tall figure had turned away and was waving one arm in frustration at some trouble at the front of the long queue. Flame's twin was only a few feet from them now, still staring straight ahead, her face cold and oblivious.

The Incarnate turned back to the queue suddenly, and Flame paused again, ducking low behind another member of the line.

'On their way?' Higgs continued, desperate to find some semblance of meaning he could cling to. 'What do you mean?'

Flame stared back at him, eyes wide with wonder. 'You really remember nothing? Coming here? Arriving?'

Higgs shook his head. His first memory was of the prison cell. Opening his eyes to find himself impossibly in his own body once more, coughing up ice water and sucking shaking breaths down into his new lungs.

'We are tools of the Novus, all of us,' Flame continued. 'We are formed from living mud, from the memories of lives lived in other times. We are tested. Judged. And if we are found worthy, we are sent on, through the long golden tunnel, into those other lives. To change what must be changed. To gain control.'

Higgs's head was still shaking back and forth but his mind was elsewhere, teasing out the memory of the time before this place. When he was with Wilt.

He felt himself sinking, impossibly heavy in the darkening waters. The shape on the ice above battered at the surface, its four paws clawing uselessly at it.

—Wilt, fight it. Stay with me!—

He was cold, so cold. So tired. He sank into the darkness, watching the light above fade out.

The memory slipped and slid away from him, slithering out of his mind's grasp. Then it lashed back again, a golden glow lighting the memory.

Wilt's eyes locked with the man and sent a black weld into his mind.

A wash of panic and fury, chaos pulsing over him, pushing into his nose and throat and choking any life away.

—No. Control it. Just like the gloomclaw, when the queen tried to use its power.—

He let the storm pass over him, ignoring the panic and pull. This man's mind was a hellscape, no human aspect remaining, all blasted away by the power that controlled him. Power that was leaving him behind.

—Find whatever's controlling him, Wilt. Before it flees.—

He raced through the collapsing mind, searching out what he knew had to be there. A connection.

—There.—

A single golden thread glittered in the distance. A weld, unlike any he had ever seen. He grasped for it, dived into it, and let it pull him free.

Higgs stumbled forward into the nearest body as the memory abandoned him, his mind ringing. 'I … I remember.'

'Then you know what it is we must do.'

Flame was moving again, almost beside her twin now. Higgs watched her, unable to move, the entire chamber seeming to swirl around him, a still central point in a gathering storm.

The Incarnate was looking this way, straight at him, and Higgs could do nothing but stare helplessly back.

Flame reached her target and grabbed her twin's hand, the other looking down calmly at her with only the vaguest recognition lighting her face.

The Incarnate was moving now, the black shadow under its hood where its face should be locked on Higgs.

'Move,' Higgs whispered, urging his frozen body into action, but it didn't respond.

Flame pulled her twin out of the line and away, the other following without protest. The Incarnate didn't see them, its attention all on Higgs as it floated toward him.

'Move,' Higgs tried again. His lips felt cold and numb, ice crystallising through his body, locking it in place.

Finally, he saw Flame and she him. She shook her head.

She's leaving me. She's leaving me here to be caught.

A bright flash of orange fire lit the room, and hot air pushed against Higgs's face, blasting the chill away and sending him sprawling backward onto the rock floor, the ceiling covered in a thick blanket of flame. The queue of figures he was crouched beside broke into disarray, bodies tumbling around him as the heat beat down, driving them all to the ground.

Higgs felt his body return, and rolled to his right just in time to avoid being crushed by a large stone column that cracked and crumbled, the weight of it shaking the world as it crashed to the floor.

He stumbled to his feet, completely free of the magic that had frozen him, and he squinted through the thick smoke and dust that filled the chamber, trying to make some sense of where he should go.

Then Flame grabbed his wrist and led him away from the chaos and fire.

Higgs tried to blink the stars from his eyes, his vision a dazzling blur of orange lit by dancing silver sparks. Flame had pulled him out of the tumult into another tunnel, but then dropped his hand, and he reached out now to feel the cool rock wall beside him as he stumbled along. His face tingled with heat, the hot air blasting out from the opening behind him, making it clear the fire that had erupted inside the chamber still burned, and he scrambled to put as much distance as possible between himself and the inferno.

His vision slowly cleared, and he could just make out the tall shape of Flame standing a few feet in front of him, her body a darker silhouette in the billowing grey and red smoke.

'Flame?' he croaked, the rough sound of his voice startling in the thick air of the tunnel.

She turned toward him, her face grim and unwelcoming. 'You know me?'

Higgs coughed and straightened up, brushing his hands over his head to make sure his hair was still all there. 'Flame? What do you—'

'You. I know you.' She looked him up and down contemptu- ously. 'The boy. The one the Novus wants.'

He stood silently in front of her, dumbfounded. For a moment, he wondered if he had really stepped back into the memory that had overwhelmed him moments before, if he was Wilt, in Red- mondis, standing in line to be inspected by the Sister.

A second shadow stepped out from behind her, and he realised his mistake.

'This is Stone. He helped to free us.'

Flame stood beside her twin, and Higgs stared back and forth between them, unable to tell them apart. 'Flame?'

'You told him our name?' The first figure turned to her twin, her anger obvious.

'It was necessary. He is necessary.' The second one—Flame, the real Flame—replied, flashing back a look that was just as furious. 'Do not question me.'

The first figure seemed to consider the words, before ducking her head in a quick nod. 'If you so insist.'

She gave Higgs one final glance before turning away. 'Do not speak to me, boy. I do not share her weakness.'

Higgs watched her walk away, feeling better with every step she took. Finally, he turned to Flame. 'Your twin?' he asked.

'I told you before, such a thing is not possible.'

'But she looks exactly like you.'

'She is me. Another me. Drawn back though the welds and formed of the living mud you saw yourself in that chamber, just as all who arrive here are. Just as you were.'

'Me?' Higgs's voice was suddenly very small as he recognised the truth in her words.

Higgs.

His lips formed the word, but no sound came out. The shape turned toward him, however, answering his call.

Higgs. It's me.

The dark walls of the tunnel pulsed with power. A cold rush of air from outside the tunnel pushed against his face, as though death itself was calling to him. He took another step, slower now, bending down and holding his hand in front of him.

Higgs. Stay here. Stay with me.

The cat trotted silently toward him, his head cocked as though listening, as though trying to understand his words. It stopped ten feet from him, and Wilt stopped as well, knowing any further movement would send it scurrying away again, into the nothingness that waited for it. Wilt dropped to his knees.

Higgs. Please.

Higgs collapsed to the ground, rocking back against the stone wall as the world spun around him, refusing to stay in place.

He was dead. Red Charley had killed him. Then Wilt had held him back, within the welds. Refused to let him go. Then—

There.

A single golden thread glittered in the distance. A weld, unlike any he had seen. He grasped for it, dived into it, and let it pull him free.

He had been pulled out of the welds, icy salt water filling his lungs, vomiting out of him as he took his first shaking breath.

'What … what is this place?'

'This is Pankesh,' Flame answered, her eyes locked onto his. 'This is the place beyond time. This is the home of the Novus. The first one. The one who reaches into the past and future and twists all threads to his bidding. He calls us, forms us, gives us duty and meaning and sends us on. Weldfarers. Back to alter the shape of the world. But he does not see all. Not yet.'

Flame peered down the tunnel to where the other one had gone. 'Even he does not realise what those he considers his servants are capable of. Come.' Flame reached down and pulled Higgs to his feet. 'We still have use for you. There are others. Others to set free.'

'Let me guess. Nine of you.'

'As many as we need.' She stopped to consider his words. 'Nine would be enough, I think.'

'And when you have them, what will you do?'

'Then we will face him. Face the Novus and let him see what his powers have wrought.'

Flame spun away and followed her other—her sister, despite her protestations—down the tunnel. Higgs watched her go, a sudden hopelessness sucking the strength from his legs.

What was he doing here, with them? What did he hope to accomplish?

'The Novus,' he whispered to himself, rising up off the wall. 'The one who called you here. You can face him, that's what.'

And then?

'And then find some way out.'

He plodded down the twisting tunnel, pushing all further thought away, another orange glow growing steadily up ahead as he moved toward it. Another opening. Another chamber.

Another Sister.

Chapter 30

Frankle sat back and rubbed his full belly, a comforting sleepiness fuzzing his brain. Sitting across from him on the low table, Heather nursed a cup of steaming chocolate, her eyes snapping between Daemi and Haddar at the head of the table as they conversed about Redmondis, Sontair, and their plans for landing at their destination.

Frankle tried to pay attention, but his mind refused to obey, his head constantly turning to face the wall in the direction of the great mountain of fire—what did Haddar call it? Pankesh, that was it.

Pankesh, the beating heart of the world.

It hadn't been marked on any map in the queen's study in Sontair. Nothing had been, other than the Eternal Sea stretching to the edge of every parchment he had found. Perhaps Heather knew more; she always seemed to.

Haddar had said that it would call to him, and he knew the truth of it. When he closed his eyes, it was all he could see now. A bright orange glow. A light at the end of a dark tunnel.

'So, we are agreed on that at least,' Haddar finished, wiping juice from his chin and pushing his plate away. 'I will continue as normal, leading some of my men off the ship as soon as we dock. You three will stay in the group, disguised, cloaked and hooded and silent. Perhaps we will be lucky.'

'But you do not believe so,' Daemi prompted.

'No.' Haddar shook his head. 'No, the Incarnate are not so easily fooled. But at least we will get you off the ship before any trouble starts.'

'What sort of trouble do you expect?' Heather asked.

'I have only seen the Incarnate confront one other. Many seasons ago now, before I even had this ship.' Haddar closed his eyes as though dredging up the memory. 'It was over quickly.'

'Can you be a little more specific?' Daemi muttered.

'You would know these powers better than me. Or at least your young friend should,' Haddar replied, nodding in Frankle's direction.

'They are wielders?' Frankle asked. 'Like me?'

'As I told your friends earlier, they are not like you. Not at all. But they do have power.'

'Welds? Do they use welds to control others?'

'This I do not know.'

'Do you see anything?' Frankle persisted.

'No, Frankle,' Heather corrected him. 'Only you wielders see the welds. But Haddar, do you hear anything? Perhaps music?'

'Music? No.' Haddar closed his eyes again, frowning at the memory. 'Though there is something … Cold. I remember feeling cold suddenly.'

'A wraith?' Daemi whispered.

No. Not a wraith. Not like me.

Frankle looked up at the ceiling where the voice had come from. The black cat sat perched on a beam, staring down at them.

'I do not know their powers, or how they work,' Haddar replied. 'But I have no doubt they will be looking for you. Especially if any see that blade you carry. What did you call it? A weld blade?'

Daemi nodded, her hand straying to the blade's handle.

'Moonsteel, in your tongue,' Haddar said. 'It has many names in ours. All know of its value. It should never have been taken to the west.'

'Like I told you,' Daemi said, 'this blade was forged in Redmondis.'

She turned her head to glare at Heather and Frankle, ready to interrupt any further information they might decide to volunteer.

'Yes, so you said.' Haddar looked between the three of them. 'And we all have our secrets still. But if what you say is true, the Incarnate will be especially keen to question you about its origins.'

'Let them try,' Daemi muttered, pushing her empty plate away. 'You mentioned disguises?'

Haddar stood up. 'You are right. It is time to prepare. Come. We shall arrive soon.' He opened the door and ushered them out, bowing as he did so.

Frankle was the last to leave. His fingers trailed along the timber of the ship, the electric tingle still there in the wood. Like it was alive.

'It speaks to you, doesn't it?' Frankle asked as he walked past Haddar. 'The ship, I mean.'

Haddar smiled and tilted his head to the side. 'I would not say *speak*. It knows me, and I know it. We live inside each other's minds, in some way.'

The black cat jumped down onto the table and darted through the door between Frankle's legs.

'You know of this too, I suspect. The call of the welds.'

Frankle simply nodded and followed the others out of the room. It was time to put such thoughts from his mind, to prepare himself. If Haddar and Daemi were right, they were about to walk straight into a fight.

Daemi shrugged her cloak up over her shoulder, making sure the strip of colour she still wore marking her as a soldier from Redmondis was covered. She adjusted the black cloth wrapped around the hilt and scabbard of her sword, scowling as she did so. Heather had given her the silky, soft cloth with a knowing grin, loudly pointing out the quality of the material, but Daemi was much more concerned about how she was supposed to be able to draw her blade without getting hopelessly caught up in it. The lightweight material seemed to want to cling to her skin like a spider's web, always getting in the way as soon as her hand brushed past her hip.

'Leave it be, Daemi,' Heather whispered from behind her. 'You'll only get it more tangled.'

Daemi forced herself to move her hand away from it. 'Just be ready. And look after Frankle.'

They were standing at the rail of the ship as it crept in slowly toward the short dock. The movement over the grass was perfectly smooth, no dips or sways as a ship moving over water would experience, and the otherworldly glide of it turned Daemi's stomach. It felt like they were flying.

She groaned as a wave of memory washed over her. The three of them clinging to the back of the great eagle as it dipped and swooped over the Tangle. 'No,' she whispered aloud, forcing the memory away before it overtook her.

'Everything okay?' Haddar glanced at her with concern, but she shook her head and he turned back to face the pier. 'You see the hooded ones? Incarnate. Two of them, at the edge of the shore.'

Daemi scanned the shoreline, the red glow from the mountain rising in front of them covering everything in a sickly, thick light that did nothing to ease the pulse of nausea in her belly. It was obvious who Haddar was talking about. Two tall figures stood unmoving at the dock, the workers breaking around them like water flowing past rocks in a stream, their hooded faces turned toward the boat, waiting for them.

Red hooded cloaks. Faceless. This time she couldn't force the memory away—it pushed over her like the tide, and suddenly she was back in Redmondis again, staring out through Wilt's eyes.

'Try to keep your mind clear. The Sentinels can sense your thoughts.'

Wilt felt a chill and a sudden oppressive pall in the air as five red-robed figures entered the room. Four were very tall, unnaturally so, and covered head to toe in red cloth. The Sentinels, Wilt guessed. Their faces were completely covered, red veils hiding their features. Their heads moved as if they were studying the students, then tilted back as though sniffing for any scent of danger.

In an instant, the Sentinels were replaced by enormous, twisting pythons, heads bobbing from side to side as their tongues tasted the air. Wilt blinked, and the vision was gone, the Sentinels back in human form, scanning the room.

She was in her own mind again, staring out over the rail of the ship. The two figures turned as one to face her.

They know. They know everything.

Daemi pushed the thought away, knowing it was useless. There was no room for doubt now.

'Do you hear it?' Frankle whispered from behind her. 'The weld song.'

'I think I hear … something,' Heather said.

'It's so loud.' The hopelessness in Frankle's voice made Daemi turn, and she grimaced at the sight. He could barely stand, shoulders hunched into himself, leaning heavily against Heather, his face pale and drawn.

'Ready the gangplank!' Haddar called out, snapping her attention back to front. A group of sailors pushed past them, sliding the heavy walkway out as the side of the boat kissed the dock, the ship settling quickly into place without so much as a sigh of noise.

Haddar started squabbling at his men in their own language, waving his arms and making as much noise as possible as the group started to move off the ship. This had been part of the plan; Haddar was to create a distraction to help them hopefully slip out unnoticed in the commotion.

Daemi looked back up at the two silent figures still staring directly at her, and her hand slipped down to the hilt of her sword.

Wait. Do not touch the blade.

Wilt's voice froze her in place. 'Where are you?' Daemi whispered.

A dart of movement under her feet gave the answer as the black cat slithered out through the mess of bodies, disappearing from Daemi's sight further down the dock.

Keep your hand clear of the weld blade. They will sense it.

'Great,' Daemi grunted. 'Now you tell me.'

Haddar was already moving forward, so there was nothing for

it but to join him. She bowed her head, hoping her hood would do something to cover her face, though she had the uncomfortable feeling the two figures waiting for them didn't need any light to see her.

A small pack of sailors artfully arranged themselves around the group, trying to disguise the fact that there were more than Daleishmen on board, and they all moved off the ship and down the dock in a group, Haddar striding ahead of them, his arms still waving in the air and his voice loud and effusive in its greeting.

Daemi kept one eye on him and the other on her feet as she followed behind, holding her breath.

One of the hooded figures stepped forward to Haddar and gestured back at the ship. Haddar moved between him and Daemi, and for a moment, the thought that the plan might actually work flared in her mind.

Then she felt her body freeze, and all hope died.

'Daemi?' Heather crashed into her back, almost losing her footing as the group of sailors suddenly broke apart around them.

It was no good. She couldn't even move her head. Her entire body was locked, as though the air itself had suddenly coalesced into ice, the chill enveloping her and holding her in place, the only movement that of her breath misting from her lips.

The Incarnate that had been talking to Haddar now stepped forward, brushing Haddar's protests aside, the dark space under its hood locked onto Daemi's face.

'Frankle! Help!' Heather cried out.

Daemi felt them shift behind her, but couldn't move a muscle, couldn't even think. All she could do was stare at the Incarnate moving toward her, as inevitable as death.

It paused suddenly and lifted its head, and Daemi caught a glimpse of shining golden eyes. The sight of them lit a memory in her mind, a golden weld hovering in front of her, just out of reach, and her thoughts spun back up to speed as she tried to shrug the oppressive pall that had fallen over her away.

'It's no good,' Frankle whispered, the strain clear in his voice. 'My welds can't penetrate. It's too strong.'

Not for me.

At Wilt's words, the ice holding Daemi in place dropped away, and her hand reached for her blade.

At the edge of the dock, the wraith coalesced into form, a writhing black shadow that rose out of nothing and reached into and through the Incarnate still standing there. As it did so, the Incarnate in front of Daemi whipped its head around, an alien screech unlike anything she had ever heard pealing from within its hood.

Daemi didn't hesitate. She drew her weld blade and plunged it straight into the back of the thing, the glowing blue blade slicing through its body and bursting out the other side. Then, just as the gloomclaw had before, the Incarnate seemed to be sucked down into a whirlpool of movement, draining into the blade itself. A moment later, an empty red cloak dropped to the ground in a heap.

Daemi stomped on the cloak and looked for the other one, but it, too, was nothing more than a pile of rags at the edge of the dock. The wraith was gone, the black cat pouncing forward to paw at the cloak in the dirt as though it was hunting a mouse somewhere hidden within its folds.

The sailors had broken into panic the moment the wraith appeared, and most of them were still running over the beach and away, desperate to put as much space between them and the nightmare that had appeared in front of them. Haddar was crouched in a ball to the side of Daemi, his head covered and knees shivering against each other, like a small child hiding in his room from the evil visions of the night.

'Haddar?' Heather whispered, placing one hand on his shoulder. 'Haddar, it's okay. They're gone now.'

He slowly raised his head, his eyes scanning each section of the world around him closely before moving on, taking in the twin cloaks piled on the ground, Daemi's glowing blue blade still shining in the red glow of the morning, and finally coming to rest on the black cat staring calmly back at him.

'This is where we leave you, Haddar.' Daemi reached down and pulled him to his feet, wrenching his attention back to her face. 'I … thank you.'

Haddar's jaw moved up and down, but no words came out as he looked back and forth between Daemi and the cat still staring up at him.

'You would do well to forget us, Haddar. Forget you ever saw us at all.'

Haddar swallowed and nodded his head, straightening his back as he gathered himself. 'Yes. Forget. Yes.' He nodded again, and a slight smile tickled across his lips. 'What was it I told you? All forget in the face of eternity. I will try to follow my own advice.'

With that, Daemi clapped him once more on the shoulder and turned away. The cat followed her, trotting along behind before leaping onto her back and curling around her neck.

Behind her, she heard Heather and Frankle bid their goodbyes, but her attention was already focused ahead, at the towering mountain of fire that reared up in front of them, the broken, rocky ground of the shoreline angling up sharply to form the base of its slope.

We are close now. Very close.

Daemi pulled the wrappings covering her blade free and dropped them to the ground as she strode on. 'And when we find what we are seeking? When we find Higgs?' she whispered. 'What then for us?'

Wilt didn't reply immediately, but Daemi could feel the thought bloom inside her mind. She wasn't sure whether it was her own or Wilt's, but then, it no longer really seemed to matter.

Then we will come to the end.

Chapter 31

In the large open courtyard within the castle walls of Sontair, soldiers struck and parried, stepping back and forth through the training regime that was becoming so familiar to them all. They had been drilling for weeks now, their muscles aching, sweat dripping down their faces as they moved through the motions. Ten, twelve, fourteen hours a day, more than any of them ever expected to have to perform when they first signed up for duty. Yet none complained. The deep grooves cut into the high stone walls where the gloomclaw had perched gave each of them a daily reminder.

They would not be caught out again. Next time, they would be ready.

The clash of steel and grunts of effort rang out through the darkening dusk, now and then a human voice calling out a word of correction or encouragement. Then, slowly at first, another sound joined them. A clack of wood on stone, a regular pace, slowly moving through the ranks and bringing with it a bubble of silence amongst the noise, as each soldier paused his strike and locked into a salute.

Lodan scowled as he paced across the courtyard, nodding to each man who caught his eye and waving to them to continue their training, to ignore him, but he knew it was hopeless. These men did more than follow him now. They worshipped him. The sound of his cane on the cobbled stone floor was enough to send training blades dropping to the ground as they hurried to arrange themselves into parade formation in front of him.

He had tried to stop such foolishness, mentioned to the captains and ranking officers that he didn't want to cause such a fuss every time he passed through the courtyard, but his words had fallen upon deaf ears. The soldiers would pay their respects no matter what. Each of them knew what the Hand meant to the city.

That was another thing. The Hand. Lodan had thought he'd finally slipped the weight of that name back in Greystone, but it had followed him here too. Whispered at first, then openly spoken, then finally worn as a literal badge by those closest to him. His personal guard had started sporting patches on their shoulders, marking them as such, an open hand insignia. Men fought each other for the right to wear it.

Lodan scowled again and banished the thought, finally reaching the base of the stairs that led to the top of the castle wall. He stopped for a moment to catch his breath, then started up, each step a trial, but one he was determined to conquer. Dizziness hit him halfway, but each day he was one step higher when it did so, and he simply closed his eyes and continued through it, refusing to slow his step.

He felt the light of the falling sun on the back of his eyelids and opened them just as he reached the top of the wall, allowing himself a pause to drink in the sight. The city of Sontair stretched out below him, still startling in its size, its winding, haphazard streets twisting away in front of him like the gnarled roots of some great tree.

Further on, beyond the city walls, the sun was already halfway below the horizon, the light shifting from blue to orange to a glowing red that was almost too much, as though the sky itself was bleeding.

'Lodan.' Griggs's voice snapped him out of his reverie, and he turned to see his old friend striding toward him along the top of the wall. 'Pretty, isn't it?'

'Pretty isn't the word I would use,' Lodan grumbled in reply.

'It seems to get redder every day.' Griggs smiled, facing the sunset, the red light throwing his features into strange relief. 'Even the soldiers have started to talk about it.'

'More gossip?'

'Oh, you know the type of thing. Signs in the sky. Everything becomes a premonition when you're facing powers you don't understand.'

Lodan grunted and glanced back at the guards in the court-yard below, moving through their drills. 'I suppose we can't blame them.'

'No. Still, I find it quite beautiful.'

Lodan looked back at his friend, and for a moment another wave of dizziness overwhelmed him so that he had to lean hard on the cane he always carried now. He was back in Greystone, the night sky stained red by the flames of the burning city, watching Griggs fall and die at the feet of the gloomclaw.

He shook his head, and the vision faded, and he forced his eyes to focus. 'It looks like fire to me. Great blazing fire, somewhere over the horizon, coming ever closer.'

Griggs flashed a grin and clapped him hard on his shoulder, almost sending him stumbling to the ground. 'You always were the cheery one, Lodan. What brings you up here anyway? No—don't answer. Let me guess. You just wanted to check if there's been any sign of these promised troops from Redmondis. I keep telling you, it would take weeks, maybe months for a force of any size to pass through the Tangle, if they even could at all.'

'They will come.'

'I think you put too much faith in your man Petron.'

'We all need faith in our friends, Griggs. That's what will save us.'

They both turned back to the fading sun as the sky slowly drained of colour, red to purple, purple to grey, grey to black. Lodan shivered silently as the night finally claimed them, the chill of the dark leaking into his bones despite his heavy cloak.

'Perhaps tomorrow,' Griggs muttered, spinning away to move back to his post.

Lodan sighed, readying himself to confront the stairs once again. As he began to leave, a spark of light flared in his periphery vision.

He looked toward it as another flared just beside it, far beyond the city walls.

'Griggs,' he whispered, not wanting to disturb the hope that bloomed at the sight of it.

'Hmm?' Griggs turned back toward him, then stopped as he too noticed the lights flickering into life in the dark.

As Lodan watched the lights spread, a blanket of them rolling across the black plains beyond the walls. Tens, hundreds of them. A vast array of light reaching out to him.

'Campfires,' Griggs gasped, not believing his eyes. 'Those are campfires.'

Lodan simply nodded and moved away to the stairs.

'Wait! Where are you going?' Griggs asked.

'Spread the word amongst the men,' Lodan answered over his shoulder. 'We're going to have to try to find room for them all.'

He started down the stairs, his cane knocking quickly against each step. By the time he reached the courtyard, he had almost forgotten it was still in his hand.

Lodan hurried back toward the castle, the lights of the campfires still blazing in his mind.

Chapter 32

Come. This way.

Higgs stumbled to one knee as the voice filled his mind, the command forcing his lips to move in time with the words. He blinked and tried to focus his eyes, but the world shimmered like a struck bell, refusing to settle into place.

Wilt. That was Wilt's voice. He was here.

His hand found a smooth round stone, and he lifted it as he stood, holding it out in front of him like an offering in the orange glow, the hot air streaming with sparks that blurred and streaked through the air, dancing around him, always just out of reach.

Higgs stared at the stone, feeling the world settle around this one point, the vision creep over him like a rising tide. The river beneath the walls of Greystone. Before Redmondis. Before everything.

Wilt began to spin his sling. 'Whenever you're ready.'

Wilt heard his own quiet tone as though he was listening to someone else. The world seemed to have shut down, all outside noise and movement slowing into a low murmur beneath him. All he was aware of was the sling moving in his hand, his senses stretched and waiting.

Then there was something more. It was as though he could feel the green of the Tangle waiting for him to act, the breath of the trees held in the silence of the moment, holding the world still for him.

Suddenly, Lodan drew back and threw his stone high out over the river. Wilt watched it move in slow motion, its arc clear. It was almost like he read it; no thoughts—stones couldn't have thoughts, could they?—but the action itself. As though each movement was pre-ordained and therefore obvious. All he had to do was play his part.

For a long moment he waited, enjoying the sense of the world around him slowing, the universe pausing for him, only him—a taut drum waiting to be struck.

He loosed his stone with another low grunt and the world sped back into life. The sounds of the river, the birds high above and the wind in the trees where the Tangle waited—it all came back in a rush as his rock speared toward the one Lodan had thrown. It met the other with a crack and shattered it in mid-air, bits of rock showering into the river.

Higgs opened his eyes as the pieces of stone clattered to the floor of the tunnel, the rock that had been in his hand now no more than a collection of shards and dust sprinkling from his fingers. He stared at them as they hit the ground, half expecting them to splash when met the floor.

'Stone!'

He looked up to where the voice hailed him, the tall figure waiting impatiently, silhouetted against the brighter orange light of the tunnel opening.

'Come. This way.'

Higgs swallowed, his mouth suddenly very dry. That had been Wilt's vision, by the river. Wilt's mind.

Flame had already turned away, unwilling to wait any longer. At least, he thought it was Flame, not one of the others. How many had she found now? Higgs couldn't make sense of it, his mind scrambling hopelessly at the sheer facade of time in this place, unable to find a grip. Tunnel, then chamber, then tunnel, then chamber. Temperature always rising, orange light growing brighter as they moved into the centre of the mountain. The heart of the flame. Vision after vision from the past swamping his senses, drowning him.

He forced himself to move, one foot in front of the other, brushing the rock dust from his hands as he walked.

Wilt was here. Close, very close.

'Flame?' he whispered as he finally reached the end of the tunnel. She turned to him, her eyes dark.

'Yes, it is me. I have sent the others away to awaken more. It should be easy enough now; the Incarnate are busy elsewhere.'

'Where are we going?' His mind was reeling, and it was exhausting to even string those few words together.

'See for yourself.' Flame nodded toward the chamber and stepped aside.

As soon as Higgs brushed past her shoulder to view the room, he felt another vision from the past well up and suck him away.

Wilt stared open-mouthed. The room seemed to stretch in all directions like a great white desert. The far wall of glass was at least a stone's throw from where he stood, and giant columns shot up from the ground at regular intervals, curving into carved forms of men and beasts, reaching up but not quite touching the high ceiling above. Wilt felt like he'd shrunk in size, or had stumbled into a giant's palace.

Higgs gasped for breath, clutching at Flame's shoulder for balance as the tide pulled at him, drawing him back under.

—It is impressive. Especially the stonework on those columns. Touch one for me.—

Wilt reached out to the first column they passed, brushing his fingers along the cold, shaped stone. As he did so, he felt something else, a spark of recognition.

—Life. This stone is alive. Crafters formed this.—

'Recover yourself.' Flame's cold voice cut through the scene and he was back beside her, one hand still wrapped in her cloak. She stared down at it, her meaning clear.

'Oh. Sorry.' Higgs pulled his hand back, resisting the urge to brush the cloth smooth. 'Lost my balance.'

'They do have an effect.'

Statues. Stone forms standing everywhere, stacked together like a milling crowd, the flashing orange light that leaked out of the rock walls sending strange shadows flittering across their angles and curves, shaping them into movement, so that the whole room seemed to surge and twist.

Higgs's eyes were unable to rest on any one form, human and animal figures morphing into each other, shapeshifting as his gaze moved across them. Familiar faces leered out at him then disappeared as he pulled his full attention onto that point. Everywhere within the chamber, the low murmur of weld song. The hot wind piping between the gaps in the statues whistling into music, dancing on the edge of hearing, teasing him with its threat.

'Others formed these. Others like you,' Flame whispered, her face locked into a frown as though what she was looking at was deeply distasteful.

'Crafters?'

'Stone.'

Flame turned back to him, watching the room's effect on him. 'You do not remember at all, do you? None of you do. You men are so weak.'

Higgs wanted to protest, but the words would not form, the thoughts losing track somewhere between his conscious and unconscious mind. The waters of the past no longer pulled at him, now he was the water itself, surging and pulsing in time with the music, unwilling to be captured or held.

'Come. We must pass through. I will help you.'

With that, she grabbed Higgs by the shoulder and pulled him along, her strength that of a man much larger, Higgs unable to resist as his boots slid and scrambled for purchase. Each statue they passed seemed to reach for him, clawing at his mind, and he shut his eyes against twisting nightmares that reared up again and again.

Stone. He was Stone. Cold. Separate. Safe.

Come. This way.

The command pulled him on, impossible to resist.

Chapter 33

Come. This way.

The voice startled Heather out of her thoughts, and she stared further up the slope, squinting her eyes to try to penetrate the roiling smoke and mist that seemed to leak up out of the ground. The cat was somewhere further up there, out of sight, but she could see Daemi easily enough, the tall, rigid figure silhouetted against the red glow of the mountain, one hand resting on the hilt of her weld blade, obviously impatient.

'I could use a hand, you know,' Heather called out, her voice lost in the rumble and crack of rock that echoed around the area, the rocky ground under her feet seeming to shift slightly with each new sound, the mountain itself threatening to break apart beneath them.

Daemi didn't move, and Heather turned back to see where Frankle was. He was ten metres further down the slope, crawling on hands and knees, his face pale and drawn, his eyes unseeing.

He had shrugged her support free as soon as they were off the dock, but he was still clearly struggling. She had tried talking to him, but it was clear straight away that was pointless. His ears were stopped, head full of the weld song he claimed filled the air completely, though she heard nothing. Whatever it was, it was real enough to him.

Wielders and their mysteries. Their power that always seemed to take more than it gave back.

Come. An opening. A tunnel.

Heather continued up the slope. It was getting steeper, and the loose rock and uneven ground made each step treacherous. She kept her eyes on her feet and moved on. One step at a time. One foot in front of the other. She tried to banish all other thought, but her mind would not be silenced. The very air seemed to leech the strength and will from her.

What were they doing? What were they hoping to accomplish?

'Enough of that,' he whispered and forced himself to follow. 'You want to go back there? Back to that cell you woke up in?'

Heather stumbled and caught herself from falling face first into the ground as the words blasted across her without warning. She stared at her hands, fingers digging into the deep red dirt, waiting for the voice to return.

'Heather?' Daemi called out, sounding very far away.

'I'm okay,' she whispered, then called back, much louder. 'I'm okay! Just … tripped.'

That had been Higgs. Higgs's voice in her mind.

He was here. Close. She could feel him.

She reached into her shirt and clasped the heartstone still hanging there, the thrum of it vibrating inside her fist.

He was here. She would see him again soon.

Heather straightened and moved on up the slope. In only a few more steps, she could make out the black scar of a tunnel opening further ahead.

Come. This way.

This was taking entirely too long.

Daemi sighed and choked back the shout she was about to unleash, her right hand squeezing the handle of her blade as though to force the anger and frustration away from her and into the weld blade itself. It helped, somehow. She stood silently, watching Heather struggle up the slope behind her, and further back, Frankle basically crawling on all fours, moving more like an animal than a man now, scuttling like a crab.

Like a gloomclaw.

Daemi pulled her gaze back to the source of the voice, perched on a ledge of rock beside the tunnel. The silent shadow of the opening in the mountainside calling her onward.

A fresh gout of steam broke out from somewhere beneath the rocky surface, and for a moment the black cat disappeared, and another familiar silhouette reared up, a looming shadow reflected in Petron's eyes, a clawed hand reaching for her, tearing at her. She shook her head and banished the memory, forcing it into the blade.

Close. He is very close.

Daemi stared into the cat's black eyes and nodded. Just as she was ready to turn back down the hill to help the others, a flash of red streaked across her peripheral vision, cutting out of the darkness of the tunnel.

Incarnate.

Daemi drew her sword and charged, the blue blade glowing brighter than ever, slicing through the mist and seeming to freeze the three figures who were coming out of the mountain in place.

The closest one, its face hidden under the cowl of its hood, raised a single finger and for a moment the ice locked around her again, just as it did before, on the dock. Then it slid away, unable to find purchase on her mind, like a glancing blow from an unskilled swordsman that she parried clear with ease. With a sweep of her blade she ducked and cut across the figure, the weld blade slicing easily through the centre of the red cloak, meeting seemingly no resistance at all, the slight blaze of power from the blade the only sign that it had encountered something other than mere air.

Another pulse of cold hit her, dead on this time, but again her mind seemed to shrug its grip free, her body not slowing at all as it moved through the routine, the first cut spinning into another, then another, the weld blade a blur of blue light as it cut down all three figures within seconds.

Daemi ended the move with her blade held out to the side, her bodyweight resting on one knee, a pile of three red cloaks on the ground in front of her the only sign of the Incarnates that had stood there moments before.

You are stronger now.

She looked over at the cat, still perched on the ledge, not having moved an inch.

'Leaving it up to me, were you?'

For now. I would rather not take my other form unless absolutely necessary. Its call is … stronger here. Much stronger.

Daemi ducked her head in acknowledgement and sheathed her blade. 'Just make sure we don't have any more surprise guests.' She nodded to the tunnel entrance and turned back to the others.

Heather's head was appearing over the crest of the slope, pulling Frankle along behind her by his cloak, both of them oblivious to the fact that three more Incarnate had fallen.

Daemi kicked the red cloaks on the ground into a pile and away, then marched back to Heather, pulling her up the final few steps and hauling Frankle into a standing position. He didn't seem to notice her at all, his eyes staring up at the mountain at something only he could see.

'Come on, you two, into the tunnel.'

Heather looked like she was about to protest, but Daemi didn't stop to hear it. She wrapped one arm around Frankle and practically lifted him off his feet, the toes of his boots dragging thin trails in the dirt as she carried him along. He seemed to weigh nothing at all.

The cat watched them move, then darted off ahead of them, disappearing instantly into the darkness within.

Come. This way.

Frankle was lost within the weld song, his ears filled with it, his eyes open yet unseeing, his body moving without thought or will, only the lightest tingling at the tips of his fingers and toes registering in his brain. He felt as though he had sunk into a weld that encompassed the entire world, the rolling chaos of the depths tumbling around him and pulsing in time with the song, the wind whipping past his face as he fell, ever downward.

'Frankle?' Heather's voice reached out to him through the fog, but he couldn't make his body react to it. Pankesh had consumed him, swallowed him whole. He was lost within its roil and flow.

And yet, there was something other. Something apart from the relentless throbbing in his mind, something separate. Cold and clear and still within the flames. Reaching for him.

Frankle felt his boots step forward, toward the tunnel, and saw the twin points of glowing blue light that were part of that coldness. The weld blade, shining blue against Daemi's side. It was one note of it. And Heather's heartstone, pulsing in time against the soft skin of her throat. It, too, joined the chorus.

'I'm fine. Keep going.'

The voice was his own, but he didn't recognise the power that forced it from his throat. He was no longer there, behind his eyes. He was elsewhere. Lost within the song.

Come. This way.

Wilt's voice was clear above the cacophony, and Frankle turned toward it automatically, just making out the shape of the cat against the darkness of the tunnel. The piled red cloaks at its feet.

He was back then, in the past, the sight of the cloaks pulling out a sharp sliver of fear from somewhere deep inside his chest. He was huddled in the corner of his room in Redmondis, covered in discarded cloaks and sheets and whatever else he could find to put between himself and the powers that stalked the corridor, hunting the wielders down, pulling them out and down to face Cortis and the wolves. He was dripping wet, fear and the stifling heat of his breath trapped underneath the clothes covering his body with sweat, lungs aching in protest against the meagre oxygen each breath could find.

'Frankle?' Heather's voice called him back again, and he was gasping against the hot steam of the air that leaked up out of the red mountain's surface, the scent of sulphur and molten rock getting stronger with each step. The cool tunnel in front of him, beckoning to him. Calling him toward silence and stillness and peace.

A shout of protest tried to make its way up and out of his chest, but the weld song tamped it down, washing it away like a wave on the beach wiping the sand clear. There was no going back now, back to that life of pain. It was so much easier to go forward.

Come. This way.

Wilt's voice called him on, and he stumbled away from Heather's grip, eyes locked on the tunnel, on the shrouded black figure that stood there now, its clawed hands formed of a thousand twisting black welds, gesturing him onward.

Chapter 34

Lodan sighed heavily and leaned back from the window he had been staring out of, clasping one hand to the bridge of his nose and closing his eyes, silently ordering his mind to stop spinning. The constant surging and pulsing of the teeming crowds in the courtyard below were too much for him. He slowed his breathing, concentrating on holding himself still, in one place, in one time.

'You okay there, boss?' Griggs stepped into the room and dropped another pile of papers on Lodan's desk, his question rhetorical. 'Another batch for you to approve. We've had to clear out most of the western edge to make more room. Got patrols pulling down the city walls on that side as we speak. It's the older section, mostly rotting timbers anyway, shouldn't be too much of a problem.'

'Good,' Lodan answered without opening his eyes. 'I trust your judgement, you know that, Griggs.'

'So you should, so you should.' Griggs slid a chair over to the desk and slumped into it. 'Perhaps we should talk about a promotion while I'm here?'

'Don't push it. Have we heard from anyone actually in charge of this Redmondis army we're opening our doors to? Any news from Petron?'

'Actually, that's why I'm here. You see—'

Griggs's words were cut off by the sudden roar of beating wings and a massive gust of wind that sent all the papers in the room flying, the entire chamber instantly a white storm of noise.

Lodan did his best to clear the air in front of his face, stepping back from the wall with two handfuls of random pages as a body leaned in through the window from outside, hauling itself gingerly through the gap. As soon as it did so, the wind died away and the papers spiralling around the room gave in to gravity, the air clearing to reveal Petron smiling brightly back at Lodan and Griggs, both of them standing dumbfounded in the centre of the chaos.

'Greetings from Redmondis!' Petron strode over to Lodan and clasped his shoulder. 'I've always wanted to make an entrance like that.'

'What was …'

'Stax, my friend and temporary steed. Much easier to get through the crowds this way. Don't worry, he'll find somewhere to settle down that won't cause too much commotion.' Petron looked around the mess he'd made of the room and nodded. 'I see you've got things under control here.'

'We did for a time.' Lodan grimaced, realising he was still clutching twin fists of paper. He set them down on the desk and brushed his hands as though to remove a stain.

He peered back at Petron, a man he hadn't seen since before the attack, before all of this had fallen into his responsibility. 'You look … well, Petron. Younger, somehow.'

Petron grinned. 'The invigorating effects of flight!' He looked around the room, searching for a chair under the blanket of paper that now covered the chamber. 'Can't say the same for you, I'm afraid. I hear you had some trouble.'

Lodan rubbed the scar across his nose. 'You could say that.' He looked down at the desk, wiped it clear with one great sweep of his arm, and perched on its edge. 'I was sort of hoping you'd help explain what exactly did happen here. It seemed to be more your department.'

'Indeed.' Petron nodded. 'I think I have just the thing.'

He stepped to the side to reveal another person standing behind him—a child, no more than ten or eleven years old, his face and cloak covered in dirt. For an instant, Lodan thought it was another of his street rats, come to report in, but the boy looked back at him with pure black eyes and a chill spike of knowledge entered his mind.

'Lodan, allow me to introduce Shade.'

Lodan froze in place as he stared at the boy. There was something otherworldly about him, something more than the unnatural eyes. Something dark and dangerous and terrifying. A moment later, he made the connection. Captain Mont. He looked just like Captain Mont had. When he'd—

You know who I am, Lodan. You've seen me before.

The boy dropped eye contact and immediately Lodan felt himself relax, as though a great fist had realised its grip on his mind.

'I—'

'Shhh!' Shade whispered, holding one finger in the air. 'Do you not hear?'

The three men all looked at each other, at a loss for words. There was no sound except the usual commotion from the courtyard far below.

They watched as the boy strode across the room, angling his head as though listening. He bent down and snatched something up from underneath another pile of papers, holding it in his fist in front of his face.

'This. Petron, you must remove this.' He threw the object and Petron snatched it from the air. It was a stone paperweight, shaped into a cat's paw. Lodan recognised it as one of Captain Mont's belongings.

'Do you not hear it? It calls back to the past, where it was formed. To the east. To that place beyond time. Are your ears so stopped?'

Shade stood in front of them, his dark eyes flashing with anger, and Lodan had the uncomfortable feeling of being scolded by a parent. Even the boy's voice was different—older, and much more threatening.

'There is.. something. A crafter formed this,' Petron muttered, turning the stone over in his hands. 'It's familiar. I wonder …'

'Remove it. Destroy it. Ensure it does not befoul any more minds.'

Petron nodded and slid the stone into a pocket within his cloak. 'I will make sure it is destroyed.'

Shade stared back at him for an uncomfortable moment, then seemed to accept his answer and all tension left the room again, and it was just a young boy standing in front of them. Not five feet tall, and desperately in need of a wash.

Lodan was still looking back and forth between them, trying to understand what exactly was going on. 'Petron?'

'Yes, Lodan. You see, my friend here is much more than he seems.'

The small boy hopped up onto the window ledge and smiled back at them, kicking his legs in the air.

'You are wondering, perhaps, how we managed to move such a force all this way south so quickly? He is the reason. He is also the reason we were able to pass through the Tangle without a single incident, though that didn't stop most of my men spending a very nervous couple of weeks marching with those trees looming down on them from either side. Shade is a part of what we know as the Guardian of the Tangle.'

'Lodan has encountered me before,' Shade interrupted, still smiling. 'Though perhaps not directly. Tell me, Lodan, do you not remember the feeling of staring out at the Tangle from the high walls of Greystone? Wondering how much protection that great unending forest would give you? Do you not remember me staring back?'

Lodan didn't answer, but a flash of another, much darker mask morphed into place on the boy's face, and a thrill of cold fear gripped his mind. 'I remember,' he whispered.

'And you have seen flashes of my other self, leering back at you from another man's bloody face, moments before he smashed his head down onto your own and gave you that uncomfortable looking scar.'

'How do you—'

'All this has happened before, you know. A countless flow of lifetimes, swirling in chaos. We are but part of its cycle.'

'Um, Lodan? It doesn't look like you'll be needing me for a while, so I'll just head out,' Griggs piped up from the far corner of the room. Lodan had forgotten he was still there at all.

Shade glanced over at the man, freezing him with a look. 'Ah yes, Griggs. You, too, are familiar. More than familiar. Tell me, do you remember that night of shadow and flame, as the gloomclaws claimed your city? Do you remember the music of it? The song at the end of that dark tunnel?'

'That's enough!' Lodan shouted, and all three faces turned to him. 'That's enough. Griggs, you can go.'

Griggs didn't need any further encouragement. He was already halfway out the door.

'You do not need to torture the man,' Lodan whispered as soon as Griggs was gone. 'What is it that you want from us?'

'Want?' Shade seemed to consider the question, still kicking his legs back and forth like a dog wagging its tail. He moved to look out the window, sniffing at the air. 'Do you not smell it? The smoke on the wind. A great fire is coming. A spark that brings the flame of change. It has happened before, long ago. When the great forest that covered this world entire was set aflame, and only the raising of the stone itself could stop its spread. A tragedy beyond understanding, yet now forgotten by all except those whose roots run deep. So much lost.'

Shade turned back to them, his face serious. 'And now the leaks spring up everywhere. What was once contained within the borders of the Tangle has spread, even here. Dark shapes sliding up from the depths of time. Unbidden. Uncontrollable. Yet you have faced such a monster. Faced it down. Remember?'

The vision swamped Lodan completely, as though Shade had whispered a spell that took control of his mind, refusing to allow him to deny it.

He was standing at the edge of the roof, looking down at another skirmish that was reaching its inevitable conclusion.

A single creature had killed eight men, surging back and forth between them faster than thought. One man was left standing, his sword held hopelessly out in front of him, trying to hold his courage in what he knew were his final moments of life. It was Griggs.

Lodan watched, knowing he could do nothing but determined to bear witness.

The monster slowed, its shape still somehow dancing between forms as it moved toward its final victim.

No.

The creature stopped, aware of another voice.

No more. Not one man more.

Lodan stepped off the lip of the roof to land on the street below. He drew his sword and pointed it directly at the creature. 'Face me.'

The dark thing didn't turn exactly, but what might have been its face appeared on its back, as though it had morphed its shape. Twin clawed arms reached out from a central point, an opening that ripped wide to form something like a mouth.

Lodan stared at it, determined not to let the fear that welled up inside him rob him of all fight.

'No!' Lodan yelled, and he was back in his room, hands gripping the edge of the desk where he leaned, Petron and Shade staring back at him. 'No,' he continued in a normal voice. 'That wasn't me. That was Wilt.'

'Yes, it was.' Shade nodded, his smile wide. 'You see more than I had hoped.'

'Wilt?' Petron asked. 'What do you mean?'

'Wilt … took control of me. Somehow. Though he wasn't there. Hadn't been seen in the city for months. According to Heather and the others, he'd left even Redmondis by then. But somehow, he was there, inside me. Taking control. Leading my arm on. Helping me fight. Helping me save Griggs.'

'Wilt has learned to do more than simply wield those connections you call welds. Connections all living things share, Petron. He can ride them. Twist them. Weave them into something more. This is why the trees have always watched him, waiting for the spark to flare into flame. This is why my other seeks him out. They have journeyed far, your young friends. Travelled over that great green sea, that graveyard of the past. Even now they edge ever closer to the centre.'

'Petron, do you have any idea what he is talking about?' Lodan asked.

Petron simply shook his head, unwilling to interrupt.

'The past seeps into the present, leeching up through the soil. It has always been so, within the Tangle. Now the barriers have weakened, and the shadows have spread. Soon, all remaining barriers will be removed, and your forces will have their hands full in this city. There are many people here, many fears. Many minds to lead astray and latch onto.'

'You mean more gloomclaws? Like in Greystone?'

'Oh, much worse than that.' Shade smiled again and hopped down from the ledge. 'But I have done all I can here. It is time for me to return to the Tangle. Perhaps there will be a way to help turn the tide.'

'You're just going to leave us then?' Lodan protested. 'Abandon us to our fate?'

'It is the nature of the cycle. You humans must make your own stand here.'

Lodan was about to step forward and actually lay hands on the boy, but Petron grabbed his shoulder to hold him back.

'We understand, Shade. We thank you for all you have done.'

'It will not be enough.' Shade said, and the mask of a young boy dropped away. An aged, saddened visage stared back at them, and Lodan felt all hope leave him. It morphed again, and the dread and despair drained away, instantly forgotten. 'It is never enough. But perhaps it will help buy Wilt and the others some time.'

He turned back to the window, and the sound of beating wings outside told them Stax had returned, following some silent command.

'You must stay here, Petron. Stay and fight. We will not meet again, in this life. But you should know by now how unimportant that is.'

With that, the strange young boy leapt up onto the ledge and stepped through the window, disappearing into the sky with another flurry of wingbeats and a whirlwind of papers whipping around the room.

Chapter 35

A circle of stone figurines, falling one into the other, each face that of someone he knew, some character from his past. Some aspect of his story.

Higgs couldn't pull his mind away from the thought. It trapped him, holding him in place as he was dragged past the stone statues, too many of them now, too real. Calling to him from the past.

He willed his eyes to close and finally managed to squeeze them shut, but that only made the memory clearer, the vision taking him away again, refusing to be ignored.

Wilt leaned forward and pushed the nearest figurine. It toppled backward, clipping the one behind it, then continued to tip completely over, spinning around to return upright. Meanwhile, the piece behind had fallen as well, knocking the one behind that, and the one behind that, until a wave of motion pushed around the circle, the faces seeming to move as they passed before Wilt's eyes, one face grimacing in pain then smiling again. The pieces were so balanced that the wave continued around the circle, never ending, each piece falling and righting itself, falling and rolling back, using the momentum to always come around to standing.

'You see?'

The single face moved through its range of expressions, and Wilt suddenly recognised the features. They were his own.

Higgs gasped and pulled his eyes open; the statue in front of him leered down with Wilt's face, before the flickering light moved again and it morphed into someone else.

'Come. This way.'

Flame's voice was cold and distant, but her hand on his shoulder guided him along, refusing to be denied.

Higgs could barely stand now, the hot air inside the crowded chamber too thick to breathe, pushing him down, draining him of all energy. He tried to lift himself back up, but another statue loomed in front of him, as if the stone itself had moved to step into his path.

It was enormous—a muscled, armoured figure, his face cruel and leering with an evil greed. A hunger. Funes. It was Funes. Red Charley's right hand man in Redmondis, the man who had hurt Heather.

Funes bent down lazily and clapped him across the mouth with the back of his hand. The blow sent him sprawling again, and stars burst across his vision.

'Smart mouths get smacked.'

'Now, now, Funes, that's no way to treat our little guest here. Come, Higgs, sit up.' Red Charley pulled Higgs into a sitting position and patted him softly on the head. 'Funes is impatient, you see. Probably best not to anger him.'

Higgs's mouth twisted, ready for another reply, but he saw Funes had stepped toward Heather and the sight stilled his tongue.

'Now, what we want, Higgs, is information. Apparently, someone has been passing messages out to the traders, skipping the middleman. Skipping us. Wouldn't know anything about that, would you?'

Higgs shook his head and glared into Red Charley's eyes; they had a yellow glint to them, as though the whites of his eyes were sick.

'Wasting time.' It was Funes again. 'Hit him again.'

Clang!

Higgs's eyes snapped open at the noise, a clash of metal on metal that seemed to ring through his mind, shattering the vision and letting the shards fall to the floor. The statue had changed again, shrunk in size, though it still leaned over him, its eyes cruel and knowing.

He tasted blood, his jaw aching from the blow that could not have come.

He was lying on the rock floor, alone. Flame had let him fall, and he tried to pull his eyes away from the statue above him but it refused to let him go, leaning closer now, whispering its past into his ear.

Cortis. His eyes were alive with power and madness, scanning the room in triumph. He was flanked by two enormous wolves, glaring coldly out at the men. Waiting.

Human guards stood nervously around them, trying to stay stone-faced and passive, yet giving themselves away with small shifts of weight. To one side stood a row of Black Robes, beaten and broken in spirit, heads drooping and some swaying on their feet as if ready to collapse at any second. From this group, one was chosen, dragged in front of Cortis, who seemed to take an age to notice his presence.

Cortis stared through his victim at something only he could see, before reaching out his hand, grasping the young man by the chin, and whispering to him. The young man instantly stiffened, his head thrown back as if trying to break free from the rest of his body. A cry of anguish broke from his throat, and his body began to sink into itself, bones twisting and snapping with sickening wet thunks. A moment later, the young man was replaced by a large dog, whimpering slightly and shaking on four strange legs.

Clang!

Again the world cracked and fell away and he was back on the floor, the statue above him having moved away. His arms and legs ached, but they were still his own. He looked frantically around the room, trying to make some sense of where he was.

'I bring him to you as requested, now for your part.'

Flame. That was Flame's voice.

Higgs tried to blink the stars and tears from his eyes. There. Just metres away, standing in front of another statue, facing into the endless dark.

You have done well, child. He is awakened, so we will deliver as promised.

The voice echoed through his mind, sending him sinking to the floor with a whimper. The Novus.

'We are ready.'

You understand you cannot return. You must travel very deep.

'We understand.'

Very well. Gather yourselves. The journey will not be an easy one.

Higgs could do nothing but watch as the others stepped forward to join with Flame. A circle of nine figures, identical.

Flame turned toward him as they formed, pulling her hood up over her face so that only her cruel smile could be seen. 'Come, my sisters.'

She moved away from him, reaching out to twine her arm around her twin, and again he sunk into the depths of memory.

A ring of figures sinking out of the roiling chaos above. Nine hooded figures, arms interlocked.

—*The Sisters.*—

—*Yes. Watch.*—

The circle of women seemed to slow their descent, then stutter to a stop, as if unable to sink any further toward the ice surface below.

—*We nearly expended ourselves just getting this far. Nine minds stretched to the limits of their endurance and still did not succeed. It was unthinkable.*—

—*But how is this possible? The Nine Sisters are no more.*—

—*Where you are is a place beyond time. What you see is part of a memory, yet here, that no longer matters.*—

Suddenly another figure appeared, flashing into being right beside the stalled Nine Sisters. It was a figure seemingly composed of shadows, no feature recognisable except a vaguely human shape. It reached out and touched the nearest Sister on the shoulder, and the group sank again.

—*They knew of our presence, and our struggle, and they gifted us the power needed to proceed. The way to draw up the serpents from below, to bend them to our will.*—

—*But ... why?*—

Why indeed?

The voice of the Novus blasted all thought clear, and Higgs was once again alone on the stone floor, his chin pressed against the rock as though he had fallen from some great height. For a moment it was freezing, the ground a slick covering of ice, the barrier between the surface world and the nightmares below.

Stand up.

Higgs was pulled to his feet by an invisible force, his body no longer his own. The only parts he could move were his eyes, and he darted them left and right to try to catch a glimpse of Flame and the others, but they were gone.

You thought she was your friend? You have no friends here. None do.

Higgs's hands were pulled out in front of him, and he was spun in place, his toes lifting off the ground and his head pulling back as the centrifugal force threatened to wrench it free from his neck. Then, just as quickly, the spinning stopped, and he was left gasping, hands still held out in supplication.

Her task was to ensure you would rediscover your power. That you would deliver on a promise made long ago. That task is now complete, so she will be allowed back into the welds. Look up.

He had no choice but to raise his eyes again and lock on to the round lump of stone now sitting in his open palms.

Her journey is of no importance. She will tread the same path once again and come to the same end. But you—you are Stone. You can shape this living rock to your will. To my will.

The stone in his hand began to warm and warp around his fingers, melting into shape.

You know what it is I will.

Higgs could see the stone sliding into place, the rock stretching and curving into a long, thin shape. A knife. A blade. A weld blade.

He blinked and tried to pull his eyes away, but they refused to follow his command. The stone was already beginning to glow, a blueish light pulsing out against the darkness.

Do not resist the memory. You have seen this before. You have heard these words.

—Forged from the very power that forms the welds themselves. A tool for merging with, and severing, every connection possible.—

He strained against it, trying to force his mind away, down

other paths, out of the words from the past. Words spoken by Cantor Cortis, long ago. Words spoken to Wilt.

What you see as your strength is now your weakness. The connection you share is a chain binding your mind. A leash. You have come too far to slip it.

The weld blade was almost complete, the curving blade sharpening and a thin trail of shadow pulsing over it all as it settled into place in the surface world.

You recognise the blade, do you not? It is what you were born to forge. It is what led you here. What ended your other life.

Higgs knew the truth of it as the weld blade fully formed, its sudden weight pulling at his numb fingers as it slipped out of his grasp and fell to the ground.

At the last moment, another hand reached out to catch it. Long, dark fingers wrapped around its handle, and black ink leaked out to cover the blade entirely, until it was nothing but a blade-shaped hole in the world.

Higgs felt the grip on his mind release and finally lifted his eyes, rising up the long arm to stare into the familiar face that leered down at him, a cruel smile twisted across it.

'Good to see you again, Meat.'

A cold shudder of pain shook him as Red Charley thrust the weld blade into his chest, then he fell away from the world and into the endless dark.

Chapter 36

Come. This way.

Daemi stumbled forward, the words pulling her on into the dark. She had left Frankle with Heather, somewhere near the entrance to this tunnel, unable to resist the call any longer. The ground seemed to slope downward, tipping her into the darkness ahead. She could no longer make out the shape of the cat in front of her, no longer see even a flash of movement within the shadows to mark its passing. She was alone again. Alone in the dark.

No. Not alone.

She glanced back to try to mark where Heather and Frankle were, but the tunnel must have curved behind her as there was nothing back there to see. Just more empty blackness, as though she was floating within a dream, unable to wake.

Here.

Daemi felt the pull and let herself drop into it, the world sharpening into a flat grey landscape as Wilt's vision took over her own. She saw herself stumbling forward, one hand held out before her, eyes blinking wildly to try to capture what light they could. A wave of vertigo washed over her as she watched herself, trying to set one foot in front of the other while viewing from a third-person perspective.

The chamber opens here. Come.

The cat moved on and she saw the tunnel open out into a wide chamber. Tall, still figures were locked in place at its entrance, watching them pass. Immediately, Daemi drew her weld blade and felt a throb of power respond as her fingers clasped its handle. As soon as the blade was free, its blue glow lit the room and the statues in the room became clear.

Daemi reached out to touch the closest statue, unable to simply trust her eyes. It was cold, hard stone, shaped with great skill into the face of a man, but stone nonetheless. She stepped closer and looked into its sightless eyes, unable to shake the feeling that it was staring back at her from somewhere behind the stone.

Come. This way.

The cat had crept further into the chamber, and Daemi forced herself to break away from staring at the statue, holding her blade high now to light the way past the long line of human forms that stood there. Each face she glanced at sent another thrill of fear into her. They were disconcerting. Too lifelike, and something more, she realised as she examined each new face. They were … familiar.

That was it. She recognised these faces, though she could put no name to them. She had seen these people before.

'Wilt?' she managed to whisper, finding herself face to face with another statue. 'Wilt, do you recognise these?'

The cat didn't reply, and she kept on after it, past rows of statues now, the darkness beyond the blue glow of her blade seeming to churn them out in an endless stream. She stopped in front of a tall statue, unable to deny what she was looking at.

'Wilt? This … this is Lodan.'

There was no mistaking it. It was Lodan's face, from before the attack, before his nose was broken. Handsome. Knowing. A face straight out of her memory.

'I thought you would like that one.'

The voice echoed to her from the darkness, and immediately she felt the chill of the wraith taking form in answer to it.

'Long time, Meat. I'm pleased to see you've brought some friends along.'

That voice. It, too, was familiar. Daemi stepped away from the statue of Lodan to try to identify its source, and her lips formed the name even as her brain struggled to understand what she was hearing.

'Red Charley.'

'Oh, very good, young Captain,' the voice replied. 'Now where is our mutual friend?'

In answer, Daemi felt herself drop into the wraith's vision again, the shapes of the statues sharpening in its grey vision, a soft glow emanating out of each stone form against the dim background of the chamber.

The wraith scanned the room, but there were no more signs of life. Just the stone forms themselves, warmed as though a single candle of life flickered within each form.

'Would you prefer this form instead, Captain?'

Another of the statues sparked into life, the dull glow within it brightening to a blaze of life that threw every other form into shadow. Daemi turned toward it just as the wraith did so, both of them cutting toward the flare of light.

Daemi reached the statue first, feeling the chill of the wraith hesitate behind her as she reached it.

It was a tall, slim man, stone shaped into the form of heavy robes that covered most of its form, except its face and the familiar, twisted grin on its lips.

'Wrex,' Daemi whispered, her heart beating loudly inside her chest. 'Cantor Wrexley.'

'A favourite of mine also, you should know. Such a simple man. So easy to manipulate.'

A cold fury dropped over her at the words, and she felt the wraith respond, blinking past her to reach into the stone statue, grasping for the fire of life that burned inside it.

'As you all are, of course. Your connections to each other. The ties that bind your minds. Oh, there you are, Meat.'

The wraith seemed to form out of the shadows beside her as it reached into the statue and froze in place, as though the stone itself had pulled it up and out of the grey void of its world, locking its black hand within the stone of the statue.

'There now. That wasn't so difficult. Now if I could just—'

Daemi collapsed onto the ground as a fire of pure pain tore into her chest. She clutched at herself, half expecting her hands to come back dripping in her own blood, but there was nothing. It was not her pain she was feeling. It was Wilt's.

'You remember this feeling, don't you, Meat? Your friend does. Come. Come join him. Come surrender yourself to death.'

Daemi tried to raise her head again, but couldn't. The fire inside her chest seemed to burn every other feeling away, a torment of flame sucking down into cold emptiness as its fuel was consumed.

Her final vision was from Wilt's eyes, the grey shadows of the world dripping away into a red glow as he looked down at his chest and the black blade that had sliced into it.

'No!' Heather screamed as they stumbled along the narrow, dark tunnel. 'Frankle!'

She tugged at his cloak and tried to pull him along with her, the sudden thrill of dread that had lit her mind unable to be ignored. Higgs. It was Higgs she could feel.

He was dying. Again.

'Higgs?' Frankle whispered, falling away from Heather's grip to lie slumped against the rock wall. 'Higgs is here?'

'Can you hear him too?' Heather asked, head moving back and forth between Frankle and the tunnel ahead, calling her onward.

'I hear …' Frankle raised his eyes to Heather's, but they seemed to stare right through her to some invisible spot above and behind her head.

'Frankle, I have to go. He needs my help.'

Heather pulled at his shoulders, trying to arrange him into an upright position. 'Wait here. I'll come back.'

'Wait.' Frankle nodded, though his eyes still drifted away from her face. 'Wait here.'

Heather couldn't delay any longer. The rush of panic that had suddenly washed over her refused to be ignored.

She turned and raced on down the tunnel, one hand tracing the wall, following its curve until she was alone in the dark, no longer able to make out Frankle's shape in the passage behind. Guilt at leaving him behind pulled at her, but her step didn't slow.

Higgs. Higgs was here. She had to save him.

The passage opened suddenly into a large chamber and she almost charged straight into the first statue she encountered, just making out an ugly grinning face as she bounced off its chest and spun past it. More statues stood behind it, each of them seeming to step into her path as she tried to push past them, as though she were forcing herself through a living crowd. The dim red glow from the walls of the chamber sent strange shadows dancing across each face until she had to avert her eyes to stop the barrage of expressions haunting her.

The panic driving her only made it all worse. She just knew she had to hurry, had to get past this fresh obstacle. Had to find Higgs.

'It's a familiar nightmare, is it not? Rushing along, never quite fast enough.'

The voice came from everywhere, but Heather refused to allow it to stop her. She plowed on, pushing through the crowd of stone figures.

'Come now. Do you not recognise old friends?'

A new, larger statue loomed up in front of her, and Heather couldn't help but raise her eyes to its face as she pushed off it. A familiar, evil grin leered down at her, and her heart froze in her chest as she recognised it.

Funes. It was Funes. The guard who—

'Wasting time. Hit him again.'

'No.' Red Charley met Higgs's look with his own, as though they were locked in a private battle of wills. 'No, there's no point. Higgs grew up in Greystone, like me.' He stood up, but kept his eyes locked on the young crafter. A slow grin made its way across Red Charley's face as he finally broke eye contact and pointed at Heather. 'Hit her instead.'

Funes didn't need to be asked twice. He stepped forward and slapped Heather across the face with the back of his hand, knocking her head sideways. The two guards holding her staggered with the force of the blow, but kept her upright.

'No!' Higgs tried to struggle to his feet, but Red Charley kicked him back down.

Funes swung again, this time into Heather's body, doubling her over.

Heather gasped as she pulled back from the vision that had overwhelmed her. Her cheek stung as though it had just been slapped, and her stomach leapt and roiled as she gulped for air.

'Ah, you see? You do remember.'

Heather squeezed her eyes closed and tried to concentrate on getting her breath back. In and out. With each shaking gasp, the pain in her stomach faded into memory.

'Surely a crafter such as yourself can appreciate the skill involved in such work. No? Well then, perhaps something closer to home.'

Heather stumbled on, keeping her eyes on her feet, refusing to allow the voice to summon any more visions of the past to disarm her.

'Now, now. You'll miss all the fun.'

She stumbled then, her toe catching on some hidden outcrop of stone and sending her sprawling forward, just catching herself on her hands before her face met the stone floor. In front of her was another statue, this one stretched out on the ground, and she let out a whimper as she recognised it.

Higgs. It was Higgs, lying dead on the floor, a deep, black gash marking his chest where the death blow had fallen. Perfectly frozen in time.

She reached out slowly to touch the statue, her hands needing to feel the cold stone to convince herself it wasn't real.

'Never let them say I'm not a romantic.'

As soon as her fingers touched the statue, its chest heaved into life, a shuddering, choking breath wracking his form as Higgs opened his eyes and stared back at her.

'Huh ... Heather?' He coughed, a thin trickle of blood leaking out the side of his lips. He looked down at his chest and the sucking wound that marked it, hands waving hopelessly over it as his lifeblood poured out of him.

Heather sobbed as she spread her arms over him, wrapping him in a hug.

It was too late. She was too late.

'Now, young wielder. It is only you and me.'

Frankle started at the words, cracking his head against the rock wall he was slumped against as he woke.

'You, too, will prove useful. A new, willing vessel.'

The world around him seemed to shimmer and flow, as if he was underwater, trapped behind glass, unable to break out of its cage. He was drenched in sweat, the air close and heavy, pulling at his lungs as he tried to breathe.

'Trapped. Hot. Hiding in the dark. Yes, you remember.'

Frankle pushed at the air above his head, his eyes unseeing, trying to force back the blankets and cloaks that covered him. That he was hiding under.

Hiding like a coward.

'They've left you alone again, haven't they? Your so-called friends. Left you to fend for yourself.'

A heavy tramp of boots moved past him and he shied his head away, desperately wishing for invisibility to save him from the patrolling guards. Cortis's guard. Come to hunt him out.

If he could just stay hidden, stay out of sight. Unnoticed.

'Yes. Unnoticed. Unnoticed by all, including the one you most desire.'

He saw them then, Heather and Higgs. Lying wrapped in each other's arms. Oblivious to anyone else.

Hopelessness washed over him as he stared at them, unable to move, unable to shift his eyes away. Inside his chest, a tornado of anger and power began to turn, the roiling chaos of the depths calling to him. Calling him onward.

'I can give you the power to change all of this.'

A strong hand wrapped his shirt into a fist and lifted him from the ground, the vision of Heather disappearing to be replaced by a new nightmare staring down at him.

Cortis. Cantor Cortis was here.

'Yes, wielder. You could be just the thing.'

Cortis's glowing golden eyes locked onto Frankle's, boring into his mind. Behind them came a shout of anger and pain, and an irresistible vision overwhelmed him.

He stood in the circle of firelight, watching as Cortis reached out to each of them in turn, his hand a wolf's paw, a golden light shining in his eyes. As the paw touched his forehead, his mind became a whirlwind of animal urgency. He was aware of pain, of his body screaming as the limbs bent and bones twisted into foreign shapes. The pain was a vehicle of change, a new presence rushing in with it, a new form taking over his consciousness. He left any thought behind and became one of the circle. One of the pack.

Frankle gasped as Cortis raised his hand—his paw—and touched it against his forehead. A shock of agony threatened to wipe all consciousness away, but the storm still turning inside his chest welcomed it. Recognised it, and pulled it into itself, the anger and fury driving it burning all fear and pain away.

This was what he had been looking for. This was power.

'Yes, wielder. That is the way. Too long have you been ignored and pushed aside. Too long has fear controlled you. Limited you. Now, though, the time for fear has passed. Come, let us teach these others the true nature of the welds.'

The boy who had been Frankle stood up and shrugged his cloak from his shoulders, his head held high as he stalked down the tunnel, black weld blade clasped in his hand.

Chapter 37

Heather lay crying in the dark, her head resting on Higgs's still chest, desperately hoping to feel some movement beneath her ear to tell her he was still alive. That she wasn't too late. Not again.

His skin against her cheek was cold, and getting colder, the pores seeming to harden as she lay there until they felt like stone once more, like the statue that had thrown this nightmare at her was now fading into unliving form.

'Higgs?' she whispered, her voice very small in the encroaching dark.

Nothing. There was no longer any movement, and as she sat back and watched, she could see his skin hardening into stone.

'Higgs!' She shook his shoulder, but he was impossibly heavy now, and no effort of hers could make the slightest movement.

He was gone. He was lost once again.

'No.' Heather sniffed and wiped her nose on her sleeve. 'No. I won't let this happen again.'

She held her hands over the wound in the centre of his chest and closed her eyes. Instantly, she felt the familiar door inside her mind open, the path that she and Frankle had discovered to merge their skills into one and form weld blades. Later, they had used the same power to knit Daemi's wounds back together. Perhaps now she could use it to save Higgs.

She reached out with all her senses to try to grasp the power she could feel pulsing beside her. The power Frankle had always helped guide her toward. But now she was on her own, and she was no wielder. That roiling chaos stayed outside of her reach, teasing her.

Wilt. Wilt could help her. Where was he? Where was Daemi?

Heather opened her eyes and dropped her hands to her lap. It was useless. She could feel the magic there, but it would not respond to her call. So much for the powers of crafters. Little good her trinkets could do for them now.

Trinkets.

The heartstone!

Heather fumbled the necklace out from under her tunic and held the jewel out in front of her, the half-heart shape spinning slowly in the air. The heartstone. Higgs had worn the other half of it—had died wearing it—perhaps it was still there, inside of him. Somehow.

She stared into the spinning stone, trying to focus her mind on it. Block out all else and feel only the heartstone. Hear only its song.

As she concentrated, the first strains of the heartstone's song began to be heard. It echoed out from the walls of the chambers themselves, as if the entire mountain had become a sounding bowl, and in moments, there was no denying it. The song was clear and getting louder.

She held the heartstone directly over the wound in Higgs's chest, not knowing exactly why but trusting her instincts. As she did so, the weld song changed, the pitch of the song dropping and warping into a deeper, more sombre tone. Low and rumbling, until the chamber began to shake with it, dust and small rocks beginning to fall from the ceiling high above and clatter on the surrounding ground.

'Higgs,' she whispered, ignoring the growing turmoil around them. 'Higgs. Come back. Follow the song. Please.'

He shook the water from his hair and wiped his eyes. He squatted on a rooftop; the rain streamed down upon him, a heavy rain that had set in hours ago and showed no sign of easing. It cut visibility to only a few feet, but that was all he needed. Below him, huddled under a poor excuse for a shelter, lay his father.

He twisted the knife in his hands, the point digging into the callus on his index finger.

It would be so easy to end it here. To never have to feel the brunt of that man's anger ever again.

Do it.

No one would see, not in this weather. There would be no consequences.

Do it.

He leaned over the edge of the rooftop and eased himself down the wall, toward his waiting victim. His feet made no sound in the chaos of the storm as they splashed on the cobbled street, and he hunkered into a squat, eyes squinting up and down the alley to spy any witnesses. There was no one. It was just him. Him and his victim.

He turned back to the man lying stretched out under the loose metal sheet that served as a shelter, slowly letting his eyes move across the man's form, waiting for some final pull of guilt to stay his hand, but he felt nothing. Not even anger, just a cold stillness inside his chest. Waiting for him to strike.

He scurried forward to the man, blade eager now to get the job finished.

For the briefest moment, a snatch of music filled the air, as though a tavern door had swung suddenly open, letting the music from inside leak out into the streets.

Then he stopped. There was something wrong. Something wrong with the man's face.

It wasn't his father at all. No red hair, no heavy, heaving chest loudly sighing up and down with sleep. This was … a boy.

—Wilt?—

The voice seemed to come from everywhere, and he ducked into a crouch and flattened himself against the nearest wall, frantically looking back and forth along the alley to identify its source.

—Wilt. You know this is not your memory. Don't let it hold you.—

The rain thickened as he held one hand over his eyes, trying to pierce the gloom. There was no movement anywhere.

—Wilt. Look at me.—

A cold dread dropped over him as he realised where the voice was coming from. He looked at the body that had been his father—he had been sure of it—and now was someone else.

The boy lay perfectly still, no movement to his chest at all, as though he was already dead. He reached out with the toe of his boot and poked at it, but there was no response.

—Wilt. You must come back. Come back to me.—

Suddenly the body surged into movement, the boy sitting up and grasping his belt, pulling him off his feet and down, until he was face to face with impossibly black eyes that stared into him.

'We have to stop him, Wilt. We have to stop him.'

The sounds of the world died, and he was suddenly in a dark, silent tunnel. At the far end, a grey shape moved against the darkness, four legged, its curling tail trailing behind it. He moved toward it and it skipped further into the tunnel, into the dark.

Wilt hesitated, only just able to see the shape against the darkness.

—Higgs.—

His lips formed the word, but no sound came out. The shape turned toward him, however, answering his call.

—Higgs. It's me.—

The dark walls of the tunnel pulsed with power. A cold rush of air from outside the tunnel pushed against his face, as though death itself was calling to him. He took another step, slower now, bending down and holding his hand in front of him.

—Higgs. Stay here. Stay with me.—

The cat trotted silently toward him, head cocked as though listening, as though trying to understand his words. It stopped ten feet from him, and Wilt stopped as well, knowing any further movement would send it scurrying away again, into the nothingness that waited for it. Wilt dropped to his knees.

—Higgs. Please.—

The cat sat on its haunches and studied him, unwilling to come any closer.

Wilt finally understood what he needed to do. He slunk forward on four padded feet, and the smaller cat sprang toward him, twisting himself playfully around his friend.

Another breath sighed out of the tunnel, and both cats raised their heads, sniffing the air. It called to them.

No. There was something more. A change in the air, a new sound chasing out toward them. Music. And inside the music, twisted within it, was a voice.

—Higgs. Come back. Please.—

It was a girl's voice.

It was Heather's voice.

Both cats trotted toward the call, away from the cold, sucking dark of the tunnel. Away from nothingness and back into the light.

She stood very still between her parents, peering at the enormous armoured foot of the man in front of them, the man who towered even over her father, her father who was the second tallest man in the village behind Fern's, and Fern's father wasn't half as handsome.

Her father gripped her hand as he spoke to the strange man, quickly and urgently, squeezing her hand harder as he went, until she squirmed against the painful grip. He ignored her, lost in whatever it was he was trying to make the man understand.

Her mother stood silently, reaching out at one point and placing a hand on her hair, brushing it back from her face.

The strange man finally shook his head and took her hand from her father's. Her father resisted at first, then seemed to collapse into himself as he admitted defeat. Her hand was engulfed in the mailed gauntlet of the stranger, and he led her away.

She looked back and saw her father, tears running down his cheeks. He seemed so much smaller now, not tall at all.

—Daemi!—

'Father?' she called out, and the world shifted sideways. The hand holding hers dropped away, and she looked down at her palm, not recognising the hand that she stared at. It was ... enormous.

'Father?' Much quieter now, just a whisper as she flexed her hand into a fist and opened it again. It was her hand. It belonged to her.

—Daemi. Come back. You cannot change this.—

She looked up from her hand and stared back at her parents' cottage. The doorway was empty now, the timber door open and swinging slowly in the wind that whipped across the village, blowing dust up from the road and blooming tears in her eyes.

—Daemi. Please.—

That voice. She knew that voice. It didn't belong here.

—We need you, Daemi. I need you.—

Wilt. That was Wilt's voice.

Daemi sat up with a gasp and rolled to her feet, hand reaching instinctively for her blade. It was still on her hip, and as she drew it forth, the blue glow of the weld blade lit up the dank chamber.

All around her stood tall columns of stone, and instantly the memory of the statues came back to her. Living stone, shaped by her memories. Shaped by the Novus.

Well, that took a little longer than I thought.

'Wilt?' she whispered, still holding her blade out in front of her in case any of the columns decided to suddenly spring back into life.

In answer, the black cat trotted out from behind one of the columns and curled itself around her legs.

Still here. Just.

'Where is the Novus?'

Gone. Taken Frankle with him, and a bit more besides. We need to hurry.

'Frankle?' Daemi gulped. She should have been guarding him. She should have—

Come. We both got taken by surprise. This way.

Without waiting for an answer, the cat sprinted away, disappearing instantly into the shadows deeper inside the chamber.

Daemi hurried to follow, darting between the stone columns and refusing to look too closely at any one of them. 'Wilt?'

Here.

A dim blue light matching her weld blade leaked out from the opening to a tunnel ahead, and she saw the cat waiting for her, glowing claws extended and moving back and forth in the dark.

'Wilt, you sound … different.'

More human than I've been in a while—the Novus saw to that. Come. I can explain once we get back to Heather and Higgs.

'Higgs?' Daemi choked back any more questions and charged after the cat, chasing the blue glow through the long tunnel of darkness.

Heather sat very still, her eyes closed, and both hands held out in the air above Higgs's chest, fingers twitching slightly as she frowned and wrestled with the powers she was trying to bend to her will. It was much harder without Frankle there to help her, but she was determined not to fail. This wound would close, just as Daemi's scars had long ago back in Sontair. She would save him. She would not lose him again.

The black edges of the deep cut in the centre of Higgs's chest morphed and rippled with movement, pulling together then slipping back apart again, and Higgs gasped with pain, his eyes closed and mind elsewhere, but body still suffering at her hands.

It was no good. It was like trying to grasp water in her fist.

'Heather?' Daemi finally slowed her sprint as she followed Wilt into the room, trying not to balk at the sight of Higgs lying there right in front of her. He looked exactly as she remembered him.

Heather. You cannot stop this. That wound is beyond any of us.

'No!' Heather opened her eyes and screamed back at the cat, all of her frustration and pain boiling out of her. 'Not again. I won't lose him again.'

You cannot fix this.

'So help me! Use your wraith form to call him back. You did it once before!'

That was different. This … this is not Higgs. Not really. Higgs died in Redmondis. I held part of him back, inside the welds, but only part. It is a memory of what he once was. A piece of the whole.

'Please.' Heather's voice was now a choked cry. 'Please help me.'

Daemi looked back and forth between the two of them, the young crafter and the cat, its black eyes glowing strangely in the blue glow from her weld blade.

Her weld blade. Heather and Frankle had forged it. Perhaps …

'Will this help?' Daemi flipped the long knife in the air and caught the blade, holding it out hilt first toward them both.

The cat stared back at her and slowly cocked its head to the side as it studied the blade.

I … I cannot promise anything.

'Please,' Heather whispered.

We will need to do it together, Daemi and I. Hold the blade, Daemi. And when I tell you, slide it into the wound.

'The wound?' Daemi gulped. 'You want me to stab him some more?'

It is the only way. Even this may not work.

Daemi nodded and stepped forward over the body, keeping her eyes averted from Higgs's face. This would be hard enough as it was.

Ready?

The cat padded up beside Higgs and raised one paw onto his chest.

Heather. You will have to help call him back. And try not to get too close.

Heather shifted herself back from the body, wiping her face clear of tears.

Now, Daemi.

Daemi reached out tentatively with the blade, slowly poking it at the black wound in the centre of Higgs's chest. As soon as the blue blade touched the skin, the cat held its paw on the hilt and Daemi was almost thrown off her feet as the sword wrenched away from her, twisting itself free of her grip and disappearing wholly into the wound.

Daemi blinked, rubbing her sword hand as she tried to under-stand what had just happened.

Heather was there, as was Higgs's still form. But the cat. Wilt. Both he and the sword were nowhere to be seen.

They were down at the riverside, slinging rocks into the river for nothing more than fun. It was their usual hangout in the off hours, when Traders Way was too bare to bother with its pickings, or when they'd had a good score the night before and could afford to spend time just being boys again.

Wilt had a natural affinity with the sling; it was the first and only weapon he'd learned to use. The only one he'd ever felt comfortable wielding. Some of the other thieves had daggers and knives, but Wilt knew better than to carry that sort of hardware. If a guard caught you with one of those, you were sent straight to the dungeons for a week at least, and who knew what you'd look like when you came out. If you ever came out. A sling could quickly become a scarf or a belt when the guards caught up with you.

Of course, if they never caught up with you, that was something else entirely.

He'd been trying to impress Higgs with the advantages of the sling. All he'd need was a length of cloth, or even better, a belt or strap of soft leather. Then whatever he could find for ammunition; rocks in this case, rotten fruit more often than not inside the city walls.

He'd been pleasantly surprised by Higgs's ability to find good slinging stones, but when it came to wielding the sling itself, Higgs was taking some time to learn the basics.

'Argh!' Higgs screamed in frustration as his third stone went fly-ing straight up into the sky.

Wilt kept his eye on it as it arced above them. The last two had landed a little too close for comfort. 'You're loosing them too late.'

Higgs muttered something under his breath and bent down to grab another perfect stone.

'What was that?'

'Nothing.' Higgs spun his sling quickly and loosed his stone, this one splashing into the water at his feet.

'Too early.'

'Thanks, genius, I hadn't noticed.'

'Don't get angry with me. Just focus on what you're doing. You'll get it eventually.'

Higgs muttered some more insults under his breath and bent down for another stone.

—The perfect stone. Perfect weight. Coming straight to my hand.—

Wilt smiled to himself and gazed over the river, toward the far bank where the Tangle waited, its green depths silently swaying. Beckoning to him. A shiver ran up his spine. The Tangle. Wild and unknown. Growing ever closer to the walls each year, waiting to consume the city.

Another splash, this time a few metres out into the river, pulled his thoughts away and told him Higgs was beginning to find his range.

—Stone. I am Stone.—

Wilt began to spin his sling. 'Whenever you're ready.'

Wilt heard his own quiet tone as though he was listening to someone else. The world seemed to have shut down, all outside noise and movement slowing into a low murmur beneath him. All that he was aware of was the sling moving in his hand, his senses stretched and waiting.

Then there was something more. It was as though he could feel the green of the Tangle waiting for him to act, the breath of the trees held in the silence of the moment, holding the world still for him.

The stone flew high out over the river. Wilt watched it move in slow motion, its arc clear. It was almost like he read it; no thoughts— stones couldn't have thoughts, could they?—but the action itself. As though each movement was preordained and therefore obvious. All he had to do was play his part.

For a long moment he waited, enjoying the sense of the world around him slowing, the universe pausing for him, only him—a taut drum waiting to be struck.

He loosed his stone with another low grunt and the world sped *back up to life. The sounds of the river, the birds high above and the wind in the trees where the Tangle waited—it all came back in a rush as his rock speared toward the other and met it with a crack, shattering it in mid-air, bits of rock showering into the river.*

Higgs let out a yell of triumph and jumped in the air. Wilt studied the ripples in the water where the rocks had landed, a strange calm having settled around his shoulders.

—Ripples. Ripples of the rock that fell.—

Wilt turned back to the shore to see Higgs standing there, waiting for him. But there was something different about him now, something … other.

'Higgs?'

Higgs didn't answer, didn't seem to hear him at all. Instead, the boy looked down at his hand and the strangely glowing blue blade that it now held.

'Higgs, what is that?'

Wilt's voice was fading, drowning in the sudden music that seemed to fill the world, wiping all other noise away. 'Higgs?'

'Stone,' Higgs answered, finally looking up from the sword and staring back at Wilt with twin black eyes. 'I am Stone.'

'Higgs. Please. Come back.'

'Heather,' Higgs answered, staring up at the sky as though addressing some hidden god.

'Higgs. Please.'

'I … I know what I need to do.'

Higgs flipped the blade in the air, catching the hilt at arm's length and closing his eyes as he thrust the blue blade directly into the centre of his chest.

Chapter 38

The boy who had been Frankle stalked along the passage, black weld blade swinging from his right hand, his eyes blazing gold in the dim red light that filled the stone tunnels. He walked on without thinking, his feet knowing the path, his mind elsewhere, in other realities, other possibilities.

A tall pair of Incarnate appeared in the tunnel ahead and froze as they recognised what was approaching.

The Novus. The Novus had taken another vessel. That meant the time was almost ripe.

'You two. Head to the Pit and ready as many as you can find. All of them. We leave as soon as I make the final preparations.' He was past them by the time he finished barking the orders and didn't pause in his stride to make sure he was obeyed.

There was no reason to. No doubt of his power here. Not now.

He raised the weld blade to his face as he walked, the black blade shimmering like liquid shadow as it moved.

With this blade. With what it now held. There was no limit to his power anywhere. There would be no one to stop him now.

The others—the wielder and his friends—they were either dead already or near so. Lost in their own dreams and memories, unable to break free of the chains that wrapped around their minds. A suitable end for such weaklings. Let them see what good their precious friendships would do for them now.

He stopped as he felt the slightest tug of protest at the pit of his skull. The boy he had taken, the young wielder, he was not yet fully consumed. Fighting back, squirming in place inside the depths, but unable to rise. He, too, would fade with time. He, too, would become dust and memory.

He held his arms out and looked over himself. Yes, this vessel would do nicely. It would last at least another fifty years before he would need to find another. Perhaps by then it would not be necessary. Perhaps by then this entire world would have faded into smoke.

He closed his eyes and smiled at the memory painted on the backs of his eyelids. Flames. Flames everywhere, fifty feet high and roaring like a living beast as they sucked all the oxygen from the air. Burning the trees, pushing them back, wiping out the lives and memories they held. Purifying the world.

Yes. They had come close the last time, so long ago now. They had come close but been foiled by the raising of the Spine. Now, though, there would be no one to stop them. No one to resist their march.

He let himself enjoy the thought for a full moment before opening his eyes once again. Ahead, the tunnel stretched into the distance, winding its way down into the heart of the mountain. He raised the weld blade again, letting the inky darkness slice through the surface world in front of his eyes.

There was no need to walk. Not now. Not with what he held in his hands.

He smiled as he realised what his body was aching for him to do. Slide back into the grey shadow realm, beyond life. Beyond death. Beyond time itself.

It had been so long.

The red light of the tunnel dimmed even further as the wraith seemed to burst out of the body that had been Frankle; the moist, steaming air freezing in place around it and dropping to the ground in the sudden chill, ice shards shattering as they hit the stone floor to leave a thousand sparkling jewels in its wake.

Inside the main chamber of the Pit, all was chaos. Long streams of shuffling figures snaked out from the central pool, some of them still clutching the buckets and tools they had been carrying when the Incarnates commanded them away from their menial tasks. They were beyond questioning any order, beyond even the glimmer of curiosity this new occurrence might provoke in any mind not completely broken and controlled. They simply followed where they were led, joined with their fellow workers in whichever long line they were directed to, and stepped forward in time with the others.

In the centre of the room, under the loftiest peak of the cavernous ceiling that stretched up into the shadows high above, beside the large swirling pool of mud that dominated the chamber, a massive stone throne had appeared. It had been raised with a word and a gesture by the Novus, called into life from the living stone of the mountain, and now the boy who had been Frankle sat upon it, eyes scanning the room, black blade twirling slowly in his hands.

He watched the dullards shuffle in their lines, watched the slow spin of the mud inside the pool, watched the Incarnates herd their charges back and forth without ever raising their eyes to face him. It was so tempting to slip back into the wraith form, back into that slice of pure pleasure between the worlds of the living and the dead, where he could simply reach out and snuff any flame of life out in a moment, savouring the rush of pain and memory that death carried with it. Drinking it in and discarding the husk.

Time. There would be time enough once the task was done. Time enough to indulge all such urges. Time enough until there was only one left standing. The Novus.

'Sire.' The bowed head of an Incarnate crept toward the foot of his throne, hands held out in something resembling a mix of a bow and a curtsy. 'Sire, the first of the … subjects are ready for you.'

'Good. Bring them to me one at a time. Those whom I judge worthy are to be led directly to the pool. From there we will make our final journey.'

'And those who are unsuccessful?' the Incarnate asked, his voice dropping into a whisper.

'They will remain here. Let them re-join the mud from which

they were formed.' The Novus waved at the Incarnate in dismissal. 'Now move, before I consider you an example worth setting.'

The Incarnate was gone instantly, disappearing into the crowd and hurrying away. The Novus watched him leave, then raised his right hand to his face, turning it back and forth in front of his golden eyes.

Such a small thing. So young and supple. It was almost a shame.

He closed his eyes and dived into the memory.

Cortis sat alone in his tent, his eyes closed, listening to the sounds of activity in the camp. Soldiers marched back and forth, breaking down the tents, moving quickly, not wasting any effort. Only the best of the guard was still here. His personal selections. Those who would not question any order.

He opened his eyes and looked at his right hand, cupped in his left, his long fingers curled into claws. He turned his hand over, and for a moment, in the flickering light of the fire, his nails were long and yellow and no longer human.

The Novus opened his eyes and looked down at the hand he now held in his lap. It was changed, no longer young, no longer human at all. Now it was the lanky, grey limb of a wolf, long yellow claws curling out from the tips of its fingers.

Yes. This would do nicely. The last vessel he had taken did leave some usefulness behind. Who knew what this new one would provide in time?

The first of the potentials was led to the foot of his throne and thrust forward, catching himself as he fell to avoid smashing his face into the base of the throne. The Novus leaned down and caught the man's chin with his left hand, cupping it and bringing him face to face with his own.

'You. I know you.'

The man seemed barely capable of thought, his eyes moving back and forth without control, his low brow knotted in confusion.

'Come. Join with me. Join my pack.'

The Novus placed his misshapen right hand on the man's forehead and a howl of pain and fury surged into his mind, blasting all other thought clear, and carrying with it a command that could not be ignored.

The man gasped in agony as his body collapsed into its new shape, and in moments, a large wolf stood before the throne, the only sign of the man who had been there a tattered rag that had once clothed him.

'Good,' the Novus whispered, reaching out to pat the wolf's head. 'Join your brothers.'

With that, he dismissed his new servant and turned to the next potential.

It was much easier this time, in this place. These minds were so much more malleable than the ones in Redmondis. Their connections so much easier to sever.

He raised his eyes once again to survey the crowded chamber. Within hours, his new army would be large enough, strong enough to take through to Sontair. Razing the city would merely be a formality. And then … so many more minds to taste. To drink from. To squeeze and break until nothing else remained. No one else.

Just him, alone.

As it should always have been.

Higgs sat up with a gasp, hand clutched to the centre of his chest and the wound that he knew should be there. But there was nothing. No blood, no pain. Just his thin shirt covering his skinny chest, his heart inside it still hammering hard in response to a blow that had never fallen.

'Easy there, remember to breathe.'

For a terrible moment, he thought he was back in the cell, coughing up frozen water and trying to get his lungs to remember how to function as his jailer thumped him on the back, but then he blinked and looked around and realised who it was that had spoken to him.

'Daemi?' He coughed, his chest still not entirely convinced it wasn't wounded.

Before Daemi could respond, he was flat on his back again, another body having flown into him and sent him sprawling in a whirlwind of long hair and choked sobs, arms squeezing him and eager hands patting him all over as if to make sure he was really there. He managed to push the body back up from him far enough to make out Heather's face, but then she leapt onto him again, smothering his face with kisses.

'Argh!' he protested, struggling to breathe under the onslaught.

'Um, Heather?' Daemi interceded. 'Perhaps you should give him some room to breathe?'

He wasn't sure Heather was going to listen, but after a few more moments and at least ten unwanted quick pecks on his cheeks, she finally seemed to tire of her ministrations and sat back, eyes glowing above tear-streaked cheeks.

'Higgsy,' she whispered, wiping her face clear.

'Don't start that again,' Higgs complained, shifting from under her and looking around. They were still inside the mountain, the dull red glow of the rock walls told him that well enough.

'Higgs? Perhaps you can explain how you're here? Alive, I mean?' Daemi smiled.

'Yes, that.' Higgs nodded and pulled himself into a sitting position. 'That's … kind of a long story.'

Now is not the time. We have to stop the Novus.

All three turned to look at the cat that had addressed them.

'Wilt?' Higgs asked, though he knew it had to be. He knew that voice better than anyone. He had spent long enough inside Wilt's mind.

'He's right.' Daemi bent down and pulled Higgs to his feet. 'Can you walk?'

'I can try.' He pushed Daemi's arm away and took a couple of halting steps toward the closest stone wall. 'Everything's numb, but it all seems to still work.'

Come then.

Wilt didn't wait for them, darting off down the tunnel like a black streak.

'Are you sure?' Daemi reached out to Higgs again, but he brushed her away with a nod.

'I'll help him,' Heather offered, stepping past Daemi without a moment's hesitation.

'No, it's okay. I can—'

'I insist.' Heather looped her arm inside his and moved close, squeezing their bodies together.

Higgs tried to wriggle his way out, but Heather was much stronger than he remembered.

'Okay then.' Daemi grinned and turned away. 'Just try to keep up. We don't have time for any long reunions.' With that, she charged after the cat, her long strides echoing down the tunnel.

Higgs watched her go and gulped, suddenly not so sure of himself.

'Come on you.' Heather squeezed his arm again and pulled him along. 'And stay close. I'm not letting you out of my sight again.'

Daemi allowed herself about fifty metres before she slowed her run to a jog. She knew Heather and Higgs would want a bit of space— Heather especially—but she didn't want to leave the two of them too far behind. This place had produced enough strangeness for her liking already; who knew what fresh dangers might spring out of the shadows?

'Wilt?' she asked the darkness as she slowed down.

I'm here. Just around the next bend.

'I'm trusting you to give me some sort of warning before we stumble into any more trouble.'

Of course.

Daemi could only just make out the voice now, and she reached for the weld blade on her hip to try to amplify the connection between them as it seemed to do, but her hand found only an empty scabbard. 'Oh. I don't suppose you have another weld blade somewhere there?'

'Fraid not.

'Because I'm not much use without a sword. And you seemed to indicate before that the wraith form wasn't going to—'

Not now. The Novus took it.

Daemi walked around the long bend in the tunnel and could see a brighter orange glow emanating from another chamber further ahead. 'Took it? How is that possible?'

She wasn't really expecting an answer, but a moment later the cat appeared in the centre of the tunnel, sitting quite still and obviously waiting for her.

The welds. They are more than just connections between minds. They are … everything. And when that power is combined into a weld blade, it can be used to do more than just kill.

Daemi slowed as she approached the cat, but there was no movement to be seen in the tunnel further ahead. 'Is that—is that how Higgs is here?'

Wilt tilted his head as though weighing her words.

Yes. When he was … when he died, in Redmondis. It was a weld blade that killed him. It took some part of him, his essence, and I used that to hold him back from the long silence of death. Used the wraith form to capture him and hold him inside my mind. Then later, in Sontair, when the Novus found me and locked me inside the ice beneath the surface world, this connection was the reason we could escape. Higgs came here, to where the weld that the Novus used originated, and he took my human form with him.

Daemi stopped and tried to understand exactly what she was hearing. 'He … took your form?'

You have to understand. The Higgs we left back there, that isn't really him. It's a part of him. A reflection of a reflection, but it's not the same boy you knew in Redmondis. It's what I managed to hold on to, what helped keep me sane those long weeks inside the Tangle, but it's not really him. Heather—

'I think she knows,' Daemi confirmed. 'I think she's known all along that she can't really bring him back.'

Yes. It's … cruel, what I've asked of her. But it is necessary.

'But then, when the Novus attacked you—'

He stabbed me with the weld blade, sucked that power into himself just as my wraith form would suck the life from a living being. Our shared connection was what saved me—saved you as well, I expect—otherwise we'd all be lost in the memories of this place. Echoes of the past.

'And Higgs?'

He knows what he is. He knows more about this place than any of us. We brought him the weld blade and he used that to bring himself back, but I think he knows that it is only for a short time.

A loud crash of steel and falling stone shot from the chamber ahead, the noise of it roiling and filling the tunnel like shockwave.

'How much time do any of us have?' Daemi muttered.

Enough to stop him. Stop the Novus before he uses the powers he took from us to hurt anyone else.

'Daemi?' Heather's voice called out from further back, and Daemi could just make out the two forms shuffling through the shadows toward them.

'Well, I hope you have some sort of plan. Two lovebirds, a cat, and an unarmed soldier are not going to get this done.'

Oh, we have more than that on our side. Come.

Heather struggled along the tunnel, her shoulder aching where she bore Higgs's weight trying to keep him on his feet, her breath rasping in and out of her throat, and her head nodding as her exhaustion turned to wooziness, but her heart sang. Higgs. She had found him. Had brought him back. Was holding him against her right now!

Higgs.

'Higgs?' she asked, trying to keep the strain out of her voice.

'Yes?'

'Do you … do you still have the other half of the heartstone?'

Heather wasn't sure why she asked, wasn't sure exactly why she wanted to know at all, but as soon as the thought occurred to her, she knew it was important.

'Yes. I do. But not like—'

'Like this?' She smiled and drew the necklace out from under her shirt to dangle in front of their faces.

'Yes. I mean, no. I don't have it like that.' Higgs pushed against her and straightened, trying to stand on his own two feet. 'It's much smaller than I remembered.'

'You see?' Heather grinned, nudging him with her shoulder before she knew what she was doing and almost sending him straight into the wall. 'It wasn't such a bad thing, was it?'

Higgs caught himself with a hand on her shoulder, then patted it awkwardly. 'No. It wasn't.'

He returned her smile then, and Heather felt her heart leap inside of her chest.

'You know, I've been hearing that song since I woke up in this place.'

'The heartstone song?'

'Weld song.' Higgs said. 'It's everywhere here. Or perhaps it's just inside me all the time.'

'Weld song. That's what Frankle called it.' The thought of Frankle tried to jam its way inside her happy glow, but she refused to allow it.

'Yes. Frankle.'

They both continued on, lost in their own thoughts for a moment.

'You know—'

'I—'

They both stopped and grinned again as they interrupted each other.

'You first,' Higgs said.

'Okay.' Heather took a deep breath. 'You know it was very mean of you to just disappear and—'

'Die?'

'And get yourself killed like that in Redmondis.' She squeezed his arm against her chest again. 'It wasn't easy.'

'I know. I'm sorry.' Higgs nodded, then grinned wickedly. 'Did you have a funeral?'

'No! I mean, not anything official. It was all very frantic at the time. The Sisters leaving. Cortis dying. Wilt seemingly vanishing.'

'And taking me with him.'

'Yes. Yes, he did that, didn't he?' Heather let the silence stretch before turning to face Higgs with the real question. 'How did he do that, exactly?'

Higgs reached out to trail his fingers along the rock wall of the tunnel and shook his head.

'I'm not sure I know. But—' He hurried to continue in the face of Heather's expression. 'But I can take a few educated guesses.'

'Okay then.'

'I think … I think it was the weld blade. The one that killed me. You know them, don't you? You know how they're formed.'

'How did you know that?'

'It was something in Frankle, when I saw him here, in my cell. He was so much like Wilt, what I remember Wilt being anyway, the same expression on his face. The same … blankness. And then later, when the Novus had me, he forced me to form my own weld blade. Then killed me with it again.'

Heather watched Higgs's face as he talked, unsure whether she should say anything to interrupt or just let him empty it out.

'It … Dying doesn't feel like you think. Like I thought it would, anyway. You hear stories, growing up, about your life flashing before your eyes and everything, but it's not like that. It's like … a pool. Like you just fell into a deep, cold pool of water, and all around you are snippets, scenes from your life, and if you could just move your arm to grab one of them, you could be back there. But you can't.'

Higgs smiled at Heather's expression. 'I don't mean to sound scary and dramatic. There's no fear, exactly. Not for me, anyway. There was just … frustration. I kept trying to reach out, trying to grab those pieces of my life, but I couldn't. Then something grabbed me instead.'

'Wilt.'

'Yes … and no. I don't think he could have unless the weld blade had landed the final blow. It took me first. Drank my entire life up in a second. Wilt just has a bit more access to that power than anyone else.'

'He said you took something from him … in Sontair. His human form.'

Higgs nodded, but continued on for a few steps before speaking again. 'I think he's right. This—' He held his arms out, looking himself up and down. 'This looks like me … feels like me … but it isn't me. Not really. Look.'

He offered his hand out palm first and Heather took it, not knowing what else to do.

'Look at the skin,' Higgs prompted. 'Notice how soft it is? How smooth? Like a newborn baby.'

Heather could feel a deep rumble inside her chest that she didn't want to acknowledge, but she examined his hand as he asked. He was right. The skin was impossibly soft.

'Like I haven't lived a day in my life.'

'But then—'

'It's this place, you see. The Novus himself. This fortress, this rock, this mountain is … more than a physical place. It's a reservoir of memory. Countless lives and stories locked inside this stone. That's what the welds are, I think—the connections between us all. The Novus reads them, sucks them in, moulds them with living stone. Just like he did with me.'

It was growing now, the ache inside her chest. Part of her knew what it was, but she shoved that thought away before it could form.

'I think he tried to capture Wilt, back in Sontair,' Higgs continued. 'Set a trap and sprung it, only for Wilt to slip away and leave me here in his place. So, he used me as bait instead.'

Higgs scowled and kicked a loose stone at their feet somewhere off into the shadows. 'It worked too. Now he has the weld blade I made, Wilt's wraith form, and Frankle, who is a lot stronger than most people think.'

Heather swallowed, trying to force the tightness in her chest away. It wouldn't fade, but she looked at Higgs's face again and consciously let the pain go. Released it to fly and land where it would. It wouldn't control her. Not anymore.

'But you're still here, Higgs. We're still here. And we're going to stop him.'

Chapter 39

The surface of the water in the viewing bowl rippled and bent as Petron's breath pushed down upon it, his eyes searching through it as he tried to will the water to show him something, anything, of what was happening to the others. Daemi. Heather. Frankle. Wilt.

Perhaps even Higgs, he mused as he gave up and sat back with a sigh, the ripples in the water reaching the edge of the bowl and bouncing back into themselves to send his reflection shimmering up at him, his elderly features the only image the waters deigned to show him.

'Petron?'

He turned toward the voice in the doorway, pushing the viewing bowl back to the far edge of the table and covering it with a cloth. 'Lodan. Come in.' Petron smiled as Lodan edged inside the doorway of the queen's study and stopped just a step inside. 'Still bothers you?'

'What?'

'This room. Where Captain Mont—I should say, whoever was controlling him—attacked you.'

'Oh.' Lodan grinned sheepishly and ducked his head. 'That obvious, is it?'

'It's perfectly understandable.' Petron slowly stood up from his chair and leaned backward to try to loosen his aching spine. 'Actually, I know the feeling well.'

'I still have the nightmares. Every night. Always the same. The golden, staring eyes looming over me. Then the smile. That twisted, evil smile.'

'Nightmares are familiar to me as well, I'm afraid. To all of us who have faced the darkness. That reminds me.'

Petron reached into his cloak and brought out a rag, then opened it on the table and spilled the stone cat's paw onto its surface.

'Is that—'

'Yes.' Petron nodded, poking the side of the stone figure with one covered finger to spin it in place. 'The paperweight from your office. Much more than that, of course.'

'Didn't the Guardian tell you to destroy it?'

'Oh yes. I'm open to any suggestions you have in that regard. Look.'

Before Lodan knew what was happening, Petron reached across the table and grabbed a heavy metal mallet, rearing back and smashing it hard onto the stone. There was a loud crack of steel on stone, and a bright flash of light that sent stars spinning across Lodan's vision, but once his eyes had cleared, the cat's paw still sat on the table, seemingly completely unharmed.

'Impressive, isn't it?' Petron mused, using the hammer to poke at the paw now, turning it slowly in place. 'Haven't even chipped it.'

Lodan stepped forward, his previous nervousness forgotten in the face of this new mystery. 'Perhaps if you—'

'Don't touch it!' Petron cried as Lodan reached for the stone, his hand freezing in place before it got any closer. 'Don't touch it, please.'

Lodan dropped his hand and nodded, then leaned forward to peer more closely at the stone. 'It's … very lifelike, don't you think? There's something about the shape of it—it almost seems to move.'

Petron dropped the cloth over the stone and slipped it back into some hidden pocket inside his cloak. 'Yes, I noticed that as well. That's part of its power, I think. It draws you in. Fascinates you. Then leads your mind away.'

'Away?'

'Like Captain Mont.'

Lodan's expression darkened again, and he ducked his head to stare at the base of the wall across from them, where a deep brown stain still marked the stone floor. 'Cleaners aren't doing such a good job in here.'

Petron followed his eyes, then reached out to pat Lodan's shoulder, spinning him back away from the bloodstain as he did so. 'Oh, don't blame them. I never let any of them in here. Too much to lose. Come.' He squeezed Lodan's shoulder and led him to another, smaller table toward the rear of the room. 'Have some tea.'

Petron didn't wait for an answer and started to fuss with the tall teapot. 'Shouldn't be too cold yet. I only brewed it a little while ago.'

Lodan slumped onto the stool Petron had just vacated and sighed, watching the old man work. *He moves faster than you do now*, he thought, and scowled to himself, angry at his own self-pity.

'And have you found anything useful in here?' Lodan asked.

'Oh, yes.' Petron turned and flashed him a knowing grin. 'Now if only I understood half of it, we might get somewhere.'

Lodan nodded wearily and looked around the room, stacks of scrolls and papers piled haphazardly across every surface, leaning towers of thick tomes looming over them. And at the rear of the room, the broken stone conduit. 'No luck at all?'

Petron handed him a steaming cup of a very strange smelling tea. 'The conduit, you mean? I've been thinking about that. Look.'

He reached into his cloak and brought out the rag with the cat's paw in it again, holding it up against the border of the conduit. To Lodan's eyes, the stone paw seemed to disappear completely, its colour exactly matching that of the conduit behind it.

'It's the same?' Lodan asked.

'From the same place, surely. And that's not all.'

Petron moved the paw slowly around the border, not letting it touch the stone but hovering just above its surface, until the paw seemed to leap out of his hand and stick right in the centre of one of the square carved panels, as though glued in place.

'Magnetic.' Petron smiled, as though that answered all possible questions.

'Magnetic? But I thought only—'

'Only metal could be magnetised. Not so, but magnetic stone is unusual.' Petron used the rag to twist the paw off the surface of the conduit with some effort and wrapped it back up. 'And now you see why I haven't been in such a rush to discard this little curio just yet.'

'Why only that part of the conduit though?'

'Exactly! You see this carving, a mountain of fire, or a volcano, or ... something. I think that's where the paw came from.'

'It's a place?'

'I think so. All these markings are, I think. See here—this fortress under a mountain. That's Redmondis.'

'But ... there are so many of them.' Lodan peered around the border of the conduit. There were at least ten individual tiles on each side of the border, each with its own carving.

Petron watched him think, sipping quietly at his tea. 'There's a good deal about this world we no longer understand. Perhaps we never did.'

Lodan leaned back again and brought his tea to his lips. 'Someone knew once. Someone made these.'

As his lips touched the tea, his eyebrows rose in surprise, and he sighed in appreciation of the sudden wave of relaxation the tea gave his mind.

'Good, isn't it?' Petron smiled. 'An old recipe a friend of mine once showed me. I've found it particularly useful lately. Helps keep the nightmares away, too.'

Lodan grunted and downed the tea in one gulp, ignoring the sear of pain it brought to his throat. 'Well, I could definitely use that. But this isn't merely a social visit.' He placed the teacup back on the table and wiped his hands on his thighs, as though readying himself for an unwanted chore. 'I'd like you to come inspect the troops with me. There's something I think you ought to see.'

Petron nodded and put his own cup down. 'Very well. Lead the way.'

Five minutes later, they were standing on a short balcony above the main courtyard of the castle, the space below filled with drilling soldiers and black-robed wielders, each armed guard partnered by an individual wielder.

Petron watched them move for a few moments, then turned to Lodan in surprise. 'You have them working together?'

'That's what I wanted to show you. It wasn't my idea, by the way. Griggs!' He shouted the last at his friend standing directly below the balcony, hands on hips and surveying the training like a drill master. 'Griggs, come up here a second, would you?'

Griggs nodded and ducked inside the building to hurry up the stairs.

'Griggs pointed it out first,' Lodan continued as they waited. 'Said it just made sense as soon as he saw how the wielders moved.'

'Indeed.' Petron's eyes hadn't left the soldiers and wielders below him. Lodan was right; each pair seemed to move together, as though following some silent music.

'Yes, boss?' Griggs panted as he reached the balcony, nodding to Petron in greeting.

'Tell Petron what you told me. About the wielders and soldiers,' Lodan ordered.

'The dance,' Griggs said, then hurried on as he realised they were waiting for him to continue. 'I mean … the way they work together. It was actually the boy—the Guardian, I mean to say—in your room the other day. He mentioned something about a song, and it stuck in my head for hours afterward. Couldn't budge it. Then, when I took a few of the new wielders in to see what the Sontair soldiers could do, it was like they each knew what to do already. The wielders seem to bind with each guard, though only the ones with weld blades. And there really was music in the air, though as soon as I tried to focus on it, it would drift away …'

'We're working on getting everyone armed appropriately, by the way. Thanks to your Redmondis crafters, of course,' Lodan interjected.

'It speeds them up, makes each soldier incredibly fast. Faster than anything I've seen except—' Griggs stopped and looked at Lodan.

'It's okay, Griggs,' Lodan said. 'Petron knows all about it.'

'Except in Greystone, when Lodan saved me from the gloomc-law. That was the fastest I've seen anyone move ever.'

'And that, as you know, was Wilt,' Lodan finished for him, turning to Petron. 'It's like each wielder and guard are making the same shared connection Wilt did with me. Though how he did it when he wasn't there physically is still a mystery.'

'Fascinating,' Petron whispered, unable to take his eyes from the moving figures below him. It was just as Griggs said, like a dance, a great open ballroom with twirling partners spinning around it, locked in motion. 'And the wielders are happy with this?'

'Oh, yes,' Griggs said, a wide smile breaking across his face. 'I doubt you could stop them now if you tried. They're taking to it like a duck to water.'

'One more Redmondis mystery,' Lodan said, his mouth twisted into a distasteful scowl. 'Perhaps this one would prove more useful than the others.'

'If you are done with me … ?' Griggs asked, obviously eager to return to the training below.

'Yes, yes.' Lodan waved him off and watched as Griggs hurried away, taking the stairs two at a time. 'Still as eager as a schoolboy.'

'Does he know, Lodan?'

Petron's tone brought Lodan fully out of his musing and he turned to face the old man.

'Know?'

'About what happened in Greystone? About what you did? Bringing him back?'

'What Wilt did, you mean. I was just the vessel.'

'Nevertheless …'

'No.' Lodan shook his head, his tone firm. 'And he doesn't need to.'

Petron was about to argue the point, but one look at Lodan's expression stilled his tongue. He turned to the courtyard below and for an instant he was back in his chamber in Redmondis, toes overhanging the cliff edge, breeze ruffling his hair, and mind elsewhere, in another form, another time, another possibility, looping and curling in the skies with his partner, wingtips almost touching.

'I understand. We've all been touched by loss. No need to pick at the scab.'

Lodan stayed silent but nodded slowly, then pushed himself back from the balcony. 'Come then, old man. Let's find something to eat and you can tell me more about your discoveries.'

Chapter 40

Daemi crouched behind a large, jagged rock that reared out of the ground just inside the entrance to the chamber, poking her head up over the edge to try to make some sense of the chaotic scene in front of her.

Heather and Higgs were still wrapped together beside her, Heather making the excuse that Higgs was still too weak to stand on his own, and Higgs not putting up much of a protest about it. They huddled beside her, wide eyed and wincing with every crack and shift beneath them.

It felt as if the mountain itself was breaking in two. Every few seconds, a fresh quake rumbled through the chamber, sending spikes of stone tumbling from the ceiling high above to smash down on whatever poor unfortunate happened to be standing beneath it. The slowly milling crowds of workers seemed to take no notice, even when a large chunk of red stone crushed an entire group of them in the centre of the floor. The workers just altered their line around the new obstacle, like a line of ants determined not to lose their path between home and whatever fresh kill their scouts had scented.

'What's wrong with them?' Daemi whispered, unable to make sense of it all.

'They're not human,' Higgs said, pulling himself shakily up to the edge of the rock to peer over. 'They're barely conscious at all. Workers for the Novus. Beasts of burden.'

Daemi watched the men move for a few more moments before

dropping back behind their shelter. 'Well, at least we won't have to worry about them trying to stop us.'

'What about the others?' Heather asked. 'The Incarnate?'

'I saw four of them, two pairs. One near the centre of the chamber, the other pair toward the back, where that platform curves up.'

'And the Novus?' Higgs asked.

There.

Wilt was suddenly beside them, tail moving slowly in the air, black eyes shifting from face to face in turn.

A flash of vision overwhelmed Daemi—Frankle sitting dwarfed in a large throne at the back of the chamber, black weld blade cradled in his lap.

Daemi bent over the edge of the rock again and tried to pierce the clouds of dust and smoke that filled the chamber. Right at the rear, she could just make out the throne before another crash and wash of dust wiped the sight away.

'What is he doing?'

Readying his army. We have to move—now. We have to stop him before he sends them through.

'Through?' Daemi asked.

'The pool,' Higgs said. 'At the back of the chamber. The Novus uses it to send his subjects through, into the welds and back. Weld-farers, he called us.'

The golden weld, dancing in front of us, beckoning us on.

'That's right.' Higgs said. 'It's how I ended up here in the first place. How Wilt ended up stuck in that form.'

And it's how we make it back.

'Okay.' Daemi readied herself to move. 'You two stay here, out of sight. Wilt and I will clear a path.'

'Are you sure?' Heather asked. 'I mean, you don't have your sword.'

'That's not going to stop us is it, Wilt?' Daemi smiled suddenly, an eager flame dancing in her eyes. 'I've always thought I should use these more.' She held up two fists and flexed them, five fingers on each hand twisting in turn.

'Daemi,' Heather piped up again. 'Your hand. It's … different.'

'No longer "One of the Nine".' Daemi's smile twisted into a hungry grin. 'Now I can fight for myself.'

'For all of us,' Higgs corrected. 'For Redmondis.'

'For Sontair,' Heather added.

For Greystone.

Daemi nodded to each of them in turn, then held one arm out to Wilt. 'Come on then. Climb aboard.' The cat leapt onto her shoulders and disappeared into the curled black locks of her hair. 'Let's see what trouble we can still cause.'

Heather watched Daemi and Wilt leave, Daemi leaping over the rock they hid behind and sprinting straight toward the line of trudging workers in the centre of the chamber.

'Uh, Higgs? Do you think we should try to help in some way?'

'Way ahead of you.'

Higgs sat back from where he had been scratching at the ground beneath their hiding place and held up a smooth, palm-sized stone.

'Where did you find that?' Heather asked. 'It looks like it came out of a river.'

'Just another one of my hidden talents. Now, you wouldn't happen to have a sling on you by any chance, would you?'

'No.'

'Thought not. Guess we'll have to improvise.'

Higgs grabbed at Heather's arm, and for a mad moment she thought he was pulling her in for a kiss, then the sleeve of her shirt tore and he yanked the strip of cloth he wanted free.

'This'll do,' Higgs whispered to himself, twisting the fabric around itself to give it more strength.

'You could have just asked.'

'Yeah. But where would the fun be in that?' Higgs flashed her a wicked grin and popped his head up over the rock they were still hiding behind. 'There she goes.'

Heather pulled herself up beside him to see Daemi charge straight into the line of workers in the centre of the chamber, knocking at least four of the large men completely over, and sending an entire bunch of them spinning into each other, a ripple of chaos spreading out around her like she was a stone dropped in a pond.

Daemi still had Wilt on her shoulders, and Heather caught another flash of movement as the cat leapt out of its hiding place to claw at the nearest unfortunate still standing near them.

'Looks like they've got things under control for now,' Higgs muttered, placing the stone in the centre of his makeshift sling and giving it a few practice spins.

'Are you any good with that?' Heather asked.

'Any good? I'm the second-best slinger I know.'

'Second-best?'

'Wilt was the expert, but like I said, I've taken part of his human form. I have a feeling that my skill might have made a sharp improvement.' Higgs grunted suddenly as he spun the sling up to speed and loosed his stone. It arced up and over the crowd that Daemi and Wilt were fighting and smacked straight into the back of the head of another worker, dropping him instantly.

'Good shot! Now you just need to find enough ammunition.'

'That won't be a problem,' Higgs replied, bending over to scratch at the ground again before pulling up another perfectly sized stone.

Heather watched him as he launched another missile, this one claiming a hooded figure in the stomach, sending him lurching to the floor with both hands clutching his belly.

Seemingly as soon as that stone was loosed, another was in the sling, spinning up to speed.

'How are you finding those so quickly?' Heather asked as Higgs let loose again.

'I told you, I'm a man of many talents. They called me Stone here, you know.'

'Stone? Your talent is finding stones?'

'Not so much finding. Here.' Higgs pulled Heather down behind the rock and turned so that she could see both his hands. 'Watch.'

He placed one hand palm down on the stone ground and seemed to push into it, his fingers disappearing entirely into the floor's surface before pulling back, clutching another perfectly sized, rounded stone.

'Now that's something I haven't seen before.'

'I know, right? It's something I remembered from Redmondis, with Cortis. When he locked me up in his fortress, I managed to form the living stone into a key to free myself. Did it again here, too. It's like the rock itself gifts you the object it knows you need.'

Higgs stood up quickly and launched another missile before ducking back down. 'Did you hear it? The music, when I pulled it out?'

'Music?' Heather asked, dumbfounded.

'Weld song. Like the heartstone's song. Here, try to listen this time.' Higgs pushed his hand into the stone again.

Heather tried to make sense of what she was seeing as his hand once again disappeared below the solid stone surface.

And just at the edge of hearing, there it was.

'I hear it!' Heather exclaimed. 'I hear the song!'

As soon as Higgs pulled his hand back out of the ground, the music faded again, as if she had lifted her necklace up and out of the sounding bowl, cutting the song short.

'Why don't you try?' Higgs stood up again and got off another shot before crouching down again. 'Here, I'll help you.'

He reached out and took Heather's hand, placing it palm down on the rough stone between them, then placed his own hand on top of hers. 'The music is key, I think. It helps open the connection. Try to listen to it, and only it. Close your eyes.'

With those last words he pushed down on the back of Heather's hand, squeezing it against the floor. Heather ignored the sudden pain and did as he asked, shutting her eyes and trying to reach out for the heartstone's song she knew so well.

It had led her here, to this place. Led her back to Higgs. Now maybe it could help lead them out.

The song was louder now, more easily picked out against the

rumble and chaos of the chamber on the other side of their hiding place. Heather let it guide her, let the music take her doubts and fears and wipe them away as her hand seemed to fall into the floor, a wet warmth wrapping around her hand as though she was pushing into warm, thick mud.

'Now, come back.' Higgs's voice called to her from within the song, and she felt her hand lifting back up and out again. 'Open your eyes.'

Heather wanted to resist, wanted to stay a few moments more in the strangely comforting song that wrapped around her, but a part of her knew she couldn't. She felt the mud around her hand harden suddenly, and as she opened her eyes, the stone seemed to grab for her, scraping the skin of her fingers as she pulled her hand fully out.

'Ouch!'

'Sorry about that. You have to be quick, or you lose a few layers of skin. Did you get the stone?'

Heather looked down at her hand, the edges of her fingers red where the rock had scraped them, and in the centre of her palm was a small pebble, cracked on one side, shaped like a heart that had been broken in two.

'Still making heartstones, I see.' Higgs stood up quickly and launched his own stone out into the chamber. 'Not so useful right now.'

'No. I know.' Heather stared down at the stone in her hand, watching it glint in the shifting red light of the chamber. It was exactly like the heartstone she had made for them. Exactly like the half that Higgs had worn around his neck. 'I guess I don't share that particular talent of yours.'

She slid the stone into her pocket and poked her head back up over the rock they were crouching behind.

Daemi and Wilt had moved past the first line of workers now, leaving a sprawling crowd of bodies in their wake. A few of them still moved, but none looked like they were returning to their feet anytime soon.

'Come on, we need to get closer.' Higgs grabbed her hand and pulled her around the side of the rock, angling across the large chamber toward another ridge of stone lining the left-hand wall.

Heather let herself be pulled along, one hand still clutching the new heartstone in her pocket. Across the centre of the chamber, Daemi and Wilt were approaching the closest edge of the large swirling mud pool, still charging forward, trying to catch any further workers or guards before they made sense of the commotion.

The stone in her hand flared suddenly, the heat of it scorching her palm, and she almost cried out in pain before she bit her lip and suppressed it.

'What's wrong?' Higgs asked, feeling her pull back against him.

Heather nodded toward the mud pool, unable to speak as her eyes tried to understand what she was seeing.

In the centre of the pool, three bubbles of molten mud had started to rise, pulling up and out to lie floating on top of it, three large spheres of shadow that flexed and morphed as the mud slew off them. The heartstone in her hand pulsed in time with them, and Heather knew in an instant what it was she was seeing.

The three bubbles popped simultaneously, sharp black claws tearing through the skin of them like a monster hatching from its shell.

Heather swallowed and forced the word out of her frozen throat. 'Gloomclaws.'

Daemi saw the three nightmare forms loom up in front of them just as she shrugged off the last of the workers who had stood in their way. The heavy-bodied men hadn't been much of a challenge. Slow moving, and seemingly only fighting back under orders, Daemi and Wilt had made short work of them. Now, though, it seemed they were in for a more formidable challenge.

'Wilt?' Daemi called, keeping one eye on the three gloomclaws that had just appeared and looking around desperately in the swirl of dust and flame to find the cat.

I'm here.

A black streak flashed between her legs and charged straight toward the pool.

Daemi ran after it, her body reacting before her fear could freeze her legs in place. The lip of the mud pool was a three-foot-high bank of stone, and she leaped up to the top of it just as Wilt disappeared over its edge. She caught herself as she landed to avoid toppling forward into the thick mud.

'You remember I don't have a sword, right?' she called, trying to pierce the thicker steam over the pool and find where the cat had gone.

Suddenly a black claw shot out of the mist straight at her throat, and she ducked and rolled along the stone lip of the pool just before it separated her head from her shoulders.

I remember.

Another large curved claw struck down at Daemi, and again she just managed to roll clear before it spiked her into the ground. She couldn't see the gloomclaw at all, but it didn't seem to have any trouble knowing exactly where she was.

A flash of silver lit the fog, and a third claw fell toward her, but this one was moving much more slowly. Daemi scrambled backward as it crashed toward her, then froze as she realised this claw was no longer attached to the monster it belonged to.

Try that on for size.

Daemi stared down at the wickedly curved and serrated limb, almost two feet in length and shining cruelly in the flames of the chamber. It rocked back and forth slowly on the stone lip between her legs where it had fallen, and it took a full five seconds before Daemi realised what Wilt was suggesting.

'This? You want me to use this?'

The arm or leg or whatever body part it had been was pointed at one end and the other opened out into a cylindrical opening just big enough for her to fit her hand inside. It looked hollow, no blood or gore leaking out of it. And it was certainly sharp enough.

'Here goes nothing,' Daemi muttered to herself, slipping her hand into the claw and lifting it easily. It was light, impossibly so. Lighter even than a weld blade.

Any further musings were banished as an entire gloomclaw loomed out of the mist and leaped over her head to land on the ground outside the pool, the creature turning as soon as it landed and seeming to morph in place so that what possibly was its face stared back at her.

Daemi rolled to her feet and found herself standing in front of it, curved black claw held out before her like a blade as the gloomclaw crept forward.

Watch it, I think I slowed that one, but it's still—

Wilt's words were forced out of her mind as the gloomclaw surged toward her suddenly, Daemi twisting to her right to spin away from it, flinging out the claw as she did so and feeling a satisfying rip as it sunk home. She continued her spin and came up ready; the claw pulled free of the gloomclaw's body with ease.

The gloomclaw seemed to stop to consider its next move, unsure about this new threat.

'Yeah, not so sure of yourself now, are you?' Daemi grinned, hefting the claw in her hand and giving it a few practice swings. 'This one has a sting.'

Whatever doubts the gloomclaw might have had were quickly banished, and it charged her again. Daemi waited for it to be right on her, then jumped toward it, low and feet first to slide underneath it, her new weapon held out above her head. It ripped across the gloomclaw's lower body, opening it up completely and sending it crashing down on top of her, a mess of hard, sharp limbs clattering around her as Daemi held her hands over her head to protect herself.

Be right there.

Wilt's words were followed by another flash of silver and the gluggy crash of something heavy falling back into the mud. Daemi didn't wait, pushing free of the mess of limbs she had caged herself inside, using her claw to slash her way clear where needed and sliding out from under the monster.

Her claw sliced into the gloomclaw easily, almost without resistance. As she cut herself free, another thought occurred to her, and she came to her feet, sliding her left hand into its own weapon.

Another thump behind her, and she spun in place, twin curved claws held out in front of her chest, ready to meet it.

But it was just Wilt, staring up at her, sitting on his haunches to try to make sense of this strange sight.

Daemi relaxed, then felt suddenly sheepish, her twin claw blades dropping to her side.

I suppose two swords are better than one.

'Where's the other gloomclaw?'

Oh, don't worry.

Wilt held up his paw and displayed his own five silver claws. *Five is even better than two.*

'Very funny. Where's Frankle?'

Come. I saw him flee as soon as the first gloomclaw fell. We must stop him.

'But the pool—didn't Higgs say he was sending his army through?'

I think he's already sent some through, but not the main force. Sontair will have to hold as best it can for now. We have to stop the Novus.

Chapter 41

Petron sat back in his chair with a groan, rubbing his aching thighs as he studied the conduit once more. He'd been at it for days now, always managing to find an excuse to disappear here to the queen's study, confident Lodan and the others had things firmly in control. And though he intended to focus on other things, rifling through the stacks of papers and tomes that filled half the room, he always found himself in front of the conduit, eyes skimming over its carved surface, trying to find whatever thread he could pick that might unravel its mysteries.

Yet no matter how much he willed it, no revelation occurred. No progress to speak of was made. The last discovery he'd stumbled on was purely by accident, and even that was only a strange trick of magnetisation. It didn't seem to have any utility.

He sighed again, feeling every day of his age, one hand still rubbing his aching muscles and the other straying once again inside his cloak to find the carved cat's paw hidden there.

It was still wrapped in its rag, Petron knowing well enough not to let it touch his skin, but even through that cloth covering he thought he could feel a change in temperature from it, a slow pulsing of heat that seemed to crescendo then fade again. Much like music, the thought occurred to him. Much like the welling of a song.

The conduit itself still seemed dead and broken. No more flashes of blue lightning arcing across its borders, no more swirling gateways of cloud filling its centre. Petron had to admit that its repair was beyond his skill, beyond perhaps all who still lived in these times. Lost to the past like so much knowledge, leaving those who remained to be pulled and tumbled by the currents without the aid of wisdom.

His right hand wrapped around the paw in his pocket, squeezing it now, as though he could eke out some answers from it through pure will.

Suddenly his palm throbbed, a blush of warmth radiating up his forearm. As it did so, a distant horn sounded from somewhere out on the training grounds.

Another pulse. Then another. Stronger now, and there was no mistaking the heat that grew with each ebb.

For a moment, Petron thought he saw the conduit flash in time with it, a dim blue light radiating out from its border, and he stood up to examine it more closely, but then another unmistakable sound wiped all such concerns away.

A howl. A wolf's howl. Just like the last time he had heard such a thing, in Redmondis, when Cortis had tried to overthrow the Sisters.

Sontair was under attack.

By the time Petron found Lodan, the entire castle seemed to be in motion. He had to push his way through columns of soldiers and servants streaming down the corridors of the castle, fear and adrenaline filling every face he passed, and he almost gave up reaching Lodan's office with the number of bodies centred around there. Then a strong hand gripped his shoulder and pulled him out of the traffic and into a separate antechamber, and he was faced with Lodan's grim visage once again.

'Come, Petron. With me.'

Lodan didn't wait for an answer, just pushed ahead through another narrower corridor and down a steep interior staircase Petron had never even known existed.

'Wolves?' Petron finally managed to ask as they reached the lower floor.

'I only hope that's all it is. Another diversion.'

Lodan's tone gave the lie to his words, but Petron thought better of arguing. They pushed through a rickety timber door and spilled out into the main courtyard, and suddenly there was no further need for talk.

Hundreds of soldiers and wielders filled the courtyard, officers trying to form them into some sort of organised defence within the chaos. Lining the high walls of the castle, looking down upon it all, were at least thirty enormous wolves, some still with their heads back, howling their battle cry to the wind, others leering down hungrily at the chaos below, long tongues lolling out of their jaws and eager drool dripping from their teeth.

The first wave of wolves leaped from the wall onto the crowd below, sending bodies flying as they landed and began to ravage all they could see.

But that wasn't the worst of it. The worst was what filled the spaces on the wall the wolves left. Gloomclaws. At least ten of them, larger even than the ones Petron had fought on the ice, each monster the height of a man, their evil claws moving impossibly quickly in the air before them, ready to tear apart any living thing that came within their reach.

'Griggs!' Lodan called out above the tumult. 'Griggs! Form the defences!'

Wherever Griggs now was, he was beyond hearing, and Lodan pushed away from Petron, drawing his sword as he did so, charging straight for the staircase that led to the top of the wall.

'Lodan wait!' Petron tried to call him back, but Lodan didn't respond. In moments, he was lost within the crowd of bodies.

Petron's hand pulsed with heat once again, and he realised he was still clutching the cat's paw within his cloak. He pulled the stone free, dropping the rag, no longer concerned if the paw touched his skin.

Instantly, the warmth and pulse of the paw seemed to fill his body, and he almost fell to the ground as he stumbled, his mind overwhelmed as a vision from the past swamped his consciousness.

Embrace the torrent. Let it free your mind from all constraint. Let it flow through you and beyond. Open yourself to me.

The words no longer filled Petron's mind. They echoed through him, but they no longer blasted all other thought clear. He kept his eyes locked on the spark as it sank toward him, still spinning on its invisible currents of air.

The serpent blurred into the background as he reached for it. Petron could feel himself pulling free of the dark mind that threatened to consume him, the connection to the howling depths shrinking into nothingness.

No! I will not allow you to escape. You will remain here! You will become my new vessel!

As his fingers closed around the spark, Petron felt the connection. Biore. Delco. Rawick. Higgs. Daemi. Heather. Frankle. All of them. All who had been touched by Wilt's power, binding them together, interweaving their lives. Linking them within the welds, entwining them in a single rope of consciousness. This was a new form of power, one never wielded before. It was what could finally save them.

Petron came to his senses, both hands out in front of him in the dirt, his right still clutching the strange cat's paw that seemed to squirm inside his fist, as though struggling to free itself.

A body jostled him and he bounced from it into another, heavy metal armour meeting his hand as he tried to catch himself. The soldier turned and shrugged him free, the man's eyes remaining locked on the gloomclaws perched on the castle walls.

Petron followed his gaze and saw what had to be Lodan, alone at the top of the staircase, sword held high in some sort of salute or battle cry as he charged straight for them.

'Lodan, no!' Petron cried out, but his voice was lost in the tumult. More bodies surged in front of him, pushing him further back, and he lost sight of Lodan once again. He retreated to the relative safety of the interior wall of the courtyard, pressing against it to leave the rushing soldiers around him as much room as possible.

Suddenly, the area seemed to explode into space, a large white body smashing down onto the soldiers and sending them sprawling. The enormous wolf turned its head to tear at the arm of the closest victim, then noticed Petron and focused its full attention on him.

Petron stared at the creature's glowing red eyes as it slowly stalked toward him, long streams of drool dripping from its maw.

He was frozen in place, unable to move at all. It was just like the nightmares that had haunted him since Redmondis. Just like he knew his death would be. All he could feel was fear. Fear and the dim, warm pulse of the paw still clutched in his fist.

All the sounds of the world seemed to fade, and in their place was a faint music, beating in time with the pulse in his hand. Weld song.

The wolf, too, seemed to hear it, raising its head suddenly to scent the wind, its waiting victim no longer its sole point of attention.

The next moment, a thick black weld struck at it, knocking the wolf to its knees with a yelp. Seemingly in the same movement, a shining weld blade swept down at the wolf's unguarded neck. A wet chop, and the great head rolled free.

'Petron!' Griggs clutched his shoulder, but Petron was unable to take his eyes from the enormous white head leaking blood into the dirt. 'Petron!'

Griggs shook him, and Petron finally managed to turn his head, trying to focus on the man's face. Behind Griggs, the wielder and soldier pair who had taken down the wolf moved on to find their next target.

'Linked. Linked within the welds,' Petron whispered.

'Petron! Where is Lodan?' Griggs shook him again, trying to make him regain his senses.

Petron swallowed, then slowly pointed to the top of the wall where he had last seen Lodan.

Griggs didn't need any more encouragement, turning and disappearing back into the crowd.

Petron was left leaning against the wall, the chaos of battle foaming all around him, the cat's paw still throbbing within his fist, a faint heartbeat within the pandemonium, stilling his racing brain and bringing with it a calmness that seemed to wash over him like a cold shower.

He looked one final time at the dead wolf on the ground, then pushed himself from the wall and surged into the battle.

It wasn't until Lodan was almost at the top of the stairs leading to the castle wall that he stopped to consider just what exactly it was he thought he was doing.

Hobbling up the staircase, long sword in hand, as though this blade wielded by that arm would do any good at all against the nightmares that stood waiting on the wall. Still his step didn't slow as he finally reached the top of the stairs and pushed past the last remaining men standing between him and the gloomclaws.

'No more!' Lodan shouted, waving his sword above his head in challenge. 'Not one man more!'

The gloomclaw closest to the staircase seemed to respond, stepping back from the broken body at its feet and turning what might have been its face toward this new threat.

Lodan felt all his bravado drain away under its gaze, only just managing to hold his sword tip up to point at the gloomclaw. He swallowed, his throat protesting as he forced down what little saliva was left in his mouth.

'Come on then, monster,' he whispered. 'Let's make this quick.'

Before he had even finished the sentence, the gloomclaw was upon him, driving him backward and almost toppling him down the steep stairs as he struggled to bat away each thrust and strike of its claws. Lodan blocked and parried as best he could, his arm moving faster than he could see, trusting the training he had forced himself to undergo each day he had been inside the walls of Son-tair. Even so, it was obvious after only a few seconds that the battle was a losing one. The gloomclaw was just too fast. Inhumanly so. Faster than thought.

Lodan felt his heel clip the top of the staircase and just managed to spin aside as another sharp thrust of a wickedly serrated claw shot out at him, threatening to take his head clean off but only grazing his shoulder as he stumbled clear. Another soldier was not so lucky, his chest taking the full brunt of a blow Lodan hadn't even seen coming, dropping the man into a puddle of dark red blood that pooled instantly around him.

Lodan gasped as the pain from the cut to his shoulder registered. His entire left arm was numb, a warm tingling radiating down from his shoulder to his fingers. He shook his arm and grimaced as a new flash of pain seared back in answer.

It was too fast. There was no stopping it. But perhaps he could delay it a little longer.

He pointed the sword back up at the gloomclaw, waiting for it to advance once again. His other arm was completely dead now, the final flash of pain seemingly the last of it.

Behind him, he could hear other soldiers retreating down the stairs, each of them seeing the truth of things. There was no stopping these creatures. It was just like Greystone.

Greystone. Where he had fought back. Where he had killed one of them.

Suddenly the gloomclaw was attacking again, its thrusts narrowing in on his wounded side, forcing Lodan to turn in place and step over the dead soldier as he frantically parried. His sword arm jolted in shock with each blow, the edge of the blade making no mark on the black shell-like armour of the thing.

Lodan's feet slipped in the blood, and he almost fell face first into the dirt, but just managed to roll clear as another claw ripped at him. He battered it away with the flat of his sword and backed up still further, trying and failing to keep the gloomclaw on the side of his good arm.

Greystone. Where you saved Griggs.

As though the thought summoned him, Lodan heard Griggs's voice call his name from the base of the stairs, but before he could answer, the gloomclaw was upon him once more, mercilessly biting in at his weak side, until he could resist it no more and another dull jolt told him it had once again struck home on his upper left arm.

His vision blurred, and he blinked sudden tears out of his eyes, trying to will the world back into focus.

'Lodan!'

He heard Griggs once again, but he seemed much further away now, his voice echoing to him as through a long, dark tunnel.

Another thrust and he managed to bat the claw clear, his sword falling free as he did so. The world was swimming in front of him now, refusing to stay in one place, the gloomclaw a growing black bruise in the centre of his vision.

'Lodan! Catch!'

He was already running, the heavy-bodied guard who had tried to take him down left sprawling in the hard-packed dirt of the flag-ball pitch behind him. On the outer wing, he saw a black streak of movement as the new winger, his name forgotten, surged clear of his own marker.

Lodan charged for the centre of the goal, knowing without looking that Griggs would deliver the ball at just the right time. He jumped, holding his right arm aloft as the ball flew into his hand.

Lodan grunted as the gloomclaw struck home once again, his left arm tugging suddenly and another sharp claw angling in at his throat. His eyes widened as he watched it, aware that it held his death.

But the blow never came. With another jerk, the gloomclaw dropped to the ground, taking most of his left arm with it. Lodan stared at the creature, not sure what he was seeing, until he realised his right arm still clutched the handle of the weld blade thrust deep into the centre of the thing.

'Lodan!' Griggs pulled him clear of the carcass and out of the way of the stream of soldiers and wielders he had led up the staircase. Lodan let himself be led, still not sure exactly what had just occurred.

'Lodan, we have to get you out of here.'

'Out?' Lodan shook his head, confused. 'But the gloomclaws—'

'Will be dealt with. Let the wielders and guards do what we trained them for. You need a doctor now. Or haven't you noticed?'

Griggs nodded down at Lodan's left side, and he turned to look at the space where his left arm used to be.

'Oh.'

The black circle in the centre of his vision bloomed wider, and he collapsed into Griggs's arms.

Chapter 42

Heather sat crouched behind another tall stone column, wincing with the rattle and crash of the chamber as heavy stones continued to fall from the ceiling and smoke and flames filled the air, now and then opening with a gust of wind to show snapshots of the battle further toward the rear of the room.

Daemi and Wilt had carved their way through to the mud pool, and the three gloomclaws Heather had watched rise from it were now either in pieces on the ground or had been sent back to whatever lay at the bottom of that swirling gunk.

'Wait here,' Higgs had said, pushing himself out from their hiding place, his sling still spinning and loosing missiles at the remaining workers and servants milling about in confusion.

Heather was quite happy to get a moment to herself, reaching inside her shirt to pull out the heartstone on its chain, and holding it in her palm to compare it to the strange pebble she had formed from the living stone of the mountain.

She stared at the two half-hearts in her palms, then nudged them together, so that the jagged edge of the break on each half met. Sure enough, the twin stones fit perfectly. She squeezed the two halves together, and the seam between them vanished completely.

'I thought as much,' she whispered, placing the chain of the now-whole heartstone back over her head and tucking it inside her shirt.

What did it mean, though? Higgs had said the mountain gives

up what it knows you need—so why the heartstone? And if it was the same half that Higgs had carried—and it certainly seemed to be—then how come he no longer had it?

She knew the answer to that one, but refused to allow the thought voice.

'Heather!' Daemi called out from behind another cloud of steam, and Heather stood up.

'I'm here!'

She waved her arms around to try to clear the smoke and steam from the air, then jumped backward with a scream as a gloomclaw popped out of the smoke right in front of her, twin claws slashing toward her chest.

'It's okay!' Daemi shouted, realising instantly what she had done. She dropped her twin blades to her side and waited for Heather's panic to subside. 'Sorry about that.'

'Daemi?'

Heather had collapsed onto the rock she had been hiding behind, but now she stood up and bent forward to try to make some sense of the sight before her.

It was Daemi all right, no mistaking her, but instead of a sword, both her arms seemed to sprout curved, jagged-edged black claws from just below her elbow to a point almost a foot past where her fingers would normally be.

'Are … are you okay?' Heather asked.

'Yes, we're fine. These—' Daemi shook her arms and both black claws dropped to the floor. 'They're very light. It's easy to forget I'm carrying them.'

'Awesome!' Higgs voice preceded him out of the smoke, and he instantly bent down to examine the claws.

'Are they what I think they are?' Heather asked, not wanting to get any closer to the cursed things.

'Gloomclaws. At least we found some use for them.' Daemi nodded. 'Higgs, I wouldn't—'

'Ouch!' Higgs sprang back from the claws, sucking his finger where the razor-sharp edge of the claw had sliced it open.

'They're incredibly sharp,' Daemi finished.

'No kidding,' Higgs said around his finger, staring warily down at the blades now, as though he feared they might come to life.

'We have to move. Frankle can't be far.' Daemi slipped her hands into the base of the claws. 'Don't stand too close.'

We have to go.

Heather looked up to see Wilt perched just above her head on top of the rock column, a vague black blur in the dim light.

'Lead the way,' Daemi ordered, and spun around, moving back into the smoke and mist and disappearing in a couple of steps.

Heather watched her leave, her body seeming to morph into a gloomclaw as the smoke wrapped around her.

'Impressive,' Higgs whispered, offering her his hand. 'Almost as impressive as my sling work, wouldn't you say? Though I didn't hear any thank you from them.'

You're a better shot than you used to be.

The cat streaked past them and vanished.

'I guess that's as good as it's going to get.' Higgs shrugged, and pulled Heather along beside him into the mist.

Higgs sucked at his finger, the blood from the cut leaving a metallic tang on his tongue. He let Heather pull a few steps ahead in the smoke-filled tunnel, then pulled the finger out of his mouth and examined it. There was an inch-long slice along the pad of his index finger, instantly filling with red and starting to bubble up and out from the wound. He put the finger back in his mouth and sucked.

Blood. So, he was human then, wasn't he? Or at least … a living thing.

Ahead of him, he could just make out the shape of Daemi, the twin blade-claws on her arms a deep, unnatural black. Bastard things. He had barely even touched the edge of one and it seemed to reach out and pull him toward it, slicing his skin easily. Hungrily. As though they were watching him and waiting for just that moment.

The blades moved back and forth beside Daemi's legs as she

walked. She'd have to be careful. One clumsy spin and she'd suddenly be a lot shorter.

Higgs had to stifle a chuckle at the thought of Daemi lurching comically to one side.

'Higgs?' Daemi turned and waited for him to part the mist between them.

'Uh-huh.'

'Still bleeding, is it?' Daemi nodded at his finger.

'It's fine. I've had worse.'

'Good. And how is the rest of you holding up?'

'I'm fine. I'm ... alive.'

Daemi seemed about to say something more, but they were both interrupted.

Dead end.

Sure enough, another few steps caught them up to Wilt, who was staring at a solid rock wall between them and the rest of the tunnel.

'But, how is that possible?' Daemi asked, stepping past Wilt and running the tip of one of her blades along the rough stone.

Suddenly, she swung back and struck hard at the centre of the wall, the black claw sending a blinding shower of sparks into the air but leaving the stone seemingly unharmed.

'Are you sure Frankle came this way?'

Oh yes.

'Maybe there was another tunnel further back we missed,' Heather said, catching up to the rest of them.

There was no other tunnel.

Daemi stepped back from the rock wall, her shoulders heaving. 'Well, rock walls don't just appear out of thin air.'

'Yes, they do,' Higgs said. 'I mean, here, in this place, they do.' All three faces turned toward him, and he hurried to explain himself. 'This mountain, this stone, it's living rock. The Novus uses it to form ... whatever he wants. Even ...' His voiced trailed away as he stared at the cut on his finger once more, leaving the rest of the thought unvoiced. 'Step back. Let me try something.'

Daemi did as he asked, and he found himself alone in front of the rock wall, one hand placed open against the cool stone.

He'd done it before, with Flame. With the Sister. Now he just had to try to do it again.

Higgs closed his eyes, placing himself back inside the memory. Instantly, he heard the weld song, as though it responded to his call. An echo from the past rolling back to him.

You see? Like this.

He reached into the stone, feeling the surface soften and accept his hand, then he twisted, and the silent command was followed.

'How did you do that?' Heather's voice snapped him back into the moment, and he only just remembered to pull his hand free before the stone closed over it again.

In front of them, there was no longer a rock wall at all. Now it was a wide, oval-shaped opening, as though an old doorway had been revealed. Beyond it, the tunnel continued into shadows, the smoke and dim red light from the stone defying any effort to pierce them.

'Nice trick,' Daemi muttered, striding past Higgs as Wilt darted ahead of them.

'Thanks,' Higgs muttered, still staring at his hand.

'Are you okay?' Heather asked, and he nodded quickly, shoving his hand into his cloak and marching after Daemi.

He could hear Heather follow behind, and he wanted to turn and tell her more, but the hand in his pocket stopped him. He could feel his fingers rubbing against each other, searching out the cut that had been there only moments before.

But it was no longer there. His finger was completely healed.

Daemi lost sight of Wilt as soon as she stepped through the opening Higgs had formed in the rock wall. The air felt different immediately. Still and cool, as though some secret pocket within the mountain had been revealed, one not opened in centuries. Smoke billowed into the tunnel from the passage behind her, filling the space immediately, sucked into the vacuum of the new tunnel like some great beast inhaling its breath, ready to shout.

'Wilt?' she whispered, still unable to avoid putting the thought into actual words, though she knew it was no longer necessary.

Watch out!

Wilt's warning was followed immediately by what looked like twin black snakes spiralling out of the tunnel toward her, dancing on the wind and snapping down at her head. What's more, the serpents seemed to sing as they swarmed her, weld song filling her mind and threatening to freeze her bones in place just as the Incarnates had on the dock.

Her blade-claws reacted before her mind could, whipping out on either side of her and sending her body into a spin that sent the surrounding smoke into a tornado of movement, the black blades slicing into and through the snakes that had attacked her, snakes she now recognised as welds. Welds she should not have been able to see.

As soon as each weld was sliced in two by her blades, they disappeared, the weld song cutting off and dying in a sudden silence. A strangled, guttural cry from further ahead told her Wilt had dealt with the Incarnates.

'Wilt?'

They're down. When you attacked their welds, their minds were overwhelmed.

'Where's Frankle?'

Further ahead. Come, there will be more obstacles.

Daemi strode on, feeling the claws on her arms pulse in rhythm with her heart, lifting her, sending a surge of warmth and energy down her spine. She felt strong, stronger than she ever had. Stronger and faster and more deadly than she had ever thought possible. And she was enjoying it.

She didn't need a warning the next time hidden Incarnates attacked. The weld song gave their positions away before the black welds could even get close. Daemi's body spun again, her claw blades whipping out and slicing the welds in two, dissipating them and sending back a pulse of pain that froze their wielders in place, leaving them ripe for the cat and its deadly silver claws.

'How many more?'

Not sure. They seem to come out of the rock itself.

Like Higgs, she thought, and turned to see if her two young companions were still behind them. A twisting cloud of smoke and a breath of breeze as a stone whistled past her head told her Higgs at least was still in the fight. She could only assume Heather was still with him.

Daemi pushed on, the rush of heat that pulsed within her threatening to burst out the top of her head as she marched, claw blades out and ready to cut down any possible threat.

With each weld they ended, they seemed to grow in strength and hunger, as though their black armoured skin absorbed the power of the welds themselves, feeding on them. Feeding yet growing in appetite.

As soon as she formed the thought, the air ahead changed again, a deep yawning chill opening up before her, like the solid ground ahead had dropped away into a deep chasm in the earth.

'Wilt?' she whispered once again, but this time there was no answer. She knew it immediately. He was no longer there. 'Wilt?'

Daemi's step slowed, a sudden doubt arrowing in at her mind like a shard of ice. She heard a crack and looked down to see a layer of white frost surging along the outside of her blade-claws.

'Wilt?'

Her breath steamed ahead of her, and the muscles in her arms shrieked with pain as the ice swallowed her blades entirely and reached her skin.

She knew before it formed in front of her what she now faced. What would end her.

The wraith reached its shifting hand into her chest and grasped the beating life within, pulling her down into the ice below.

The boy who had been Frankle sat perfectly still on his stone throne, watching his forces fall. The girl and the cat cut through them like a whirlwind—gloomclaws, wolves, Incarnate. It didn't seem to make any difference. Each piece he sent to face them was toppled and moved past, the two of them getting ever closer to him.

He felt a twist of nausea rise in his stomach, a spasm he had to close his eyes to focus on and resist, thrust the life within back down into the dark to be forgotten. This was his vessel now. He would not give it up.

The girl cut down another gloomclaw, the twin black blades she wielded slicing through its armour with ease. He felt the briefest flash of regret as the gloomclaw fell; a part of him called up from the past and given form, now ended in a moment before it could start the task for which it had been summoned.

He watched the girl, saw how inhumanly fast she was, how she and the cat twirled together in a dance of death, joined by more than thought, and knew it would have to be him who faced her, who finally ended the resistance. He had thought they were already dealt with, lost in the realm of dreams and memory, but somehow they had been brought back. Hauled into the present by their shared connections.

It reminded him of another time, long ago now but still only a moment away, when he sat alone on the peak of this mountain, witnessing the fires consuming the forest below. All those lives and memories turned to smoke and ash. The silent, still moment of victory. Then seeing the stone itself rise up in the distance, denying the cleansing flame. One last obstacle thrown up in his path.

It seemed no matter how he tried, he would never be able to remove the stain of them. Remove it all from this world so he could remain alone in the dark, pure and untouched, unsullied by love. There was only one thing for it.

He stared at the hand holding his black weld blade as it slowly fade from being, the world dropping into the grey shadow realm of the wraith. All else faded from notice, just two dancing flames of life in front of him, sparks in the wind, waiting to be snuffed. He watched the spark flare as it ended another creature, then moved.

In a blink, he was in front of her, the twisting snakes of his hand reaching past her defences and grasping the heart within. Watching her face drop into that knowing expression of death that was so familiar.

A flash of light lit the side of his face, and he saw the other—the cat—reaching out for him again, its silver claws exposed as it reared back for a second strike. Another thought, another grasp, and it too was within him, the last seconds of life fading from its eyes.

Daemi!

Wilt? Where are you? I can't see anything.

Daemi, hold on. Try to resist.

It's so cold, Wilt.

The boy who had been Frankle heard their final words and squeezed harder, determined this time not to let any light remain.

Another spasm of nausea rocked him then, collapsing his leg and almost wrenching him away from his victims. The boy, the one within, he was still fighting him. Resisting.

He felt the wash of memory tug at him, the boy trying to cling to some part of his mind as he struggled. Trying to blow some life into the flames of life he clutched.

The boy would not succeed. All light would be extinguished. All connections severed.

The wraith would stand alone.

Heather felt the chill before she saw them, the air thickening with cold as she pushed through the smoke. Inside her tunic, the heartstone rumbled with life, seeming to pull her onward into the cold, not allowing her to resist.

In a step, she was upon them, Daemi's body arched backward in pain, her features frozen, the black claws on her arms covered in a thin, crackling layer of ice. Beside her, Wilt too was immobilised, floating in the air at Daemi's shoulder height, as though time itself had stopped just as he launched into a leap. And between them both, twisting arms holding them in place, stood the wraith.

It took all of Heather's will not to turn and flee at the sight of it. A grey shadow, floating on the surface of the world, clawed hands reaching into its victims' chests and sucking the life from them.

The heartstone rumbled again, almost pulling itself out from under her shirt, and she clutched at it, needing the throb of life within it to give her strength and allow her feet to keep moving.

As soon as her fingers touched it, she knew what she had to do, and what the consequences would be.

'Higgs.' She turned toward him, the boy she had spent so long pursuing, the one she had lost too many times already.

'I know.' He smiled at her and placed one palm on her cheek. 'We both know it has to end here.'

Heather didn't trust herself to speak and bowed her head to pull the heartstone and its chain over her head.

'The stone gives us what we need,' Higgs whispered. 'Go. And look after Frankle. He's not as clever as I was.'

Heather felt his hand drop away from her face and turned back toward the wraith.

It didn't seem to notice her as she approached, or it simply saw her as no threat, but once she was within reach of it, her heart sank as its haunted face turned full toward her.

'No!' Higgs called, stepping past her to take its attention. 'We're the ones you want.'

An evil grin twisted the features of the wraith, and a spark of hunger lit its eyes as it registered Higgs.

Heather stepped around it, out of its sight as it reached once again and froze Higgs in place, the dancing serpents of its claws slicing into his chest. Higgs's body bucked, but his expression never changed. He stared into the face of death without fear, and that is what gave Heather the final push of strength she needed.

She stepped forward, ignoring the searing pain of cold, and looped the heartstone over the wraith's head.

A flash of blue light blinded her, and all she knew before she fell into unconsciousness was the sight of a small boy standing in front of her, the wraith form melting away from him, his eyes glowing with life as the heartstone's song filled the chamber, wiping all other sound away.

Higgs knew these would be his final moments in this place. This form. This life. He knew it and accepted it and felt no sadness. No bitterness or anger at the fate he had been dealt.

He remembered the pain of the blade that had killed him in Redmondis. The rush of memory that had overwhelmed him. There was none of that now. He could be at peace.

The wraith's hand entered his chest just where the weld blade had burst out of it so long ago, and there was only the briefest breath of cold as he felt it grasp his heart. Then Heather stepped behind it and placed the heartstone over the wraith's head, and the entire world seemed to explode in a blue flash of power.

The sounds of the world died, and he was suddenly in a dark, silent tunnel. At the far end, a grey shape moved against the darkness, four legged, its curling tail trailing behind it. He moved toward it and it skipped further into the tunnel, into the dark.

Higgs hesitated, only just able to see the shape against the darkness.

—Wilt?—

His lips formed the word, but no sound came out. The shape turned toward him, however, answering his call.

—Wilt. It's me.—

The dark walls of the tunnel pulsed with power. A cold rush of air from outside the tunnel pushed against his face, as though death itself was calling to him. He took another step, slower now, bending down and holding his hand in front of him.

—Wilt. Stay here. Stay with me.—

The cat trotted silently toward him, head cocked as though listening, as though trying to understand his words. It stopped ten feet from him, and Higgs stopped as well, knowing any further movement would send it scurrying away again, into the nothingness that waited for it. Higgs dropped to his knees.

—Wilt. Please.—

The cat sat on its haunches and studied him, unwilling to come any closer.

—Wilt. You have to let me go.—

The cat stared back at him, its head cocked to one side.

—You have to take back your form. You have to let me go.—

Higgs knew the cat would not abandon him, no matter how much he begged. It would wait for him to act, and so he did.

He turned away, back toward the darkness of the tunnel and the cold air that breathed out of it. There was no smell to it, no sense of loss or death. Only silence and ice and the frozen eternity of the world without him.

Higgs felt the cat change, but did not turn to witness it. He strode down the tunnel, away from life, away from love and worry and all the links that held him back within the welds.

He smiled as he walked into the unknown wonder of the world beyond life.

You. I know you.

Wilt felt his consciousness return as his body morphed back into humanity, his mind filling with thought like a mould topped up with soft clay, ready to be fired in the kiln and cracked free, revealing the true form underneath.

Some part of him watched as Higgs walked away, but he felt no more than a pang of regret. Higgs was a memory now. A good one, a true one, but no more than that for those still alive and active in this world. He turned his attention back to the voice that called to him, that filled his mind and cradled him within its fist.

You.

He knew Daemi still stood beside him, frozen in a wrench of pain. He stepped toward her, grasping the hand of ice that held her in this place and sliding it free. She too dropped away, not into death this time, but into the wash of time the wraith held within it, a storm spinning endlessly inside its heart. He knew what he had to do.

With a thought, a golden weld appeared, a shining, dancing ribbon inside the darkness, a string of sparks joined in train, a flame dancing with song. He turned Daemi toward it and saw her dive into it, away from him, back to the place he had first seen the golden weld, as the ice wrapped around him in Sontair and he thought all hope had gone.

You. Me.

Still he ignored the voice that called him, that shook the universe around him. He saw Heather and Frankle standing together behind the wraith, their hands joined and eyes reflecting back the same golden weld. He sent them on, too, back into the life ahead, away from this place beyond time.

Then there was only him remaining. Him and the wraith.

Me. You are me.

Wilt knew the voice spoke the truth of it. It was the chill dread that ran underneath life like an underground river cutting through rock and stone, wearing it away and shaping the world above with its meanderings. It would never be defeated, never stopped. It could only be rerouted. Back into the past. Back into a place where it could pool around itself, its turbulent waters stretching out and calming into a still pond. Calming and cooling until a thick layer of ice crusted over it, locking the doubt and fear and yearning for oblivion underneath.

The wraith was death itself, and death is timeless.

Finally, you see.

The voice of the Novus squeezed his mind, trying to force out every last drop of life, but Wilt did not need to resist any longer. He knew this mountain of fire, this beating heart of the world, was a forge. He would allow it to shape him, but he would not allow it to break him in two.

He felt the tug of the connections to others he still held and felt the fire of anger and pain each one caused the Novus. The wraith. It wanted oblivion. It wanted to answer the call of the void. But Wilt knew that such desire was pointless now. That life would not be cut away.

We are the same. You cannot leave me.

'I know,' Wilt replied, his lips moving yet no breath pushing past them. 'But I can take you with me.'

Clang!

The mountain of fire collapsed upon them with the sound of metal on metal, the sound that called back from the past and gave Wilt the path.

He reached into the wraith and held it, pulling it into himself as they vanished into the wash of time and space that only the wraith could truly control. It came willingly. It cast itself into Wilt, into the past, to try once more to sever all connections. To fail once more.

The boy crouched beside the flames, his face cast in shadow, waiting for the hammer to fall.

Heavy wooden beams ran along the ceiling of the blacksmith's hut—long fingers hanging above his head, waiting to snatch him into their fist. He watched the burly blacksmith at work, the man's massive back sweating in the heat of the forge, the muscles in his shoulders bunching and twisting with each powerful swing.

Clang!

Epilogue

Lodan stood alone at the top of the castle wall, staring at the land outside Sontair's high fortifications, watching the building sites slowly break into movement in the soft golden glow of the sunrise. The forces sent from Redmondis to protect them had done their job and more, and now spent their time expanding the borders of Sontair to help find room for all its people.

His fingers rubbed the deep gouges in the stone wall that the gloomclaws had left behind, the only sign remaining of their brief time in this place. As he did so, he felt the tingle of his ghost arm, the arm that had been taken from him in the battle they had all waged against the strange dark forces that had tried to overwhelm them. That they had beaten back and defeated. Together. Wielder and soldier, crafter and common man.

Far below, the beginnings of movement were gaining pace, and he knew the change of the guard was due as the first curve of the sun rose above the horizon. He knocked his knuckles one final time on the cold stone of the wall and turned away. Back to work. Back to the endless list of tasks and duty that now stretched out in front of him in his role as Protector of Sontair.

As he started to descend the stairs, his eye caught another familiar figure, striding tall and proud across the training courtyard. Heading away from the castle and the city. Daemi. Daemi was leaving.

By the time he caught up to her, she had reached the small, half-hidden gate that led out from the side of the courtyard and into the warren of the city below. He almost held himself back, almost let her leave in the silence and solitude she obviously wished for, but he couldn't help but call out one final goodbye.

'Daemi!'

She turned at the voice, a frustrated scowl twisting her features as she recognised it.

'Not going to leave without saying goodbye, are you?' Lodan grinned as he caught up to her.

'I was hoping to do exactly that,' Daemi grunted, shifting her shoulders so that Lodan caught the briefest glimpse of the black cat curled around her neck, hiding within her curled locks.

'So, you are leaving?'

'I am.' Daemi turned completely to face Lodan. 'We are.'

'Yes, I see. And not bothering to even take a blade with you?' Lodan nodded toward her hip where the weld blade once hung from her belt.

'Not exactly.'

Daemi raised both arms from her sides, and with a metallic snap of some hidden mechanism, sharp black blades as long as her forearms appeared from each hand, curved claws that seemed to grow out from her flesh.

Lodan simply stared, his words dying in his throat.

'Heather and Frankle's work, of course,' she explained, turning the evil-looking blades slowly in the air, before another shift and the blades disappeared back into her sleeves with a smooth, mechanical click. 'Had to give them something to do.'

'You're leaving them as well?'

'Those two have more than enough to keep them busy here. Which is a good thing, I suppose. They're completely inseparable now. Besides, I'm sure Sontair's new Protector will find plenty of work for them.'

'No doubt. I'll have plenty of work for Sontair's greatest warrior as well, if you'd only stay.'

Daemi paused then, the eager glint in her eye fading. 'We cannot stay here. There's too much—'

'Memory?'

'Perhaps.' She smiled, and the cat on her shoulders peered out once again from behind her hair. 'You can't expect us all to stay.'

'No. No, of course not. You sound like Petron. He said almost the exact same thing before he flew out of here on his eagle, back to Redmondis.'

'I know. I will miss him. And you.'

Lodan dropped his head into a bow and let it go at that. She had seen so much, this young adult girl who carried herself as a warrior. Done so much for them all. Lost so much more. Who was he to lay claim to any more?

'Well then, travel safely. And try not to stir up too much trouble with those nasty-looking blades of yours.' Lodan stepped past her to hold the gate open. 'I hope to one day see you again. Both of you.'

Daemi smiled then, a warmth spreading across her face that almost reached her eyes before fading. She nodded once more, then walked past him, out the gate and onto the narrow path that led down the steep hill into the city below, and beyond that, the world.

About the Author

T.R. Thompson is an Australian speculative fictions author. He lives in Belgrave on the outskirts of Melbourne with his wife and two young sons.

When not writing or reading he spends too much time gaming and taking long meandering walks through the forest that always seem to end up at a tavern.

www.trthompson.com